MW00931788

THE N.O.A.H. FILES

SHOCK THE MONKEY

THE N.O.A.H. FILES
SHOCK THE MONKEY

NEAL SHUSTERMAN
&
ERIC ELFMAN

LITTLE, BROWN AND COMPANY

New York Boston

Little, Brown and Company
Hachette Book Group
1290 Avenue of the Americas, New York, NY 10104
Visit us at LBYR.com

First Edition: May 2024

Little, Brown and Company is a division of Hachette Book Group, Inc. The Little, Brown name and logo are registered trademarks of Hachette Book Group, Inc.

The publisher is not responsible for websites (or their content) that are not owned by the publisher.

Little, Brown and Company books may be purchased in bulk for business, educational, or promotional use. For information, please contact your local bookseller or the Hachette Book Group Special Markets Department at special.markets@hbgusa.com.

Library of Congress Control Number: 2024932037

ISBNs: 978-0-7595-5527-3 (hardcover), 978-0-7595-5529-7 (ebook)

Printed in the United States of America

LSC-C

Printing 1, 2024

PART 1

• •

A SKY FULL OF STARS

1

With Claws Like That...

THE CREATURE WAS CLEARLY NOT OF EARTH. IT DID NOT EVEN bear the slightest resemblance to anything that had ever legally been on this planet.

Wherever it was from, it was obviously an apex predator. Even its teeth had teeth.

"Can't you go any faster?" asked Andi, clinging to Noah's back as he raced through the Latvian forest to escape the hellish creature.

"Maybe if *you* weren't so heavy."

"Oh, so now it's *my* fault?"

Noah was pushing himself as hard as he could. He had employed cheetah-speed and tried to use horseshoe bat echolocation to anticipate trees, boulders, and other obstacles in their path—but using two complex animal traits simultaneously? Impossible! It was like trying to do math while someone was shouting random numbers at you. He could do them one after the other, but not simultaneously—so they ended up bouncing off a tree, taking critical seconds away. The neon-blue monstrosity was almost on them now.

"Slime trail!" shouted Andi.

"I tried that already!" Noah shouted back. "Twice! I slopped our trail with hagfish slime, then snail slime, and it didn't even stumble!"

The creature's scales, each with its own miniature mouth, screeched as the creature galloped toward them. Although "galloped" wasn't quite the right word for a thing with five legs. "Gallolloped" was more like it. The rhythm of its hooves cut a five-beat cadence that just felt wrong on so many levels.

"You're the brainiac!" Noah yelled to his sister. "Think of something!"

"I'm not a miracle worker!" shouted Andi. "In case you haven't noticed, I'm a product of science, not a magical being."

Andi was, as her name suggested, an android. Not the phone, but an actual android, although she was also a phone, but that was a very small part of her functionality. Most of the time she was in humanoid form, indistinguishable from an actual human. But once in a while, she was a suitcase.

She had already tried all her countermeasures against the monstrosity closing in on them, from dark-energy quan-

4

tum lasers to self-doubt torpedoes. But nothing had worked.

"Fractillian Abysmal Beasts are extremely difficult to discourage once they get their mind set on something."

"Is that what it is?"

"Duh—isn't it obvious?"

Noah leaped into a tree with gibbon agility to clear an unexpected bog—but the Fractillian Abysmal Beast stomped right through the bog as if it weren't there.

"Maybe," said Andi, "we should find out what it wants."

"It wants to eat us!"

"Not *us*," reminded Andi. "*You*. My metallic alloys are not digestible to it. But that aside, we're not certain it *does* want to eat you."

"Are you kidding me? *Look* at it!"

"All that drool discharging from its primary mouth does not necessarily indicate hunger. Fractillian Abysmal Beasts tend to have issues with saliva overproduction."

Noah dropped back down to the forest floor and called up cheetah-speed again. While he had still not mastered all the defense mechanisms of the million-plus species held within his DNA, there were several hundred he could summon at a moment's notice—if not simultaneously, then at least one after another. For instance, he could go all poison dart frog on the monster, forcing his skin to secrete a deadly neurotoxin—but there was no guarantee it would work. And even if it did, the thing wouldn't die until *after* it had eaten Noah, so that was a nonstarter.

Had Noah been able to effectively echolocate while also running like a cheetah, he would have known about the granite face of a mountain in front of them before it could be seen. And although Andi's radar did catch it, she couldn't communicate the threat in time.

Noah hit the mountain face at nearly sixty miles an hour. That would have killed a normal human, but his body responded like a tardigrade—a microscopic creature that could survive bullet-speed impact. Of course, that didn't stop it from hurting.

But he didn't have time to yowl. He swallowed the pain of his near splat and, realizing he had to climb the sheer cliff, called up some gecko. Gecko was easy—it was, in fact, one of his favorite traits. His fingers spatulated, and he began to scale the rock wall, but just a few feet off the ground, he realized his critical error.

Shoes.

To successfully gecko, he needed all ten fingers and all ten toes to climb. Quickly, he kicked his shoes off and tried again, but to no avail.

Because he was also wearing socks.

How pathetic to have survived an entire alien conspiracy trying to kill him, only to be defeated by a stupid pair of socks. The irony that they were from "Target" was not lost on him.

• ● •

Noah Prime never expected he'd be spending his time running from aliens. To be honest, he had never believed in aliens, until a team of them blew up his house and his parents informed him that they were not, in fact, human, but were emissaries of an advanced species trying to protect him and save his life. Of course, what they failed to tell him was they also wanted to destroy all life on Earth.

Turned out that the aliens trying to kill him were the good guys, and his parents were forces of evil. Even the name of their species—Fauxlites—screamed that they were not what they appeared to be. That sort of thing messes with your head, sending your moral compass spinning into strange, dizzying places.

All the more reason to make everyone think you're dead and then disappear.

But being devoured by a Fractillian Abysmal Beast was not the kind of disappearing Noah had in mind.

• ● •

The painfully blue beast gallolloped closer, reaching for Noah. Its stubby little fingers squirmed in anticipation of grabbing Noah and thrusting him into its toothy maw, where the teeth on the teeth could rip him to tiny bits (which the teeth on the teeth on the teeth could break down even further).

If Noah offered up an arm or a leg, that might buy him and Andi the time they needed to escape—and he could use his axolotl salamander regenerative ability to grow new limbs. He'd used it before, but it was as painful as . . . well, getting your limbs chewed off. So he was not too keen on that plan.

Andi hopped off his back and turned to the creature. "Okay, you caught us," she said. "Are you just going to stand there drooling, or are you going to tell us what you want?"

And to Noah's surprise, the creature said, "I'm not entirely sure yet."

"So," said Andi, "you just randomly chase people through the woods without even having a clear endgame?"

"I'm trying to decide whether to turn you over to the Anusians or to the Fauxlites."

Which meant there was nothing random about this encounter. "Then . . . you know who I am," said Noah.

"And I know that there'll be quite a reward for alerting either side to the fact that you're still alive."

Well, the good news was that Noah was now off the day's menu, but the alternatives to being eaten weren't much better. If the Anusians knew Noah was alive, they would kill him, while the Fauxlites would keep him alive, put him on some interplanetary wildlife preserve, and destroy all life on Earth.

"One might assume there'd be a reward," Andi said,

8

"but think about it...the Fauxlites hate Fractillians. They'll probably send you on your way without even a thank-you. And the Anusians? Well, correct me if I'm wrong, but weren't you a prisoner of the Anusians who escaped in the Volcanic Portal Disaster a few months ago? If you go to them, their mission leader will probably oysterize you again and put you back on her pearl necklace."

The creature's mouth seemed to drool just a little less fervently. "Nascent Organic Aggregate Hybrids are valuable. Maybe giving them this N.O.A.H. will buy my freedom."

"Yes," said Noah, "but you seem pretty free to me already."

"Ha!" scoffed its many scaled mouths, then its primary mouth said, "Free? How can I be free when most of the time I have to squeeze myself into a human skin just to fit in?"

Noah shrugged. "But not when you're rampaging."

Its scale mouths sighed. "True," it said. "But there's more to life than rampaging. And like your android said, I'm still a fugitive, and I'm tired of hiding. But if I bring the Anusians your limp, lifeless body—I'm sure they'll let me off for good behavior."

"Killing me is NOT good behavior!" Noah insisted.

"Depends on who you ask."

"And besides—*I'm* the one who broke Vecca's necklace and threw you into the pond to rehydrate!" said Noah. "If it wasn't for me, you and all the other prisoners would still be pearls around her neck! And this is the thanks I get?"

9

That gave the Fractillian pause.

"If you let us go," said Andi, "we'll give you something more valuable than anything our enemies can give you."

"And what would that be?"

Then Andi turned to Noah. "Tell him, Noah."

And the creature looked at him, waiting expectantly.

It was so like Andi to lead him from a cliff wall to a cliff edge. Great. He had nothing.

"Uh...Uh..."

"Well," said Andi, feigning impatience. "Are you going to *illuminate* him or not?"

And Noah figured out what Andi was suggesting. It wasn't going to be easy—he had only managed this particular trait of the broadclub cuttlefish once before. Noah closed his eyes. And when he opened them, they spilled out bright bioluminescence of the exact wavelength needed to hypnotize the Fractillian. Noah didn't know how long it would last—but it gave him a momentary advantage. Now that it was hypnotized, Noah shifted gears. Turning off the bioluminescence, he dredged up the harpy eagle. His fingernails elongated into the world's sharpest claws—as did his toenails, completely shredding his socks, as if in karmic punishment for preventing his earlier escape. Just as the trance wore off, Noah leaped at the Fractillian Beast, clawing at it. The creature roared. All its scale-mouths roared, all its terrible teeth in teeth in teeth gnashed in fury. It tried to turn, shake him off, but instead succeeded only in flinging him onto its back, where Noah dug in his claws again, even deeper than the first time.

Then the creature stopped thrashing. And it shivered. And it said:

"Oooh, that feels *good*."

This wasn't what Noah was expecting. He redoubled his efforts, clawing and shredding deeper, sending wailing scales flying—but no sooner had the creature's flesh shredded than it healed, and new scales came in to replace the old.

"Ooh . . . Now a little to the left . . ."

"Andi, it's not working!"

"Actually, I think it is," said Andi. "Do as he says."

So Noah moved a little to the left and dug furiously at the creature's back with his hands and feet.

The beast rolled its shoulders. The new scales all seemed to be smiling and deeply relaxed.

"Oh my Universal Deity!" said the creature. "That feels amazing. Please don't stop."

And since the creature was not eating him or turning him over to his enemies, Noah kept it up for a whole twenty minutes, until the Fractillian Abysmal Beast was as relaxed as a kitten on its favorite rug.

"That," said the beast, "was the absolute best back massage I've ever had. You should go to the Fractal Abyss and start a business. With claws like that, you'd make a fortune!"

11

"I'll keep that in mind," said Noah.

"Pity you'll never get a massage like that again," said Andi.

Now that the creature had been massaged into submission, its primary mouth and all its scale mouths puffed their lips into a profound pout. "Aww, why not?"

"Because," said Noah, picking up on Andi's lead, "if you turn me in, I'll either be killed or put on a protected wildlife preserve. Either way you'll never see me again. But on the other hand . . . if you let us go, I'll be happy to give you free massages for life."

The creature was silent.

"Well," asked Andi, "what do you think?"

"Quiet," said its many thousands of mouths, "I'm thinking."

• ● •

In the end, the Fractillian, who formally introduced himself as Murdrum, agreed to the terms. But not without insisting that Noah make himself available for massages whenever Murdrum had a hankering.

"I don't like it," Noah told Andi.

"Hey, a Fractillian isn't the worst friend you could have."

The mention of friends made Noah's heart sink a little.

"Of course, I do think it's time to move again," said

Andi. "Because if one rogue alien was able to find us, others could."

Move. That was easy for Andi to say. She spoke every earth language that ever existed, as well as a few that had yet to emerge, and her database was well-equipped with the cultural norms of every society, allowing her to adapt in ways that Noah could not. Right now they were in Latvia—and not only didn't Noah speak the language, he had never even heard of the place before they set up house there. And to make it worse, on the rare occasions they went into the nearby town of Ludza for food and supplies, Andi introduced him as *mans brālis idiots*, which Noah quickly learned meant "my idiot brother." And all Noah could do was offer a blank smile and play the part.

"It's not appropriate to call someone an idiot!" he had reminded her.

To which she had responded, "In your case, it's the *only* appropriate word."

Mr. Ksh, their rich benefactor, assured them that he could move them to a new location every few weeks, since he had an endless supply of real estate holdings, but for Noah, all the moving around was getting old.

"I miss Sahara and Ogden," he told Andi, as they sat in their secluded cottage, or *kotedža*, in front of a fire that Andi kept having to relight with her optical lasers, since the wood was so damp.

"So I'll set up a virtual hangout room for you."

But Noah shook his head. The holographic rooms Andi could set up were cool and all, but it wasn't like being there in person. And besides, it was getting harder and harder to make all their schedules match up. Sure, Noah could meet anytime, since hiding from the known universe didn't exactly fill one's social calendar. But Sahara had school and gymnastics, and now had started volunteering to help K-i children. And Ogden—well, Ogden's schedule was filled with uniquely Ogden-esque things.

"I want to go back to Arbuckle," Noah announced. "I want to visit my friends in person."

"Not a good idea," said Andi. "Arbuckle is still ground zero for alien fugitives, as well as for 'the Kratz Incident.' And let's not forget Agent Rigby and all her 'Nowhere Men' are still trying to figure out why there's a volcano in the middle of town." Nowhere Men—that's what they'd come to call Agent Rigby's dark-suited government henchmen— were almost always male, wore the same cologne, and had an identical lack of any sense of humor whatsoever.

"I don't have to go back as me," Noah pointed out. "You could make me a skin to wear, and I'd be undetectable."

"What if Ogden and Sahara are still under surveillance?" countered Andi.

"What if they're not?"

"What if there are Anusians and Fauxlites still hanging around?"

14

"And what if there aren't?"

"What if Ogden and Sahara are trying to get on with their lives and don't want to see you anymore?"

That one stung . . . because as much as Noah wanted to deny it, that was a very real possibility, too.

"Well, the best way to know that for sure is to face them and ask them," Noah said.

Andi stood her ground for a few moments more, but in the end, gave in—because she knew that Noah, much like a Fractillian Abysmal Beast, could not be discouraged once his mind was made up.

2

The Tyranny of Memory

ARBUCKLE WAS GOING TO BECOME A TOURIST ATTRACTION. Eventually.

How could it not, after the inexplicable emergence of a hundred-foot volcano, alien sightings, and an unprecedented episode of mass hysteria where hundreds of people believed they were a middle school science teacher?

Regardless of how it all shook out, Arbuckle would be a mystical place that people would flock to, like Roswell or Stonehenge. In fact, Arbuckle had its own identical replica of Stonehenge, which, like the volcano, had appeared out of nowhere one day. Someone should definitely start charging admission.

Mr. Ksh was not greedy, but he knew an opportunity when he saw one. Which was why, even before the dust had settled, he had purchased all the property immediately around the volcano, where he planned to build a new town center once the debris was cleared out—and the volcano at the town center's center would be its centerpiece.

The government had reluctantly lifted lockdown two months after the event, even though they still had checkpoints monitoring all comings and goings. Of course, they still had a fenced-in area marking a hundred-yard radius around the apartment belonging to one Dr. Quantavius T. Kratz, who was technically no longer present in Arbuckle, in spite of how many people still believed they were him. As if one Kratz wasn't enough, now there were hundreds.

• ● •

Sahara Solis found it amazing how one's life could make room for the strangest things and just go on as if it were all normal. People adapt. *She* had adapted. So now when she went to school, she rode her bike around a volcano, and then around the Quantavius Zone (where people still believed they were Dr. Kratz), stopped at Starbucks, and went to class. She also belonged to a very small secret club who knew what had *really* happened. But she couldn't tell anyone.

And in spite of what Andi might think, Sahara wasn't avoiding Noah. Not really. Okay, maybe she was, but not because she didn't want to see him. It just hurt to see him, knowing that she would probably never be in the same actual room with him ever again. It wasn't so much moving on as it was tending to the wound left by his absence.

"Sahara, come down or I will feed your breakfast to the cat."

It was a Monday morning, just like any other since her parents had become Kratz.

"Mom," she called downstairs. "That's Kratz talking, not you."

"I know, I know," her mother said in frustration. "It's just that I haven't had my coffee yet. Sorry, I'll be fine in a few minutes."

It was normal to be cranky in the morning, Sahara tried to tell herself. Of course, Kratz-cranky was crankiness on a whole new level. Still, both her parents were emerging from that bitter fog a little more each day.

"There are whole days where I don't feel like him at all," her father had told her. "His memories are starting to fade, like some old, bad dream."

Memories, yes, but attitudes are harder. She knew she had to be patient, which didn't always come easy for Sahara.

The omelet her mother made her was good, which meant that her mother remembered what their standard family breakfasts were, although she did occasionally serve Sahara a bowl of Cheetos, either by mistake or by a sudden spike of Kratz-driven malice. But when her mother realized what she had done, she would be embarrassed and mad at herself. "Baby, I'm sorry—but that man gets into every corner of your mind like an overflowing toilet. I'll be glad when we can just flush him out."

She had to remember that her parents were the lucky ones. They had been outside the event horizon when Kratz had activated the memory cube and projected himself upon unsuspecting neighbors. Which meant that eventually Kratz would be gone from their minds and they would be fully themselves again. But for everyone inside the Quantavius Zone, their old selves were completely gone. All their memories, personalities, everything. Those were the ones whom Sahara felt truly sorry for. Which is one of the reasons why she spent several afternoons a week volunteering to help Kratz-identifying children learn to be someone other than Quantavius Kratz.

That afternoon she assisted one of the government therapists on an art project intended to spur the children's imaginations, the theory being that if they could imagine themselves as someone other than Kratz, then they could *become* someone other than Kratz.

"I hardly see the point," said a ten-year-old, whose nametag said Ryan Rosenstein. "Art is just busywork for lesser minds."

"That's not true, Ryan, and you still need to do it."

"What a cruel trick of fate this is, that a girl who was once my student now looms over me giving me orders."

Sahara took a moment before answering him calmly. "I

was not your student. I was Mr. Kratz's student, and you are not Mr. Kratz."

"Dr. Kratz," the boy said. "I am not *Dr.* Kratz." And that was actually a breakthrough, because, without realizing it, he had admitted who he wasn't. Now it was just a matter of getting him to accept who he *was*, even if his memories would always tell him otherwise.

"Ryan, Dr. Kratz is an unhappy middle-aged man without many prospects for his future. But you are a ten-year-old boy who can be anyone you want to be. So why choose to be him?"

And then she pointed to the sign that had become a Q-Zone motto over the past few months. "Fight the tyranny of memory."

The boy heaved a very middle-aged sigh. "Fine," he said. "Give me the paper and I'll draw whatever you want. But I can assure you I'll be thoroughly bored."

Well, thought Sahara, it was a start.

• ● •

Kratz-identifying children weren't the only headaches Sahara had to deal with, because there was, of course, Ogden. He was also a member of their secret I-know-what-really-happened club, and that bonded them in ways that she wished it hadn't.

Lately he had been coming to her for romantic advice, as if she were an expert on such things.

20

"If you were Claire Jensen, what could I do to impress you?"

To which Sahara had responded, "Absolutely nothing. Because, frankly, Ogden, Claire Jensen is not in your planetary group, if you catch my meaning."

To that Ogden shrugged. "Orbits change, celestial bodies plummet from the sky, and someone needs to be there to catch them."

Sahara couldn't help but be a little bit impressed by Ogden's practical approach. Not that she thought he'd be successful, but his combination of naivete and skillful analysis was charming in its own way.

"Besides," said Ogden, "if I don't get to her, Raymond B.S. will, and that simply cannot be allowed!"

"I promise you, Ogden, Raymond B.S. doesn't have a chance with her, either. He's too creepy."

"Don't be so sure. Mesmer and Rasputin were super creepy, and they succeeded where less creepy people failed."

Sahara found it best not to argue with Ogden, because arguing with him was like playing Jenga on a Tilt-A-Whirl. But it still annoyed Sahara that Ogden had this puppy-eyed crush on Miss Popularity.

"Why Claire Jensen?" Sahara had to ask. "She's the shallowest, most entitled, most self-absorbed girl in school!"

"She's only that way because deep down she's insecure," Ogden insisted. "But when she's my girlfriend, she'll be as secure as a prison for the criminally insane."

• ● •

There are certain people with names so unfortunate it's like a strange alignment of planets. Ogden and Sahara's history teacher was one of those. Mr. Balding was doomed from the moment the first clumps of hair began to clog his shower drain. The inevitability of the prophecy put forth by his very name was too powerful to ever escape. On the first day of school every year, there were always students who couldn't stifle their snickers. Mr. Balding was used to it. He took it in stride. He was even patient with that one student who, with the unwavering conviction of a flat-earther, insisted for weeks that his last name had to be a joke. But if it was a joke, then the man's parents were in on it. Because his first name was Spalding.

One might think that Spalding Balding was the be-all and end-all of unfortunate names, and yet he was just the tip of the iceberg.

Because there, in the English department, was Miss Stalker.

While "Adeline Stalker" was only mildly problematic as a name, it all became a whole lot worse when she and Mr. Balding fell in love and got married. Individually, they kept their own last names, but they absolutely insisted that their children be hyphenates.

And thus, Raymond Balding-Stalker was born—and was doomed from birth.

But rather than despising his parents for the name, Raymond went with it, embracing his name on every level. Now that he was a student in his parents' school, he accepted his role as "the Creepy Dude," and excelled in the position, knowing that, in the fullness of time, he'd grow out of his name. Or more deeply into it. Or maybe just have it legally changed.

As anyone can tell you, the Creepy Dude is a time-honored position in every school. It doesn't even have to be a dude, because the creep factor is not gender specific. But regardless of the particulars, someone always filled the position in every school, because nature abhors a vacuum.

Raymond Balding-Stalker was quiet. He had more thoughts than most people realized, but he kept them to himself. And for as long as he could remember, his arch-nemesis had been Ogden Coggin-Criddle.

Although Raymond always felt their rivalry was on a level playing field, it was not. While Ogden was unique and generally spent his life in left field, at least he was in the ballpark. Raymond, on the other hand, was out in the parking lot trying to see over the fence. But there was something about the whole volcano incident that gave Ogden more confidence than he'd ever had. The fact that he now had an interest in Claire Jensen infuriated Raymond, because Raymond had harbored a secret crush on her since kindergarten. The very idea that Ogden might actually make some inroads, and maybe even *talk* to her, gave Raymond many a sleepless night. He was determined to somehow, in some way, make his feelings to Claire known, and leave Ogden crying and humiliated in the dust.

• ● •

Ogden's parents had been at the far edge of the memory-field when Kratz accidentally projected himself out to his neighborhood—which meant they only lasted as Kratz for just a couple of weeks. Now they were long back to their old selves.

Which meant they weren't talking.

Ogden still shuttled between identical bedrooms in identical homes across the street from each other—aptly named House Coggin and House Criddle. He still honored the custody arrangement, which was all about prime and non-prime numbers. This was Ogden's version of normal. His comfort zone.

As it was the fourteenth of the month, he had three days in a row at his mother's house, since the next prime number wasn't until the seventeenth, when he'd spend a day with his father. Usually he didn't play favorites unless it suited a particular agenda, but lately he'd liked being at his mom's house more, because she had a new boyfriend of whom Ogden heartily approved.

Mr. Ksh.

Ogden had come to respect the man who helped him, Noah, and Sahara save the world. Ogden admired the calm, sensible way Mr. Ksh dealt with everything from being hurled twenty years into the past by his own future self, to his car being hurled a hundred feet into the sky by a rogue alien with him inside. *This is a man I could learn from*, Ogden had concluded.

Not that he couldn't get fatherly advice from his actual father—in fact, it was quite the opposite. Professor Coggin was thrilled on the rare occasions that Ogden asked him for advice. So thrilled that he would drop everything, and turn his response into a research project resulting in a lengthy dissertation, when all Ogden usually wanted was a simple yes or no.

When it came to his hypothetical relationship with Claire Jensen, he thought Sahara would give him good advice, being a girl and all. But clearly Sahara had an anti-Claire bias that made anything she said suspect.

And so that evening, before his mother got home from the university (for she, too, was a celebrated mathematics professor), Odgen put his question to Mr. Ksh, who had been spending more time with them than not.

"Mr. Ksh," Ogden asked, "how do you win the affection of a girl who doesn't know you exist, or if she does know you exist, sees you as a lower life-form, perhaps invertebrate?"

Mr. Ksh nodded knowingly and gave him a wide grin.

"Ah, yes, the great question of the ages. The question of love!"

"Let's not get carried away," Ogden corrected. "We're talking holding hands in public, arm-over-the-shoulder in movies, and, in time, the requisite pressing of lips that tends to accompany these activities."

Still the man didn't stop smiling. "You try to make it all so clinical, yes? But it's not, is it?" Then he wagged a finger. "I've seen that look of infatuation in your eyes, Ogden. I've been wondering who the lucky classmate might be."

"From her perspective, I don't think she sees it as lucky."

"Well then, you'll need to offer her a new perspective."

"But I don't know how!" Ogden sighed. If Noah were here, he would know. Or at least he would tell Ogden not to waste his time—which would be helpful in its own tough-love sort of way.

But Mr. Ksh was a man who believed all things were possible, because experience had shown him that all things were.

"You must talk to her like there's nothing unusual about you talking to her," he advised. "You must present the best true version of yourself at all times. You must shine like the worthy young man that you are!" Mr. Ksh said. "And then buy her something nice."

"Uh . . . like what?"

Ksh shrugged. "Well, where I come from, a yak—but

this is a different time, a different place. You'd know better than me what would have deep and significant meaning for a fourteen-year-old American girl." And then he leaned closer and whispered, with his eyes wide. "But whatever it is, it should make her see stars!"

3

A Twinkling Ball of Burning Gas

It was an unpleasant day in the Latvian forest. Rain buffeted the windows of Noah and Andi's cottage, which had sprung multiple leaks.

Andi stood in the one dry corner, seeming to stare off into space.

"Aren't you done yet?"

"Quiet! I'm still downloading the pattern for your artificial skin."

"You've been standing there for hours."

"Sunspot activity," she said. "It makes the dark-and-stormy web glitchy."

"Don't you mean 'the dark web'?"

"Don't be stupid, that's totally different." Then Andi took a step closer to the window to get better reception.

As everyone in the enlightened universe knew, if you

needed something and had no idea where to find it, there was one place you looked. The dark-and-stormy web.

While Earth's dark web is a virtual den of all sorts of criminal activity, the dark-and-stormy web was perfectly legit—a great trans-universal network sparking with dark energy. True, it had unseen tendrils that reached into every aspect of life throughout the universe, but that didn't make it illegal. It was simply the universal equivalent of Amazon.

It was, quite literally, a web that was spun by the Cosmic String Spider—perhaps the most malevolent entity to ever exist. It would lure unsuspecting life-forms into its web with promises of endless amounts of useful information, then ensnare and devour them. (In other words, the universal equivalent of Google.)

In the end the spider was killed, and to this day its rotting carcass remains at the center of the web, becoming one of the most horrifying artifacts of the universe. Now the dark-and-stormy web is a wealth of trade and commerce. At least until the Cosmic String Spider's egg sack opens, releasing thousands of its offspring into the universe in a few million years, or next week.

As for the artificial skin that Andi was buying, it was listed by a certain Beverly Hills dermatologist, who just happened to be a shape-shifting alien with a side hustle. His human patients never knew why their treatments were so painful, but they endured it because they all went home completely cured of whatever skin ailment they had, never knowing that their skin had been copied by the good doctor. It was, therefore, a win-win for everyone but the dead spider.

"Can't you just go into town and copy someone's skin for me, like you did before?" Noah asked.

"What, in *this* weather?" Andi replied.

Noah dropped himself down into a thoroughly drenched sofa. He really couldn't complain because Andi was doing him a favor. It had been his idea to go back to Arbuckle, and his idea to do so in disguise.

"Is it a good skin?" he asked. "What will I look like?"

"Stop distracting me."

Noah sighed and felt his butt become porpoise-like in response to the wetness of the cushions. Patience was a virtue that Noah lacked. He supposed he could dredge up a little sloth to make the time appear to move faster, but sloth was so hard to snap out of. So he busied himself with thoughts of meeting up with Sahara and Ogden, and how much fun it would be.

Unfortunately for Noah, none of the creatures woven into his DNA had an ability to predict the future. If one did, then he'd be more prepared for the type of "fun" he and his friends were headed for. Which was no fun at all . . .

• ● •

It was always strange getting used to a new skin. It wasn't like a rubber costume that stretched to fit you—it was

30

more like the skin stretched and shrank the fabric of space itself, so that anything could fit inside it, from a human to a giant multi-tentacled alien. It itched, and it chafed, and it tingled.

"Okay," Noah said, not even bothering to check in the mirror to see if his face was straight, "I'm ready for the portal."

"Sit your porpoise-butt down, I'm still calculating."

"How do you know I have porpoise-butt?"

"I can smell it. It's not pretty."

Andi turned, then turned again, facing in different directions. "Hmm...sunspot activity is making a direct portal too difficult to manage. Are you sure you want to do this?"

"Yes," said Noah. "Whatever it takes."

"All right, then," said Andi. "We're going to have to do a lunar-transfer."

Andi had mentioned this once before. "You mean a portal that bounces off the moon?"

"The portal doesn't bounce—we do. We jump to the moon through one portal, then into a second portal that gets us to our destination. Kind of like connecting flights at an airport. But without oxygen."

"Oh. Okay."

Andi positioned herself. "Hold on to something nailed down," she said. "Unless you want to get sucked through the portal, go bouncing across the airless surface of the moon, and die."

"Point taken." So Noah employed gorilla strength to hold on to the cabin's central support beam and took a deep, shuddering breath. He knew Andi was programmed to protect him, so he doubted she'd put him in any real danger. Even so, this didn't sound good.

"You seem a little worried," Andi said, looking him over. "Take this." She handed him a little purple pill. "It'll help protect you from explosive decompression."

Noah swallowed it. "Okay, ready," he said.

"There'll be a moment of airlessness when you reach the lunar surface and leap to the second portal. Whatever you do, don't miss the entrance to that second portal."

"Wait, which direction do I leap?"

"It'll be obvious when you get there."

Andi touched her finger to the wall and inscribed a large circle that began to glow. Then the center of the circle disappeared, replaced by the gray and grainy expanse of the lunar surface—and there came a rush of wind so powerful, it nearly ripped Noah free from the beam. Everything—everything in the cabin—was sucked through the hole. The waterlogged sofa, the pots and pans collecting rainwater from the leaky roof, the big pot-bellied stove, which bounced off Andi before careening through the hole. Andi, on the other hand, didn't seem affected by the wind at all. She just stepped through onto the surface of the moon.

That's when everything went sideways. Literally. Because

the support beam ripped loose, and the entire cottage began to collapse. With nothing stable to grab onto, Noah was sucked out onto the surface of the moon—and in spite of what Andi had said, the second portal was *not* obvious when he got there.

He could see the earth shining bright blue on the lunar horizon, but he had no time to appreciate the view, because the air had been sucked out of his lungs, and it felt like his lungs were about to be sucked out of his chest. His animal instincts instantly enlarged his lung capacity like a loggerhead turtle, which could hold its breath for nearly ten hours, but that was entirely useless on the moon, where there was no breath to hold.

He realized he probably would have died if Andi hadn't given him that pill. Then instinct kicked in, and he began to exhibit a trait he later learned was the naked mole rat, which could exist for a time without oxygen—but it was too little, too late. Dizzy and disoriented, he looked around desperately for the transfer portal. He was already feeling consciousness beginning to slip away when he felt a hand tug at his arm. He turned and saw Andi, shaking her head angrily. She was moving her lips, but without air to carry the sound, Noah couldn't hear her string of insults, which was probably just as well. She pulled him a few steps to the left, and Noah found himself falling into the connecting portal. Before he knew it, he and Andi landed in muddy earth. Which was fine because it was *Earth* earth.

The portal closed behind them, the roar of escaping air stopped, and Noah rose to his feet. He knew exactly where they were. They were smack in the middle of "Stonehenge-West," the replica that had replaced their house in Arbuckle, Oregon, three months ago—although it felt more like a hundred years.

After a few deep breaths, and puffs of moon dust, Noah began to feel better.

"Good thing you gave me that pill," he said. "What was it? Some kind of oxygen infusion?"

"It was a Skittle." Andi shrugged.

"What?!"

"It's called the placebo effect. Fake medicine for impressionable minds. It helped, didn't it?"

"Only slightly," Noah told her, both relieved and annoyed that it had helped at all.

Before they headed off to find Sahara and Ogden, Noah took a moment to look around. This was the place where he had lived most of his life—and even though the house was gone, the terrain was the way he remembered. The trees, the hills, the little dirt road that once led from their house to the highway that always got his parents' cars so muddy when it rained.

His parents. The loss of them still ached and he knew it would for a long, long time. Not just the loss of their presence, but the loss of his image of them as fine upstanding people. Because they *weren't* people. Not in any human sense. They were Fauxlites. And they certainly weren't upstanding, considering their mission to end all life on Earth. He wondered where they were now. Was Vecca still wearing them as a pair of pearl earrings? Did he care? Of course he cared. No matter what awful beings they were, he still loved them. And he had to believe that, in spite of their murderous mission, they still loved him. Wherever they were.

"Looks like you're still on the moon," Andi commented.

"I was just thinking about Mom and Dad," he told her.

Andi sighed. "Sorry, bro—I don't have a Skittle for that."

• ● •

Meanwhile, Ogden, having no idea yet that Noah was in Arbuckle, busied himself with his advice from Mr. Ksh.

Talk to her like there's nothing unusual about you talking to her. Present the best true version of yourself.

To the old Ogden, it would be a terrifying prospect, but he was a new man. He had survived alien captivity and countless threats from various malevolent forces. Talking to a girl was easy. At least that's what he told himself.

And so, while Noah and Andi were portalling their way to the moon and back, Ogden sought out Claire Jenson during lunch and, finding her in the cafeteria line, paid off the kid behind her to let him slip in. The next person in line complained about giving cuts—but technically it wasn't cuts, it was a legitimate business transaction, so the complainer had no case.

Then Ogden tapped Claire on the shoulder, and she turned to him, blinking those deep, soulful, if overly outlined, eyes.

"So, Claire," he said. "It's lunch!"

"Uh . . . Yeah, so?"

"Always my favorite meal! Some like breakfast, others dinner, but lunch is the most powerful meal, because it divides the day in two!"

"Do I know you?"

"I'm Ogden Coggin-Criddle. How could you forget, Claire? We've known each other for years."

"Uh . . . I don't think so?"

"Well, I have many fond memories," Ogden told her. "And I look forward to making more."

"More what?"

"Memories—didn't I just say that?"

"Sorry, I really wasn't listening."

"Oh—and let me be the first to wish you a happy birthday!" Ogden said.

"Uh . . . you're not the first."

"Well, almost the first."

"Not really."

"Well, one among the many, then—and I look forward to your party tonight."

"I . . . don't think you're invited. . . ."

"I'm sure it was an honest mistake, as we go way back. By the way, I've been studying current dance trends, and I think you'll be impressed." Then he took her hand, spun her out of the line like a top, and spun her back, leaving her noticeably dizzy.

"Was that really necessary?" she asked.

"Absolutely," Ogden responded.

"BURGER, PIZZA, OR VEGAN LASAGNA?!"

Both Ogden and Claire were jolted by the voice of the food server, who, for some reason, always yelled out the food choices, even though there was no reason to yell.

"Do you mind? We're trying to have a conversation," Ogden snapped.

"I'll have the vegan lasagna," said Claire, "but with a burger patty on top."

"CAN'T DO THAT!"

"Aw, pleeeeeease?"

"OKAY JUST THIS ONCE!" said the server. "NEXT! BURGER, PIZZA, OR VEGAN LASAGNA?!"

"I'll have what she's having," said Ogden.

"CAN'T DO THAT!"

"But you already made an exception."

"AND I REGRET IT."

"This is completely unfair! You're favoring her because she's pretty and has the perfect smile!"

"AND BECAUSE SHE SAID PLEASE. YOU DIDN'T SAY PLEASE."

"Okay, please."

"TOO LATE, THAT SHIP HAS ALREADY SAILED. NEXT!"

Ogden was so infuriated by this clearly preferential treatment that he forgot for a moment why he was there, and by the time he remembered, Claire had already left and was sitting at the popular table with other popular types.

"YOU RUINED MY OPPORTUNITY!" Ogden yelled at the server.

"NOT MY PROBLEM," he yelled back, then the next kid in line elbowed Ogden out of the way to get his lunch.

Ogden stormed out of the cafeteria, having completely lost his appetite, and skipped school, because his singular focus would make education impossible today. It was becoming increasingly clear that if he was going to win Claire's heart, he would need to follow Mr. Ksh's next bit of advice and get her his own version of a yak. The perfect birthday gift. It was only a matter of deducing what the perfect gift would be.

• ● •

There was only one game store in Arbuckle. Merlin's Games and Mischief. The guy who ran it, Miles "Merlin" Miller, was dedicated to his clientele.

"I feel it's my moral responsibility to get gamers out of their mothers' basements," he often said—and was very successful

in the endeavor. In addition to selling just about every kind of game imaginable, the place was filled with tables of active board-, card-, and role-playing games, all day, every day.

This was Ogden's domain. These were his people—and also the guinea pigs on whom he tested his own game creations. He considered himself the Mischief of Merlin's Games and Mischief.

It was here that Ogden went to find a gift for Claire—because it was the only place he could think of in Arbuckle that sold anything remotely interesting.

Merlin himself was a large Hagrid-looking man—basically just eyes and a nose in a big, bearded face. He knew every game, old and new, and was skilled at picking the right one for the right person. But when Ogden explained the situation to him, Merlin shook his big, hairy head, and said, "Sounds to me like this girl isn't the game-playing type. Or at least the kind of games I sell."

"I know," admitted Ogden, "but everything else I can think to get her is ordinary and boring. Flowers, chocolates, gift cards—anyone could get her that. I want to get her something that makes her see stars!"

Merlin tapped a pensive finger to his lips. "Stars, you say.... I think I know just the thing." Then he pointed to the shop's bulletin board, where people advertised things like open spots in quest parties and basements for rent. There, slightly off-center, was a gold-edged card that read:

McGuffin Observatory—Star Registry.
Buy your sweetie a Star!

Ogden had to admit he was intrigued. He had heard of star registries before. And while flowers die, chocolates melt, and gift cards magically disappear in junk-drawers, a star will be there forever. Or at least for a few billion years until it goes supernova. *Yes ... but was it a "yak"?*

"I don't know, Merlin—there are more stars out there than people on Earth, so there's nothing all that special about it."

"Ah!" said Merlin, leaning in a bit closer. "That's where you're wrong. Most registries have stars you need a telescope to find—but McGuffin Observatory specializes in stars that can be seen by the naked eye. Just glance up into the night sky, and there it is."

That snagged Ogden's interest. He imagined himself at Claire's party, looking up at the stars and pointing out the twinkling ball of burning gas he had purchased for her. It would be a very romantic moment.

"Can I buy it here?"

Merlin shook his head. "Gotta go to the observatory. It's about twenty miles outside town."

• ● •

Ogden was no stranger to ride-share apps. Sometimes self-propelled wheels like a bike or skateboard were too inefficient or labor-intensive—and riding his bike twenty miles up a mountain simply wasn't going to happen. So he took out his phone and requested an Unter—the ride-share app for drivers that were rejected from Uber. It was cheaper, faster, and occasionally more thrilling. Their motto was "Why take your life into your own hands? Let us do it for you!" And while a surprising number of Uber drivers were aliens, Ogden suspected Unter had an even higher percentage. So when the dented little Kia jumped the curb to pick him up, he asked, "You human?"

To which the driver responded, "As human as I need to be."

Which was good enough for Ogden.

• ● •

Noah decided to walk his old path to school from where his home used to be.

"Wouldn't you much rather swing through the trees?" Andi asked.

And although Noah was excited to be here, he wanted to slow down and savor being home. Besides, school hadn't let out yet, and he didn't want to just hang out front, since the overzealous school security guard had a major issue with loitering. Fake skin or not, it would draw unwanted attention. A leisurely walk would get him there by the time school ended.

Neither of them paid much attention to the careening

41

Kia that sped past them, heading out of town, toward the mountains.

Halfway to school, they came to a shop-lined street far enough from the center of town to be spared from the volcanic disaster. With the old town center gone, this spot was bustling with activity. Restaurants and quaint boutiques that never got much traction were suddenly full of people. Even the ever-empty Arbuckle Fashions now appeared ever-full.

"It's time for me to make myself inconspicuous," Andi said. "Just in case people recognize me."

"You should have made a skin for yourself," Noah pointed out.

She glared at him. "I'm perfectly happy to be a suitcase." Then she looked toward the crowded street. "Are you absolutely sure you want to do this?" she asked.

"Of course I do," Noah said. "We're here, and I'm doing it."

"Fine," said Andi, preparing to take suitcase form. "But don't blame me if everything goes terribly, horribly wrong."

4

Everything Goes Terribly, Horribly Wrong

THE MCGUFFIN OBSERVATORY WAS PERCHED ON A MOUNTAIN-top at the end of a long winding road; it was a simple square brick building with unusually narrow windows and a green dome. *Oxidized copper*, thought Ogden, *like the Statue of Liberty.*

There was no parking lot, just a gravel roundabout. Clearly, this was not a tourist-friendly place. It appeared closed, perhaps even deserted, but Merlin was never known to steer anyone wrong.

"Wait for me," Ogden told his Unter driver, and although the man grumbled, he agreed to wait, because the only fare he would find in this remote spot would be Ogden.

The large door, also weathered copper, had neither bell nor knocker, but that didn't matter, because as Ogden approached, the heavy door creaked open.

"Come, come," said a raspy voice, "you're letting all the good air out," and a bony finger extended out of the darkness, beckoning.

The moment Ogden stepped inside, he realized there was nothing good about the so-called good air. The place smelled vaguely vinegary with chemical overtones and earthy undertones that tended toward foul.

At the other end of the bony finger was an equally bony old man, who closed the huge door behind him.

Ogden peered into the dim observatory. He could see the cylinder of the telescope positioned at a steep angle, its business-end poking through a gap in the dome. Like the narrow windows, the gap let barely any light in at all.

"Welcome to McGuffin Observatory," the old man said. "Have you come to view the heavens or to peruse our gift shop?"

"I'm here to buy a star."

The man smiled, revealing teeth that were best left undescribed. "Splendid!" he said, then turned and called out, "We have a customer!"

A woman stepped out of the shadows. She wasn't old but was weary in some fundamental way, like a socialite who had seen everything, was impressed by nothing, and whose flesh was now succumbing to the gravity of her own disappointment. Ogden was quick to realize she was the source of the unpleasant under-smell. It reminded Ogden of the time a pigeon had fallen into the dryer vent and croaked.

44

His clothes had smelled like the left armpit of death for weeks until they found the body of the tragic bird, and for years he insisted he could hear the mournful cooing of its ghost in the rumble of the spinning dryer drum. It made him wonder if she was not long for this world. Only much later he would realize how true that assessment was.

"Is the star for yourself or for someone else?" the woman asked, hefting a sizable document.

"It's a gift."

"And can you pay the price?"

Ogden held up his phone. "Do you take Apple Pay?" he asked. And although these didn't seem like people prepared for digital exchange, she nodded and extended her hand, instructing him to tap his phone to her bracelet. *New technology?* thought Ogden. Perhaps he could get one for Claire next Christmas, once they were a couple.

The purchase went through without the slightest hitch. Fifty bucks on the emergency credit card account his father gave him. Easily done.

"Proceed this way," she said.

Ogden followed her to a desk, where she spread out the pages of the registry document—two copies—then handed him a pen.

"Sign here, and here," she said, indicating several different spots in the lengthy contract, "and initial here, here, and here."

But Ogden hesitated. "I was told I'd be able to see the

star in the night sky without a telescope," he said. "Is that true?"

"Oh yes," said the old man. "The star's celestial position is noted on the certificate you'll receive. Although its planet can only be 'seen' through spectral analysis."

"Wait—it has a planet?"

The man nodded.

"Can I name that, too?"

"Of course!"

Ogden leaned over the document, signing and initialing where indicated, and then, in his best printing, he wrote in his chosen names. The star would be "Jensen." The planet would be "Claire."

When he was done, the woman handed Ogden his signed copy, keeping one for herself. Then she went to a small safe, unlocked it, and removed a fancy-looking scroll, which she then handed to the old man, who then handed it to Ogden with a ceremonious bow.

"Your star certificate!" the old man said.

Ogden spread the certificate out on the table. It was fine parchment, with lettering etched in gold. There was a signature line at the bottom, and Ogden moved to sign it. But the old man stayed Ogden's hand.

"That's not for you," the old man explained. "That must be signed by the recipient of your gift. Her signature will make it official."

And so, with the paperwork complete and his impatient Unter honking outside, Ogden said thank you, made a quick exit, and the strange couple closed the heavy door behind him with the resonant gong of a sealing crypt.

Ogden smiled as the car careened down the winding road back home. *Tonight*, he thought, *will be a night to remember!*

• ● •

Meanwhile, back in Arbuckle, Noah strolled down the street, his suitcase/sister in tow, confident in his disguise. A passing woman gave him a double take, nearly tripping on a crack in the pavement. He didn't give it much thought. At first.

He paused when he reached the local coffee house, Grounds Zero, noticing some high school kids sitting out front. There was a football player in an Arbuckle High letter jacket, and his girlfriend wearing a school baseball cap. But he realized the mascot was different. Arbuckle High had apparently abandoned their old dinosaur mascot. Now they were, for obvious reasons, the Roarin' Volcanoes.

That's when things started to get weird.

The high school couple, who had been enjoying their lattes, were now staring at him like a pair of deer in headlights.

"Uh . . . cool! So you're the Volcanoes now," Noah said.

And then the girl screamed at the top of her lungs.

Her scream made Noah flinch so powerfully, his entire fake skin went numb with pins and needles, like he had hit his funny bone, but all over his body.

Needless to say, the scream drew everyone's attention on the street.

"Oh my god! Oh my god! Oh my god!" the girl said. "You're . . . You're . . . You're—"

It was her boyfriend who had enough wind left in his lungs to get the rest out.

"You're Jaxon Youngblood!"

And suddenly people began to chatter and crowd around Noah.

"Jaxon Youngblood? *The* Jaxon Youngblood?"

"I heard he shows up in random places, but *Arbuckle*?"

"I love your music, Jaxon!"

"You're so hot!"

"That was such a cool Grammy acceptance speech!"

"Can we get a selfie?"

"I want one, too!"

"So do I!"

"I saw him first!"

And that's when Noah caught his reflection in the window. The million-dollar hair, the perfect teeth, the ridiculously long eyelashes, everything down to the ten-karat diamond in his nose—which explained that particular itch. He was, without a doubt, teenage heartthrob and pop superstar Jaxon Youngblood.

"Sing 'My Love Is a Charging Rhino' for us, Jaxon!"

Noah shook his head so hard, his brains hurt. "Nope. Not me. Wrong guy."

He turned to Andi—but in little pink suitcase form, she was providing no help in this celebrity-spotting moment. So, grabbing Andi's handle, he ran across the street feeling like maybe he actually was channeling a charging rhino, while Andi's wheels were just as uncooperative as an actual rolling suitcase.

"Andi," Noah said, when they reached the sidewalk, "what have you done?"

A digital read-out appeared on the handle of the suitcase, with the words, YOU ASKED FOR A SKIN, I GAVE YOU A SKIN.

"You do realize this is the very opposite of inconspicuous, don't you?"

DEAL WITH IT appeared on the handle.

And now, not only were the girls from Grounds Zero tittering about him and snapping selfies with him from a distance, they were also watching him talk to a suitcase—which would draw even more attention to himself, even if he wasn't one of the most recognizable celebrities on the planet. So he slipped into Arbuckle Fashions, quickly finding himself a Roarin' Volcanoes baseball cap, which were everywhere, and a pair of oversized dark glasses to hide his famous Jaxon Youngblood eyes.

But he didn't get the new disguise over his old disguise fast enough, because the cashier said, "Hey, aren't you—"

49

"No!" said Noah. But it was too late. Word had already spread, and people had raced across the street from Grounds Zero as well as a few neighboring stores to peer in the window—some not even knowing what they were there to look for, except that something exciting was happening, and FOMO had taken over.

"Pleeeeeeze, Jaxon!" someone squealed. "Sing us 'Love Me, Baby, Like a Tree Loves the Rain'!"

"Does this place have a back door?" Noah asked the cashier.

And luckily it did.

• ● •

Arbuckle Middle School hadn't changed much since the volcano incident. There were some kids and teachers who had yet to return and were still held within the Q-Zone, being re-educated and de-Kratzed, but other than that it was business as usual.

Avoiding the mob of starstruck fans searching for him took some time, so Noah ended up arriving after the end of the school day. Ogden, he figured, must have already left, but he knew exactly where Sahara would be. Gymnastics practice.

Noah pulled his hat as low as he could and entered the gym, taking a seat in the bleachers where some other kids and parents were hanging out, too focused on their own business to notice that a superstar in disguise had just entered the building. He spotted Sahara on the parallel bars, doing an elaborate routine. She was a wonder to watch. She dismounted and before she got back into it again, Noah picked up a crumpled piece of paper he found by his feet, compressed it in his hand with crab-claw strength, and hurled it in her direction. It landed right at her feet, which was intentional. He didn't want to bean her with it.

It got Sahara's attention, and she turned to the bleachers. He gave her a little wave, and she zeroed in on him, looking more suspicious of him than anything. Then she cautiously approached.

"Do I...know you?"

Noah pulled off his hat and removed the dark glasses.

"Don't you recognize me?" he said with a signature Jaxon Youngblood smile.

"Not at all. Should I?"

It figured Sahara wouldn't know Jaxon Youngblood. Pop culture was never her thing.

"Wait," said Sahara. "Your voice sounds like..." Then she gasped. "Noah? Noah, is that you?"

"In the flesh," he said. "Or at least someone else's."

Sahara rushed forward and threw her arms around him, almost knocking him off balance in more ways than one. Then she took a moment to look into his eyes. "I see you in there," she told him. "That's quite the pretty-boy skin you're wearing."

"Tell me about it." Then he tapped Andi's handle. "Blame it on my sister."

Sahara grinned. "I like your real one better." Then suddenly her expression darkened. "Wait—why are you here? What's wrong? Is the world ending again? What's going on, Noah?"

"No, nothing like that . . . ," he said, then shrugged. "I just kinda . . . really wanted to see you." He could feel himself blushing—full-mandrill, red and blue—and wondered if it went all the way through his Jaxon Youngblood skin.

Then her coach called to her. "Sahara, this isn't social time."

"Sorry—my cousin's here from out of town. He came by to surprise me!"

"Cousin?" said Noah.

"Well, she wouldn't cut me any slack at all if I said boyfriend."

He gave her another Jaxon Youngblood smile. "Boyfriend?"

"Semantics," she said. "You're a boy, and you're a friend. Let's leave it at that for now."

"For now?"

"For now." Then she relaxed a bit and smiled. "I've really missed you, Noah. The virtual visits were okay . . . but to be honest the VR makes me kind of nauseous."

"So . . . is that why you've been avoiding them?"

"Yeah . . . I didn't want to identify you with wanting to hurl."

"That may be the nicest thing anyone's ever said to me."

They hugged again, and the digital readout on Andi's handle read UGH, SPARE ME.

•　●　•

Used to be Ogden spent his free afternoons hanging with Noah, but since Noah's "death," there was only one place he went after school.

"We'll definitely find him at Merlin's Games and Mischief," Sahara told Noah and Andi, who had reverted to human form once they had left the school and was no longer in danger of being noticed. Andi, however, chose not to go with them to Merlin's.

"I'm going to do some reconnaissance," she told them. "I want to check with some local resident aliens to see if the Anusians or Fauxlites have shown their faces around here since Noah's horrible death."

"Aren't you afraid you'll get recognized?" Sahara asked.

Andi shrugged. "I'll stay away from humans. And I'm sure the local aliens already know I got abandoned as scrap when the Fauxlites left. So me showing up alone just reinforces the narrative that my dear brother is dead."

After Andi left, Noah offered to tree-swing Sahara to Merlin's, but while that might work in the woodsy outskirts of town, Sahara pointed out that Jaxon Youngblood swinging through trees in populated areas would probably go viral on someone's social media.

"I thought you didn't know who he was," Noah said.

"Of course I know who he is," Sahara answered. "I even have 'Kiss Me till I Turn Purple' on a playlist—but if you tell anyone, you're dead to me."

That made Noah laugh.

"It's just that pretty boys like him kinda all look alike to me," Sahara said. "But at least your eyes shine through. Even though they're trapped between those Venus-flytrap lashes."

And so Noah and Sahara walked to the game shop, which was fine with both of them because it gave them more time together.

"I've gotten pretty good at a whole bunch of traits and defense mechanisms," Noah told her. "Watch this!" He took off his dark glasses and looked at her.

Sahara gasped. "Noah, did the color of your eyes just change?"

"Yep! Brown to green."

"And now they're turning blue!"

"It's a reindeer thing," he said. "Just call me Rudolph."

"Then your nose would have to shine."

"I can do that, too." Then he called some Atolla jellyfish luminescence to the tip of his nose. It glowed right through his Jaxon Youngblood skin.

Sahara smiled. "So now that you can control it, I guess there aren't any more blubber-fests or penguin dances."

Noah simultaneously winced and grinned, remembering that time he developed walrus blubber to keep them from freezing to death and had to wrap Sahara in it. And the time at the school dance when he began flapping his arms like an emperor penguin. And yet, as embarrassing as those moments were, there was something satisfying about them, too. Because they hadn't scared Sahara off. In fact, those strange moments of animal weirdness actually brought them closer. Call it animal magnetism.

"Once in a while, when I get startled, something strange pops up," Noah told her. "But it keeps life interesting, y'know?"

"I'll bet."

"Those were fun times, though, weren't they?"

Sahara gave him a sideways look. "Fun? We nearly died like five or six times!"

"Yeah, well, sure, it wasn't fun while it was happening—but afterward."

The conversation lagged for a moment. Then, before it could become awkward, Sahara said, "So, why are you here, Noah?"

"I told you, I really wanted to see you."

"And then?"

"And then to see Ogden."

"That's not what I mean." She stopped walking for a moment and really looked at him. Suddenly, he felt like he wasn't wearing a Jaxon Youngblood skin at all. No disguise, no hiding. He didn't like the feeling, and he didn't know why.

"So we see you, and it's great," said Sahara, "and we talk about all the wild stuff that happened. And then what?"

Then what? The question made Noah uncomfortable enough that he felt he might spike like a hedgehog— but that would rip right through his celebrity skin, so he quelled the urge. He remembered the conversation he and Andi had had back in their Latvian shack.

What if Ogden and Sahara are trying to get on with their lives?

Noah had forced the thought away, but now it came back like a boomerang, with enough force to make his whole brain ache.

What if they don't want to see you anymore?

And finally, Noah realized the real reason why he had wanted to come back. As painful as that reason was.

"I came here . . ." He stopped and took a long breath. "I came here to say goodbye."

Sahara nodded, and tears began to pool in her eyes. It took a moment before she could bring herself to speak.

"I know," she said. "In a way I knew it from the second I saw you." She took his hand and squeezed it. "I don't want to say goodbye any more than you do . . . but it hurts too much. It hurts knowing that you can only be here an hour or two—and even then you can't even be here as yourself."

Noah felt his own eyes getting moist. He tried to stop

it by blinking but only succeeded in batting those stupid long eyelashes, which gathered even more tears like morning dew on grass. "Running and hiding is not the way I want to live," Noah told her. "It's not who I am."

"But it's the only way you can save the rest of us," Sahara pointed out. And she was right. He hated that she was right. "It's...the most noble sacrifice I could ever imagine," she told him. "And I...kinda love you for it."

Then she held him like she would never, ever let him go. But he knew she would. Just as *he* had to let *her* go.

And although he knew it was selfish, he secretly wished that a whole world of brand-new awful things could happen. The kind of awful things that would keep them from having to say goodbye.

• ● •

The foyer of Merlin's Games and Mischief was lined with plaques, awards, and framed articles about heroic gamers, with headlines like "Gamer Saves Family and Xbox from Burning House" and "Gamer Solves Cold Case Through Role-Playing Campaign."

In the entranceway of the store, under an intricately carved sign that snarkily read ABANDON SOAP ALL YE WHO ENTER HERE, stood Merlin himself, who greeted them with a hearty "Well met, fair maid and young bullyrook! How fare ye this fine day?"

Noah took off his dark glasses since the place was so

dim. "Yeah, bullyrook and whatever to you, too. We're looking for Ogden."

The large man rubbed a hand across his bushy beard, as if he might pull Ogden out of it.

"Any friend of Ogden's is a friend of mine," he said. "Especially those of celebrity status!"

Noah sighed. "Let's keep that between us."

"Aye! Ixnay and mum's the word," Merlin whispered, although it still sounded a bit like shouting.

"So, is he here?" Sahara asked, looking around at the tables of gamers, eyes not yet adjusted to the half-light of the place.

"Indeed he was! He was looking for a gift for a girl he fancied."

Sahara sighed. "That would be Claire."

"Claire *Jensen*?" said Noah.

"Yeah—it's her birthday," Sahara added. "Big party tonight. And I can guarantee he wasn't invited. Because I wasn't invited—and I would certainly get invited before him. Not that I care."

Noah shook his head. "Claire Jensen. Hooo boy! Ogden doesn't aim low, does he."

"Delusion is his comfort zone," said Sahara.

"Shoot for the stars and reach the moon, I always say," bellowed Merlin.

"Or bounce off of it," mumbled Noah.

"Unfortunately, he was unable to find an appropriate

58

gift for his lady-love here, so he took his leave to search elsewhere."

"Do you know where he went?"

Merlin paused and stroked his beard a bit more. "Nay. Have nary a clue." Then he turned away to resolve an escalating dice dispute.

And although Noah had a sense that the man wasn't being entirely truthful, he dismissed it as his own unfounded suspicion of people with too much facial hair.

Had Noah followed his intuition, things might have gone quite a bit differently.

5

A Miserable Murder of Crows

CLAIRE JENSEN LIVED IN THE NEW NEIGHBORHOOD OF HIGH-brough Hill, where homes were unnecessarily large and minds were unnecessarily small. Not that its residents were particularly dimwitted—they weren't. But, like Andi, they were able to narrow their focus to laser precision. While in Andi's case it was to burn holes in titanium walls and such, for the residents of Highbrough Hill it was so they could see only what they wanted to see and only when they wanted to see it. And mostly what they wanted to see were green lawns and clean windows and well-polished cars.

As for what went on inside the unnecessarily large homes themselves, it was just as disorganized and cha-otic and troublesome as in any other home. But as long as no one could see it from the curb, that was just fine and dandy.

Claire's party was set for 6:00 PM, but Ogden was going

to be late, because his Unter blew a gasket and had to be towed, making his trip back from the observatory longer than expected. That was fine; cool kids always arrive fashionably late—and he definitely needed to project coolness tonight.

Now, with the star certificate in hand, his replacement Unter was careening back down the winding mountain road toward Arbuckle—and destiny.

•　●　•

When Noah and Sahara arrived, they assumed Ogden was already there, since he tended to be painfully punctual. There was someone at the door checking the guest list because, this being the social event of the season, the long line of potential party crashers was beginning to assume theme park proportions.

"Do you really think Ogden made it through Checkpoint Jensen?" Sahara asked Noah.

"One of Ogden's superpowers is getting into places he doesn't belong," Noah answered. "He's probably in there. But how are *we* going to get in?"

Sahara looked at him pensively.

"Have you ever tried frog's legs?" she asked.

"Yeah, once. It's not true—they don't taste like chicken."

"No, that's not what I mean." Then she pointed at the house next door, where it looked like no one was home. "If you can jump over the neighbor's fence, you could hop into Claire's backyard from theirs."

"Yeah, but what about you?" asked Noah.

Sahara put her arms around his neck and, trying not to be too awkward about it, said, "I don't mind coming along for the ride."

They arrived in Claire's yard unnoticed, and without incident.

"Do you see Ogden?" Sahara asked Noah.

He looked around. "Not yet."

"Let's hope it's not too late to save him from himself."

• ● •

Ogden arrived a few minutes later—just as the stars were coming out, which would provide the perfect setting for his gift—and, as Noah had said, he was well-practiced in attending events he hadn't been invited to. The trick was to simply stride in like you knew exactly where you were going, and if someone stopped you, you just mumbled something specific but slightly incoherent, such as "They need me to hoist the thing, or you can forget about dinner." It was a Jedi mind trick that always worked. He never knew precisely what he would say until he was in the moment, but he trusted the universe to guide him.

The line of the unhappily uninvited was long, but Ogden knew that getting in that line was the kiss of death, because once you became one among many, you lost any hope of advantage. So Ogden bypassed the line like it wasn't even there and attempted to stride past the party coordinator who was checking names against the guest list.

"Excuse me? Are you on the list?"

"I'm not a guest, I'm running the digital piñata," he said. "I've got to reprogram the candy or it's going to be a disaster."

And once again it was proven that Ogden had a strong effect over weak minds.

He got all the way to the backyard without anyone else stopping him. Which was, in its own way, disappointing. He was looking forward to a challenge.

There were kids doing cannonballs in Claire's pool, splashing water onto other kids' plates of food. There were adults, presumably Claire's parents, and more professional party staff, trying to serve food, clean up messes, and prevent the inevitable medical emergency that typified a middle school house party.

And there was Claire, radiant as a mermaid without fins or slimy scales.

He would have made a beeline to her if the pool wasn't between them, like a moat between a knight and his princess. He had to go around it, passing the barbeque and the birthday cake. One thing led to another, and Ogden's priorities temporarily changed, as he hadn't had a thing to eat since breakfast.

• ● •

Unbeknownst to Ogden, or anyone else at the party for that matter, a figure lurked in the perfectly manicured bushes of Claire's backyard. Dressed all in black, Raymond Balding-Stalker fancied himself a manga-style ninja. If only he had a sword to cut out the heart of his rival and serve it up flaming on the barbeque.

Ogden heart, medium-well.

Whoever said revenge was a dish best served cold had never been to a barbeque.

Raymond was not as skilled as Ogden at gaining admittance to places he wasn't invited, so he showed up a few hours early, before anyone would notice. He climbed the fence and secured his place deep within a dense shrubbery almost as unremarkable as himself.

Only now, as he spotted Ogden entering with a gilded scroll that was clearly some brilliantly conceived gift for Claire, did Raymond realize his folly. Because while getting into the bush was no trouble at all, getting out was proving to be problematic.

Its prickly branches were like fish hooks gripping his ninja outfit and wouldn't let him go. His every attempt to free himself made the bush shake and shimmy. Around him, anyone who happened to notice the unruly bush assumed it was just a make-out spot and made note of it for later use during the party.

Finally, he won the battle with the bush and pulled

himself out of it, but the momentum of his heroic escape launched him headlong into the pool.

• ● •

Noah scoured the party for Ogden, but it wasn't made easy by his dark glasses, which he didn't dare remove. There were already rumors going around that Jaxon Youngblood had made a surprise appearance in Arbuckle earlier that day, and people were on the lookout.

Meanwhile, Sahara had slipped off to have a word with her former friend.

When Claire went inside to check the status of guest arrivals, and the turn-away line, Sahara caught the birthday girl before she returned to the backyard, making sure they were alone. Claire was surprised to see her—and a bit guarded.

"Sahara? What are you doing here?"

"Used to be I actually got invited to your birthday."

"That was a long time ago. People change."

"Not always for the better," Sahara pointed out.

Claire put a former-friendly hand on Sahara's shoulder. "Don't be so hard on yourself, Sahara. So, you got a little antisocial and disappeared into your gymnastics. Those are still valid choices."

Sahara wanted to smack her for that but realized Claire wasn't being sarcastic; she sincerely believed what she was saying. It was more sad than anything else.

"I'm happy with my choices," Sahara told her, shrugging Claire's arm off her shoulder. "Are you?"

Claire didn't answer; instead she glanced to the activity outside, clearly in a hurry to get back to all the adoration. "Well, as long as you're here, have a burger and some cake. Enjoy the party!"

"I'm not here to enjoy it," Sahara told her. "I'm here because a friend of mine is going to show up uninvited, manage to get around your security measures, and give you a gift. I'm asking you to please, *please* be decent to him."

Claire offered a smile that she probably believed was genuine. "When have I ever, ever not been decent?"

And although Sahara could have listed off every specific instance, she didn't. Instead, she said, "Just try to make your birthday special for others, too. Not just for yourself."

• ● •

Ogden was still stalled at the grill and, having already eaten, was instructing Claire's father on proper grilling technique, because clearly the man was an amateur.

"You have to make sure the flame is not so high that it chars the burger, but high enough to keep the center from being a barbeque bomb of deadly bacteria."

"Uh, wouldn't you rather be enjoying the party?" Mr. Jensen suggested.

Ogden looked down at the gilded scroll in his left hand, and suddenly remembered why he was there before being so rudely distracted by food. He reached out and shook Mr. Jensen's hand. "I'm Ogden," he said, "your daughter's future boyfriend. We'll talk."

Then he scoured the party for Claire.

He spotted her helping/not helping someone dressed entirely in black who had fallen into the pool. "Um, the ladder's over there," she said, pointing, but stepping back from all his splashing so as not to get her party dress wet. "Who are you anyway?" she said to the possibly drowning boy. "Are you even supposed to be here?"

By the time Ogden reached her, the waterlogged party crasher had run off into the bushes in utter embarrassment, leaving an opening for Ogden.

• ● •

Claire Jensen was not surprised that kids crashed her party. It was only to be expected. And although those who weren't on the official guest list were turned away at the door, anyone who managed to get in anyway was rewarded by being allowed to stay. As far as Claire was concerned, they had earned their admittance through their intrepid determination. It was her way of obliging the unwashed masses of Arbuckle Middle School—although one of the unwashed had now not only been washed, but also chlorinated.

"Ew—it's Raymond Balding-Stalker!" someone beside her said as the unfortunate boy struggled to free himself from the bush he had rushed into. "What's *he* doing here?"

67

"Doing whatever it is he does," responded Claire, magnanimously. And since the bush seemed to have him well restrained, she decided to just let it be. Because she was just that kind of girl. And also because the boy's mother, Ms. Stalker, was her English teacher—so it wouldn't hurt to show kindness to her son.

But now there was another uninvited guest begging her attention, coming toward her from the grilling area. She recognized him as the boy who had bothered her in the lunch line. Claire sighed. Shouldn't one's birthday party be more than humoring those who didn't belong? And yet humor she must—because in the end, every potential vote counted if she hoped to remain student body president once she got to high school. She knew that all too often elections are decided by the people who don't matter.

"Oren! You said you'd be here, and here you are!" She was particularly pleased with herself that she remembered his name. "Did you bring a bathing suit? I wouldn't want you to have to swim in your clothes like that other boy."

"Actually no," he said, having his focus so hypnotically on Claire, she doubted he even saw that other boy. "But I'm flattered you want to see me in a bathing suit."

"I didn't say that."

"Yes you did—but that's for another day. Right now, I'd like to give you a birthday gift I know you're going to treasure!"

Claire then remembered Sahara had said something

about an uninvited guest bearing a gift. "Good for you for getting this far!" she said. "Usually party crashers don't bring gifts—they just bring their appetites."

"Well, I brought that, too—but to be honest, I'm really not a party crasher. I'm more of a party whisperer."

By now some of Claire's actual invited guests had taken notice of the conversation and were migrating over—which was the last thing she wanted.

"Well, there's a gift table inside," Claire said, pointing. "Just make sure you write your name on it so my mother can write you a thank-you note."

"This can't wait for a gift table," Oren said. "You have to open it right here, right now, beneath the clear, starry sky."

"It's partly cloudy," pointed out Claire.

"Which means it's also partly clear," countered Oren.

"Is this scrawny dude bothering you, Claire?" asked Thayne Smith. He was captain of the boys' volleyball team, and at the forefront of Claire's collection of friends, even though he was an absolute tool—because as her mother once said, "*Tools can be wielded to great ends. Just look at your father.*"

Also joining the growing cluster was Jess Elizondo, a girl who was not quite as popular as Claire, however, like a cactus in a photo of the desert, needed to be there in Claire's background to provide perspective and scale.

"Ogden?" she said. "You invited Ogden?"

"It's Oren," corrected Claire. "And I didn't invite him."

"But fate had other plans," Oren said, and he held up a gilded scroll, which caught Thayne's eye more than anyone else's—but that was just because he tended to be easily distracted by shiny objects.

Then Oren unrolled it to reveal it was some sort of fancy certificate.

"I don't understand," said Claire as she looked at it. "What is it?"

"I know! It's a diploma from Nerd University," said Luke Hooten, who only aspired to be a tool but was more like a drill bit. "Get it? NERD University?"

Claire ignored him and read the gilded certificate. "So this is like for a star? In the sky?"

"And not just any star!" Oren said. "It's one you can actually see at night—especially this time of year!"

"Seriously?" said Jess, taking it from Claire and waving it in Oren's face. "You show up to a party and give her something like *this*?"

Oren grabbed it back, starting to act a little more agitated. "Look at it, Claire—it even has its own exoplanet! You know what an exoplanet is, right?"

"More like ex-zero-planet," said Luke. "Get it? Ex-ZERO-planet?"

There was something about the desperate look on Oren's face that started to weigh on Claire. She took the certificate again and looked at it more closely. "Actually, I think it's kind of sweet," she said.

70

"Sweet?" said Jess "Are you kidding me?

"Look," Oren said, pointing at the certificate. "I even named it after you!"

Then Claire noticed that there was a place toward the bottom—a blank line begging for a signature.

"It's ridiculous!" sneered Jess. "What would she even do with it?"

Now Oren began to lose his temper. "She would sit in her ginormous yard in front of her ginormous pool and look up at it, shining down on her from seventy-three-point-five light years away, and know that her boyfriend thought enough of her to get her a yak!"

"A what?"

"It's a metaphor!" yelled Oren.

"Wait," said Claire. "Did you say 'boyfriend'?"

That brought silence to the whole group. Until Thayne said, "Hey, I thought *I* was your boyfriend." Which wasn't true either, but that was a different conversation.

"Oren . . . ," said Claire.

"It's Ogden," he told her. "And I got this for you because you're like this star, Claire. And I'm like the exoplanet, trapped in your orbit, spinning closer and closer, longing to burn up in your radiance."

More silence. Someone cannonballed in the pool, splashing them, but nobody else moved.

And then Jess began to giggle . . .

. . . and Thayne began to chuckle . . .

71

...and Luke let out a guffaw...

...and before long everyone around Claire and Ogden was laughing.

It's not like Claire really wanted to laugh, but sometimes when your friends laugh, it's contagious—and even though Ogden's eyes were filling with tears, and his face was looking like he really was about to burn up in the heat of a sun, she just couldn't help herself. She just laughed and laughed, and finally struggled to get a grip.

"I'm sorry, Ogden," she told him, handing him back the certificate. "It's just...it's just..." But she lapsed into another fit of laughter.

Then from somewhere else in the party someone screamed, "Oh my god! It's Jaxon Youngblood!"

And suddenly Ogden's star was the last thing on anyone's mind. Because it had just been eclipsed by a brighter one.

• ● •

Noah and Sahara saw the whole thing. Every last humiliating moment of Ogden's fail. Although they both agreed Ogden wasn't really the one who failed. His attempt was valiant, and beyond anything that either Noah or Sahara thought him capable of. It was Claire and her friends' failure of humanity. The kind of thing that made Noah wonder if his parents had the right idea after all about wiping out life on Earth.

72

Noah would have broken into that miserable murder of crows and pulled Ogden out before they got their claws into him, but just as the whole thing started, Sahara convinced him to let it play out.

"A few months ago, Ogden wouldn't even have had the nerve to talk to a girl," Sahara pointed out. "And now look at him! We owe him the chance to see this through."

Noah had to admit she was right—they had come here to save him, but maybe that's not what he needed.

"Claire's changed since we were friends," Sahara said, "but I can't believe she's as awful as people say. This might not end as badly as we think."

So they lingered back and watched . . .

. . . and were both horrified when Claire began to laugh along with her brutal friends.

Now it was Sahara who wanted to rush in and rescue Ogden, but Noah stopped her.

"I have a better idea," he said. And he pulled off his shades, flipped off his cap, and tossed his hair. Then he turned to the nearest girl and batted his eyes.

• ● •

Word shot through the party faster than a trans-lunar portal that the rumors about the superstar being in town were true—and not only in town, but right here at Claire's party!

"Wow, Claire," one of her friends said. "I can't believe your parents actually got Jaxon Youngblood to come sing

73

you 'Happy Birthday'!" And her parents were so befuddled, they didn't deny it.

Of course, no singing had begun yet—because as sophisticated as alien skin technology was, it didn't go all the way down to the vocal cords.

While the crowd surrounded the counterfeit superstar, Sahara went over to Ogden, who sat dejected by the pool, looking at the star certificate, which had gotten bent and dog-eared in the clumsy hands of Claire and her minions.

"Hey," she said tentatively.

He looked up at her and was even more miserable. "Are you here to laugh at me, too?"

"No, never, Ogden."

Ogden pursed his lips and shook his head. "You warned me. I should have listened to you." He looked over at all the kids clamoring around the unexpected guest like pigeons at a crumb spill.

"Claire's father is under-cooking the meat," Ogden said. "I hope they all get the runs for a month."

"You know what, Ogden? Claire doesn't deserve that star."

"Yeah," agreed Ogden. "The way she blew the whole thing up, I should have gotten her a supernova."

"Or a black hole," suggested Sahara. "Then you could watch her collapse in on herself."

Ogden gave a half-hearted chuckle at that.

"Listen, Ogden . . . people who are super popular like

74

Claire made a choice. They chose to believe that what people *think* matters more than who people *are*. And in the end, it always comes back to bite them."

"Why should that matter when you're so popular that Jaxon Youngblood comes to your birthday party?"

Sahara smiled. "He didn't," she told him. "I'll give you one guess who that really is."

• ● •

With so many people pressing around the famous singer, Claire had to practically claw her way through the autograph seekers and selfie-takers to get to him. He was here for *her*, why couldn't her guests realize that? Finally, she managed to push everyone else out of the way and stood before him. She felt like she might faint and wondered if he'd catch her in his arms if she did.

"Jaxon!" she said. "I can't believe you came all the way to Arbuckle to sing me 'Happy Birthday.'"

He offered her his heart-melting smile. Then he said, "I didn't. I'm here to hang with my friend, Ogden."

"Wh-what?"

"The kid you and your friends just laughed at—and all because he bought you a gift that actually means something, instead of some waste of money that'll end up in the back of a closet."

Claire felt like her brain was short-circuiting. "I . . . I . . ."

"Let me finish that sentence," Jaxon said. "You, you . . . are self-centered, self-important, egotistical—"

"Don't forget over-accessorized," suggested Jess, who was already sensing a popularity void that she could readily fill.

"Right, that too," said Jaxon.

Claire's lower lip began to quiver.

"But it is your birthday," Jaxon said, "so I'll forgive you just this once . . . if you apologize for what you did."

"I'm so sorry, Jaxon!"

But he shook his head. "Don't apologize to me." He pointed behind her. "Apologize to my man Ogden."

Ogden waved, a big smile plastered on his face. "Hey, 'Jaxon.' Good to see you."

"Same here, Ogden, same here."

Claire looked around to see that everyone at the party was staring at her. This was, by far, the most humiliating thing she had ever experienced.

"If you want me to sing, Claire, then you'll accept Ogden's gift, and you'll *never* laugh at my friend again." And then Jaxon crossed his arms, waiting.

Stunned, Claire toddled over to Ogden. The self-centered, self-important, over-accessorized part of her wanted to shout at him *You've ruined everything! Now Jaxon Youngblood hates me because of you!* But another part told her to do what she should have done in the first place and accept the gift graciously. Or at least as graciously as she could still manage.

"Give me that thing!"

She snatched the star certificate from Ogden, shared a glare with Sahara, then turned back to Jaxon, giving him her best fake smile, and a thumbs-up. "All good here!"

"It's not official until you sign it," Ogden reminded her.

"Fine! PEN!" she yelled. Three people came running with pens. She chose a pink sparkly one, and she signed her name on the signature line.

"There!" she said to Ogden. "Are you happy?"

And once the document was signed and official, that's when the *real* party crashers arrived.

6

Rip, Tear, Rupture

THE PROBLEM WITH HAVING AN ANNUAL BIRTHDAY SPECTACLE IS that each year one had to top it. Such was the case with Claire Jensen's birthdays. It began when she was young, with an appearance by SpongeBob SquarePants, and it only went uphill (or downhill, depending on your perspective) from there.

Last year her birthday featured a troupe of Polynesian fire dancers that nearly set the whole neighborhood on fire, and a flyover from one of the Blue Angels who owed her father a favor.

So, when the aliens showed up at her front door, no one batted an eye; all the attention was still on Noah and his highly recognizable skin, fending off the throng of adoring fans. Which meant he was at an immediate disadvantage when the attack came.

The aliens at the door were wearing humans. Not

human skins, but *actual* humans. They were a species of puppet masters, and human beings were easy puppets to wield, dead or alive. The bony old man and foul-smelling woman at the door seemed a bit old for the party, and like Ogden, had cut the line. The party planner asked them if they were on the guest list, and the man responded by pulling out a pacifier. He said, "Don't make me use this."

"I'm sorry," the party organizer said, "but I can't let you in unless—"

The man cut her off by placing the pacifier in her mouth, and she instantly reverse-aged into a baby and crawled away, crying.

"The gate guard has been neutralized," the anemic man said. "Proceed with the extraction." And he stormed through the house to the backyard.

• ● •

Claire turned away from Ogden and was racing back through the crowd to show Noah/Jaxon that she had indeed accepted the star, when the exceptionally unwell-looking couple came out into the backyard.

Ogden spotted them immediately. "Wait, I know those two," he told Sahara. "They're the ones who sold me the star."

"What are they doing here?" asked Sahara. And then they watched as the couple pulled pacifiers out of their pockets and proceeded to turn anyone in their way into a baby.

"Uh-oh," said Ogden. "That can't be good."

But so involved were the people fawning over Jaxon Youngblood, no one noticed until Claire's father was pacified and the flow of food off the grill suddenly stopped.

"Hey," somebody yelled, "what's with all these babies? And where's my burger?"

Sahara was the only one with the presence of mind to realize who they were after. "They're here for Claire!" she said. "Something about that certificate she signed!"

Sahara raced to Claire and Noah. "Something weird's happening," Sahara told them. "Claire, you need to run!"

"Weird how?" Noah asked.

"Out of this world weird. Volcano in Arbuckle weird!"

"Cool," said Thayne Smith, who was listening in. "Sounds like fun." Then a pacifier got shoved into his mouth and he turned into a baby.

"Claire Jensen," said the unwell woman. "You need to come with us."

And, having just seen both of her parents turned into babies, Claire decided it was best to take Sahara's advice. She turned, and she ran.

Sahara tried to hold the two party-crashers back, pressing her lips together so as not to be pacified as well, but they evaded her and Ogden much more nimbly than such unwell-looking people should.

Noah, who finally managed to escape from his throng

of adoring fans, took in what was happening, but not enough to fully understand it.

"Use your powers!" Sahara shouted to Noah, less worried at exposing him than stopping whatever was going on here.

"To do what?" he asked.

"Anything!"

But then a girl with long nails grabbed his head to pull him close and squealed, "I'd do anything to have a kiss from Jaxon Youngblood."

Noah resisted, she pulled a little too hard, and Jaxon Youngblood's face ripped right off, leaving the girl screaming in the depths of what was now her own personal nightmare.

"My god! I killed Jaxon Youngblood!"

Leaving her behind, Noah moved closer to the action while using his golden-cheeked warbler vision to get a clearer view of the chaotic situation. In the commotion, someone bumped against him, and to steady himself, Noah accidentally put his hand on the hot grill, causing him to leap completely out of his Jaxon skin. He inflated like a puffer fish and landed in the pool, where he floated like a beach ball.

Ogden never took his eyes off of Claire as she ran across the expansive yard, so he was the only one to see the swirl of birthday napkins, cups, and plastic silverware beginning to rise. Not as if blown by a wind, but swept up by a soft blue ray of light—shining right in the spot that Claire was running toward.

"Claire! No!" he shouted, and took off toward her. "Stop!"

He was inches away from her, his hands just about to reach her and save her from the tractor beam, when he was suddenly tackled.

• ● •

Raymond Balding-Stalker had been waiting for the perfect moment to make his move. Watching from the bushes, he had reveled in Ogden's complete humiliation as he was rebuffed by Claire and her friends. And then Raymond suffered the misery of seeing Jaxon Youngblood redeem Ogden.

The jealousy of seeing Claire accept that star certificate was almost more than Raymond could bear. He didn't notice the aliens. He didn't notice the sudden abundance of babies. All he saw was Claire running, the wind in her hair, and Ogden running after her.

And that's when he made his move.

Using his mostly imagined ninja skills, he launched from the edge of the treacherous bushes and hurled himself at Ogden just before Ogden reached Claire, taking him down to the ground and pinning him there.

"You don't deserve her, Coggin-Criddle!" Raymond shouted, going all Ninja on Ogden.

• ● •

The moment Claire hit the edge of the tractor beam, her stomach began to tingle and her hair began to swim around her face like she was underwater. She never actually felt herself leave the ground, but when she looked down she was already five feet in the air—and although she wanted to scream, the beam seemed to freeze her vocal cords, and made her limbs go limp. All she could do was hang there, in midair, rising higher and higher.

• ● •

Her party guests didn't know what to make of all this, and in the commotion, logically assumed that this skyward display was the show-stopping finale of another spectacular Claire Jensen birthday party. And as she ascended into the light, people began to applaud the quality of the special effect. Yay! The Jensens have done it again. Then someone began to sing:

"Happy birthday to you . . ."

And as herd instinct kicked in others joined along:

"Happy birthday to you . . ."

And soon, almost everyone not a baby was singing:

"Happy birthday, dear Cla-aire . . ."

And then they brought it home in the enthusiastic, painfully off-key manner of every birthday song sung since the very beginning of recorded time:

"Happy birthday...toooo...youuuuuuu...."

Then the lights of the spaceship above them came fully on, shining in everyone's eyes. They couldn't see much of the ship, other than that it was massive and directly above them. Suddenly, it became clear to most, if not all, that this was not part of the planned festivities.

• ● •

Noah, useless in swollen pufferfish form, finally managed to deflate himself and climb out of the pool. The unwell woman had leaped into the beam of light and was rising toward the ship beneath Claire—but the woman's conspirator hadn't made it to the tractor beam yet. Noah leaped at him with the full force of a pouncing panther and took him down, trying not to be overpowered by what must have been the man's cheap cologne—a chemical stench not entirely unlike the mutant animals Mr. Kratz used to keep in jars in his classroom.

"Who are you?" Noah demanded. "What's happening?"

"The deal is done!" the man said. "Whatever you do, you can't change it!"

"What do you want with Claire?"

But instead of answering, the man opened his mouth and tilted his head back. "Ah...ah...ahhhh..."

84

The man was about to sneeze, and the thought of this unwell-looking man sneezing on him was such an unpleasant thought that Noah turned his face away, just as . . .

"Ahh . . . Ahhh . . . CHOOO!"

. . . the man let off a juicy sneeze, and a tiny green worm no longer than a fingernail blew out of his nose, missed Noah entirely, and sailed in an arc across the yard.

• ● •

"Let me go!" yelled Ogden. "Get off me, Raymond!"

Ogden never considered himself a fighter, but Raymond's sudden attack had prevented him from saving Claire—and that brought Ogden to a level of rage he had never before experienced. He hit back, giving as good as he got. They rolled and threw punches, only some of them connecting. Ogden imagined that his adrenaline might give him some of the animal strength that Noah had—and maybe it did, because he definitely delivered Raymond a black eye.

But still Raymond wouldn't stop. He had not been expecting Ogden to fight back, and it just made him madder. Raymond was so focused on fighting his archrival that he never saw Claire rising skyward, never heard the misguided chants of "Happy Birthday," never saw the spaceship above them . . .

. . . and Raymond never noticed the little green worm as it landed on his left eyebrow, then crawled down into his tear duct, squiggling its way deep into his sinuses.

But he *did* notice when the worm reached his brain. Because that's when he stopped fighting and stood up without telling his legs to do so.

Stop, he told his legs. *What are you doing?*

But they didn't listen or obey a single command he gave them. Because they weren't *his* legs anymore. Now Raymond Balding-Stalker was nothing but a powerless passenger in his own body. A puppet for the little green worm to use.

• ● •

Ogden stood up the instant Raymond let him go. "Yeah, you'd better run away!" Ogden yelled after him.

But Raymond spared a glance back, long enough to say, "Thank you, small, naive biped. You have been most helpful."

Then Raymond leaped into the light, which lifted him to the ship, and then the ship powered away with such force it blew the windows out of the house and tore up half the trees in the yard.

Everyone was left stunned. Well, almost everyone.

"Wow," said Luke Hooten, his hair pointing in all unearthly directions. "Best party ever!"

• ● •

Noah instinctively took an elephant stance, and so he was the only one not blown over by the wake of the spaceship's departure—and the only one who actually saw it distort the space around it as it engaged its warp drive, or whatever it was actually called by the beings that invented it. The craft seemed to expel itself from Earth as if by slingshot, disappearing into the heavens.

Ogden picked himself up off the ground. "Well, that's not how I expected tonight would go," he said. "But it's great to see you, Noah."

"Same here, Ogden."

"Noah! Ogden!" Sahara called. "Could you guys help me?"

She was standing near the pool, trying to round up crawling babies, of which there were at least a dozen. "Keep them away from the pool!"

Ogden hesitated. "I'm not good with babies," he said.

"You don't have to be good with them—you just have to keep them from drowning!"

So they hurried over to Sahara and helped her gather more infants and deposit them in the arms of teenagers, who were already stunned and bewildered, and now were holding babies.

Ogden glanced at one he had picked up, noticed her abundance of eyeshadow, and came to the conclusion that this was Claire's friend Jess, who was much less thoroughly obnoxious in infant form. Considering that they were all "pacified," it only made sense that the way to return them to normal was to pull the plug. So he removed the binky from her mouth. But all that succeeded in doing was to make baby-Jess wail. So he reinserted the pacifier and decided this was an issue best resolved by an actual parent. *Anyone's* parent.

Meanwhile, Noah tried to bring comfort to the troubled situation. "Don't panic!" Noah said to the non-pacified kids groaning and beginning to lift themselves from the ground. "It's going to be okay!" And while Noah had no actual proof that everything was going to be okay, isn't that what you're supposed to say in a situation like this? Then he realized that that rule didn't really apply, because there never had been any situations like this.

A few yards away, a kid rose to his feet, dazed and disoriented, and pointed at him. "Hey, aren't you Noah Prime—"

Suddenly, Sahara jumped in and shook the kid hard enough to rattle the thought away. "WAKE UP! YOU'RE DREAMING!" Sahara screamed at him.

"Wh...what was that for?"

Sahara stood in front of him, completely blocking his view of Noah, and pointed at someone else. "Over there! That girl needs your help!"

"Oh my god!" wailed the girl in question, who was holding the face of Jaxon Youngblood. "I just wanted to kiss him, and now I've torn his beautiful face off! I'm a monster!"

And so, forgetting all about Noah, the kid went over to

help her pick up the pieces—literally—of the pop super-star's skin.

"Noah, you can't be seen here," Sahara reminded him. "If people realize you're alive, it could get back to the Anu-sians or the Fauxlites!"

"Hold on a sec," Noah said. Then he looked down and concentrated. When he looked up again his face was gone. Well, not entirely gone. His skin and bones had gone completely clear, like flavorless Jell-O. But Sahara could see his eyeballs and his brain.

"Ew."

"Glass fish," Noah explained. "It has a see-through body. If I take off my shirt, you'll see my internal organs."

"Thanks, but no thanks."

That's when Ogden approached with the Roarin' Volca-noes cap and sunglasses that Noah had come to the party with. "Hey, it worked for Jaxon," he said. So, Noah let his skin go back to normal, and put on his original disguise.

By now neighbors had run over to see what the trouble was—looking for Mr. and Mrs. Jensen, but not finding them, since they had both been pacified.

"What happened here?" one of the neighbors asked.

"Fireworks accident," another one concluded. "I've already called 911."

That's when Andi came bounding over the back fence, landing right next to Noah, Sahara, and Ogden. "I came as soon as I heard the RTR."

"The what?" asked Noah.

"The RipTearRupture—it's what we call a faster-than-light engine."

"Ah," said Noah. "So *that's* what it's called!"

"RTRs should never be gunned this close to a planet's surface. Whoever it was, they wanted out of here fast."

They quickly told Andi what she had missed.

"Claire Jensen?" she said, incredulous. "Why would anyone in their right mind want Claire Jensen?"

"I do," said Ogden, "And I'm in my right mind."

"That's highly debatable," said Andi.

Then Andi approached the strange-smelling unwell man on the ground, who appeared even more unwell than before. "Who's this?"

"He's one of them!" Noah told her. "I knocked him unconscious."

"Uh, he's more than unconscious," Andi informed him. "He's dead."

"What? I killed him?"

"No," said Andi. "My scan shows advanced cellular necrosis. He's been dead for a long time but preserved with formaldehyde...."

"So...we're dealing with an attack of the living dead?" asked Sahara.

"Possibly...," said Andi. "But it could also be Usurpers. Did anyone see a small green worm come out of him?"

"No," said Noah, "but he did let off a nasty sneeze before he went limp."

"And," said Ogden, "I did see something green on Raymond Balding-Stalker's unibrow before he got weird and jumped into the antigravity beam—but I just thought it was a booger."

"Yes, it was Usurpers," said Andi. "Now we know *who* . . . but we still don't know *why*."

Somewhere far off, but getting closer, they heard the approach of emergency vehicles. Their classmates were now all congregating in groups to discuss the trauma/thrill of whatever it was they just experienced, and all the pacified babies were in arms.

"It looks like things are relatively under control," Sahara surmised. "Maybe we should get out of here before we get asked questions we don't want to answer. . . ."

But just before they slipped out through the side yard, she caught Noah grinning.

"How could you possibly be smiling at a time like this?" she asked.

"Sorry—just some dolphin bubbling up," he said.

But that wasn't exactly the truth. The fact was, Noah couldn't help but feel a twinge of guilty pleasure in all of this. Because as long as there were terrible, horrible extraterrestrial things going on, he and his friends wouldn't be saying goodbye.

PART 2

• ● •

BRICK HOUSE

7

Kratz Actual

QUANTAVIUS T. KRATZ SAT IN HIS CELL, AS GLUM AS THE DAY WAS long. And his days were *very* long.

He tried to convince himself it wasn't really a cell at all. It was more like a studio apartment. With an extremely firm bed. And a toilet directly next to the bed for convenience. And a nice little slot in the door through which food could be given and plates removed. Why, a space like this would sell for over a million dollars in New York City!

But it was no use. He couldn't forget that the door was locked from the outside.

On the plus side, there were no runny-nosed middle school brats he had to govern with no allowable weapons beyond his superior mind. Of course, that also meant he could no longer entertain himself by making their lives as miserable as his own. The only person he could irritate these days was his former assistant, and now jailor, Agent

Rigby. He took immense pleasure in refusing to answer her endless, pointless questions that he didn't have the answers to anyway, in spite of her horrifying methods of torture.

He heard the locks activating, and a moment later the door slid back, revealing two muscle-bound, unsmiling government agents in black suits. *That time again*, he thought. Well, no reason to make it easy for them.

However, the two agents had no trouble dragging him out of his room and down the long hallway, in spite of his attempts at resistance. "Kratz Actual on the move," they radioed to their superior. It was what they called him here. Because there were far too many counterfeit Kratzes these days.

They hauled him into the interrogation chamber, where they strapped him to a chair. A moment later, Agent Rigby entered with another agent: a stoic Black woman, with a name badge that identified her as Agent Knell. He'd seen her before. She was being trained in interrogation.

"Welcome back, Dr. Kratz," said Agent Rigby, grimly. "I hope you'll be a little bit more cooperative this morning. Shall we begin?"

Kratz refused to give her the courtesy of a reply, or even a nod, but that didn't stop her.

"What can you tell me about the 7-Eleven on Arbuckle Boulevard?" After a moment of silence, she continued, "Nothing? Perhaps this will remind you."

She lifted a typed report from the desk in front of her and began to read.

" 'In the days prior to the volcanic anomaly, multiple individuals—including one dressed as a Roman gladiator and another in the robes of the Spanish Inquisition—entered the aforementioned 7-Eleven, and never came out again. In addition, a wave of spatial distortion has been detected around the building so powerful, it could buckle titanium.' " Rigby looked up at Kratz, one eyebrow raised. "Anything you'd care to add?"

Kratz said nothing. The silent, frowning agent Knell loudly cracked her knuckles in preparation for today's torture.

"And maybe it's time you told us what you know about the advanced robotic weapons system, code name: Andi Prime?"

Kratz sighed. Same old questions. "Perhaps you should ask her brother. Oh, that's right, you had Noah Prime, and he escaped within hours of his capture. Bet that didn't go over well with your superiors, Eleanor."

"Who told you that?" Agent Rigby snapped.

"I have my sources," Kratz responded. Actually he had been holding his ear to the little food slot and overheard two guards talking about it—but Rigby didn't need to know that.

"One last chance, Quantavius," Rigby said. "The family

who lived in the apartment above yours. They were hospitalized with internal injuries and broken bones after claiming that they were tossed around their apartment as if 'gravity kept switching directions.' And they were actually the lucky ones—because they were still at the hospital when everyone in the immediate vicinity of your apartment suddenly claimed to be you! You, Quantavius Kratz, are the epicenter of *all* paranormal activity in Arbuckle, and although ignorance is your defining trait, you cannot claim ignorance about it!"

Kratz struggled against his bonds. "I've already told you everything I know!"

"You mean all that garbage about demons?"

"It's true! I know what I saw!"

Rigby sighed and pinched the bridge of her nose as if warding off a migraine. "We've already managed to determine that the beings you claim to be demons were actually extraterrestrials. And your so-called 'gateway to hell' was nothing more than a portal that opened to the earth's mantle—which explains the volcano, but not how or why it was accomplished."

This was all news to Kratz. But he maintained his poker face, because this indeed was a game of poker. Even if he wasn't playing with a full deck.

"Well then," said Kratz, "there's nothing I can tell you that you don't already know." Which was true. But Agent Rigby was still convinced he was bluffing.

"Very well," she said. "Have it your way." Then she turned to Agent Knell. "He's all yours."

Agent Knell gave an awful grin, cracked her knuckles again, then left the room, returning with a crate overflowing with papers. Kratz began to sweat.

"What," he asked, "is that?"

Agent Rigby smiled. "We've collected for you five hundred of the absolute worst student science essays ever written," she said. And Agent Knell, her jaw hard as nails, slammed the first one down in front of him.

"No food, no drink, no sleep until you've graded them all," said Rigby.

Feeling a wave of nausea overtake him, Kratz looked at the title of the first paper. It read "Atom and Eve: When Molecules Fall in Love."

His eyes rolled in abject agony; all his attempts to be coolly resistant fell before this new horror. *"For the love of God, Eleanor! This is inhuman!"*

But she just looked at him without the slightest bit of pity. "It's called torture for a reason, Quantavius." Then she handed Kratz a red pen and patted Agent Knell on the shoulder. "I'll leave you two to your 'business.' Perhaps after a few hundred of these, he'll be more open to a meaningful discussion."

"Nooooooo . . ."

But she was gone, leaving Kratz alone with Agent Knell, and essays like "Pluto: Dog or Planetoid," and "The Chemical Composition of the Zit I Just Popped."

Kratz dropped his head and gave himself over to sobs of misery. But then Agent Knell spoke. It was the first time she had ever spoken in his presence.

"Suck it up, Kratz," she said. "Today's your lucky day. Or should I say *our* lucky day."

And she reached over and unlocked his restraints.

• ● •

The secret regional headquarters of the Federal Office of Biological Experimentation (FOBE) was not an easy place to escape from. Only once—when Noah Prime flushed himself into the sewer and his sister simultaneously blasted her way out of the armored north wing—was there ever a security breach.

But if Agent Knell had her way, today would be another embarrassment for Agent Rigby, and her so-called secure facility.

"Who are you?" Kratz asked as they ran down the hall. "Why are you helping me escape?"

"All you need to know is that I'm on your side," Knell said. "And that your freedom brings me one step closer to mine."

She took a sharp turn down an adjacent hallway, and Kratz followed, his mind awhirl with possibilities. Was this a trick? A pretense to get him to cooperate? Or was she actually an ally?

As for Agent Knell, she didn't care what he believed, so

long as he did as he was told. She used her thumbprint to open the door of a stairwell and pushed Kratz through first. Then she fired her weapon at the door's scanner, rendering it inoperable just as the door slid shut behind them.

A minute later, with alarms blaring, agents scrambling, and a full lockdown in progress, a sports car came careening out of the parking garage seconds before the security gate slammed shut, successfully preventing high speed pursuit.

"Ha!" laughed Agent Knell, as they sped toward the highway. "Precisely as I planned! Their own lockdown protocol foiled any attempt to chase us!"

"Ha!" echoed Kratz. "I couldn't have planned that better myself."

"Very true!" said Knell with another laugh. "You would have done quite the same."

"So, who are you, really? And where are we going?"

Knell was surprised that Kratz, being the genius that he was, hadn't figured it out already. But perhaps keeping him in the dark was better for both of them. Or at least better for her.

Kratz, however, was a man also motivated by pure self-interest, and he knew that Agent Knell wasn't telling him the full story. But the truth would come out in due time. For now, their goals were in alignment. It seemed Rigby was their mutual enemy, and as they say, *"My enemy's enemy is . . . not my enemy anymore."* Or something like that.

The mysterious agent continued to drive evasively, making quick turns and occasionally doubling back, to confound anyone trying to track them. He approved. They were the exact tactics he would use under the circumstances.

Once she was certain that they weren't being followed, Agent Knell turned them toward Arbuckle—but made sure that they approached from an unexpected direction that avoided checkpoints into town. It was a route only an agent of FOBE would know. She didn't share their ultimate destination with Kratz just yet, though. Best to keep him guessing.

"As I'm sure you've figured out by now, Agent Rigby wants to get her grubby little hands on the technology left behind by the alien incursion," Knell told him. "But they haven't yet found anything they can use."

"And what makes you think you can?" Kratz asked.

Knell smiled. "Because *I* know that *you* know where the portal gun, antigravity wand, and memory projector are hidden."

Kratz gasped. "How do you know about those? I never told anyone about them!"

Once more Knell offered a humorless smile. "Let's just say I know what I know."

And although Kratz was annoyed by her secrecy, he found himself admiring her.

Almost as much as he admired himself . . .

8

I Know a Thing Who Knows a Thing

"REAL ESTATE," SAID MR. KSH, WHEN THE KIDS TOLD HIM WHAT had happened at Claire's ill-fated party. "As I told you once before, it's always about real estate."

While the star certificate got sucked up into the spaceship along with Claire and the Usurpers, Ogden still had his copy of the detailed contract he had to fill out at the observatory—an observatory that didn't actually exist on any map. The contract was full of disclaimers, and waivers, and terms of service—all the things that you never really read.

Mr. Ksh flipped through page after page. "Yes, yes—this is a full-fledged, legally rendered real estate transaction," he said. "When Claire signed that certificate, she became the official owner of that star and its planet."

"But why would someone do this?" Noah asked.

"Well, whatever their reason," said Mr. Ksh, "they

must have been highly motivated sellers. How much did this star system cost?" he asked Ogden.

"Fifty bucks."

"Ah. Sounds like quite a deal," he concluded.

"How did Ogden even find out about it?" Andi asked.

The other kids looked at one another and realized where they had to go next.

• ● •

"I swear, I don't know anything about it," said Merlin, completely dropping his olde-timey way of talking. "I'm just a guy who runs a game shop."

But Andi saw through that, quite literally. "Well, Merlin, my bio-scan says that your brain is where your liver should be, your liver is where your spleen should be, and instead of a spleen you have a secondary stomach for digesting plastic. And also, your beard hides an extra set of lungs that filters carbon dioxide and other greenhouse gasses out of the air."

"So?" said Merlin.

"So," said Andi. "You're obviously an Enviro-nerd—a genetically manufactured species introduced into the eco-systems of planets with climate issues." She turned to the other kids. "He, and thousands like him, have been placed here on earth to clean up your human mess, while pretending to play Dungeons and Dragons. Without them, this planet would have been a dead rock twenty years ago." Then she turned back to Merlin and put her hand over the place where her heart would be had she been human, and bowed slightly. "We thank you for your service."

Noah stepped forward, pointing an accusing finger. "But that doesn't explain why you helped the little green worms abduct Claire Jensen!"

"Okay," said Merlin, "I'll admit I knew they were up to something—but they threatened to turn me over to the Federal Office of Biological Experimentation. And if FOBE got ahold of me, I'd be cut up into a thousand little pieces! So I agreed to let them post their card on my bulletin board." Merlin sighed. "I thought they were just looking for fresher hosts, because the bodies they were in had seen better days. And knowing you, Ogden, I figured you wouldn't mind being the living host of an advanced species."

"It would have been enticing," Ogden admitted, "but they never asked."

"Well," said Sahara, "as it so happens, we know Agent Rigby—the head of FOBE. A single call to her, and it'll be scalpels for you.

"Yeah," seconded Noah. "You'll be the subject of their next alien autopsy."

Merlin began nervously nibbling on an empty plastic soda bottle. "What do you want from me?"

"We need a way off-planet," Andi told them. "In a ship

105

with an RTR drive big enough for all of us to catch up with the Usurpers."

"Whoa, whoa, whoa," cried Sahara. "When did this become a 'we' thing?"

Noah sighed. "Sahara's right. I mean, she can't just drop everything and go off-planet; she has a life."

"Well, I've got a semblance of one," Ogden said, "and I'm willing to go. . . ."

"Of course you are! Because this is your mess!" Sahara pointed out.

Ogden glared at her. "Sure, just abandon your closest friends when things get a little stressful."

Sahara glared right back. "(A) you are not my closest friend, and (B) taking a blind leap into outer space where we all might die horrible deaths is a bit more than 'things getting stressful'!"

"I'll make sure nobody dies," said Andi. "At least not immediately."

"And my powers can help protect us, too," Noah pointed out. "That is, if we all decide to go."

Sahara crossed her arms, understandably huffy. "Well, none of this matters anyway, because we don't have a ship!"

Then they all turned to Merlin, who had been happy to be left out of this conversation. Now he backed away at the prospect of their combined attention.

"Don't look at me—I don't have a trans-stellar ship,"

Merlin told them, then took a moment to consider. "But I know a thing who knows a thing who might be able to help you...."

• ● •

The UFO event of the previous evening was already bringing government types flooding into town. They wandered the area around the Jensen home, waving radiation detectors and taking soil samples, and questioning neighbors in an ever-widening circle. Reports of missing people—mostly party guests—kept law enforcement busy, as did the inexplicable abundance of babies, who were all now in the overwhelmed hands of Child Protective Services.

"We need to be off the streets," Noah said, as they left the game shop. "With FOBE agents poking around everywhere, it'll be hard to avoid them, and we can't risk them seeing me or Andi."

"And I don't want to have to go into defensive mode," said Andi. "They already think I'm some sort of doomsday weapon."

"Aren't you?" asked Ogden.

"Oh, please! I might be able to turn a building into a smoldering crater, but that's hardly an extinction-level event."

"So, what now?" asked Sahara.

"While we're waiting for Merlin to contact his sources,

I can tune my sensors to look for interstellar residue and traces of RTR exhaust, in hopes of finding a ship we can get passage on," Andi suggested, "but it'll take time."

"We don't have time," whined Ogden.

"Well, that star isn't going anywhere," Andi pointed out. And apparently neither were they.

• ● •

They went to Ogden's mom's house to regroup and plan their next move. His mom was off at work, but Ogden's cat seemed glad to see them. And alternately not. The cat wove in and out between them, meowing, begging for attention but seemingly annoyed whenever anyone gave it some. Like Ogden himself, the cat was a bundle of contradictions.

Andi moved around the room pacing as she scanned the neighborhood for a ship, but so far had come up with nothing.

Merlin showed up at Ogden's door and said he had news but seemed a bit guarded.

"Through my contacts, I've been able to confirm that there's an RTR ship here in Arbuckle." But then he hesitated.

"So where is it?" Noah prompted.

"I don't know," said Merlin, looking sheepish. "The thing who knows a thing wants payment for information. And so does the second thing."

The kids looked to one another. "Will this thing take Apple Pay?" Ogden asked. "The other aliens did."

Merlin sighed. "The first thing is demanding payment in human souls."

"Fine," said Andi, barely blinking. "How many—and do they have to be decent ones, or can they be really bad people?"

Merlin shrugged. "Probably a nice mix."

"Andi!" shouted Noah, then turned to Merlin. "Sorry, that's not an option!"

"Maybe we can go straight to the second thing and skip the middleman."

"Middle-*thing*," corrected Ogden.

"Whatever," said Sahara. "Just tell us what the second thing wants."

"Human brains," Merlin informed them.

"How many—and do they have to be smart ones?"

"Andi!"

She threw up her hands. "Can you at least let me negotiate?"

"No!" Noah said, standing firm. "Tell your things no deal."

"Well, I did my part," said Merlin, "so you can't expose me."

"Don't worry," said Ogden. "This town wouldn't be the same without you, Merlin. Your secret's safe with us."

Merlin was visibly relieved. "There's one bit of information my guy slipped. Wherever this ship is, it's old and hasn't been used for a while."

"Hmm," said Andi. "Probably why I couldn't find any residual trace of its engine."

"I'd be careful if I were you," Merlin warned. "Even if you find it, a ship that's been out of use that long might not be very spaceworthy."

"Noted," said Noah.

Merlin turned to Ogden. "May your quest be attainable without loss of life and limb, Sir Ogden of Coggin-Criddle." Then he bowed and left them no better off than when he had arrived.

Andi sighed. "He hath left us with nary a clue."

Sahara glared at her. "Don't you start talking like him."

"Sorry," grumbled Andi. "I couldn't help myself."

"This is terrible," moaned Ogden. "We're never going to find her! This is all my fault!"

"Agreed," said Sahara.

Which irritated Ogden no end. "You're not supposed to agree with me! As a supportive friend, you're sup-posed to say it wasn't my fault at all and that it couldn't be helped!"

"But it *was* your fault, and it *could* have been helped."

"You're not making me feel any better! What happened to the friendly comforting Sahara from last night?"

"That was before I found out you fell for an obvious scam by people who were clearly aliens!"

"Guys," said Noah, coming between them. "Let's just

bring it down a notch, get ourselves some warm milk, and relax."

"Warm milk?" said Sahara, looking at him funny.

"Sorry, it was the first thing that came to mind. Must be an animal thing. Ogden, maybe get us some snacks so we're not all so cranky."

"Best idea I've heard all morning." Ogden went into the kitchen but couldn't let it go. "It could have happened to anybody," he insisted. "How was I supposed to know?"

"Maybe because the 'people' who sold you the star looked dead . . . and smelled dead?" said Sahara.

"My parents are university professors—that describes half the people they work with." Ogden returned from the kitchen with what he thought were snacks, but when he looked at the plate, all he had done was open a can of tuna. Disheartened and wondering how he could have been so distracted, he gave it to the cat, who was more than happy to devour it.

"If we can't find ourselves an RTR ship," said Sahara, "we may have to find a way to accept that Claire is gone."

Ogden buried his head in his hands like it was, once more, the end of the world.

"Don't worry, Ogden," Noah said. "We'll find her." Then he sighed and leaned back. "But first, I just want to lie down on a big green sofa in a big blue house and forget all about it for a while."

That got Sahara's attention. "Did you say a big blue house?"

Noah considered that. "Yeah, I did. Why did I imagine that?"

"Does the blue house have yellow trim?" she asked.

"And wind chimes...," said Noah, sitting up. "How did you know?"

The cat meowed and brushed between them.

Sahara took a good look at it. "Ogden, where did you get this cat?"

"Mittens is a rescue," Ogden told her. "We found him after the volcano blew."

"Right—I remember now," said Sahara. "At first you thought it was a female cat."

"Only because I have a tendency to see dogs as male and cats as female," Ogden explained. "Anyway, since no one came looking, we adopted him." Then Ogden furrowed his eyebrows. "Not sure where we got the name Mittens. It just kind of felt...right."

Sahara looked at Noah. The cat meowed. Both of them suddenly had an image come to mind. More of a feeling, actually.

"Sudden urge to go outside?" Noah asked.

"And to come right back in." Sahara said. "That's definitely cat."

"So was that thought of warm milk," said Noah, "and

112

Ogden opening a can of tuna without realizing it." Noah turned to his sister. "Andi?"

Her eyes snapped open "Can't you see I'm busy?"

"I need you to do a scan of Ogden's cat."

She looked at him with faint disgust. "It's a cat," she said.

"Run a scan anyway."

She sighed. "Fine." She raised a hand, moved it about in the air above the cat . . .

. . . and suddenly her weapons systems came online. Her eyes turned red, and laser bolts shot out. The cat yowled and jumped just in time, as Ogden's mother's favorite chair was reduced to ash.

"Andi!" yelled Noah.

"That's not a terrestrial feline!" shouted Andi. "That's Mittens the Disgruntled. He has the death sentence in twelve star systems." Her eyes began to power up again.

"Andi! Stand down!" demanded Noah.

A moment of laser-sharp tension, and Andi's eyes went back to normal. "I'm supposed to protect you from threats—and *that's* a threat."

"Actually," said Noah, "he might not be. He might be trying to help us."

Mittens was now on his scratching post, back arched, fur on end. Suddenly, everyone got a very distinct image of being attacked by merciless claws, then a sudden craving for mouse.

"Ogden—he's your cat. Could you get him to... de-escalate?" said Noah.

"Mittens, come here," Ogden said. "I'm sorry that the big bad robot stressed you out. Let me scratch behind your ears."

Reluctantly, Mittens slunk down from his perch, pausing only to hiss at Andi, before climbing into Ogden's lap for the aforementioned ear-scratching.

"Mittens is clearly telepathic," Noah said. "And when we were talking about the RTR drive, Sahara and I had the identical vision of a blue house."

"I had a vision of a vegetable garden," Ogden said, "but I think it was in the yard of a blue house."

"Mittens," Noah asked, "do you know where we can find an RTR drive?"

Again the image of the house and garden came, almost as vivid as a photograph.

Sahara shook her head. "I know Arbuckle backward and forward—there's no house like that in town. It must be somewhere else."

"How do we know it's anything?" Andi said, annoyed that, as an android, she couldn't get telepathic projections from a criminal alien cat. "It could just be the last place he lived."

"If he's really trying to help us, then he must want something in return." Noah turned to the cat in Ogden's arms. "Mittens—what do you want for helping us?"

And although Sahara and Noah got nothing, Ogden got the full picture.

"Uh...He wants this whole house. To himself. And a human whose sole purpose in life is to serve him."

Sahara looked around at the house, then at Ogden. "Um, doesn't he already have that?"

"Well, yeah," agreed Ogden, "but it's not official."

Noah considered it. "Tell him...you'll work on it?"

Just then Andi jumped up. "Hey! I've got something."

"You found a ship?" Noah asked.

"No...but someone just opened a portal right here in Arbuckle!"

9

My Thoughts Exactly

HALF AN HOUR EARLIER, AGENT KNELL AND DR. KRATZ ARRIVED in Arbuckle. As they approached the town, Agent Knell insisted that Kratz slink low in his seat as not to be seen. "No need to advertise your presence," Knell said.

After months of captivity and interrogation, Kratz didn't have the will to argue, so he lowered his seat back and continued refining his plan, such as it was, to gain the advantage.

"Getting into the Quantavius Zone won't be difficult," the agent said, "and FOBE will have no idea we're heading there—because I left clues suggesting we're headed south, so Rigby will be off on a wild-goose chase."

They arrived in Arbuckle by an unpaved, unguarded road—but hit unexpectedly heavy traffic once they were in town, and Kratz dared to poke his head up slightly to look around.

"What's going on?" he asked.

"In case you forgot, thanks to you, a volcano popped up in the middle of everything, messing up all the roads," the agent grumbled. "You can't get anywhere from anywhere in Arbuckle anymore."

"Not that you ever could," quipped Kratz, "since anywhere in Arbuckle is basically nowhere."

They both chuckled at that, for precisely the same amount of time.

The detour took them past a small, freshly built park at the base of the new volcano, featuring four gleaming bronze statues that had been draped in flowers and surrounded by candles.

"The Prime family," Agent Knell said, even before Kratz asked. "They're missing—presumed dead. Officially, they're the only casualties from the volcanic eruption—but unofficially, we know that the boy and his robotic sibling are still at large. Not sure about the parents, though."

But none of this addressed his primary concern.

"What about me?" railed Kratz. "Did no one notice I was missing, too? I demand to be presumed dead and given a statue!"

"The world is fickle and cruel," said Agent Knell. "With so many other people claiming to be you, no one wanted to hear about 'Kratz actual.'"

"People are imbeciles."

"Agreed. All the more reason to take what's ours."

"What's mine," Kratz corrected.

"If you say so."

When they reached the Quantavius Zone, they drove past the guarded entrance and down a side street. "We can't risk the main entrance, but I arranged alternate access," Agent Knell said.

Her "alternate access" turned out to be bolt cutters in the back seat. They hopped out at a spot where trees hid them from view, and Knell proceeded to cut a hole in the chain-link fence that surrounded the Q-Zone. "Guards walk the perimeter once an hour. We have about forty-five minutes to get in and out before they find the breach." Then she went back to the car and grabbed something from the back seat. "We can't risk that any of the sub-Kratzes we pass will recognize you. Put this on."

It looked like some sort of rubber Halloween mask but felt too soft to be rubber. He felt he should have recognized the face but had no clue who it could be.

"In case you're wondering, it's a likeness of Noah Prime's father," Agent Knell said.

"Why would FOBE make a mask of Noah Prime's father?" Kratz asked.

"We didn't. We found a damaged artificial skin in the woods the day of the eruption. We suspect Noah Prime's parents were aliens using sophisticated disguises."

"Won't people recognize him from the statue?"

"*You* didn't—and since anyone we run into in the Q-zone

will be a sub-Kratz, we can assume they won't recognize him, either. Now shut up and put his face on!"

While Kratz hated being told what to do, there was something he liked about being ordered around by Agent Knell. Her harsh directives reminded him of his own inner voice. He slipped the strange mask over his head, and immediately his face felt odd and tingly. He reached to touch his face, and he could actually feel his fingertips. It was as if the mask had fused with his own skin.

"A shame to hide that handsome face," Agent Knell said. "But we do what we have to do. Just try not to rip it when you take it off."

Once through the fence, they proceeded to Kratz's apartment building, passing boarded up storefronts and several people with supremely irritated expressions on their faces.

"Even after all these months, their frustration hasn't faded," noted Agent Knell as they went to the building's back entrance. "Many of them still insist that they are you and want to be back in your body. But others have come to appreciate being you, but with the benefit of a better body."

That made Kratz pout a bit. "My body is adequate," he grumbled. Which was really the best he could say about it.

They made their way up the dim stairwell to Kratz's floor without encountering any neighbors, then down the hall to his apartment. Crime scene tape was across the door, but it was old and frayed. FOBE had already done a full forensic analysis of the place and had concluded long ago that there was nothing left to find. How wrong they were!

Agent Knell, who had prepared a copy of Kratz's keys, ripped off the crime scene tape and opened the door.

Once inside the empty apartment, Kratz stopped and looked around, bewildered. "What happened to all my things?"

"The government took it all to test for unusual electromagnetic energy but found nothing. Now I'm sure it's all crated in a warehouse in Area 51, or some such place."

Gone was the painting that hung on the living room wall, hiding the safe. And gone was the safe, ripped out of the wall.

"They found the safe pretty easily," said Agent Knell. "It didn't help that it was behind a painting of a bank."

"Yes, I assumed they would find it."

"Which is why," said Agent Knell, as she reached back into the hole in the wall, "you hid a second safe behind the first one." And she tugged loose a board to reveal the truly *hidden* hidden safe. "As you know, it's a biometric lock, so now we just need your thumbprint to open it."

But something suddenly began to click into place for Kratz. "If FOBE didn't find the safe, how do you know about it?"

"Why does it matter? Give me your hand!"

Finally, Kratz put two and two together, and, for once, came up with something other than five. "You were one of the FOBE agents who was in town investigating the volcano when I activated the memory projector! You were near my apartment when it happened! That's how you know about the devices, and the safe! *You're just another sub-Kratz!*"

"Don't you *dare* call me sub-anything!" she bellowed. "I am every bit the Kratz you are, but with a stronger, more agile body—much better than 'adequate'! So who's the sub-Kratz now, hmm?"

But Kratz wasn't done adding things up—this revelation had yet another layer! "So, being me, you were smart enough to say nothing, laying low and gathering intelligence until you could set me free to help you retrieve those alien devices."

"Of course," Agent Knell said, smiling her devious smile. "Just as you would have done. And once I get my hands on them, I'll be unstoppable!" Then she cleared her throat and corrected herself. "We'll be unstoppable, I mean."

It was the same thought Kratz had had himself, but now there was a new wrinkle: He needed to get rid of Agent Knell. The same way she needed to get rid of him.

"Open the safe!" she commanded.

Kratz looked at the safe, then looked at her.

"No," Kratz said. "As soon as I open it, I'll be useless to you."

"I could just cut off your thumb and open it myself."

"You could have done that a long time ago, but you didn't. Why didn't you, Agent Knell? I'll tell you why! You couldn't bring yourself to damage the actual Quantavius Kratz—because you couldn't bear to disfigure yourself!"

And they both knew it was true because they were quite literally of one mind.

She sighed. "I'm afraid you give me no choice." She gave him a sharp karate chop to the neck and Kratz dropped to the floor in excruciating pain. "I might not be willing to disfigure you, but I don't mind putting you in a world of hurt. And you forget, I might be you up here," she said pointing to her head, "but I still have the strength and muscle memory of a highly trained FOBE agent!"

Kratz felt Agent Knell drag him across the floor, closer to the safe. But Kratz had once been a trained FOBE agent himself, many years ago. And although he had gotten a bit flabby over the years, he still managed a simple escape maneuver: Dropping out of her grip, then turning and lunging at her, he knocked her off balance just enough to pull her to the ground.

She immediately reached for her taser and jammed it against his neck. Kratz heard the click of the trigger and heard a loud buzz . . . but felt nothing.

"Ha!" he screamed at her. "Foiled by an alien mask!"

Refusing to be deterred, she rose to her feet, dragging him up with her, put him in a choke hold, and pushed him

122

toward the safe. Kratz, completely exhausted from his first maneuver, didn't have the strength to stop her.

"This is happening whether you like it or not!"

Kratz felt her press his thumb against the safe, and he heard a click. As Agent Knell swung the door open, she said, "At last!"

But Agent Knell's smile faded as she peered into the open safe.

"It's . . . it's empty!"

In her moment of befuddlement, Kratz pulled away, and, with a safe distance between them, he crossed his arms in defiance and held his head high in triumph.

"Do you think me so short-sighted?" Kratz said. "You received my mind, but clearly not my superior intellect! You forget that my memories were projected upon you, and all the other fake versions of myself *before* I actually hid the three items—which means you only assumed they'd be in there."

Then Knell began to fill in the blanks herself. "The moment you realized your memories had been projected on others, you knew the safe-behind-the-safe was no longer a secure hiding spot—because they would all know of its existence!"

"Yes," said Kratz. "I'm sure dozens of sub-Kratzes have snuck in here trying to open it. But you're the only one who actually had me and my thumb here to do it."

"So where are they, Quantavius? Where did you hide them?"

"Wouldn't you like to know!"

Her shoulders dropped in exasperation. "We're getting nowhere, and we're running out of time," she said. "Once they find that breach in the fence, the Quantavius Zone will be in lockdown, and we'll never get out. We have no choice but to work together."

Kratz said nothing. Because as much as he hated to admit it, he knew she was right.

"Think about it," she said. "Haven't you ever wished there were more of you so you could accomplish twice as much? We're the perfect team! Two Kratzes are better than one!"

"Why should I trust you?"

"You can't! But I know that I can't trust you, either, so that makes us perfect partners!"

He thought about it—realizing that since their minds mirrored each other, she wouldn't betray him until the exact moment *he* would betray *her*. Which meant they couldn't successfully betray each other at all. It was a perfect balance.

"I hid them in the stairwell," he said.

"In the wall sconces," Knell realized, with a grin.

"Precisely! Half the lightbulbs are out, and the super never changes them—"

"—and now since the super is just another version of you—"

"We know for a fact they'll never be changed!"

"And the other Kratzes won't think of it—"

"—because they'll assume it's all in the second hidden safe, just as you did!"

"Genius!"

"Genius!"

"Let's go."

The two of them went back to the stairwell, and Kratz pointed out the three lighting sconces. "One object in each. But I can't remember which one I put where."

"Let's each get one at the same time, okay?" said Knell. "For balance of power."

"My thoughts exactly."

They each put a hand into the sconces closest to them. Kratz withdrew the pocket portal gun, while Knell pulled the antigravity wand out of her sconce, pointing the objects at each other in the exact same instant, like it was some sort of high tech quick-draw.

They both stood there a moment, without firing. A stand-off. Then they both smiled simultaneously.

"We'll grab the memory device together," Kratz said.

"Agreed."

They went to the middle sconce, reached in, and came out with a cube that somehow had seven faces. They were both holding it, and Kratz's hand was resting lightly against hers.

"There," she said, "it's done." Kratz noticed she didn't move her hand away.

"One of us needs to let go," he said. Then, as a gesture of good faith, he did so, letting her hold the cube. Then the moment became a little awkward.

"What's your name, Agent Knell? If we're going to be partners, we should be on a first name basis."

"It's Janelle," she said. "Although my friends call me Nell. Or Knell. I'm never quite sure."

"Well, it's a pleasure to meet you, Nell."

Kratz had to admit this was going very well. In fact, he was beginning to like her more and more. She was, after all, *him*. So what was there not to like?

• ● •

When the coast was clear, Kratz and Knell left the building, only to realize that they were too late. The hole in the fence was now guarded by a pair of armed guards, with a third one closely examining the sports car they had escaped FOBE's maximum security facility in. An unmarked black helicopter zoomed overhead, and they could only assume it was all about them. They ducked behind a tree, then simultaneously reached the same conclusion.

"Why are we hiding——" said Kratz.

"When we have superior weapons?" said Knell.

Then one of the guards noticed them lurking behind the tree. "Hey! You there!"

There was only one move they could make now. Kratz reached into his coat for the portal gun.

"Do it!" said Knell.

Kratz jumped out from behind the tree, aimed the portal gun, and hit the button.

Unfortunately, his aim was off—because the portal opened about five feet above the guards' heads. Kratz had no idea where the portal went, but through it, Kratz could see the tops of trees far more exotic than anything that grew in Arbuckle, accompanied by dense humid air that flowed out.

"Great. You gave them a window to a tropical paradise."

It was, however, distracting enough to grab the guards' attention for the moment.

"Quick, Nell," said Kratz. "You need to—"

"Already on it!" said Agent Knell. She pulled out the antigravity wand, aimed it in the guards' general direction, and flicked her wrist. In one burst, all three guards were ejected up and through the paradise window. Along with the sports car.

"No!" cried Nell. "I just finished paying it off!"

"Forget it," said Kratz. "If we find the right buyers for these weapons, you can purchase a hundred sports cars." But, of course, right now, they were going to need another vehicle.

They went over to look up at the portal. There was an unfamiliar smell flowing out with the warm, sultry air. Slightly sweet and slightly foul. Like fruit slowly rotting. "Where do you suppose we sent them?" Kratz asked.

And in response, an enormous T. rex poked its head out of the portal and attempted to eat them.

They fell to the ground just in time, avoiding its snapping jaw. "Do something!" yelled Kratz.

"No, YOU do something," screamed Knell.

Kratz fumbled with the portal gun as the beast opened its toothy maw again, preparing to chomp. He pushed random buttons—and finally, the portal closed, severing the T. rex's head and leaving its body back in the Cretaceous Period. The massive head hit the ground with an earth-shaking thud. Its eyes blinked once and seemed to say *Really? Do I deserve this?* And then it was dead.

Kratz and Knell, splattered with dinosaur blood, got to their feet. The scene was a mess—which was typical, because Quantavius T. Kratz had an astounding talent at creating monumental messes that someone else had to clean up. And now with basically two Kratzes in play, it was double the mess, double the misery.

"Excellent," said Knell. "We found another practical application for the device. Bladeless Guillotine!"

Kratz looked at the head of the hideous beast and sneered. "Mess with Kratzes and pay the price!" he said. He kicked it and yowled because its teeth were much harder than his toes.

"Now to find another vehicle," Knell said.

"As I recall," said Kratz, raising an eyebrow, "we've hotwired a car or two in our youth."

128

But as it turned out breaking into modern vehicles wasn't as easy as it used to be. They were still trying to steal themselves new wheels, when a group of kids showed up at the T. rex head. A group of kids who looked very, very familiar ...

• ● •

"Yeah, I don't think this is supposed to be here," said Noah, looking at the severed T. rex head in the middle of the street.

"Yuck," said Sahara. "We'd better be quick, because as soon as someone else discovers it, this place will be swarming with FOBEs."

Andi held up a hand, looking up to where the portal must have been, then she shook her head. "I'm picking up way too many shredded subatomic particles," she said. "Whoever did this didn't know what they were doing. It's like raccoons got ahold of a portal device. And not even smart racoons. Definitely not the kind of beings that'll have something as advanced as an RTR ship."

So this appeared to be another dead end. But then Ogden, who had been lingering back, holding his cat, stepped forward. "Uh ... guys ... I've been in serious ongoing negotiations with Mittens ... and we've finally reached an agreement," he said. "He'll tell us the location of that house if I officially dedicate my life to his service."

And Mittens purred in satisfied approval.

Noah went up to them. "Mittens—can you swear to us that the owner of that house has an RTR ship?"

The cat nodded—and although Noah didn't really trust him, they had no other options if they were going to go after Claire. Noah looked at Ogden. "If you're okay with it, Ogden, then so are we."

And so, with everyone in agreement, the cat proceeded to project the location of the house directly into their minds.

What the kids didn't know was that the telepathic projection also reached Kratz and Knell, who were hiding behind a nearby bush. Mittens knew, of course—he could smell them and hear them whispering to each other—but he projected the information anyway.

Because he couldn't be bothered to care.

10

You're Sitting in It

As far as anyone in Arbuckle knew, the blue house had always been there. Not that it had—but no one could remember it *not* being there. It was, therefore, the opposite of stealth. Not invisible, but so visible that it was taken for granted. Just a part of the scenery that you don't notice—like the color of your neighbor's front door, or the types of trees on your own street. Sahara, who claimed to have never seen the house, had actually passed it many times—but it was as if something told her not to pay it any attention, so she didn't. That was because the house was surrounded by a "naught-abnormal" field that tweaked people's minds into ignoring it.

It was a stately Victorian—a style that could have made it the neighborhood's haunted house were it not so well kept and so unnecessarily jolly. It was made of sturdy brick painted a cheery blue, with pink cupolas sprouting on the sides like ladybugs, bright yellow trim, and a grand tower that could have been a lighthouse had it been anywhere near the sea. A porch swing and well-tended garden completed the picture.

As for the grandmotherly woman who lived there, she was well-loved for her kind words, her peach pies, and her remarkable vegetables that always won awards at the Oregon State Fair. She had always been grandmotherly. Even grandparents who as children had trick-or-treated at her door never noticed she didn't seem to be growing older. Something told them not to trouble their minds with it. So they didn't.

• ● •

Noah opened the gate of the white picket fence, and they all stepped into the yard.

"Yup, this is the garden I saw," Ogden said. "Just look at those eggplants."

The eggplants in question were disturbingly large. About the size of watermelons.

"Are they alien?" asked Sahara.

Andi waved a hand over them. "Nope. Just big eggplants."

The garden featured zucchini the size of baseball bats, tomatoes the size of pumpkins, and kale the size of kale.

"Take anything you want."

They looked up to see the smiling, grandmotherly woman sitting on the porch swing, her hair pulled up in a loose silver bun. "All my produce is free, as long as you promise to cook it into something delicious." Her voice was friendly, and her smile was genuine. She looked like what one might imagine Mrs. Claus would look like, without all the red velvet and white furry frills. Just a flowery house-dress and an apron.

They approached the woman on the porch.

"We're actually here on other business," Noah said.

"Business can wait." She stood up. "I'm Miss Luella. And who might you all be?"

"I'm Noah Prime. This is Sahara Solis; that's my kinda, sorta sister, Andi; and the boy with the cat is Ogden Codden-Criddle."

Miss Luella gasped. "Mittens!" She clasped her hands together in joy. "Well, any friend of Mittens is a friend of mine."

And the cat meowed.

"Wait," said Ogden. "You know Mittens?"

"Oh yes! We've had many great adventures together, Mittens and I."

And although none of them could wrap their minds around this kindly woman in cahoots with a wanted feline criminal, they decided to just let it go.

"Come inside, come inside, my house is your house." She

gestured them up to the porch. "I have a peach pie ready to come out of the oven. And some mackerel for you, Mittens."

So they followed her inside, and she closed the door behind them but didn't lock it, because at Miss Luella's house, neighbors were always welcome.

• ● •

Keeping a safe distance, Kratz and Agent Nell Knell had followed the kids from the edge of the Q-Zone to the elegant Victorian and watched them enter the house with the old woman. But the moment they looked away, they forgot the house was there. They had to keep it in their line of sight just to remember where they were going. Kratz found it annoying—just as he found everything else involving Noah Prime annoying.

"If it weren't for Noah Prime, none of this would have happened!" Kratz spat. "I can't see why we should waste our time with him now."

Knell smiled. "You have no idea how much Rigby wants to get her hands on that kid," she said. "We bring her Prime, and we're both suddenly her best friends again."

"Or she throws us both in cells and takes all the credit."

Knell shrugged. "Then we send her to Jurassic Park, too."

That made Kratz actually giggle.

Their course of action seemed clear. Nothing could stop them now. And then they came to Miss Luella's prize-winning garden.

"Oh no . . . ," said Kratz.

"Sweet Fancy Moses, this is bad," said Knell.

Because before them . . . were vegetables. Dozens and dozens of vegetables.

Kratz had long suffered from lachanophobia—the irrational fear of vegetables. It stemmed (no pun intended) back to his mother, who would refuse him the slightest kindness unless he ate all the vegetables on his plate. She would scream at him, torment him, and threaten him with all sorts of horrific consequences. "They're called squash for a reason," she would say. "Pray you never find out why." Or "Potatoes have eyes! Better eat them, or they'll just keep watching you!" But artichokes were the worst. Because "choke" was right there in its name—and his mother took good advantage of that.

Thus, he had never eaten a vegetable in his adult life and avoided the produce section of the local Fresh and Funky supermarket like a vampire avoided garlic.

Knell couldn't help him, because being Kratz herself, she had the exact same vegetable terrors—and this particular garden of giant veggies was beyond their worst nightmare.

"My God, Nell . . . what do we do? *What do we do?*"

"Just keep your eyes forward," she said. "Find your happy place."

"I don't have a happy place!"

Agent Knell took a deep breath.

"Me neither." Then she took his hand. "We can be each other's happy place."

And together they strode forward into the unthinkable horror of torturous tomatoes, egregious eggplants, Brobdingnagian brussels sprouts, and the kale...the kale...

They were almost to the porch steps when something appeared before them that they hadn't noticed before. Three stalks, crowned with nasty, prickly leaves. Bulbous things molting malevolence.

They both shuddered. Artichokes. Why did it have to be artichokes?

"Close your eyes, Nell," Kratz said, the grip of her hand giving him strength. "Close your eyes, and in five steps we'll be past it." And so together, eyes closed, they passed the great gagging monstrosity and achieved the porch.

But then they realized that once they captured Noah, they would have to cross the garden again to get out....

• ● •

The pie was, without question, the best the kids had ever tasted. Except, of course, for Andi, who had no actual taste buds and only ever pretended to eat. Naturally, she was a little resentful.

"Fruit, fat, flour, and sugar. Big deal. My power source is a lot more efficient and long-lasting."

Miss Luella patted her on the head. "Not everyone has the luxury of a beryllium sphere, my dear."

But it still didn't ease Andi's sour grapes, which she wouldn't have been able to taste, either.

"Now then," said Miss Luella, "what is this business you speak of?"

Ogden practically leaped across the table, wired on the aforementioned sugar. "We have to go after Claire. They took her into space, and we have to get her back."

The wizened woman raised her eyebrows. "Ah, that troublesome kerfuffle last night on the other side of town," she said. "Sorry to hear your friend was mixed up in all that."

"We're pretty sure it was Usurpers," Sahara told her.

"Usurpers!" said Miss Luella. "Well, that's a fine kettle of fish."

To which the cat meowed, and she got up to get him more mackerel.

"Oh, I completely forgot to put the kettle on," she said. "What type of tea would you prefer? Earl Grey? Chamomile? Or Relativity T'oolong—that one's my personal favorite. Of course, it takes forever to brew, but it's always done before I start!"

Noah took a deep breath. "Miss Luella, we're kind of under a time crunch here."

"Well then," she said brightly, "let's go for the T'oolong. Oh look, it's ready. Let me pour you a cup so I can begin brewing it."

Noah knew if this woman was going to give them

assistance, they needed to play by her rules and in her own time. The last thing they wanted to do was alienate the one alien who might be able to help them. So Noah and Sahara dutifully drank their tea—but Ogden's patience ran out after his second sip.

"The Usurpers already have a twelve-hour lead on us," Ogden blurted. "We don't have time for this."

"My dear boy," said Miss Luella, settling into her chair. "As long as you drink my T'oolong, time in the outside world slows to a crawl, providing us all the time we need."

And sure enough, when they glanced out of the window, the trees had almost stopped moving in the breeze.

"Now," said Miss Luella, "tell me everything."

• ● •

Well, they didn't tell her *everything*. She didn't need to know about Noah being a N.O.A.H., and his Fauxlite parents being turned into a pair of pearl earrings, and how he was the last surviving human ark—or that he had been the one who had freed Mittens and hundreds of other imprisoned alien criminals—or how their imbecilic science teacher, Mr. Kratz, had fouled everything up, and may have even been responsible for the volcano.

But even without all that, the story of Claire's abduction and the events leading up to it took twenty minutes to tell, because everyone had something to say about it. Yet only ten seconds passed in the world outside the kitchen. And so involved were they in the tale, that no one saw, or sensed, the two individuals coming in the front door and moving extremely slowly through the front parlor. Not even Miss Luella.

"Well," said Miss Luella, once the tale had been told, "that's quite a tempest in a teapot. Sounds like you could certainly use a friend right about now. I'm in!"

"Great," said Noah. "Andi, can you pilot a faster-than-light ship?"

"Duh," she said. "I'm insulted you had to ask."

But Miss Luella rose from her seat. "Sorry, Andi—nobody flies my ship but me." Then she turned to the cat. "Ready for another adventure, Mittens?"

And the cat purred.

"Okay," said Noah, "take us to your ship."

To which Miss Luella replied, "You're sitting in it."

• ● •

The "naught-abnormal" energy field that surrounded Miss Luella's quaint home was more than just a countermeasure against curiosity. It protected Miss Luella from attention that might be drawn from sudden arrivals and departures of her home—which was, in a way, a motorhome, in the purest sense of the word, because its basement housed a powerful RipTearRupture drive. The same basement in which Kratz and Knell were currently hiding.

•   ●   •

"If you're going to leave, Sahara, you should go now," Noah said. Even though he was up for this adventure, he wouldn't push Sahara into joining it—or guilt her into it the way Ogden had tried to do. For her sake, he was willing to say goodbye, even if he wasn't ready.

But Sahara didn't say goodbye. She just stood there looking at him. Until Miss Luella said, "Sahara, dear, would you accompany me up to the flight deck? I could use a copilot."

The cat hissed, and the woman gave Mittens an apologetic shrug. "Sorry, my love, but she has opposable thumbs."

Noah could see in Sahara's eyes the moment she decided. Such a huge decision, quietly made during a single swing of the grandfather clock's pendulum. She offered him a tiny but mischievous smile, then went to join Miss Luella.

"The rest of you find a comfortable seat," Miss Luella said, pointing to the overstuffed armchairs and loveseat in the parlor.

"Don't we need seat belts?" asked Ogden as he sat down.

"Not to worry," said Miss Luella as she and Sahara went upstairs. "The furniture knows to hold you down."

Which is really something you don't want to hear under any circumstances.

Out of all of them, only Mittens knew there were two unexpected guests in the house. Not only could he smell them, but he had seen them trying to secretly cross the

140

living room while Miss Luella and the kids were talking. They had taken refuge in the basement, leaving the door slightly ajar. So the cat gently leaned into it to close it and used his telekinetic mind to lock the deadbolt, for no reason other than his own amusement.

And in so doing, unknowingly sealed the fate of an entire planet.

• ● •

Interstellar ships are fairly common throughout the universe, because every advanced civilization makes such a mess of their home world that they need to find a way off their planet to "somewhere other than here." Spaceships were originally sleek and aerodynamically streamlined to make it easier for beings to escape their worlds' atmospheres—and also because every civilization goes through a big-things-that-look-cool stage, which is where planet Earth is currently stuck. However, once the RipTearRupture drive was invented, shape was no longer an issue, and spaceships took on fantastic and frightening forms ranging from simple cubes to crystalline fortresses to terrifying titanium beasts. It all depended on the taste of the owner.

That being the case, a blue Victorian house rocketing through the cosmos was barely worth a raised Megaloptican eyebrow. And since Megalopticans had 193 eyes, a single eyebrow raise was really nothing at all.

• ● •

The little tower room on the top floor, which appeared to be nothing more than a quaint architectural flourish, was, in fact, the flight deck. To Sahara, it didn't appear much like the bridge of a ship. It looked more like a little reading room, where one might sit on a rainy night and read a nice cozy mystery. It was full of embroidery and lace, two comfortable chairs, and a counter with antique perfume bottles that were actually the ship's controls.

"Hold on," said Miss Luella.

"I am," said Sahara.

"I'm not talking to you, dear."

Then the paisley fabric of the chairs grew tendrils of yarn that wrapped around their legs, holding them in place. Noah's and Ogden's distant shouts from the first floor indicated that their furniture had done the same.

"Would you like to do the honors?" Miss Luella asked an astonished Sahara.

"I would love to!"

Sahara took hold of the tallest bottle and slowly pushed it forward.

• ● •

When the launch engines engaged, the ground shook so violently neighbors thought that Mount Hood, twenty miles away, had finally erupted, as geologists have claimed it was about to do for years. But the rumbling didn't last long enough to cause any major concern—and since the house itself was surrounded by the "naught-abnormal" field, no one much noticed its ascent, or even its absence after it was gone. People did see the expanse of freshly roasted vegetables, and the smoldering crater where the house had been—but no one remembered there *not* being a smoldering crater there, so people just accepted it as a standard feature of their neighborhood.

Unlike the Usurpers, Miss Luella waited until the ship was a responsible distance from the ground before she took the controls back from a thoroughly stoked Sahara and engaged the RTR drive.

The ship ripped a hole in the fabric of space-time, tore into the gap, and ruptured the very laws of physics. The universe, being much like a cranky neighbor yelling at kids to get off his lawn, then proceeded to boot the ship toward its designated exit point in an attempt to rid itself of the annoying disruption. Thus, "nuisance control" was the guiding principle of all faster-than-light travel.

• ● •

Down below, Kratz and Knell were unaware of what was going on—but were horrified by the noise coming from the large metallic object in the center of the basement.

"I've never heard a furnace so loud!" Kratz shouted over the device's ear-splitting roar. "It's clearly malfunctioning!"

"Yes," agreed Agent Knell, covering her ears. "An accident waiting to happen!"

It got even louder, its powerful vibrations seeming to rip, tear, and rupture the very cells of their bodies. Then they were both thrown to the ground by some force they couldn't even begin to understand.

Yes, thought Kratz, *this furnace is definitely in need of repair.*

11

To Serve Claire

EVEN FARTHER FROM EARTH, CLAIRE JENSEN WAS MORE FURIous than frightened as she paced in her cell. Okay, so it wasn't exactly a cell since her quarters on the alien spacecraft did have a separate bedroom. And a living room. And a grand bathroom with its own spa. Okay, it was more like a luxury suite, with her own personal robot-butler to attend to her every whim—but a gilded cage was still a cage, wasn't it?

"I demand to know what's going on!" she said to the robo-butler.

"It is a sizeable universe; many things are going on," he said. "You'll have to be more specific."

She grunted in frustration. Trying to get answers from this robot was like trying to find the right prompts for ChatGPT. She had never been good at that.

"Just take me home!"

" 'Take Me Home,' " the robot said. "A song by Phil Collins circa 1985. Would you like me to play it for you?" And a drum riff began.

"No! Alexa, *stop!*"

"Alexa: a primitive artificial intelligence program from Earth. Would you like me to mimic her voice?"

And he did. It was all so annoying.

"Shall I draw you a bath, or retrieve a bowl of fine human food for you?" the now gender-fluid butler said.

"No!" Claire shouted. "I want to speak to a person! Or whatever passes for a person in this place!"

"As you wish, Your Highness," they said, and rolled out.

She wanted to throw a crystal glass at the robot as it left, but she knew a robo-maid would come to happily clean it up. At first she thought "Your Highness" was the robot just being sarcastic, the way her father would call her that whenever she was being, quote, unreasonably demanding, unquote. But she sensed no sarcasm in the robot. She didn't even know if it was capable of it.

She hurled herself down on the plush velvet sofa and looked out the two-story circular window, upon a shimmering vista of passing stars that looked like Christmas lights.

All she knew for sure was that she had been abducted by aliens, but they had yet to tell her of their intentions. The stories she knew of alien abductions involved things like cow mutilations, painful probes, and human-alien hybrids. It did not bode well for her immediate future. Then there was that old *Twilight Zone* episode that always seemed to pop up during holiday marathons, where the aliens' great manifesto of service to humanity turned out to be recipes for how to cook them. Is that why the robot wanted to bring her food? To fatten her up for dinner? So irritating.

Just then a human, or at least what appeared to be, entered her suite. It was only when he got close that she realized who it was.

"Raymond?"

"Yes and no," he said. "The Raymond Balding-Stalker that you know is no longer in charge of this body. My name is Ø, but you can still call me Raymond if you like, or perhaps Raymønd, as that would be more accurate, Your Highness."

"Why does everyone keep calling me that?"

"All will be made clear once we arrive on Claire."

"Excuse me?"

"The planet that you now own. Your friend Ogden, who facilitated the purchase, officially named the star 'Jensen Majoris,' and named its planet 'Claire,' in honor of you, Your Highness."

"Seriously?"

The Raymond-thing looked a bit confused. "Do you mean I should repeat what I just said in a more serious manner?"

"No . . . just . . . forget it."

"I'm sorry, Your Highness, but I'm not currently in possession of a memory eraser."

Claire sighed. "Never mind, just take me home. I want to go home."

"But that's precisely where we're going, Your Highness. To your new home."

• ● •

Ø returned to the bridge, where his accomplice, ≠, was waiting for him.

"Is it quelled?" ≠ asked, shifting her very dead jaw so that it didn't hang at such an awkward angle.

"The subject is as quelled as possible under the circumstances," Ø told her, then reached up to remove a bit of flaking skin from ≠'s face. "You really should have chosen a host that's still alive while you had the chance," Ø said. "It might be less aromatic, but it's much warmer and more agile."

"Nonsense," said ≠. "A living body feels pain. Plus you have to constantly contend with the resident anima."

Ø shrugged. "The boy Raymond is barely a blip on my radar," Ø said. "He stopped struggling hours ago and is content to sit back and watch as I control his body."

"In that case," ≠ said, "you chose wisely."

"Are you in touch with the coronation committee?" Ø asked. "Is everything on track?"

"Yes, they are awaiting our arrival."

Ø gave a satisfied sigh. "What a fine day it will be when she takes the throne."

"Do you think she will cooperate?"

"Of course," said Ø. "I firmly believe this is the fulfillment of all her dreams."

≠ clapped her hands together, releasing a puff of pulverized skin.

"Imagine, just a few more planetary revolutions, and we can celebrate. All our hard work finally rewarded upon the coronation."

"Yes," said Ø, "but I'm more excited about what happens immediately *after* the coronation."

"As am I, Ø, as am I."

PART THREE

• • •

PLANET CLAIRE

12

Bad Kitty

"Woo-hoo!" yelled Sahara in absolute joy. "Take that, gravity! Because this girl is hotter than a heat shield on re-entry! Woo-hoo!"

"That was a wonderful blast-off, dear," said Miss Luella, with the calm of someone who had done this a hundred times before. "Especially considering it was your first!"

Down on the ground floor—which was no longer technically a "ground" floor anymore—Ogden jumped up and climbed the stairs all the way up to the tower room the moment the chair let him go.

"Are we there yet?" Ogden asked. "Are we traveling by teleportation or wormhole?"

"Neither," said Miss Luella. "It's more like we're crawling around in the guts of the universe."

"So . . . we're basically waiting for the universe to poop us out?"

Sahara sighed. "Only you, Ogden, would think of that."

"I was just going with the existing metaphor."

"Stay up here as long as you like," said Miss Luella. "Enjoy the view of 'intestinal space.' It's on autopilot now—just be careful not to touch anything."

There were windows on all four sides of the little tower room, displaying a startling vista. Sahara, still feeling the rush of the launch, was mesmerized by the shimmering lights, which didn't look like guts at all, and although Ogden would normally have been impressed, he was all about one thing now. Finding Claire. Everything in between here and that goal was just empty space. He had arrived at the party last night with a mission. Yes, the mission had changed, but he still had one.

Miss Luella then reached over to a little shelf full of tchotchkes that, miraculously, hadn't fallen during liftoff. She grabbed a small snow globe with a non-descript figure standing inside. "We'll be needing this!" she said.

"A snow globe?" Sahara couldn't imagine why they—or anyone, for that matter—would ever need a snow globe.

"It's a bio-locator to help us find your friend. Once we reach the planet, it will point us in her direction—but we're going to have to prime it with a sample of her DNA."

"Well, good luck finding that," said Sahara.

"How about a lock of her hair?" suggested Ogden, who then reached into his pocket and pulled out a small clump of hair tied together with a little pink ribbon.

Sahara gaped at him in horrified astonishment. "Why do you have a lock of Claire Jensen's hair?"

"I refuse to answer that question. Best to just move on."

Ogden handed Miss Luella the hair, and she inserted it into a small slot in the snow globe and closed it. "It'll take a while to process, but by the time we're on the planet, it will take us right to her!"

Meanwhile, down in the living room, Noah had still been in the loveseat, which maybe was a little too loving and did not want to let him go. When he finally pulled free from its embrace, he heard Sahara way up in the tower room, whooping for joy. He wanted to run up there, too, to share this moment with her, but then Andi spoke.

"Something's wrong."

She had ripped herself free from her armchair without waiting for it to release her. Now it was full of torn threads and seemed to be nursing its wounds.

"We're flying through space in an old house," Noah said. "I think if you look up 'wrong' in the dictionary, that might be like the second or third definition."

"Quiet!" snapped Andi. "I'm picking up a biomass anomaly—an imbalance—as if there's more organic matter on this ship than there should be."

"Is that a problem?"

"I don't know yet. Leave me alone and let me concentrate."

Noah turned to the window in the living room. A few minutes ago, it had looked out on the woman's lush garden, but that garden was now probably millions of miles away, replaced by a view that was truly spectacular—beyond what he imagined traveling in an interstellar craft would be. Lights danced like the Aurora; stars zipped past in glistening rainbows. He touched his finger to the window—but it wasn't glass. It was some sort of membrane as sheer as cellophane, yet sturdy enough to keep the inside in, and the outside out.

It occurred to him as he hurtled away from Earth, that if he had never found out the truth about himself, he would have gone on a journey like this with his parents. They would have revealed their extraterrestrial nature to him, but not the nature of their mission. Noah would have been blissfully unaware of the dark fate of Earth—all he would have known was the joy of the stars. Part of him wished for that kind of ignorant bliss, until he realized...

My friends and everyone I know would be dead.

Thinking—even for a moment—that he wanted that nearly manifested in a tortoise shell to protect him from the crushing guilt.

"Well, we're on our way," said Miss Luella, coming down the stairs, satisfied with their launch. It was smoother now that they had punched into whatever's beyond the beyond.

"How long will it take?" Noah asked.

"Time's different out here," she told him. "It will feel like twelve hours, but also like twelve minutes, and twelve days, all at the same time."

Noah found himself feeling uneasy. Not that any of this was easy, but this was something more. At first, he thought it might be some animal trait expressing itself, but then he realized that it was just him. The feeling got worse when he thought about Sahara and Ogden, who were enjoying their wild ride. He got what he wanted—an adventure with his friends. So why was he so unsettled?

Miss Luella patted down the frayed fabric of Andi's wounded armchair, like soothing an anxious pet, then she sat in the one Ogden had occupied. The chair seemed much happier to have her in it than Ogden, who had kept squirming and picking lint from its arms.

"Something on your mind?" she asked.

Noah didn't really have an answer except to say, "Sahara's and Ogden's parents are going to worry."

"Yes," agreed Miss Luella, "that does tend to be an issue when children your age leave the planet. Can't be avoided, I suppose."

Noah sighed. "I don't have that particular problem."

"Yes, I know," said Miss Luella.

"You do?"

"Oh, yes—I knew all about the N.O.A.H. program. Can't say I was a fan of it. Creating a human ark, then wiping out all life on the planet?" She shivered. "Brrrr—nasty business. I wasn't looking forward to having to relocate and find another reasonably pleasant world. So when I heard through the grapevine that you had been terminated, and the program scrapped . . . well, I must admit I was relieved."

"Yeah. Sorry I'm not dead."

"I'm not sorry," said Miss Luella. "You found a way to 'game the system,' as they say. That makes me much happier than your demise!"

There was a long moment of silence that would have felt awkward with most people, but not with Miss Luella. "It was your friends' choice to make this journey," she said, reading Noah's feelings if not his mind. "You feel responsible, but from what I can see, they're not doing it because of you."

She was right. But on the other hand, they'd never be going off-planet if it wasn't for him—they'd never even know it was a possibility. Maybe Noah didn't put his friends on this ship, but he *did* drag them into his orbit—an orbit that was wildly unstable and dangerous.

Then Miss Luella smiled. "Comets have a wildly eccentric orbit, and yet their coming is always celebrated."

It was then that Noah looked over at the cat lounging on a windowsill and realized what was happening. It was taking his thoughts and projecting them to her. Who needs to read minds when you have a cat that can do it for you?

"Is it wrong for me to be . . . kind of glad that this is all happening?"

Miss Luella raised her eyebrows and gave him a knowing nod. "Adventure can be habit-forming. And I'll wager the four of you have had some good ones."

"Yeah, they were pretty solid."

Then Miss Luella took a long moment. Noah couldn't tell whether she was still getting his thoughts from Mittens, or if she was looking to a place in him that went deeper than conscious thought.

"As a Nascent Organic Aggregate Hybrid, the whole world revolved around you and whether you lived or whether you died. Even before you knew, I'll wager there was a sense that something was up—something larger than just you and your family.

"I don't know . . . maybe . . ."

"As the last N.O.A.H., you were the most important person in the world," Miss Luella said. "And now . . . you're not. That must be hard to get used to."

"I'm not anything now. I'm not even supposed to be here."

"Just because people don't know you exist doesn't mean you're not supposed to."

It left Noah with a lot to think about—and he began

to feel a bit sick to his stomach. But that had nothing to do with his thoughts. *Perhaps it's the artificial gravity*, he thought—but honestly, it didn't feel all that different from Earth gravity.

Suddenly, Andi snapped out of analysis mode. "Something's definitely wrong," she said.

"Yeah," said Noah. "And I'm feeling a little queasy."

"We're like a ship on the waves," said Miss Luella. "You've got yourself a wee bit of space sickness." She stood still, taking a moment to feel the motion herself. "Must be those pesky inertial dampers. They're always slipping out of alignment."

"I think it's more than just the inertial dampers," said Andi. "I'm sensing a .07 degree lateral wobble."

"Still within acceptable parameters, dear," said Miss Luella. "Noah, the bathroom is through the kitchen, and just off the mudroom, if your tummy gets too upset." Then she went to adjust the works of the grandfather clock, which apparently controlled the inertial dampers.

Noah pushed open the door to the mudroom. His old home, being a farmhouse, had one of those, a little room between the kitchen and the back door to take off muddy boots and hang comfy flannel winter coats. Or, in this instance, space suits disguised as comfy flannel winter coats. He turned into the bathroom and splashed water on his face, hoping he wouldn't have to hurl from space sickness, or whatever this was.

The thing is, Noah was not a motion-sickness kind of kid. He could read in cars on winding roads and was fine on the one rough-weather boat ride he'd ever taken, so he wasn't sure why some wobbling motion would affect him. Maybe it was an animal thing, but he couldn't figure out what animal thing it might be.

The truth, although he didn't know it at the time, was that his peptic unease was a whole menagerie of critter-cringings. For instance, the golden-cheeked warbler, whole flocks of which can sense the coming of devastating storms, even when the sky is sunny and clear. And the green sea turtle, known to swim from volcanic eruptions days before they actually happen. And the Indian elephant, entire herds of which have been seen racing for higher ground long before anyone knows a tsunami is coming.

In other words, if Noah could have read his own intuition, he might have known that something was coming. Something very bad, and very soon.

That's when one more critter entered the picture. Mittens the cat. He just stood there at the open bathroom door, which Noah had neglected to close, his tail slowly undulating like a cobra.

"Get lost," Noah, said. "I don't need a cat watching me hurl."

But Mittens just stood there watching. And waiting.

• ● •

Kratz finally felt the pressure that was pushing him against the dusty floor begin to dissipate enough to sit up straight. He looked at the bulbous metallic object in the center of the basement where the noise was coming from. Now he was scared. Faulty furnaces can and did explode. They could fill a house with carbon monoxide, killing everyone inside. They had to get out, and fast.

Kratz and Knell climbed the stairs, only to find that the door was locked from the other side. Which meant they had no choice but to shut down that terrible furnace.

"If we don't want to die in a house explosion, we'd better figure out what's wrong with that thing," Agent Knell said.

The object was hot to the touch and still rumbled in a most threatening way. Kratz noted that the joints were held together by unconventional screws. They didn't have a simple flathead groove or the engraved X that required a Phillips head. The indentation looked more like a multidimensional amoeba.

"Hmm. Must be European."

So Knell frantically scavenged for the proper tool. She found a rusty old toolbox in a corner, amid a pile of yarn and knitting needles—but most of the tools in the box were entirely unrecognizable: stainless steel instruments that seemed vaguely medical in nature, a small saw that had literal teeth, a claw hammer where the claw was actually a claw. There was nothing at all that resembled a screwdriver. She did, however, find an ordinary, if some-what heavy, monkey wrench.

"Here," she said, handing it to Kratz. "When in doubt..."

"Bang it out!" he concluded. And began to repeat-edly smash the most vulnerable joint of the device with the wrench hoping he could shut the thing down before it blew up.

• ● •

It is a well-documented and time-honored fact throughout the universe that technology responds to abuse. You can fix a pesky TV by smacking it. A faulty starship cockpit? Give it a well-placed punch. And while computers don't do well when struck, who hasn't fixed their laptop by scream-ing at it? For this reason, monkey wrenches are the same everywhere. The only difference is the grip, as they are dependent on the type of appendage that is meant to hold them, be it hand, tentacle, flipper, or pseudopod. The pur-pose of monkey wrenches, however, is always the same: to strike machinery that isn't doing what it's supposed to do—usually by people who don't really know what the machine is supposed to do anyway, only that it's not doing it.

The device in question, however, was not misbehaving in the least. It was functioning precisely the way a RipTear-Rupture engine was intended to function, and, like most technology, did not appreciate the uninvited abuse. Which explains why so many biological civilizations have been destroyed by robotic uprisings—but in this instance, the RTR drive was in no position to wage war against carbon-based life-forms. Instead, rather than allowing itself to be beaten into submission, it simply got louder and even more testy.

• ● •

"Miss Luella, my sensors are telling me we're off course," said Andi as she wandered the living room, trying to figure out what wasn't right.

"That can't be, I've got fail-safes within fail-safes—because I don't even trust myself," said Miss Luella with a carefree chuckle.

Andi, however, was never free of care. Especially when she knew she was right. Which was always.

Suddenly, the grandfather clock began to chime a heavy G-sharp, although some might call it A-flat. It was a deep almost funerary toll that brought no solace to anyone—especially because it wasn't anywhere near the hour.

"That's the general alarm," said Miss Luella, finally sparking the tiniest bit of concern. "Perhaps someone altered our programmed coordinates."

"Or it's the biomass anomaly throwing the ship out of balance," suggested Andi. "Are you sure there's no one else onboard?"

And as if the chiming clock wasn't enough, a metallic

clanging began to ring out from the basement that was even more alarming than the alarm.

"Hmm," said Miss Luella. "That engine does make strange sounds, but this is a new one." She began to walk toward the basement door, when suddenly the entire house started to quake. Anything not nailed down began to crash to the ground.

"Oh fiddlesticks! The inertial dampers have failed!"

Ogden and Sahara came bounding down the stairs, nearly falling over each other.

"What's happening?" asked Sahara.

"Nothing to worry about," said Miss Luella. "Ships will be ships. Better strap in until we figure out what's what."

But Ogden shook his head. "No way am I letting that chair grab me again!" he said, just as the ship took a lurch that sent him sprawling onto it. This time the piece of disgruntled furniture grabbed him with more force than it had before.

"Ouch! Stop that!" But it only increased its spiteful grip.

Miss Luella stumbled to the kitchen and out into the mudroom to check on Noah—because while most of the furniture could hold a person in place, the toilet was not very grabby.

"Noah, you'll need to come out!" she said. "It's too dangerous not to be upholsterized for the duration."

The entire ship lurched again, knocking Miss Luella

off balance. It didn't help that Mittens was at her feet. She tripped over him and fell sidelong into the bathroom. Noah caught Miss Luella before she could hit her head on the sink, and the moment he caught her, the cat pushed the door closed with his paw.

Noah's feeling of nausea was replaced by a tingling sensation of something inevitable.

"Lordy, what botheration!" Miss Luella tried to open the door but couldn't—and with good reason: It had been locked from the outside by Mittens, in the same way he had used his mind to lock the basement door.

"Mittens!" yelled Miss Luella, banging on the door. "Mittens, what are you up to? Let us out of here immediately!"

Noah opened his mouth to speak but instead found his tongue flicking out several feet and catching a large horsefly on the wall, in an unasked for, and unappreciated, animal moment. Just as suddenly, his tongue was back in his mouth, along with the fly, and his gag reflex made him swallow. It was the fact that he had just eaten a fly that had been in a bathroom, probably having eaten what flies eat, that finally made Noah hurl. He knelt and puked his guts into the toilet. Literally—he ejected his stomach like a starfish and then had to open his mouth even wider to push his stomach back in. It wasn't pretty, and there was no fun to be had.

Meanwhile, Miss Luella, who had until this moment

been the model of calm, considerate patience, was getting, shall we say, slightly irked.

"Mittens, don't you dare!" she yelled through the door. "Bad kitty! Bad kitty!"

While in the kitchen, Mittens casually closed the door to the mudroom, a small room with two doors—one to the outside, and one to the kitchen. In other words...an air-lock. Then, without a second thought, Mittens jumped on a counter and pushed a little red button next to the garbage disposal switch, ejecting the ship's escape pod—which happened to double as the downstairs bathroom—into the unknowable expanse of space.

· ● ·

Andi heard the pod being launched, but with her sensors already overloaded by the ship's various other sounds and malfunctions, she couldn't identify what that particular noise had been. Even so, she hurried to investigate.

Once in the kitchen, she saw the cat pawing at the door to the mudroom and urgently meowing. Andi was not par-ticularly fond of felines, and even less fond of this one.

"What is it? Are Miss Luella and Noah in there?"

The cat just meowed again in response and pawed at the door.

As an android, she could not be influenced by the cat's telepathic powers—no images were projected into her mind, or thoughts pulled out of it. But the creature's behavior seemed to indicate some urgency—and maybe it was trying to tell her that Miss Luella and Noah were in trouble.

She shooed the cat out of the way, opened the door, and stepped into the mud room. And immediately found that something was very wrong. Because to the left of the door, there was just a big empty corner. Hadn't there been a little bathroom there?

Then the cat pushed the mudroom door closed behind her. Only then did Andi realize her folly. Because the moment the mudroom door was closed, the cat hit the button that opened the house's back door.

Andi was sucked out of the airlock into the emptiness of space, proving that Mittens was, indeed, a very bad kitty.

13

Carnivorous or Noncarnivorous?

CLAIRE WASN'T BEING TREATED BADLY BY THE THING THAT HAD taken over Raymond Balding-Stalker's body—but his associate, the woman who looked and smelled like death, was horribly rude.

"What is your problem?" she snapped. "Why won't you eat these perfectly good nutritional pellets we've given you?"

"It's dog food!" complained Claire.

To which the rotting woman just scoffed. "So? Earth mammals are Earth mammals. I don't see the problem. The bowl even has your name on it. You're just too picky."

The Raymond-thing was much more accommodating. "Explain to us what kind of nutrition you require, and we'll do our best to provide it."

The rotting woman rolled her swollen, puffy eyes. "Why must you coddle her?"

"Because," said the Raymond-thing, "if she is to take her rightful place, she must be treated with courtesy and respect."

The woman waved her hand dismissively, and the hand promptly fell off.

"Ew," said Claire. "Like big, fat, supersized ew."

"Oh, get over it," said the woman.

"Don't mind UnEqua," said the Raymond-thing. "As you say on Earth, her bark is worse than her bite."

"UnEqua," said Claire. "Interesting name."

The woman stiffened. "My name is ≠," she said. "Only friends get to call me UnEqua—and certainly not a lowly human."

"Claire will call you whatever she likes! We will treat her with respect!"

UnEqua grumbled, then stormed off with her hand, looking for some underling who could sew it back on.

"Thank you," said Claire, then circled back to their original conversation. "So, can we ditch the dog food?"

"Certainly," said the Raymond-thing, and he removed the plastic pet food bowl. "What would you prefer?"

"Well, lately I've been vegan," she said. "So maybe an açai bowl."

"I don't know what that is."

Claire huffed in exasperation. "Fine. Then a salad."

"And what might that be?"

"Plants! Just bring me plants!"

170

"Of course. Carnivorous or noncarnivorous?"

"Noncarnivorous!" she shouted, getting increasingly annoyed. "I want to eat them; I don't want them to eat me!"

"Well, I just thought you might like the challenge. I'll be back shortly, Your Highness."

He left, and Claire crossed her arms, still not sure whether or not he was mocking her by calling her that.

• ● •

Raymond Balding-Stalker—the actual one—was awake, alert, and aware of everything that was happening. Yes, the Usurper had taken over his body, but it could only push him down, not out. He still felt everything, from the black eye that Ogden had given him, to how uncomfortably yucky his black ninja outfit had become. Apparently, these Usurpers didn't understand the concept of a change of clothes. It was a concept that Raymond himself often failed to grasp, but now he resolved that, if he survived this, he'd listen to his mother and change his clothes on a regular basis.

The Usurper had tried to lull him to sleep, but Raymond wasn't having it. Eventually, it just accepted that Raymond would be there, watching and listening. He was now just a spectator within his own body—which wasn't all that different from how he usually felt, so it wasn't that hard to adjust.

And besides, there were advantages.

For instance, he had never had the nerve to speak to Claire in any meaningful way—but this alien body-snatcher was a commanding presence, charming in a way that Raymond was not. He quickly came to realize that this whole body-snatcher thing could work in his favor.

Hey, he shouted from deep down in his spine, or wherever it was his consciousness had been pushed. *Hey, alien body-snatcher, I want to talk to you.*

"Quiet," it said, "or I'll kick you down even harder."

You could do that, said Raymond, *but wouldn't you rather know how to make Claire happy?*

"I can manage without your assistance."

Really? said Raymond. *You know, I could have told you that Purina Dog Chow was a mistake. But you didn't ask.*

Ø sighed. "And we bought a thirty-pound bag."

Well, it just so happens that I'm not just an expert on human stuff—I'm an expert on Claire Jensen.

That got Ø's attention "Is that so . . ."

Oh, yeah! I know everything about her. What she likes, what she hates, what she does when she thinks no one's looking.

"So . . . you are a student of the observational sciences!"

You could say that, Raymond said. *Let me help you . . . and maybe we can both get what we want. . . .*

• ● •

172

Claire found herself pacing with nothing much to do and getting hungrier by the minute. They hadn't even told her how long it would take to get to this planet that she now supposedly owned. Earth must have been billions of miles away by now. She wondered what her friends must think, and worried if Jaxon Youngblood had seen her abducted. And if he had, would he write a song about it?

When the Raymond-thing returned, it had a silver tray with actual human food.

"Here you are," he said. "A pulverized-and-baked sheet of grain, rolled over shredded plant matter and congealed bean-scum."

"A Caesar tofu wrap!" said Claire. "My favorite!"

Then he pulled out a scroll and unrolled it to reveal a digital screen no thicker than a single sheet of paper. "On this device, you'll find the fifth season of *Angry Debutantes* already loaded and ready to watch."

Which confused Claire. It was her favorite show, but a fifth season? "Can't be," she said. "*Angry Debutantes* was canceled after season four."

The Raymond-thing smirked. "Here, perhaps. But we downloaded it from a parallel universe where there were two more seasons!"

That made Claire actually gasp. Sure enough, when she tapped the screen, season five, episode one popped up. This was definitely worth being abducted by aliens!

"We'll be arriving on your planet shortly. Everyone at the palace is anxiously awaiting your arrival."

"A palace?" said Claire. "I have a palace?"

"Of course you do," said the Raymond-thing. "And a planet full of subjects for you to rule with gentle benevolence."

Well, that certainly changed things, didn't it. It gave Claire a lot to think about.

Satisfied, the Raymond-thing turned to go, but Claire reached out and grabbed his hand in unexpected gratitude— unexpected even to her.

"Thank you, alien thing," she said.

"As I said, my name is Ø. But my friends call me Slash," he said. "And I certainly hope I can count you among my friends."

"All right then. Thank you, Slash."

While deep inside, Raymond shivered with joy that Claire Jenson was finally holding his hand.

14

"⊕ςΦ↓δψ§!"

IN THE BASEMENT OF THE BLUE HOUSE THAT WAS CAREENING wildly through space, Quantavius Kratz put down the wrench, having had no success shutting down the noisy "furnace."

"It's no use. This blasted thing must be controlled by a thermostat upstairs."

Agent Knell folded her arms. "I'm beginning to think this may be more than an issue with a furnace."

"Occam's razor, Nell. Occam's razor."

Kratz was referring to the elegant and simple concept that suggested that, more often than not, the obvious answer is the correct one. And in this case, a furnace-looking thing doing a furnace-like thing was, more often than not, a furnace. Occam's razor, however, is also a fine recipe for answers that are spectacularly wrong.

• ● •

When Ogden and Sahara had hurried back up to the flight deck, they thought Miss Luella was right behind them. When she didn't show, they began to worry. Neither of them could even drive, much less pilot an out-of-control interstellar starship. The closest Ogden had ever come to driving was the Autopia at Disneyland—and even then, he had somehow managed to launch his car into the *Finding Nemo* submarine ride, sending Dory into the mouth of Bruce the Shark, to the horror of little children watching through the submarine's windows.

"Look at the controls," Ogden said. "They look like two joysticks—I'll bet one controls pitch and yaw, and the other one looks like a throttle."

"You don't need to mansplain, I see it myself!" said Sahara.

"It's not mansplaining—I expound the same way to males and females."

"Great, so can I throttle and expound *you*?"

The ship's wobble was taking on epic proportions. The Christmas lights that had just a few minutes ago seemed so calming were spinning wildly before them.

"Why don't you control thrust, and I'll control attitude?" suggested Ogden.

"There's already too much attitude!"

"Not that attitude—I mean the angle at which we're flying."

"Tumbling, you mean."

"Right, and we have to stop the tumbling!"

Which neither of them knew how to do. Miss Luella should have been up here by now—it didn't bode well that she wasn't. "I think we'd better find Miss Luella!" said Sahara. "I'll stay here to . . . to not make things worse. You go find her!"

Ogden didn't argue. He ran downstairs, leaving Sahara to deal with the controls on her own. Sahara's virtual driving skills far surpassed Ogden's—in fact, she always killed at *Mario Kart*—but flying a house was an entirely different proposition. And while Ogden was willing to experiment with the joysticks, Sahara didn't want to touch anything unless she knew precisely what it did. It was a wise decision, because the thing that Ogden thought was the throttle was, in fact, the self-destruct lever.

Half a minute later, Ogden came racing back up the stairs, out of breath, with Mittens trailing behind.

"It's no use! They're gone!"

"What do you mean 'gone'?"

"I mean disappeared, vanished. Noah, Miss Luella, and Andi are nowhere in the house!"

Sahara tried to wrap her mind around this but just couldn't do it. "You mean to tell me that it's now just you, me, and a cat hurtling through space?"

"Pretty much, yeah."

Around them, the guts of the universe buckled and

twisted and squirmed, and finally spat them out. The shooting multicolored lights were gone. Now they were tumbling end over end through regular space, which wasn't any better at all.

Just then Mittens jumped up and strolled casually across the control panel as cats are wont to do, randomly stepping on buttons with his paws. But perhaps it wasn't as random as it seemed, because the sound of the engine changed, and the tumbling house stopped tumbling. In a few moments it had stabilized and flipped itself facing foundation-first toward a rapidly approaching planet.

"Do you think that's the planet we're looking for?" Sahara asked. "Where they took Claire?"

In response, the cat projected into their minds an image of itself giving them a thumbs-up—which was both disturbing and confusing, because it didn't have thumbs—but they got the idea.

"We'd better strap in," said Sahara. "I think we're landing."

"Or crashing," said Ogden.

"Well, either way this trip is about to end."

So they dropped their butts down into the flight deck chairs, which immediately gripped them in terror. Then Sahara and Ogden gritted their teeth as they hit the planet's atmosphere, hoping beyond hope that Mittens knew what he was doing.

• ● •

Meanwhile, the escape pod tumbled through the void, in a completely different direction from the house, and Noah didn't have any idea of what void it tumbled through, because the little bathroom/escape pod had no windows.

"Well, this is a fine mess," grumbled Miss Luella as she sat on the edge of the bathtub. "I can't imagine what Mittens was thinking."

"He was thinking, 'I'm gonna steal this ship, and eject its owner into deep space.'"

But Miss Luella waved her hand dismissively. "Oh, pishposh, that crafty feline is more elegant than that. Plans within plans within plans. Mark my words, there is more to this than you think!" Then she chuckled. "That cat is going to get an earful when I catch up with him."

"*If* you catch up with him," Noah pointed out. "How do you know we'll even survive? Is there enough air in here? Water? What happens when we get hungry?"

The old woman smirked. "I'm sure you'll be able to catch a few more flies."

That only served to make Noah feel that his stomach might invert again. He swallowed. Hard.

"My dear boy, this escape pod is designed to sustain us as long as necessary. There's running water, the medicine chest has dehydrated food rations, and we have a commode to relieve ourselves, with the shower curtain providing a wee bit of privacy. In short, we'll be fine."

"We could be out here forever...."

"Nonsense! My escape pod is programmed to find the nearest inhabitable planet. And since we were traveling deep within the universe's unthinkables, it will likely spit us toward a planet in no time. Give or take a theoretical eternity."

Noah sighed. He thought of his friends, who still may not have any idea that he was gone. Andi would put two and two together, and tell them exactly what had happened, though. That is, unless that miserable cat had found a way to disable her. He wanted to pound the walls. He hated being helpless, but right now, he had no choice but to tumble blindly through space in a bathroom that had become an outhouse. A *way*-outhouse.

"I do love an adventure," said the old woman with an excited little shiver. She had said as much when she first encountered them. "And," she added, "we already know that you do, too."

He gave a blue-red mandrill blush, remembering how he'd been moaning and groaning about how uninteresting his life-as-nobody had become. Even so, adventures were always better after you knew you had survived them.

"My friends need me...," he insisted.

But Miss Luella gave him a very pointed look. "Do they really?"

"Of course they do!"

"Seems to me it's more about *you* needing *them*."

Her words must have struck a chord because they made Noah uncomfortable. "So? We need one another."

"True, true," Miss Luella admitted. "But I get the feeling that you're so used to them being part of your fiascos that you won't let them have a fiasco of their own."

"But . . . but what if they're lost without me?"

"Well . . . considering our current position, I'd say we're the ones who are lost."

Noah couldn't argue the logic of that. Yes, he felt protective of Ogden and Sahara, but was it because he believed they wouldn't make it without him . . .

Or was he afraid they might actually be fine?

Even without a telepathic cat to tell her what he was thinking, Miss Luella seemed to know. She put a gentle hand on his shoulder. "Friends don't let friends be sidekicks," she said. "Let them take care of their business. You and I can have our own adventure. . . ." Then she paused for a moment, sensing at the same moment Noah did, a slight change to their environment. "And, as it seems to be getting a bit warm in here, our new adventure is about to start. Because the heat shields have encountered an atmosphere!"

• ● •

With all the heat and vibration of reentry, Noah expected the landing to be rough, but it wasn't. Just a smooth touchdown as the bathroom/escape pod's landing struts kissed the ground.

"Well, that could have been worse, all considered," said Miss Luella. "Can't expect more from an escape pod."

"No? How about blasting back off?"

"Sorry, dearie. I'm afraid escape pods are only designed for one-way trips."

She glanced in the mirror over the sink, which now displayed strange symbols in some unearthly language.

"Ah! An argon and oxygen atmosphere!"

"Is that bad?"

"Not at all! It's a little more oxygen than you're used to—you might get a bit giddy, but otherwise, it's perfect!" Then she went to the medicine chest. "Oh—before I forget." She pulled out a little vial, opened it, and fished out what Noah at first thought was a pill. But it was moving. The little vile was full of little pink moving bugs.

"Here you go!" she said cheerfully. "Don't eat it—it probably won't taste as good as that fly."

Noah grimaced at the thought and looked closely at the little beetle-like insect. It seemed harmless enough. "It looks like a ladybug."

"Look closer," said Miss Luella.

Noah brought his hand closer to his eyes and noticed that there were little grooves in the bug's back. Familiar-looking grooves. It took a moment for him to realize what it reminded him of. The bug looked like a tiny little brain.

Then suddenly it crawled up his wrist, bit him, and burrowed under his skin.

"Aaaaah!" screamed Noah.

"Oh, don't be a baby," said Miss Luella. "It only hurts for a little bit."

• ● •

Ixodita Cerebri—better known as brain ticks—are the most plentiful insects in the known universe, and an integral part of the galactic educational system. A well-educated brain tick can hold entire courses of higher learning from literature to theoretical physics in their miniature brains— but, by far, their greatest use is in communication. Because, throughout the better part of the Milky Way galaxy, language is not learned; it is spread by parasitic infection.

After all, who would want to spend endless hours in a classroom, repeating bland phrases like *"Este es el sombrero de Guillermo"* or *"Detta Ikea-bord saknar en skruv"* when one could let a language-trained brain tick burrow into their nervous system and give them an entire language in just a few seconds?

While there are countless languages in our galaxy alone—from the blood-spatter speech of Arcturus to the trillion-taste vocabulary of Draconian tongue-snakes— there are four that are widely spoken, having been spread along the spiral arms of the galaxy by uncontrolled brain tick infestations.

The four great Galactic languages are: First Spiralese, Second Spiralese, Third Spiralese, and French. There are those on Earth who will argue that French, like many European languages, evolved from Latin. This is entirely untrue. It arrived in a meteorite.

• ● •

Having a brain tick bite you and burrow under your skin is not the most pleasant sensation in the world. It reminded Noah of that first shot of anesthetic at the dentist's office; the idea being much more painful than the actual pain. He could feel the moment it plugged into his nervous system like a shock shooting through his arm and out to the rest of his body.

"Just wiggle your toes and count to five," Miss Luella said. "It'll pass."

So Noah did, and by the time he got to five, the pain on his forearm and that weird electrical misfire faded away, although he could still see a little lump under his skin where the thing now nested.

"Why did you do that?" Noah asked.

"You had to be schooled," Miss Luella said. "How do you feel?"

"⊕ςΦ↓δψ§!" said Noah.

"Excellent! You're speaking First Spiralese now!"

"I am?"

"Yes! And with perfect diction—which is hard to accomplish with only one mouth."

She grabbed a few items from the bathroom's medicine chest, then turned to the door.

Now that they had landed, the lock on the door had disengaged, allowing Miss Luella to turn the knob. There was a hiss of escaping air, and Noah flinched, suppressing a sudden urge to quill-up like a porcupine.

It's just the pressure equalizing, he said to himself, feeling the need to tell his startled DNA that quills were entirely inappropriate and unnecessary at the moment.

The door swung open, and the little bathroom/escape pod filled with sweet-smelling humidity as if they had just arrived in Hawaii, but when they stepped out, it was clear no travel agent had ever booked a vacation here. Or at least no *human* travel agent. The lush foliage looked like something one might see in a Dr. Seuss book: towering, leggy flowers with oversized petals, shrubs that grew perfectly round, tall grass that undulated in the wind even though there was no wind, and a tree that dangled with fruit that seemed to be made of blown glass. "Whoa..." was all that Noah could say.

He took a step toward the tree but stopped short as he saw a creature peering down on him from the limbs. Actually, several of them. They looked like a cross between a squirrel and a monkey, with large, anime eyes, and multicolored fur. They seemed both inquisitive and meek. But before he could approach the little creatures, a sonic boom rang out from high above, and they were scared away. Noah looked up to see a ball of fire streak across the sky. A few moments of silence, and the sound of the impact reached them—a hefty BOOM!

"Oh dear," said Miss Luella. "Brace!"

She grabbed onto the doorframe, and Noah did the same, just as the shock wave hit. The ground shook like an earthquake, and a sudden blast of wind tore several over-sized petals from the tall flowers. Then the shock wave passed, and all was quiet again.

But the shock wave lingered in Noah's gut, resonating as he realized . . .

"Your house!"

"Possibly . . ." said Miss Luella, which was not the answer Noah wanted to hear. Because if it was the house, it meant his friends had just been incinerated.

"Sahara and Ogden!"

"Perhaps they got out," suggested Miss Luella.

"Was there another escape pod?"

"No . . ." Then, seeing Noah's distress, Miss Luella took an optimistic turn. "But on the other hand, we were ejected in mid-flight, which means the house could be millions of miles away. And Mittens wouldn't have ejected us just to burn up himself entering the atmosphere."

"So it's not them?"

"All I'm saying is that we can't be sure either way."

Noah held on to that tiny spark of hope, wishing he had more.

"We need to find out!" insisted Noah. "We need to know!"

Then Miss Luella looked off toward the strange forest. "It looks like we may have some help."

Noah followed her gaze to a creature. Not a small squirrely thing, but a creature almost their size.

The sight of it made Noah's neck expand like a frilled lizard, which made the creature back off. Noah felt more embarrassed than anything—because it didn't look threatening at all. He reached up and pushed his expanded neck back into place, but it was unwieldy, like trying to close an umbrella.

The creature was humanoid, with two legs—but it had three arms: the two usual ones and a third growing out of its back ending with a six-fingered hand plopped palm-down on its head like it had no better place to be. Its body was covered in silver fur that caught the light and shimmered.

"Was it you who made the ground shake?" it asked in a voice that was almost musical. "You're not supposed to be here."

"No, we didn't make the ground shake," said Noah, "but we need to find out what did."

"And," added Miss Luella, "we're here by accident; we

187

don't mean to trespass. We were ejected from our ship in mid-flight, and this was the closest habitable planet."

"That must have been awful—but at least you landed safely." Then the creature reached its third hand forward, placing it gently on top of Noah's head—which must have been a form of greeting—so Noah did it back. It was the right response.

The creature—who Noah was finally beginning to see as a person, and not a creature—called its species "Triastral," and was not from here but from a different world entirely.

"I'm Jadoon, or Jad for short. I don't have a ship, so I guess you're stuck here."

But Noah knew where there was a will there was a way—and he had the will of every creature he had left behind on Earth.

• ● •

If it was up to Noah, they'd have headed straight to whatever had fallen from the sky—but they had no idea what dangers they'd face. They needed a guide, which meant they needed to win Jad's trust.

Jad led them through a crazy alien Eden, filled with a mind-boggling array of strange plants and critters.

"Is the whole planet like this?" Noah asked.

Jad shrugged, which was weird with three shoulders.

"Different parts look different. This part looks a lot like my home world."

Finally, they reached Jad's home, a structure that appeared to be carved out of a giant piece of glass-fruit. Noah thought they'd be meeting Jad's family, but it was only Jad.

"Are there many others? I mean of your kind?" Noah asked.

"Oh, tons and tons, back on Triastra, where I'm from," Jad told them. "But here, it's just me, except when my parents bother to visit."

While Miss Luella busied herself with Jad's garden— which was even more unusual than the huge vegetables she grew back home—Jad took Noah inside to show off a home that was clean and organized, although Noah couldn't tell what most things inside were.

Getting to know an entirely new sentient species was exciting for both Noah and Jad. Jad found it strange that humans were "missing an arm," and wondered how they shielded their heads from the sun without a third hand. Until that moment, Noah had never even considered how helpful a third hand might be. Pity he didn't have any of Jad's DNA, or he might have been able to grow one.

It was hard to tell Jad's age. Time, as measured by Earth's rotation and revolution, didn't mean much on a different planet. But Jad seemed the equivalent of a teenager.

Noah also wasn't sure if Jad was male or female, and trying to find out proved to be awkward.

"I'm sorry, I don't understand the question," Jad said, when Noah finally asked.

"I mean, biologically," said Noah, feeling his words starting to stumble. "Or non-biologically, because there's that, too."

"I still don't follow."

Noah grimaced, realizing this conversation was going off the rails. "Okay, let's try this another way. Tell me about your mom and dad. Or your moms, or your dads, or whatever it's like where you're from."

Still, Jad just said, "I'm really confused."

"Your parents! Tell me about your parents."

Understanding finally bloomed in Jad's eyes. "Oh— you mean my endo, my ecto, and my exo."

That caught Noah by surprise. "Wait. You have three parents?"

"Well, duh, of course!"

Now Noah's brain was starting to hurt. "Sooo...how does that work?"

Jad gave a big old smirk. "Seriously? You need me to tell you about the birds and the bees and the turtles?"

"Turtles? No, there aren't any turtles in that equation!" blurted Noah. "It's just a birds-and-bees situation. Or birds-and-birds. Or bees-and-bees. But no matter what, there are no turtles!"

Jad squinted just a bit. "Are you telling me your species is non-trinary? How does that work?"

"I'd rather not get into it!"

And then, mercifully, Miss Luella came in with flower cuttings that she put into a vase that also somehow seemed to be alive. "You live in paradise, Jadoon!" she said. "An absolute paradise."

Jad glanced back at Noah and shifted all three shoulders—not in a shrug but in the universal body language of awkwardness. "Should we continue this conversation later?" Jad asked.

"Absolutely not," said Noah.

"Agreed," said Jad.

And it was filed away in a place that neither of them would dare go again.

"You poor thing, it must be hard to be on your own," Miss Luella said as she arranged the flowers.

"I'm used to it," Jad said.

You adapted, thought Noah. In a way, he and Jad weren't all that different.

"So . . . your parents come and go?" Noah asked, hoping there was a ship, or some sort of teleportation going on.

Jad sighed. "Mostly they go. They've only visited once since they brought me here."

"Hmm . . . curious," said Miss Luella, considering Jad more closely than before. "And why did they bring you here?"

Jad became a bit uncomfortable. "Well, because my parents all thought it was a good idea."

"What about friends?" Noah asked. "Do they visit?"

The question pained Jad even more. "I have lots back home...but they don't come here. They've probably forgotten me by now." Jad turned to look wistfully out the glass face of the bulbous home. "My parents said there'd be neighbors. I keep waiting for them to move in."

Noah's mention of friends reminded him of his own, and the fact that he still didn't know their fate. Small talk with a friendly alien was all well and good, but there were far more pressing things.

"Jad...could you help guide us to...to whatever it was that crashed?"

Jad seemed taken aback by the question. "Why would you want to do that? It's probably just a burning mess."

Noah swallowed hard, trying not to think about that. "It...it might have been the rest of our ship, and...and our crewmates. We need to know...."

"There's a barrier at the edge of my property. You won't be able to get past it."

"We have to try...."

Jad reluctantly nodded. "Okay, I'll take you there. And once you realize trying to get out is pointless, we can come back and have lunch! And after that we'll go find a big-enough crystal fruit for you to live in. Best day ever!"

Noah opened his mouth to tell Jad that, no, they

weren't about to stay here, but Miss Luella gently touched Noah's arm.

"That sounds like a fine idea, Jadoon," she said.

Noah figured she was being kind and wanted to let Jad down easy. But on the other hand, maybe she meant it. Because without a ship, they could be stuck here for a long, long time.

• ● •

While the property was expansive, Jad's home was near its eastern edge. Jad took them to the fence, if only to show them it would be too difficult to climb.

"As you can see, there's an impenetrable security perimeter," Jad said. "Now that that's settled, let's go back and have lunch!"

"It's just a fence!" said Noah. "Not a problem."

Through the fence, Noah could see that the foliage on the other side, while still tropical, was different. No more leggy flowers and grass that waved like tentacles. Instead there were ferns and palms and roses and gardenias. He became acutely aware of how familiar the flowers smelled. And weren't those mangoes growing on that tree? "It's like . . . Earth," Noah said.

"What's Earth?" Jad asked.

"My home world."

"Yes," said Miss Luella. "It's just like Earth on the other side of the fence. . . ." She pursed her lips as if she had more to say but wasn't saying it. "Maybe we need to rethink this...."

"What's to rethink?" Then Noah dug deep down, knowing exactly what the moment needed. A fence was nothing. All it took was a little bit of spider monkey.

In a moment he felt the familiar tingling in his fingers and toes. He felt limber, he felt agile. Suddenly, the top of the fence that seemed so daunting a second ago wasn't even an obstacle. This was going to a piece of cake!

"Noah! Wait!" yelled Jad as Noah leaped—

And felt the ten thousand volts of the electrified fence shoot through him.

15

The World of Last Life

FOR NOAH, ELECTROCUTION WAS DIFFERENT THAN IT WOULD have been for any other human being—because every single creature wrapped within his genetic soup responded in its own powerful and particular way. In an instant he lived every path of evolution along every single evolutionary tree. Biology's trial and error, eons of success and failure, were encapsulated in that moment. The survival cry of every earthly species was played out across the high voltage conductivity of Noah's body and soul.

He could have died—*should* have died—because living flesh was not designed to withstand a jolt so severe. But millions of years of survival was not about to throw in the towel now. In that moment something extraordinary happened; because, for an instant, Noah wasn't a conglomeration of different animals battling for the right to express themselves. He was, for the first time, all of them all at once.

He never exactly lost consciousness. It was more like he jumped to the other side of consciousness. Like passing through a black hole, only to discover that somehow you still existed.

"Noah! Noah, can you hear me?" He could hear Miss Luella's voice, but it seemed distant. "Noah, are you all right?" She sounded closer this time. Bit by bit he returned to the here-and-now. He was lying on his back in the strange wavy grass. He knew without looking that his hair was part crowned crane spikes, part urchin spines, and part jellyfish stingers. Each time he blinked, his eyes saw different colors and different levels of depth and clarity. Miss Luella knelt over him.

"Stay back," Noah said. "I could hurt you!" He could sense every part of him from stem to stern was venomous. So he took a deep breath, then another, willing the surge of animal defensiveness to pass. Reasserting his humanity. In a moment he came back to himself, but somehow felt more than himself.

He sat up and saw that Jad had backed away in shock. "You're . . . you're—"

"I'm fine," Noah said, but when he tried to stand up, his legs felt like they had no bones, and he fell back down, right into Jad's arms.

Then Jad smiled. Purple tears formed in those slightly oversized eyes.

"You're . . . like me . . . ," Jad said. "You're just like me. . . ."

• ● •

Noah couldn't help but to look at the world from an earth-ling's point of view. It never occurred to him that there might be other Nascent Organic Aggregate Hybrids out there. Other N.O.A.H.s. Now it made perfect sense. The Fauxlites were all about terraforming—so obviously their efforts wouldn't be limited to Earth. His parents' mission was just one of many missions. Could one of those missions have been Jad's home world?

In fact, it was. Jadoon was a Juvenile Aggregate Dynamically Optimized Organic Nexus. In other words, a Triastral N.O.A.H.

• ● •

Still weak from the massive electric jolt he had taken, Noah found it hard to put thoughts together, but things were slowly dawning on him. Meanwhile, Jad, full of excited joy, couldn't stop talking and waving all three arms.

"I knew I couldn't be the only one!" Jad said. "You've got weird animal stuff happening to you, just like me! It's why my parents brought me here—they told me no one would understand, so we had to leave home. They promised me I'd be safe here."

Jad dragged up a huge spongy mushroom cap for Noah to lie on. It was kind of like lying in a beanbag chair, although it smelled funky. Then Miss Luella sent Jad off to fetch first aid supplies for Noah's wounds, leaving her and Noah alone.

"This place...," Noah said. "It's not just any old planet...."

"No, it's not," agreed Miss Luella. "This must be the Fauxlite's biological preserve. The World of Last Life."

"Which means the other side of that fence..."

Miss Luella nodded. "Is the habitat that was meant for *you*."

Noah shook his head in disbelief. Their luck couldn't have been any worse! To wind up on the very planet his parents were going to bring him to. What were the chances? Unless of course it was no accident...

"Mittens!" shouted Noah.

"Yes, Mittens," agreed Miss Luella.

The cat had not ejected them into random space; it had ejected them at a very specific moment, with very specific intent. To send them to the Fauxlite's biological preserve. Was the cat working for the Fauxlites all along? No—more likely he saw an opportunity and took it. Mittens would now seek out a Fauxlite ambassador and tell them that Noah Prime had been delivered. Then demand a reward.

"We have to catch that cat before it tells the Fauxlites!"

"One step at a time," Miss Luella said. "It might not matter. Because if it was my house that crashed so spectacularly in the distance, poor Mittens would have been killed."

Along with my friends..., thought Noah, but he shook the thought off. He had to take this one step at a time, just as Miss Luella had said.

Jad returned with squirming things that looked like a cross between leeches and Band-Aids.

"Hey!" Jad said, even more excited than before. "If all the things on the other side of the fence are from your planet, then you were supposed to be my neighbor! Why didn't you say so?"

Jad's excitement seemed so wrong, so disconnected from the harsh reality of the situation...and all at once Noah realized...

Jad's world has been terraformed...

...and Jad doesn't know.

Triastra, the world Jad came from, was gone. Wiped and terraformed into a completely different planet. Every last living thing, from the plants to the animals to the insects to Jad's friends...they were all dead. Hadn't Noah wondered what it would be like to never know the truth? To be taken on a great cosmic adventure by his parents, without ever knowing the fate of Earth? Jad was exactly what Noah could have been, had things gone differently. And Jad's parents never came to visit. Of course not. Because Jad's "parents" were just Fauxlites wearing skins of Jad's species. Just like Noah's parents.

Noah felt his eyes get moist as he watched Jad so obliviously applying the leechy Band-Aids to Noah's burns. But

Jad took Noah's expression for pain. "Don't worry," Jad said. "It only hurts a little, but they'll help those wounds heal really quick."

"Jad ... I'm so sorry ... ," Noah said.

Jad just looked at him, blinking. "Sorry for what?"

"Noah, dear," said Miss Luella, interceding before Noah could say too much, "maybe we should leave all that for another time and focus on getting over that fence."

Noah took a deep breath and nodded. "Yeah. Yeah, of course we should." Because how do you tell someone that their very existence caused the death of everyone they knew? Noah found himself unable to look in Jad's big, trusting eyes. So instead he patted his hand comfortingly on top of Jad's head, and Jad did the same to Noah with that strange third hand, smiling.

"Friends and neighbors," said Jad.

"Friends and neighbors," echoed Noah.

And Noah hoped that Jad never learned the truth.

• ● •

With the help of the Leech-Aids, and his own axolotl salamander DNA, Noah healed remarkably quickly. In just a few hours he was ready to take on that fence again.

"Are you sure?" Miss Luella asked. "After what it did to you the first time?"

"I just wasn't ready," Noah told her as he stood before it, charging himself with adrenaline.

"I don't know about this...," said Jad.

But Noah knew it wasn't just blind confidence. Something had changed. It was as if that first jolt had galvanized him. His defenses—his abilities—had been fused. He wasn't just a collection of creatures. He was all of them at once.

"Trust me," Noah said, surprised by the resonance of his own voice. "I got this."

Then he launched himself against the fence—and this time when he grabbed it and felt the deadly electric surge, he was ready. Electricity? That was nothing. It was his to mold. He simultaneously channeled the powerful current of an electric eel, the indestructibility of a tardigrade, and the fearless fury of a honey badger! Noah met that current with an electric pulse of his own, sending it surging back through the fence with energy enough to melt electrical towers on a lesser world. But here, it managed to blow out a sizeable section of the Fauxlite fence in a glorious shower of sparks.

He clung to that fence until the last of the current had died. He was smoking, his clothes were half burned off, but he was awake, alert, and undamaged.

"Whoa...," said Jad. "That was amazing!"

"Not done yet," Noah said. Then he called forth claws that were the combination of a dozen different animals— the grizzly bear, the mountain lion, the alligator, and more— and ripped a hole in the fence large enough for them to climb through. "There. *Now* I'm done."

They made their way toward the rising smoke in the distance. It wasn't as ominous a plume as it had been when they first set out. Whatever it was, it had almost burned itself out.

By the time we reach it, there'll probably be nothing left.

Noah tried to get that thought out of his mind.

The landscape was by no means friendly. They had crossed from a tropical zone into a temperate forest with pines and thorny thickets. He much preferred the tall flowers and whimsical trees of Jad's domain. Noah thought Miss Luella would have trouble keeping up, but for a woman her age, she was pretty spry. Although to be honest, there was no telling what her actual age was. Just because she looked grandmotherly didn't necessarily mean she was.

"Are there animals?" Jad asked, wary to be in an unknown ecosystem. "Are they dangerous?"

Were there? Noah wondered; he hadn't heard as much as the chirp of a bird, or skitter of a lizard. Then he realized—of course there weren't animals! Because the animals would have been grown from *him* after he had arrived.

"Only one animal," Noah said. "Me. And yeah, I can be dangerous."

"But don't you think it's weird?" Jad said. "There are plants, and there are insects, but nothing else...."

Noah remembered the orchid his mother cultivated

202

that contained the DNA of every plant on Earth and the weird bugs that Ogden called manslaughter hornets that contained the genetic material of Earth's insects. All that genetic material must have been extracted to fill this place with plants and bugs. But it was missing the creatures that Noah was supposed to provide.

"My habitat isn't complete," Noah said—but that opened the door to more questions.

"Habitat? What do you mean habitat?"

"Oh! Will you look at that!" said Miss Luella, jumping in to change the subject. "What lovely wildflowers! I'm sure they're different from the ones you're used to, Jad. So much smaller!"

The distraction worked. But whether Jad realized it or not, habitats were exactly what these enclosures were. Was this planet a zoo, then, with the biological diversity of every planet the Fauxlites had destroyed? If so, where were the zookeepers? Why were there no gawking alien visitors? What were the Fauxlites really up to with this place? Noah would have to ask his parents if he ever found them. One of many things he wanted to ask them. He wondered if his parents were still pearls hanging on Vecca's ears. Did Vecca even have ears in her natural form? All Noah had seen were tentacles, but no ears. He shivered thinking about it. Best not to go there now. First things first.

For a while Jad got quiet. Preoccupied. Finally, Jad asked, "Noah ... what did you do back there at the fence?

203

You didn't just glitch—you actually *used* your animal stuff."

"Yeah, of course I did," Noah said, like it was nothing. But it wasn't nothing—and he knew that more than anyone. It had taken Noah a long time to get his traits and defense mechanisms under control. Every once in a while, he still "glitched," as Jad had called it, but for the most part, wresting his inner alligator and gorilla was getting easier. Although now he supposed he was wresting alligator-gorillas because his traits had fused in weird ways.

"I could teach you . . . ," Noah suggested.

"I'd like that," said Jad. "When it started happening, I didn't know what was wrong with me. Suddenly, I'd go all blue like a Sky Thorg, or liquefy like a Spillrat, and go down the drain. That one was the worst! It took my parents forever to fish me out of the sewer—it was gross!"

"Been there, done that," said Noah. "I feel your pain." He shuddered, remembering the time he had to go boneless and flush himself down a toilet to escape being the subject of government experiments. Then he asked, "Did you ever wonder if your parents weren't telling you everything?"

"All the time," said Jad, giving him a three-shouldered shrug. "Maybe they'll tell me more when they come back."

Miss Luella cleared her throat and shook her head at Noah. Right. Now wasn't the time to ruin Jad's life. But maybe he could make it a little bit better.

"All right, lesson one," Noah said. "Are there any

creatures on your world that are good at hitting things with their head?"

"Yeah! The Banded Batteroid."

"Okay, great. You see that boulder over there? I want you to run toward it as fast as you can. Don't think about the bando-battery thing, just think about how that big rock is in your way, and how much you want to break through it to get to the other side. Imagine yourself on the other side."

Jad looked a little worried. "Yeah, but what if . . ."

"No what-ifs," said Noah. "Trust your body to do what it has to do."

Jad took a deep breath and charged toward the boulder.

"Noah, are you sure this is a good idea?" asked Miss Luella.

"It'll work," Noah told her. Although he did remember that one time he tried to use his head like a Rocky Mountain ram, only to get schooled in pain—but that failure was part of his learning curve. "Even if Jad can't pull up the bando thing, some protective trait should pop up." Or, thought Noah with a grimace, some healing trait if this leads to a cracked skull . . .

Head lowered, Jad made contact with the boulder—

And promptly disappeared.

"Huh?" Noah ran up to the boulder. "Jad! Where are you?"

"Over here!" Then Jad came around from the other side.

Noah stared at Jad, bewildered, and Miss Luella just laughed. "How'd you get there?" Noah asked.

"You told me to imagine myself on the other side. So I did."

Noah shook his head. "But how—"

Jad gasped. "The Quantum Loper! It's a creature that teleports short distances when in danger!"

"Well," said Noah, "there you go! Now you know how to call up Quantum Loper!"

Jad grinned like a little kid who just got a gold star.

"Stick with me," Noah said, "and you'll be a pro in no time!"

· ● ·

They passed from one Earth environment to another. A gnarled oak forest to an African savannah, to a large salt-water lake that was clearly intended for an abundance of sea life. Every environment on Earth was represented some-where in this habitat. Finally, they came to a scrub-covered plain . . . and to a smoldering crater at least fifty yards wide. Most of the scrub was scorched, and the ground had buck-led from the impact.

"Well, we made it," said Jad, probably ready to turn around and go home.

Noah steeled himself for what he might find in that crater. He wanted to know—needed to know—but at the same time was afraid to know. He slowed down, and finally stopped before he could get close enough to see inside. Then Miss Luella came up behind him, and said, very gently, "You don't have to look in that crater until you're ready."

But he knew that waiting wouldn't change the truth, whatever that truth was. So Noah took a deep breath.

Please let it not be the house. Please let it not be the house. Please let it not be the house. Then he stepped forward and peered over the lip of the crater to see . . .

That it wasn't the house.

What he saw—or more accurately what he didn't see— took Noah's breath away. No smoking timbers, no charred remains of the old Victorian. No dead Sahara. No dead Ogden. That billowing plume of black smoke had merely been from the brush that had been set aflame by the mysterious impact. Suddenly, Noah began to feel weak at the knees. Tears of relief started to fill his eyes, but he quickly wiped them away because he didn't want Jad or Miss Luella to see them.

"What is that?" asked Jad, pointing down at a soot-stained object at the very center of the crater, wedged half-way into the ground. "It looks too small to have made a hole so big."

"Small things make big craters, dear," said Miss Luella.

The object was glowing red hot but was still intact.

"It looks like some kind of box," said Jad.

"No, it's not a box," said Noah. "It's a suitcase."

16

"You're Ugly and Your Parental Units Clothe You Strangely."

ON ANOTHER PLANET, SEVERAL LIGHT-YEARS AWAY, OGDEN AND Sahara made their way through the mess of the living room, which had not fared well in their landing. While Noah and Miss Luella's touchdown had been easy, Sahara's and Ogden's was not. Pictures had fallen off the wall, china had leaped out of cabinets to its death, and quite a few knick-knacks were beyond repair. But in the end, it was still technically a landing, and not a crash.

Looking out through the window, Sahara could see they had landed in some kind of alien wasteland. The sky was orange—like it might be when there are wildfires on Earth, but she suspected it always looked like this.

She turned at the sound of pounding on the basement door—but it was only Ogden banging on it. "Hey—are you guys down there?" he yelled, rattling the doorknob, and pounding on it again. It was locked from this side—which meant that Noah, Andi, and Miss Luella couldn't be down there, but it was the only place in the house he hadn't looked. He unlocked it and tried to pull it open, but it wouldn't budge. It was as if someone was holding it closed from the other side. Ogden figured the doorframe must have been knocked out of alignment by their landing, and the door was just stuck.

"What could have happened to them?" Sahara asked. Then she turned to the cat that had followed them down from the flight deck. "Do you know?"

Mittens just weaved between her feet and projected an image of a question mark into their minds. Sahara had a feeling the cat knew more, but no matter how she tried, she couldn't get past that big fat question mark to see what might be behind it.

"From what I can tell, this RTR drive completely breaks down the laws of physics," said Ogden. "Anything could have happened to them. They could have been displaced in time or bounced into a parallel dimension. Or maybe they're still here, but invisible to us, because they've phase-shifted."

"Or," said Sahara, looking off toward the kitchen, "they bailed in the escape pod before we crashed."

"What escape pod?"

Sahara pointed to the big red blinking button in the

kitchen just above the coffee maker that said ESCAPE POD EJECTED.

"Oh," said Ogden.

It was a relief to know that Noah hadn't left the universe entirely, but even so, Sahara found it hard to swallow. "I refuse to believe that Noah would just abandon us."

"Maybe he didn't have a choice," suggested Ogden. "Andi's programmed to protect him at all costs, right? Maybe she realized we were going to crash and did it to save him."

"And not us?"

"She's not programmed to save *our* lives."

Sahara crossed her arms and huffed. "Even so, that's just rude."

"And Miss Luella must have gone with them."

That just made Sahara even more annoyed. "Isn't a captain supposed to go down with the ship?"

"Maybe not when it's a house."

A wind rattled the walls, and through the window, they saw a huge purple tumbleweed blow past. In the hazy distance were mounds that, from here, looked like rolling hills. Only later would they find out what those "hills" were actually made of.

Mittens was pawing at the door to get out, and Sahara moved toward it, but Ogden stopped her.

"We have no idea if the atmosphere's breathable," said Ogden.

Nevertheless, Mittens gave up waiting for them to open the door and opened it with his mind instead. It swung wide to the sound of a moaning wind. A blast of warm air made it clear that the atmosphere wasn't going to kill them. Or at least not right away. But Mittens ran out, going his merry way. They figured Mittens wouldn't have taken off like that if the air was bad. Besides, they sensed his thoughts—he was in search of edible extraterrestrial critters. Although for some reason a sudden flash of a scowling Mr. Kratz popped out of the feline's mind and into theirs. (It was, on Mittens's part, a careless brain-burp, and might have sent up a red flag for Ogden and Sahara, were the current circumstances not so overwhelming.)

Sahara and Ogden went out onto the porch, which had made the trip mostly intact, although their landing had buckled it a bit. The porch swing had collapsed on one side. But other than that, it looked like the house had survived the landing.

"Look," said Ogden, pointing at a huge crimson sun, "Jensen is a red dwarf!"

"Dwarf?! That sun is gigantic!"

"That's because the planet is so close to it. The fact is, most Earth-like exoplanets are—"

"Listen, let's focus on the reason we're here," Sahara said. "We can take an astronomy class later." Then, remembering what Miss Luella had told them, she ran back in, and all the way up to the tchotchke shelf on the flight deck.

211

This time all the tchotchkes had fallen and many lay broken on the ground, but luckily the snow globe hadn't. She picked it up. When the swirling snow cleared, the little ceramic figure inside that didn't even have a face before now looked an awful lot like Claire. And it was pointing.

Sahara rejoined Ogden, and they stepped down off the porch to the gritty hardpan and followed Claire's little pointing finger down into a gulley that looked like it had once been a riverbed. There were still little pools of water, but they looked gunky, like tar, and smelled like spoiled milk. There were insects swarming around the pools, although they didn't appear too intimidating.

"They kind of look like ladybugs," Sahara noted. She and Ogden quickly discovered that the insects bit. One got into her shirt and bit her in the universal itching spot— that one small place on your back that you can't reach.

"I got bit by one, too—it really hurts," Ogden noted. "I think it burrowed, but I can't see it anymore."

"We should have brought bug spray," she grumbled.

"Well, hopefully they don't have venomous neurotoxins," said Ogden. "But if they do, we'll know soon enough."

The only effect of the bug bite was that they suddenly felt more knowledgeable in a way that was hard to define. . . .

Up ahead were more of the purple tumbleweeds, but they looked different—more solid, and a little more colorful. It was only as they got closer that they realized why.

The "tumbleweeds" were entirely made of bits of paper and plastic, wrappers and packaging material. One intact bag had an image of something that looked like a corn chip with thorns. Another object looked like a soda can, with an opening designed for a very different sort of mouth.

"What's with all the trash?" asked Sahara.

"It's not trash," said Ogden. "It's an art installation. It looks like some of the pieces in Arbuckle University's art gallery."

"Or it's trash," said Sahara.

Ogden sighed. "Or it's trash—but don't you think an advanced alien species would have solved the problem of waste? If it's trash, I'll bet it's *ironic* trash."

Claire's little porcelain finger still pointed ahead but the gulley turned left, and they had no choice but to follow the gulley. Claire's porcelain face seemed to become a bit miffed that they weren't moving in the direction she was pointing, but she'd just have to deal with it for now.

There was a sign up ahead. Sahara could tell it wasn't written in any Earth language, and yet amazingly she could read it. She couldn't even begin to understand why. But, in translation, the sign said:

WARNING!
PROTECTIVE LENSES REQUIRED BEYOND THIS POINT.
VIOLATORS WILL BE PERSECUTED.

"I think they mean 'prosecuted,'" said Sahara.

"Maybe we should take a different route," suggested Ogden. "We don't have protective lenses."

"So?" said Sahara. "If we see anything too bright, we'll cover our eyes and look away."

"That would only work if light is the problem. For all we know, we might be about to encounter eyeball-eating creatures."

That unpleasant thought gave Sahara pause. "Ogden, your mind really must be a very frightening place."

"Yes," Ogden admitted. "Which is why I've had to become so remarkably brave."

Just then, the sound of engines drew their attention. They looked up to see two motorcycles descending into the ravine. Instead of wheels, vibrating magnets kept them hovering above the ground. Riding the two hoverbikes were figures in intimidating uniforms. It didn't take a genius to figure out they were either military or police, or security guards wishing they were military or police.

"Hold your positions!" one of them said.

"Did you not read the sign?" said the other. "No one may enter the city of B'Light without protective goggles!"

They hopped off their hoverbikes and approached Sahara and Ogden. Although the guards weren't human, they were humanoid enough; they each had two legs and two arms, although those appendages had more than the usual number of knees and elbows. Their mouths were way too large, and their eyes way too high on their foreheads—at least by Earth standards. But since they weren't on Earth, it was Sahara and Ogden's mouths that were too small, and eyes too low.

"What are you wretched creatures doing disobeying the law?" said the one on the left.

"Are you of subpar intelligence or are you scofflaws?" said the one on the right.

"Probably both," said the left.

"We're sorry," said Sahara, trying as best as she could to be diplomatic. "We didn't have protective goggles, so we thought—"

"Clearly you didn't think!" interrupted the left officer.

"They're obviously incapable of thought!" said the right.

"Look at you both!" said the left. "You're scrawny and sickly in appearance."

"And," added the other, "you're ugly and your parental units clothe you strangely!"

"Hey!" said Ogden, his temper beginning to flare. "I dress myself! My parental units haven't picked out my clothes for years!"

"And that awful grating voice!" said the left officer.

"Yes, it's like a mewling animal asking to be put out of its misery!" said the right.

Sahara held back any and all retorts, because in that moment she realized something that Ogden hadn't. "Just tell us where we can get protective lenses," she said.

The left officer reached into a small pack on his waist and pulled out two pairs of goggles. Or two triplets of goggles, as it were—because they were meant for beings with three eyes.

"All we currently have are Blearian tri-focals!" said the left officer. "But if you pull them tight, and let the central lens hang down over your miserable excuse for a nose, they should work."

She grabbed the goggles and handed one set to Ogden. "This will solve everything," she whispered to him.

"I really can't stand looking at these two," said the right officer. "Both of my stomachs are nauseated at the sight of them."

"As are mine," agreed the left. "Do you two realize that you are repulsive in a rare and precious way?"

Ogden looked ready to burst. "Is this how you treat all visitors to your world?"

"Ugh! That horrible voice again! Do all of your kind sound that way?"

"Ogden," said Sahara calmly. "Put on the goggles."

"We don't have to stand for this!" demanded Ogden.

"Ogden!" shouted Sahara. "Put! On! The! Goggles!"

"Fine!" Ogden grunted. He slipped on the goggles, as did Sahara. With some adjustment, and with the central lens dangling, they were able to make them fit.

Then, when they looked at the guards, their large mouths were no longer scowling. In fact, they looked pleased.

"Ah! Much better!" said the left officer. "Now you are in compliance."

"That was unpleasant, wasn't it? Sorry about that," said the right.

"But rules are rules."

"Can you forgive us for speaking to you in such a disrespectful manner?"

"Of course they can forgive us—they know we were just doing our job."

But Ogden was still fuming. *"What are you talking about?!"*

Sahara put a firm hand on his shoulder to calm him down. "It was the sign," she told him. "Don't you remember? It said 'Violators will be persecuted.'"

"Precisely," said the left officer, maintaining his good-natured smile. "But now that you are no longer in violation, our discourse can now be completely civil."

"Unless, of course, you find other laws to break," said the other.

"In which case our persecution shall resume."

Ogden groaned. "Could you please stop talking back and forth like that? It's like watching Ping-Pong. It's making me dizzy!"

"Sorry," said the left.

"But we can't stop," said the right.

"We have one brain to share between us."

"Linked wirelessly."

"More efficient that way."

"I speak while he inhales."

"And *he* speaks while I inhale."

"I just said that."

"Well, I'm sure they get the gist."

The wind picked up, blowing down the gully and filling the air with the smell of feet—although they couldn't be sure what feet would smell like here, and they really didn't want to find out.

"Can we assume that you were in that otherworldly abode that fell from the sky?"

"Yes," said Sahara. "We're looking for a friend—she was abducted from our planet and brought here."

At the mention of it, their eyes raised a bit higher on their foreheads. "You must mean our new landlord!"

"Landlord?" said Sahara.

But Ogden understood. "Sahara, I bought this planet for Claire. Word must have gotten out to the locals."

"Yes," said the left officer. "We were recently informed about the sale—and I certainly hope the new landlord is better than the old ones."

Then the right officer leaned in close to his companion. "Perhaps treating these two well will put us in good standing with the new landlord. It's always advantageous to have the landlord's ear."

"Except when we had the last landlord's ear, they came to take it back."

"I thought we agreed never to talk about that."

"My bad."

"Uh...sorry to interrupt," said Sahara, "but do you think you could bring us to our friend?"

"We don't have the authority," said the left guard. "But we'll bring you into town and let our First Citizen decide."

"First Citizen?" asked Sahara.

"The city's chosen leader," one of the guards responded.

"Oh, so like a mayor, then."

"Great," said Ogden. "Sounds like a plan."

Which confused the guards. "As we said, we don't have the authority to make plans. We just follow orders."

• ● •

The place might have smelled bad, but the perfume that had been poured into the bilgy muck that ran through the town camouflaged it, and after a while Sahara and Ogden became noseblind. As for the town itself, it was a glorious village of light and life. Even the citizens' clothing seemed to be woven out of light, and the streets were paved with shimmering gold brick. Stunningly beautiful butterflies with smiling, almost human faces fluttered past like a tiny welcoming committee. It was quite a difference from the arid wasteland where Miss Luella's house had landed. The goggles were to protect them from the radiation that all the bright lights of the city put out.

"Without them, you'd be blind within the hour," one of the officers told them. "Good thing we found you when we did."

"This place is amazing," said Ogden, starstruck by everything he saw.

"Yes, it is," Sahara had to agree, although her suspicious nature kept making her wonder if there was something she was missing. Something about the town felt familiar, and the thought kept gnawing at a distant corner of her mind.

They rode on the backs of the hoverbikes through the town until the two officers dropped them off at what appeared to be a fancy hotel, with bright blinking lights, gaudy and titillating.

"Uh, I don't know if we can stay here," said Ogden.

"We don't have any local currency," said Sahara.

"Which means we can't afford it."

"Ogden, you're talking back and forth like them."

"I can't help it—it's contagious."

"Stop it!"

"No, *you* stop it!"

Sahara took a deep breath and said nothing, reminding herself that she did, indeed, have her own brain and did not need to share one with Ogden.

"Not to worry," said the left officer.

"All expenses are paid," said the right.

"Least we could do for friends of the new landlord."

• ● •

Ogden was impressed by the hotel lobby. It reminded him of some of the really expensive hotels he'd seen when he went to Las Vegas with one parent or the other. Everything was at the elegant end of glitzy and garish—if anything glitzy and garish could be called elegant. There was a multipaneled glass atrium letting in light from outside and refracting it like a prism to create shimmering colors everywhere. In front of them, a three-headed swan swam in a little pond, gliding under a diamond-paved footbridge that led to a golden front desk. Behind the desk was a bored receptionist, but she perked up as they approached.

"Welcome to the HydraCygnus Hotel! How may I help you?"

"Hi—we were told there's a room for us," Ogden said.

"It's supposed to be comped," Sahara added.

"Ah," said the woman. "You must be the friends of the new owner."

"Best friends," said Sahara, because that had once been true.

"That's right," Ogden seconded. "In fact, I'm the one who bought this place for her." Then he added, "By 'this place,' I mean this planet, your star, and whatever else might be orbiting it."

The clerk never lost her smile. It was unnerving, and since she was wearing those odd protective goggles, her eyes seemed to bulge. Ogden couldn't be sure if the clerk had naturally bulging eyes, or if it was caused by a lifetime of wearing those goggles.

"When can we see Claire?" Ogden asked. "I mean, Miss Jensen, your supreme . . . landlord."

"The palace is some distance from here. But I'm sure the First Citizen will provide you with transportation. In the meantime, we have you both in the honeymoon suite."

"Yeah, no," said Sahara. "There won't be any honeymooning!"

"Not unless it's required," said Ogden.

"No, not even if it's required," said Sahara.

"Right. That being the case," said Ogden, "is there an only-friends-and-barely-that suite?"

"The honeymoon suite is the best we have," the clerk informed them. "Honeymooning is only suggested, not required, and there's enough room for the two of you to keep your distance, if distance is the norm for your species."

Then she handed them a marble that was somehow a key. "Enjoy your stay here at the HydraCygnus. We'll let you know when the First Citizen arrives. As you're the only friends of the new owner we've encountered, I know he'll be excited to meet you." Then she tapped a little bell and a bellhop appeared almost immediately. "Please show our guests to their suite," she instructed the man in the uniform and cap.

"Of course," he said, bowing to Sahara and Ogden. "Right this way!"

As he led them back over the diamond footbridge,

Ogden took a moment to study the swan in the pond. He felt his neck hairs begin to stand on end.

"There's something about that swan that bugs me," Ogden whispered to Sahara, "but I can't figure out what it is."

"It has three heads," Sahara reminded him.

"Yes, but that's not what I mean. There's something else...." He tried to adjust the protective goggles on his face to get a better focus but found that they were stuck to him like suction cups. He would have stayed studying the swan longer, but the bellhop and Sahara were already in a crowded elevator waiting for him.

"Room for one more," said the bellhop. Which, Ogden noted, was what someone always said in every elevator nightmare he'd ever had.

• ● •

The suite was spectacular. Just as the clerk had said, it was roomy, with a stunning view of the city, which looked even more amazing from this view—ornate architecture, marble arches, and huge balconies filled with blooming flowers.

"Why would someone sell a world like this for fifty bucks?" Ogden said.

"You're right," said Sahara. "If something seems too good to be true, it usually is. There's something off about all this." Sahara threw herself on a comfortable-looking sofa. "But at least we can rest awhile. And take these goggles off."

"Good luck with that," said Ogden. "They're kind of snug."

Snug was an understatement. They were form-fitting to her eye sockets and cheekbones, and when she tried to pull them off, it was as if they were glued to her face. She pulled so hard, she felt her eyeballs might come off with them.

"Why would they make us wear them in our own hotel room?"

"Rules are rules here, I guess."

"No. It's like that swan, Ogden. This whole city is off . . . and what's more—it . . . reminds me of something."

"Of what?"

"I don't know. But there's something familiar about all this. . . ."

But neither of them had the brain power at the moment to unravel the mysteries of Planet Claire. They were just too exhausted. Ogden face-planted onto one of the beds and yowled because face-planting while wearing an over-sized pair of protective goggles is never a good idea. But a minute later, he was snoring. As for Sahara, she fell asleep where she was on the sofa, which wasn't nearly as comfortable as it looked.

• ● •

Just after Sahara and Ogden left the fallen blue house, Kratz and Knell emerged from the basement. The noisy furnace had finally turned off—although, coincidentally, the moment it shut down, there was a ground-shaking jolt that threw him and Agent Knell to the ground. After all that racket from the furnace, their ears rang in the sudden silence.

"That's the second seismic event today," Knell had noted.

They both heard the pounding on the door, and that annoying boy, Ogden, calling out for Noah, Andi, and someone named Miss Luella. When Ogden unlocked the door, and tried to open it, Kratz held it closed to keep them from being discovered. Then it was quiet.

"We can't let them leave," said Knell. "If we're going to catch Noah Prime, we have to make our move now." But when they opened the basement door, they found that the house was empty. Everyone had left.

"They couldn't have gone far," said Knell, and led the way out the front door, both of them steeling themselves to face the dreaded vegetable garden once more—but the second they stepped outside, they realized that the garden was gone. And so was the street. And so was the whole neighborhood. They stopped short on the porch.

"What's going on?" asked Knell. Then she turned to Kratz as if this was all his doing. "Quantavius, where are we?"

Kratz thought about all that had befallen them in the basement: the strange vibrations, the sudden jolts, the noisy furnace that might not have been a furnace at all . . . and he arrived at the only possible conclusion.

"The house is a time machine! We've traveled back millions, maybe billions of years to when the world was new. . . ." He pointed up at the red sky. "Look at that prehistoric sky. What more proof do you need?"

Knell squinted toward the sun. "I would agree . . . except for the fact that the sun didn't look like that in its early days."

Kratz took a look at the gigantic red sun and came to the only other possible conclusion.

"Aha! So we've traveled into the distant *future*—when the sun has expanded to a red giant!"

"Makes sense to me," said Knell. "The question is, why did they come here? If Noah Prime and his delinquent accomplices are in league with aliens, what do they want with the future?" Then she smiled. "I see a long, slow, painful interrogation in store for Noah Prime."

"Agreed, but we have to catch him first."

And so, armed with the levitator, the portal gun, and the memory cube, they took off down a gully, following footsteps in the sand, still not having the slightest idea that they were on a different world. . . .

17

The Jadoon Cipher

\ - - _ _ \ |

In a house that was an exact replica of the one Noah once lived in, beside a field that was eerily similar to the one by which his original house once stood, Noah tended to the suitcase that was his sister.

/ - | \ - \ - - /

Andi's wheels had melted off. Not that they would have been any help hauling her across the faux Earth terrain. Noah and Jad had found the house a few miles from the impact crater, and now Noah was using tools from his father's coffin-making workshop—which was also perfectly recreated—to try to pry Andi open.

- - | / \ _ - __

Her handle and unlock button had been fused, and most of the lights were out on her digital display, making it impossible to read what she was saying. Noah couldn't even be sure if she was actually saying anything at all. Those random dashes and slashes on her digital display could have just been a malfunction, for all he knew.

-|-. . .

"I don't know why you're so worried about it," Jad said, a bit irritated by all the attention Noah was giving the little roll-aboard. "Your house has everything you need. You probably don't even need any of the stuff in your luggage."

"It's more than luggage," Noah tried to explain. "It's . . . it's an android."

Jad looked confused. "A what?"

"A kind of a robot."

"Kind of a *what*?"

That made Miss Luella chuckle. "Noah, not all civilizations are arrogant enough to create AI in their own image," she said. "I imagine the Triastrals never found much use for such things." Then she went back to the kitchen. Since the house was fully stocked, she was baking bread, as if settling in for a long stay. The smell of fresh bread would have been comforting to Noah, had they not been in a replica of a home that no longer existed. The fourth version of that home, in fact. The original, of course, had been in Arbuckle, but had been destroyed in an alien attack. The second was in a cornfield in Iowa, the third was on a Himalayan mountaintop. And now this. When they had first arrived at this one, Noah half expected to find another set of backup parents pretending to be his real ones.

"Can't you just forget about the suitcase?" whined Jad. "Whatever's in there is probably ruined anyway."

Noah let off an exasperated huff. "I can't!" he said finally. "It's my sister in there!"

That gave Jad serious pause for thought. "Uh . . . Noah, I hate to tell you this, but if your *sister* is in there, I don't think she survived."

Noah almost laughed. "Trust me, Andi could survive a supernova. Although it might tick her off."

\ \- —. _ | - /

If she really was trying to communicate, there had to be a better way.

"Andi," he said, "if you can hear me, blink once."

The display on the handle went dark.

And then, a single mark appeared.

" _ "

Noah blew out a breath of relief. So it wasn't just random misfirings. Andi was still alert, and probably extremely annoyed!

"Hey," said Jad, "she really is alive in there!"

"Sort of," said Noah. "It's complicated."

By now Miss Luella had come back out of the kitchen, curious about this new development.

"Andi, your display is broken, so we're going to have to talk this way," said Noah. "Do you understand? Blink once for yes, twice for no."

" _ "

"Good. So, first—are you okay?" Noah asked.

Andi responded with " - " and then " - - " and then " - " again.

"So . . . that must mean maybe?" said Jad.

"Or it could mean she's not sure," said Miss Luella. "She probably can't run a systems diagnostic in there, the poor thing."

"Did Mittens eject you, too?" Noah asked.

" - "

"And do you know what happened to Ogden and Sahara?"

" - - "

"Do you know how we can get off this planet?"

Andi gave them a very long pause, and then a very slow " - - ". Leave it to Andi to find a way to "blink" sarcastically.

"Why are you asking her that?" said Jad. "You just got here! Why are you talking about leaving?"

Jad nervously tugged at a few ear hairs with that third arm. Noah understood Jad's anxiety. Jad's ecosystem was a paradise, but alone in paradise was still alone.

Andi waited for the next question, and Noah sighed. There had to be a better way than playing a slow game of twenty questions to communicate. Then something occurred to Noah.

"Miss Luella—do you happen to know Morse code?"

"Oh, heavens no," she said. "All that buzzing and beeping drives me to distraction. I never cared for it."

The only Morse code Noah knew was what everyone knew: dot-dot-dot, dash-dash-dash, dot-dot-dot. SOS. That wasn't going to be very helpful, since SOS was pretty much the synopsis of their entire week. But on the other hand, it didn't matter what the code was as long as both sides knew it.

"We need to create our own code," Noah said, "then teach it to Andi."

"I can do that," said Jad. "I'm good with secret codes." But then Jad hesitated. "If I help you... will you promise not to leave?"

"I promise... that we won't leave you here alone," Noah said. Which was enough for Jad.

• ● •

A / B // C /// D - E -- F --- G | H || I ||| J /- K //- L /|
M //| N -/ O --/ P -| Q --| R |/ S ||/ T |- U ||- V /-| W -/|
X |-- Y -|- Z -/-

• ● •

They called the code the Jadoon cipher. Since the language of First Spiralese—which they had been speaking—had over five hundred letters, they decided to go simple and create the code in English, which Jad learned quickly, even without the benefit of a brain tick.

"My whole species is really good with languages," Jad told them. "Maybe someday I could take you to my planet."

Noah took a deep breath, and offered no response, other than, "Yeah, maybe."

The cypher used combinations of three symbols: a dash, a slash, and a vertical line, all of which Andi was able to create using the limited functional lights on her readout. Although Noah needed a cheat sheet, they only needed to explain the code to Andi once.

" | --/ |- ||| |- " Andi wrote.

Got it.

And then she offered up this:

" -/| || -- -/ ||| | -- |- --/ ||- |- ||| //| //| / //- ||| /| /| |- || / |- /// / |-"

When I get out Imma kill that cat.

Noah tried a screwdriver, a crowbar, even a hammer and chisel to get Andi open, but nothing worked, and Andi was increasingly annoyed.

" ||- |/ | --/ -/ -/ / // |/ -- / //- //| --"

She kept pulsing out her frustration in Jadoon cipher symbols—which was much easier for her to do than it was for Noah to decipher. He couldn't find a single animal in his genetic repertoire that had the cognitive ability of instant translation. Jad could do it but was too busy checking out everything in the house to be bothered. So Noah had to rely on his own very human brain, which required him to write it down and consult the cipher key. He wished there was a brain tick around that could learn it instantly.

"Ur gonna break me" is what Andi had said.

"You're already broken," Noah responded. "We might need to break you more before you can be fixed."

"I'm not broken, I'm jammed. There's a diff."

"Maybe we could grease your seams."

"Don't u dare."

Noah dropped his tools in frustration, and they hit the ground with a clang. "So what do you suggest?"

No response but "——_——". Which wasn't part of the cypher, just a digital glare.

Throughout all of this, Jad continued to explore the house, pulling things out of cabinets like an overstimulated child. "What's this? What's that? What's this?"

Miss Luella, with endless patience, answered all Jad's inquiries.

"A muffin pan. A laundry basket. An XBox."

"What do you put in an XBox?"

"Every last bit of your free time."

Noah tried not to be irritated by Jad's lack of anxiety over their whole situation. After all, this was the first time in ages that Jad had seen anyone. How could Noah fault his new friend for being excited? And knowing the fate of Jad's world . . . well, Jad's ignorance certainly was bliss.

Miss Luella went on with a litany of labels. "That's a

potato peeler, that's a roller skate, and, good lord, I have no idea what that is."

"It's a Roomba," Noah called out. "It cleans floors and trips you."

Noah stepped away from his compacted sister, rethinking his whole approach.

Then Andi pulsed out, "Fine. I'll do it myself." Suddenly, her damaged LED screen went blank.

"Andi?" said Noah, but the screen stayed dark. "Great. She's pouting."

"Or maybe she's thinking," suggested Miss Luella.

"No, I know my sister. She's pouting." And then he went off into his room to do the same thing.

Noah's room was, of course, just as he remembered. Same motocross posters, same messy desk, same pile of laundry in the corner. The Fauxlites were obsessive when it came to attention to detail. But Noah didn't feel comforted by the familiarity. More than anything, it was an unsettling reminder of what he'd lost. He knew if they couldn't find a way off this planet, this could be his room again, permanently. And if the Fauxlites ever found out he was alive, and was exactly where they wanted him to be, that would be the end of Earth.

There was a timid knock. Noah turned to see Jad standing by the open door, waiting for permission to enter.

"You can come in," Noah said.

Jad stepped in and looked around, no longer asking

234

what everything was for. There was a sense of respect now. Of reverence for Noah's personal things.

"My parents did the same thing yours did," Jad said. "They copied our home—and my sleep space—perfectly. I thought it was weird. Do you think it's weird?"

"Yeah, it's weird." Noah took a moment to gauge the level of Jad's wide-eyed innocence. But then, Jad's eyes were always wide.

"What did your parents tell you?" Noah asked.

Jad shrugged and looked away. "My...*problem*... was getting worse. People were starting to notice the way I was behaving like different animals, and my parents were..." This part was clearly hard for Jad. "My parents were embarrassed and ashamed. They said they'd take me to a place where no one would make fun of me. I didn't know they meant off-world until we got to the spaceport." Jad took a moment to wipe away a tear. "They never told me why they left me alone, or why I never heard from my friends...." Jad's eyes began to tear up even more. "I'm sorry...it's just hard to think about, so I try not to."

"My parents were a lot like yours," Noah said. "They didn't tell me stuff, either. They lied to me for a long time."

"Did they go away, too?"

"They got taken away."

"Who took them?"

"People who wanted to kill me."

Jad gasped. "So your parents were protecting you?"

"Kind of . . ."

"Maybe my parents were protecting me!"

"I'm sure they were, but . . ."

"But what?"

Noah realized he'd already said too much, but Jad wasn't about to let it go. Noah had to choose his words carefully.

"That 'problem' that made you have to leave your world . . ."

"Is the same one you have," Jad said. "But for you, it's not a problem, is it?"

"I used to see it as a problem, too. But once you learn how to control it, it's more like having special powers that no one else has."

"But *why*?" asked Jad. "Why are we like this? No one else is like this. . . ." Then Jad took a dangerously deep look at Noah. "You know something! What is it? What are you not telling me?"

"Jad . . . uh . . . I . . ."

"Lunch!"

Never had Noah been so relieved to be interrupted. Miss Luella stood in his bedroom doorway, defusing what could have been a disastrous situation.

"The fridge and pantry are fully stocked, so I made grilled cheese sandwiches on freshly baked bread. Are either of you lactose intolerant?"

"No," said Noah.

"I don't even know what that is," said Jad.

"Well, we'll find out soon enough, won't we?" said Miss Luella, brightly.

Jad threw Noah one more glance, as if to say, *This conversation isn't over*, then headed toward the kitchen. But Miss Luella held Noah back.

"Noah, you mustn't tell Jad," she whispered.

"I know, but it's so hard to keep my mouth shut."

She sighed. "Think about it this way; if it were you, and Earth had been destroyed, would you want to know?"

Noah was about to say that, yes, he would absolutely want to know. But then, what good would knowing do? It would serve no purpose other than to make him miserable for the rest of his life. So then, would he rather live in blissful ignorance like Jad? Noah didn't like either option.

"Let's just keep trying to figure out a way off this planet," he said.

And at that, Miss Luella smiled. "I think I might have found a way," she said. "But first, lunch!"

• ● •

Noah hadn't realized how hungry he was until he bit into his grilled cheese.

"This is delicious," Jad said, devouring it in just a couple of bites and asking for another that Miss Luella was happy to provide.

The meal brought memories to Noah, as tastes and

smells sometimes do. He remembered sitting in his original kitchen, eating grilled cheeses with Andi—and Andi did eat them, but it was all for show. She had a little ejection port on her side for all the food she chewed and swallowed. Those days before he knew the secret truth of things loomed large in moments like this. He could almost pretend that he was just sitting at home, eating lunch with one of his friends. Except that this particular friend was covered with silver fur. Things change, and moments of nostalgia weren't going to help him now.

"So what did you find?" he asked Miss Luella as he rinsed his dish in the sink.

"I'll show you." Then she opened up one of the things she had taken from the escape pod's medicine chest: It looked like a little makeup compact, but when she opened it, Noah could now see that it was a small radar dish, which cast a holographic map in the air. "As you can see, there's a small launchpad about twenty miles from here," she said.

Noah pointed. "Is that a ship on the launchpad?"

"Looks like one," she said.

Jad began to look nervous. "I don't think we're supposed to go there."

"Don't worry," said Noah. "Going where we're not supposed to go is kind of my specialty."

"Yeah," said Jad, "but it's not mine. And if we get caught..."

"If we get caught," said Noah, "they'll just take you back home. They won't hurt you. They can't."

Jad's bushy eyebrows furrowed. "What do you mean they can't?"

"I mean they're not allowed. We're important to them—no matter what we do, they won't hurt us."

Still, Jad wouldn't let it go. "Important to who?"

Noah could only stammer "Uh..." And with Noah's brain suddenly on pause, Miss Luella chimed in.

"It's a mystery!" she said cheerfully. "But whoever 'they' are, they wouldn't have brought you here and set you up in such a splendid home if they wanted to hurt you!"

"They brought me here?" said Jad. "No, my parents brought me here. Didn't they?"

Now it was Miss Luella's brain that was on pause. "Uh..."

The truth about Jad was a minefield. Every conversation tiptoed around it, but eventually it would blow up in their faces.

"Your parents...may have had other reasons than the ones they told you," Noah offered.

"You don't even know my parents."

"You're right," said Noah, gently bringing his foot back from the mine. "So let's focus on what we do know." He turned to the projection of the launchpad. "What's the terrain like between here and there? Can we walk it?"

"I'm sure you two can," said Miss Luella.

Noah didn't like the sound of that. "You're coming with us, right?"

Miss Luella sat herself down at the kitchen table. "This adventure has been a bit much for me. I'm afraid I'll only slow you down. I'm already growing quite attached to your little farmhouse. It'll be a wonderful place to settle down, don't you think? I bet I'll be able to grow an even finer vegetable garden than before!"

"So, you're just going to stay here?" asked Noah. "What happens when the Fauxlites come back and find you here?"

"Oh, I've got a few tricks up my sleeve," said Miss Luella with a sly grin.

"Wh-what are Fauxlites?" Jad asked.

Yet another mine to step back from. "It doesn't matter," Noah said. "They're not important."

He could tell Jad wasn't buying it but wisely chose not to press for an answer in the moment. Instead, Jad said, "You can go to that ship. But I've got to get back home. Because what if my parents come back, and I'm not there?"

The question hung heavy in the air. Noah could read such lonely desperation on Jad's face, he had to ask a question he'd been avoiding. He put a hand on one of Jad's three shoulders.

"Jad . . . have you considered . . . that maybe your parents aren't coming back?"

Jad's wide eyes narrowed in anger. "Don't say that! Of course they're coming back!"

"Jad..."

"I know what you're thinking! You think they're dead. But they're not! Because if they were, someone would have come and told me!"

"I don't think they're dead, Jad... but there could be other reasons why they haven't come back...."

"No! I don't want to hear this!" Jad turned away, but not before Noah saw heavy tears begin to flow. "You've ruined everything! It was all fine before you showed up! I wish you never came."

"I'm sorry."

"Nothing was supposed to be like this!" Jad yelled through the tears. "It was all supposed to be better. Just me and them, in a great new place. Away from the crowds and the noise—a place where my 'problem' wouldn't be a problem anymore. That's what they said! This isn't how things were supposed to be!"

Noah took a seat beside his new alien friend, who suddenly didn't seem so alien at all. "Sometimes things happen that are out of our control," Noah said. "And thinking about it just makes things worse. Better to focus on the things you *can* control."

"Name one single thing that's in my control!"

Noah took a moment to consider his answer before he

spoke. "Whether you spend your life waiting for something that might never come ... or get out there and actually live your life. That's in your control."

It seemed to strike a chord, because Jad calmed down, considered it, and offered Noah a bargain.

"If I go with you ... then you have to promise to tell me what you know."

Noah tried to protest, but Jad wouldn't let him.

"I'm not stupid—I know there's something you're not telling me. So, promise me you'll tell me, and I'll go with you."

Noah looked at Miss Luella as if he needed her permission. But she just pursed her lips, and offered neither permission, nor veto. This decision was up to Noah.

"Okay," Noah said. "Let's find my friends. And then I promise I'll tell you everything."

"Good," said Jad, heaving a satisfied breath. "Then what are you waiting for? Let's get moving."

18

I'll Be Your Cocoon Today

WITH ANDI STRAPPED TO NOAH'S BACK, THEIR JOURNEY TO THE launchpad would have been next to impossible if he hadn't had his animal traits to give him strength and stamina. She was an extremely heavy and awkward piece of luggage. Noah experimented with his newfound skill of fusing traits. Like closing his eyes and fusing bonobo agility with flying fox echolocation.

"You're so good at using your animal things," Jad said. "I'll never be able to do what you do."

"It's just practice," Noah said. "I bet you were good at sports because of it!"

"I was the high scorer on my SphereBash team," said Jad, with a nostalgic grin that quickly turned to melancholy. "I wonder if I'll ever play again."

Noah knew if this was a Triastral sport, Jad probably wouldn't.

"You could teach me, and we could play it together," suggested Noah.

Jad snorted at that. "You need three arms and there are seventeen to a team, so..."

"Well," said Noah, "that's a skill I'll never have, so you've got me beat there."

The twenty-mile hike took Jad and Noah across all sorts of earthly terrains, from a miniature mountain to an Arctic tundra so cold it made Jad's fur grow extra dense.

"It's another stupid animal response I can't control," Jad said. "Chillax Bear."

"Practice," Noah reminded Jad. "Use it when it's helpful. Suppress it when it's not."

"Easy as that."

"I never said it was easy." Although Noah's body threatened to grow a hefty layer of walrus blubber (as it had done once before), he had learned to belay that biological order. Instead, he turned cold-blooded like a fish—in particular, the Arctic snailfish, which basically has antifreeze for blood.

They made their way through all the various engineered microclimates, until coming to a fence that marked the end of the fake-Earth habitat. And since no one was supposed to be in his habitat, this fence wasn't electrified. They climbed it with ease.

On the other side of the fence was a flat, featureless plain—a region that had not yet been prepped for an occupant. There was nothing there but beige gravel, like an empty aquarium—and there, just a few miles across the expanse, was the launchpad.

"Maybe we should wait until it gets dark so we're not seen," suggested Jad. But this planet revolved slowly, and the sun was nowhere near the horizon.

"If we wait, that ship might launch—we can't take that chance," Noah said. Then he dug down deep and dredged up some natural camouflage. Cuttlefish crossed with a bit of chameleon. It made him look exactly like the gravel, but less shiny than the cuttlefish camo alone would look. His new electrically charged ability to combine traits had endless possibilities!

He turned to see Jad gawking at him. "I can't do that."

"Yes you can." Noah sat Jad down on a rock, and they both focused.

"All animals have ways of hiding from predators," Noah said. "But don't just think of the animal. Instead, imagine the most embarrassing situation you can think of. One that would make you want to vanish."

Jad's big eyebrows furrowed. "Being caught in public with my fur shaved off," Jad said. "I knew a kid who that happened to."

"So imagine you're that kid. Feel like they must have felt."

Jad concentrated—and for a moment, all that thick silver fur went clear as glass. Not just the fur, but Jad's entire body. Noah could see right through.

But in a moment the effect was gone. Jad released a frustrated sigh.

"Just keep practicing," Noah said. "For now, stay behind me."

They made their way across the gravel plain. As they neared the ship, they could see how impressive it was. It was silver and sleek, with an insignia that not even Noah's brain tick could decipher.

"I know that symbol," said Jad. "It's the logo for Virgo Galactic—they're the best spaceline. Much better than WarpBlue or Final Frontier."

The launchpad was just a single pad, and a small terminal that was barely a terminal at all. Noah supposed the planet didn't have many travelers. Just Fauxlites bringing in new N.O.A.H.s or checking on the ones that were already here. The fact that it wasn't crowded would make it easier for Noah and Jad to get inside but also harder to go unnoticed once they were.

"Ooh!" said Jad. "Look at that!"

Noah followed Jad's gaze to two Fauxlites near the entrance. Noah had only seen one Fauxlite in its natural form. It was when his "backup father" was shot on the day of the volcanic eruption. The laser blast had blown Noah's backup father right out of his human skin. The species was humanoid but glowed as if they were made of light.

"They're so beautiful!" Jad said.

"They might look beautiful on the outside," warned Noah, "but inside they're monsters."

Even saying that made Noah's heart sink, because it only reminded him that his own parents were members of this monstrous world-killing species. And so were Jad's.

Once the two Fauxlites had left, Noah and Jad were able to sneak inside and hide behind a column, so as to not be seen. The terminal was little more than a waiting room. Just rows of benches and a vending machine full of little living things. A sign above the ramp that led up to the ship read FINAL BOARDING IN PROGRESS.

"Looks like we got here just in time," Noah said.

"So we're really gonna do this?" asked Jad.

"Too late to turn back now."

The gate area was already empty, except for an agent and a single passenger arguing with her about his ticket. Although Noah's camouflage had changed to mimic the color of the wall, at this close range, it only partially hid the suitcase strapped to his back and barely hid Jad at all. They'd be spotted if either the gate agent or the passenger happened to look directly at them.

At the counter, the disgruntled Fauxlite was getting increasingly frustrated, as evidenced by the reddening shade of his glow. "But I specifically requested a window cocoon!"

"I'm sorry, sir, but the window cocoons are all taken."

"Then MOVE someone!"

"If you'd like, you can wait until the next transport, seven planetary rotations from now."

"No! This is completely unacceptable!"

There was a small alcove to the right, and Noah saw exactly what they needed. It was an alien equivalent of a cloakroom, but instead of jackets and coats, there were artificial skins hanging on hooks. It was disturbing, but he supposed it would have been worse if any of them had been human. These were the skins of different alien species.

Noah grabbed two of them at random. "These skins will disguise us," he told Jad. "Quick! Put one on!"

Jad looked at the limp thing in disgust. "Ew!"

"It's easier if you don't think about it."

"But it's not going to fit!"

"Trust me, I have experience with these things. They bend space, so no matter how small they look, you'll fit inside."

And with the sound of someone approaching, Jad had no choice but to comply.

The skins were two of the same species but not humanoid. Once sealed in the skins, Noah and Jad were giant eyeballs on thin stalks, with half a dozen crab claws for feet. The bending-space thing had compressed most of their bodies into those stalks, which couldn't be more than three inches wide. But even with space-bending, Andi couldn't fit inside with Noah.

"This feels weird," said Jad. "I have no arms."

"You have a tendril," Noah pointed out. "Just roll with it." Noah's single worm-like tendril was all he had with which to drag Andi.

Just then, a Fauxlite came around a corner and stopped short when he saw them.

"Gleeb? Seymour? What are you doing here? I thought you left on last week's transport!"

"Uh . . . yeah, we were supposed to," said Noah, "but we had trouble with our Nascent Organic Aggregate Hybrid. It had an infection, so we had to take care of it, since it still believed we were its parents."

That brought a slow eyeball turn from Jad, and Noah instantly regretted saying it.

"Your N.O.A.H. had an infection?" said the Fauxlite. "How troubling. What kind?"

"Pink eye," said Noah.

"Really! Isn't that fatal in Occuloids?"

"It can be," said Noah. "So you can see why we had to miss last week's transport."

"Well," said the Fauxlite, "I hope you cloned it in case it dies—or we'll be in violation!"

"Of course, of course," said Noah. "We cloned it the moment it got sick, right, Gleeb?"

"Uh . . . right," said Jad. "And we cloned the clone just in case."

The Fauxlite nodded his approval. "Good. Because

those blasted inspectors look for every excuse to revoke our terraforming license. Well, good to see you both. Don't forget to hang up your skins before you go, so they can be cleaned."

"We'll clean them when we get there," Noah said. Wherever "there" was.

"Wearing your disguise off-planet!" said the Fauxlite. "That's dedication!" Then he sauntered off, chuckling.

All at once it occurred to Noah that getting off this planet might mean a trip to the Fauxlite home world. Out of the frying pan into the fire. But when he mentioned that to Jad, who had traveled commercial starlines before, Jad dismissed that particular concern.

"Virgo Galactic doesn't fly anywhere direct," Jad said. "Have to change ships at Elgafar, which is light-years out of the way—and you're always missing your connection. Ugh, don't get me started."

The Final Boarding sign was now flashing in earnest, and the disgruntled traveler was demanding to speak to someone in charge. The gate agent was so involved in the drama that she didn't seem to care that the two crab-legged eyeballs weren't presenting her with boarding passes. She just waved them up the ramp.

On board, a flight attendant greeted them. She was not Fauxlite, but of a different species. And she had two heads.

"Hi, we're Beatrice," said the two heads in unison. "Welcome aboard!"

"Thank you," said Noah to one. "And thank you," he said to the other.

"Do you need help finding your cocoons?"

"That's okay, we'll manage."

Then one head whispered into the other one's ear, and they both took a pointed look at Andi, who was still being dragged along by Noah's root-like appendage. "I'm afraid that piece of luggage appears damaged beyond regulations."

"Uh...right," said Noah, fumbling for a way out of their scrutinous gazes. It was Jad who came to the rescue.

"I know, isn't it awful? Our last trip was with Final Frontier. That's what they did to it."

One of the flight attendant's heads shook in sympathy, while the other nodded knowingly. "I'm not surprised. With those discount starlines, you get what you pay for. Of course, that would never happen with us," they said. "Enjoy your flight!" Then they went off to help a traveler who had somehow gotten turned upside down in her cocoon.

The cabin was circular like a barrel, rather than long and thin like an airplane fuselage. Green cocoons hung from the ceiling looking gooey and limp. The ones near the windows were all taken, but there were empty ones toward the center.

"I don't like the look of those things," said Noah.

"Don't worry," said Jad. "Travel cocoons are fine once you get used to them. Much better than cranial hooks."

Just then, the disgruntled Fauxlite who had been arguing with the gate agent came aboard, glowing red with anger. He said something rude to Beatrice, then pushed his way past Noah and Jad, toward the center, clearly having not negotiated himself a window cocoon. He did pause, however, to be rude to them, too.

"What are you two staring at?" he sniped.

"Nothing," said Jad.

"Yeah," said Noah. "When you're a giant eyeball, it's your nature to stare." Then he stared some more just to annoy him further.

"Those skins are hideous!" the man grumbled. "You should have taken them off before you boarded! Some people!" Then he reached out to a cocoon, and it sucked him inside.

Noah stowed Andi in the under-foot bin beneath the cocoon he had chosen, and when he looked up, Jad was already ensconced in an adjacent cocoon. Noah could only slightly make out Jad's giant eyeball through the veiny green membrane of the cocoon. "All good," said Jad's muffled voice.

Noah leaned his own giant eyeball toward his cocoon, and it drew him in. He was now encased within a stretchy, rubbery membrane. It felt like a slimy green hammock and seemed comfortable enough, until it opened its eyes.

"Hi, I'm Kyle! I'll be your cocoon today."

Noah yelped in surprise.

"First time?" asked Kyle the cocoon. "Don't worry, I promise not to digest you. Honestly, I couldn't if I tried—all my acid glands have been removed in order to serve you better! Please let me know if there's anything I can do to make your trip more comfortable!"

"Just leaving me alone would make me comfortable," Noah said, not at all happy to be inside something alive. He felt a whole host of animal reactions swarming within him, but if any of them presented themselves, it would not end well for him, or for Kyle, so he suppressed them.

"Are you sure there's nothing I can do? I can provide entertainment, if you like. I can sing a large variety of popular tunes."

"No!" said Noah. "Please don't sing!"

"Fine," said Kyle, a bit miffed. "If silence is what you desire, then that's what you'll receive." But not before Kyle gave the obligatory safety talk, which must have been mostly the same throughout the known universe.

While Kyle talked, Noah let his mind wander. Jad had said all outbound ships first go to an interstellar flight hub where travelers catch their various connections. It was hard enough to gain passage on a ship departing from a quiet planet—it would be much harder to do at a busy travel hub. Plus, they had no idea of their destination. If Ogden were with them, he could have identified it from star charts... but then maybe not, because star charts only showed celestial positions as they appeared from Earth.

Andi would know. But Andi wasn't talking—and only now did Noah suspect that she wasn't just pouting. She had said she had an idea before she went silent—but she never told them what that idea was....

The cocoon suddenly tightened around him, and for a moment Noah thought that maybe he was being digested after all—but then came the rattle of the engine, making it clear that Kyle was just giving Noah a protective embrace to smooth out the turbulence and g-forces of launch. It was much more pleasant than being held down by furniture.

Not a minute later, they were free from the planet's gravity. Noah floated in freefall, which was oddly soothing within a travel cocoon. With no sense of up or down, it felt like being in a womb. A comforting sense of peace came over him as he floated in his own private void. In no time at all he was asleep. And he remained asleep until the ship was attacked.

• ● •

Noah was awakened by a violent blast followed by the blaring of an alarm. For a moment he panicked, having no idea where he was. All he saw were green veins and a pair of terrified eyes.

"Ooh, this is bad!" said a frightened voice. "This is really, really bad!"

Noah found himself growing wolverine claws, and

feline fangs. He tried to speak, but it came out as a lion's roar.

"Ooh, that's bad, too!" warbled the voice.

Noah remembered where he was, just as another blast rocked the ship. His claws were already beginning to shred his artificial skin. If he lost that, it would make everything a whole lot worse. He swallowed and pushed his various animal traits as far down as they could go—and although it felt like trying to get toothpaste back into the tube, he managed to get the claws to retract, and the fangs to recede. His voice, however, still sounded rather lion-like, which wasn't helpful at all.

"What's going on?" he roared.

"I don't know!" said Kyle the cocoon. "And why do you sound like that? Stop sounding like that! It's freaking me out!"

Noah cleared his throat, and his voice normalized. "Just calm down. Whatever's wrong, it's going to be okay."

"You don't know that!" wailed the terrified cocoon.

Noah tried to find the seam and peel himself out, but Kyle was clinging to him like someone who was drowning. Then the flight attendant's voices came over the loudspeaker.

"Attention passengers! It is our duty to inform you that we are under attack. Please exit your cocoons and proceed in an orderly fashion to the escape pods."

Escape pods, thought Noah. *Why is my life now plagued with escape pods?*

"Wait, did they say 'exit your cocoons'?" wailed Kyle. "Are we being left behind?"

Then another cocoon responded. "Don't worry—whoever's attacking us, they probably just want to eat the passengers. We'll be fine."

Noah finally found the seam and shimmied out of the cocoon, even more disoriented now by the weightlessness. Jad was already floating there, eye wide and bloodshot. "We have to move before the escape pods launch."

They started to propel themselves through the throng of panicking passengers and cocoons, but then Noah remembered—"Andi!" He doubled back and grabbed Andi from the under-foot storage compartment...and realized that he had grabbed her with his *actual hand*, not a root tendril. He had managed to tear a hole in his skin, and his arm was now fully exposed. Anyone who saw that arm would know he was an impostor!

"Wait! Take me with you!" yelled Kyle.

"Noah, we have to go!" called Jad, nervously clicking a dozen crabby legs.

"Pleeeeeeease," begged Kyle.

And then Noah realized something. "Maybe we can help each other...."

Noah grew a single claw on his index finger, then reached up and cut the cocoon from the roof.

"Ow! That hurt!"

"Do you want to get out of here or not?"

"Just try to be more careful!"

Then Noah wrapped the cocoon over his exposed human shoulder, hiding it from view.

"Wait!" yelled another cocoon. "Take me, too!"

"And me!"

"And me!"

"And me!"

They all began to undulate, trying to reach for him, but Noah forced his way past them, until he reached Jad.

"About time!" Jad said. "Why'd you bring a cocoon?"

But another blast rocked the ship before Noah could answer. The lights flashed off and on. There were still dozens of Fauxlites floating around the cabin, glowing a panicked purple, trying to propel themselves toward the escape pods—but without gravity, it wasn't an easy task. Or at least for beings that couldn't grow octopus suction cups. Even so, it wasn't easy for Noah to cling to the bulkhead and hold Andi *and* help Jad toward the pod while a cocoon wrapped around him like a big, ugly Christmas scarf.

Right by the entrance of a pod, they encountered the flight attendant. One of her heads had passed out, so the other one had to pull double duty.

"This pod is still available," she said. "Thank you for flying Virgo Galactic! I hope this won't prevent you from giving us five stars on our app!"

Noah and Jad jumped into the escape pod, which was already occupied by one other individual. A panicked family of Fauxlites tried to pile in behind them, but the other occupant sealed the door before they could get in.

"What did you do that for?" yelled Noah. "There's still room for more!"

"Their problem, not mine!" said the passenger. Only then did Noah realize that this was the annoying disgruntled traveler, the last person they wanted to share an escape pod with. He hit the launch button before anyone could even find, much less buckle, their safety harnesses—and the ejecting pod tumbled them all like a clothes dryer.

"Quick, get inside me!" said Kyle. "I can protect you."

So Noah and Jad squeezed inside the cocoon, which buffered them from the worst of the tumbling.

"See," said Kyle, "aren't you glad you brought me along?"

The disgruntled traveler, who had not been invited into the cocoon, was now even more disgruntled.

"I saw that!" he yelled. "I saw that appendage! You're not Fauxlite! What are you?"

Then Andi, who was also tumbling around the escape pod, struck him in the head, knocking him unconscious. And even though Andi was in suitcase form, Noah couldn't help but wonder if she had done it on purpose.

19

Worldless

SAHARA TOSSED AND TURNED ALL NIGHT. IT WASN'T EASY SLEEP-ing with goggles clamped on her face. She had tried to remove them—because did these people really expect her and Ogden to sleep with them on? What if she had an itch? Or what if she had contact lenses and had to take them out? This arrangement was clearly not intended for anyone's convenience.

When she did doze, she had the strangest dreams. Houses falling from the sky. Evil people being crushed beneath them as they came down. Oblivious townsfolk in a bright Technicolor village. Sahara knew what those images were, and where they came from. She'd have to be clueless not to see the connection—and how her current reality res-onated with her favorite childhood story. But it was more than that. There was a voice in her head that kept whisper-ing to her that this connection was worth investigating.

Dig deeper, the voice said. But frankly she was too tired to dig at all.

She had no idea how long it had been since she had collapsed exhausted. Dawn was peeking through the windows, but who knew how quickly the planet rotated? It could have been dark for just a few hours, or for days. All she knew was that Ogden was still snoring across the room, and these blasted goggles were making her whole face hurt.

She went to the balcony where the rising red sun painted the beautiful towers in shades of crimson. Everything glistened and glowed. It was beautiful, but something about it was unsettling.

Dig deeper . . .

She gripped the goggles and tried to pull them off, but that sent a surge of pain through her eye sockets, and veiny squiggles filled her vision. She sighed and began to fiddle with the dangling third lens. Perhaps the key to removing them rested with that third lens. . . .

Their ornate hotel suite had a kitchen, and although the appliances were odd, they were mostly recognizable. This triangular one was an oven; that cylindrical one was a refrigerator. The drawers held eating utensils for various sizes and shapes of mouths. There were spoons, forks, and even sporks, which Sahara had always suspected had alien origins.

And there were knives—which were the same throughout the universe.

She grabbed the sharpest knife and took it to the band that connected the third lens to the others. And she began to saw.

• ● •

"Ogden, wake up!"

Ogden heard Sahara's voice in his sleep, but his subconscious refused to acknowledge it. He was having the most amazing dream and didn't want to be disturbed. In the dream, he was in a flying kayak preparing to swoop down and rescue Claire from the clutches of a headless T. rex. To his right and left, in their own flying kayaks, were astrophysicist Neil deGrasse Tyson and a remarkably buff Albert Einstein. Like most dreams, it made perfect sense to itself, although Ogden was beginning to suspect that its logic might not hold up under scrutiny—which made him want to hold on to it even more.

"Ogden!"

Now Sahara was shaking him, and he felt the dream beginning to evaporate. Neil deGrasse Tyson dissolved into a swirling galaxy of cosmic dust, Einstein went up in a mushroom cloud, and Stephen Hawking, who had only just arrived, collapsed into a singularity, wheelchair and all, before he could utter a single computer-generated word.

As Ogden surfaced from the dream, he swore to himself that he would remember it, but it was entirely forgotten by the time he opened his eyes, leaving him with a vague sense of loss and feeling very, very annoyed.

"What do you want?" he croaked. "Can't you see I'm sleeping?"

"You need to get up and smell the roses. Because they're not roses! We've been lied to!"

"Lied to? How?"

He looked up to see her eyes, which he shouldn't have been able to see. "You took your goggles off! You're not supposed to do that!"

"The question is why, Ogden," Sahara said. "Why aren't we supposed to do that?"

"Because the people who live here said so," Ogden snapped. "And I don't want to get yelled at again by two officers with half a brain!"

"Forget about them! Ogden, I think L. Frank Baum was an alien."

"Who?"

"Not just an alien," continued Sahara, "but I think he must have come from here!"

"Who are you talking about?"

Sahara grit her teeth in exasperation, as if it was obvious. "The guy who wrote the Oz books!"

For a moment Ogden wondered if he had woken up from one bizarre dream into another. "Oz? What does that have to do with anything?"

"Oh, trust me! It has to do with *everything*!"

Ogden sighed. As much as he didn't want to admit it, he had been struggling with an overwhelming urge to say *I don't think we're in Kansas anymore* from the moment their house came crashing down on this planet. But he had flatly refused to say it, because it was too blatantly obvious a thing to say. Well, maybe the time had come to just go with it.

"Okay, I'm listening," Ogden said, crossing his arms and shaking his head, betraying the fact that he really didn't want to listen at all.

"Did you ever read the books?" Sahara asked.

"I saw the movie."

"Forget the movie, I'm talking about the books!"

"Why would I read the books if I can see the movie?"

Sahara just stared at him. "Did you actually just say that?"

He shrugged. "Once in a while, there's a movie that's as good as the book."

"Name one!"

"Well, let's see . . . there's—"

"No!" Sahara said, shutting him down. "You just did what you always do! You've derailed the conversation."

"It didn't have any rails," Ogden pointed out. "It was more like a self-driving car."

"My point," said Sahara, slamming her hand down on

the nightstand, "is that in the Oz books, the Emerald City wasn't actually emerald. It only looked that way because they made people wear special green glasses to 'protect them from the glare.'"

She waited for Ogden to put it together.

"Oh . . . so, you think—"

Then she brought a knife to his face. "Hold still." And before he could even flinch, she cut the band that dangled between the second and third lenses. The instant the band was broken, the goggles unclamped from his face and fell off, revealing a truth that Sahara already knew.

"Wait . . . where are we? What is this place?"

The first thing Ogden noticed was the sofa across the room. The one that had appeared so velvety and plush when they had arrived. Now it looked like the kind of sofa people leave by the curb, hoping against hope that the trash collectors will actually take it away. The fabric was rotting, and bare springs poked through the cushions. And that velvety feel? It was moss. Around them the walls of their so-called hotel suite were cracked and peeling—and a glimpse toward the bathroom revealed that the grand golden toilet wasn't golden at all. It was . . . it was . . .

"Ew" was all Ogden could say.

"Exactly!" said Sahara. "Ew."

He picked the goggles up off the floor. "Augmented reality!" he concluded, intrigued almost as much as he was nauseated. "These are augmented reality glasses! They take what's actually there and project something else over it! A digital makeover!"

He hurried to the balcony and looked out over the city. Without the goggles on, what had been glorious towers and rolling green hills were now crumbling concrete ruins and piles of garbage.

"This city . . . it's a dump!"

"Exactly," Sahara agreed. Then she grimaced. "Even the butterflies aren't what they seem."

And when one of them came fluttering in the open terrace door, Ogden saw what those butterflies really were. They were spiders. Hairy. Flying. Spiders.

There was a knock at the door, and Ogden and Sahara looked at each other.

"So what do we do now?" Ogden asked, still reeling from their revelation. But before Sahara could answer, the door opened—because in this dump, none of the locks actually worked.

Half a dozen people entered. Each appeared to be of a different species. That was something both Ogden and Sahara had noticed—there was an abundance of different sentient species here—but with so much thrown at them so quickly, they hadn't yet wondered to ask why. Immediately, the group began gasping and whispering to one another, noticing that the two earthlings were not wearing their goggles.

They were all dressed in shredded, stained rags, and

265

while torn jeans might have been fashionable on Earth, these ruined garments were by no means a fashion statement. Ogden held one lens to his face and was not surprised to see that, through the augmented reality lens, they were clothed in glowing garments of light.

"What do you think this is all about?" Sahara whispered. But before Ogden could even guess, a member of the party puffed up (literally) and said, "All rise for the First Citizen of our fair city!"

"We're already standing," Ogden pointed out, but Sahara shushed him.

The First Citizen entered—a slim creature with gaunt, sunken cheeks. He was of a species that had little bud-like horns and spots like a leopard, although even his spots seemed faded, as if they had seen better days. The scene reminded Ogden of "The Emperor's New Clothes" but with aliens. The First Citizen wasn't naked, of course, but he might as well have been. He carried himself with the pride of a man in a tuxedo, despite wearing rags no better than any of the others.

He stepped forward to greet Ogden and Sahara. "Pleased to meet you, I am Forlo, the First Citizen of—" But he stopped short when he realized their goggles were off. "Oh no!" he gasped. "Quickly! Quickly! Put your goggles back on before you go blind!"

"Actually," said Ogden, watching a winged spider flutter past, "blindness might be the better option."

Sahara was neither impressed nor intimidated by Forlo. "We know!" Sahara said simply and plainly. "We know, so you can drop this whole charade."

Then the herald—or whatever he was—puffed up and announced as pompously as he could, "I'm sure the First Citizen has no idea what aspersions you are casting upon his integrity!"

But First Citizen Forlo waved a hand to silence the herald, and he deflated mournfully. The creature stepped forward, peering through his goggles at them, scrutinizing them. Ogden wondered if they were now to be executed for knowing the truth. Sahara, on the other hand, didn't sense danger. First Citizen Forlo had an air of wisdom, not malice.

The First Citizen heaved a sigh and dropped his shoulders. They fell halfway to the ground, leaving him with a very long neck. Now, with those spots, he looked more like a giraffe than a leopard.

"How unfortunate," he said. "It was our hope that you would see our town as we've come to see it."

Sahara looked at the entourage. "So, everyone in the city knows it's all a lie?"

"Of course everyone knows," First Citizen Forlo said. "What kind of fools do you take us for?"

"But if you know, then why do you wear those goggles?"

He sighed again. "If you lived in a place like this," he said, "wouldn't you?"

Reality is never truly objective. Whether on Earth or on a faraway planet, reality is what everyone agrees it to be. Money is just worthless paper, unless everyone agrees it's not. Seconds and minutes and hours only exist because we believe they exist. And beauty? Beauty isn't in the eye of the beholder at all; it's in the *mind* of the beholder—which is much more easily fooled than the eye. Certainly, some things are constant. Two plus two will always equal four . . . but four of what will forever be in question.

The city of B'Light was a glorious shining metropolis for all those who agreed it was. And those who didn't buy into the communal lie? They wore the goggles anyway, to save themselves from despair and persecution.

"We pump the smell of flowers into the air to mask the worst of the odors," the First Citizen explained as he walked through the wretched streets of B'Light with Sahara and Ogden. Ogden continued to hold a single lens to one eye so he could see both the real world and the augmented one at the same time.

"Incredible!" he said. "That fancy car is just a rusted hovercar up on blocks! And that waterfall is a broken pipe! And the dog that woman is walking is just a giant cockroach on a leash!"

Sahara was still having trouble wrapping her mind

around all this. "But aren't there other places you could live?" asked Sahara. "Another city?"

First Citizen Forlo scoffed at the suggestion. "As if it's that easy," he said. "I'll wager that you've never known poverty, that you have the privilege of being from a planet with natural beauty, rich in resources. But this world? It has nothing of value to anyone."

Sahara bristled at the idea that she came from a privileged planet. She considered herself sensitive to the struggles of others. Her parents had risen from poverty, and although they had given Sahara a better life, they made sure she never took it for granted. But to argue against the man's point would just prove it.

"Every city, town, and settlement on this planet is the same," Forlo explained. "Gray, downtrodden, and crumbling, without the resources to do anything about it. But at least in our city, we have the goggles."

"That flower garden is just crabgrass!" exclaimed Ogden. "With actual crabs!"

"Ogden!" snapped Sahara. "Stop being impressed. It's disrespectful!"

That made Forlo laugh. "What civilization doesn't engage in window-dressing?"

"Yeah," agreed Ogden. "It's like capped teeth, or designer clothes, or tattoos, or even wearing makeup."

"Precisely," said Forlo. "The face we present to the

world is never what we see in the mirror when we wake up. Why should a city be any different?"

But Sahara still couldn't buy into an entire philosophy of self-deception. Perhaps things like makeup and body modification were their own forms of augmented reality, but there had to be limits. There had to be an objective reality.

"Instead of dressing up cockroaches and crabgrass, why not see the world for what it is and try to make it better?"

Now the man seemed offended. "Then perhaps you should be First Citizen. Maybe then you'll see how difficult the task is!" He took a moment to regain his composure. "What you fail to realize is that this city—this entire planet—is the last stop. Not just for things that no one wants, but for people with no other place to go."

They had reached a promontory—a hilltop that afforded a view all the way to the horizon. Between here and that distant horizon, there was nothing worth viewing at all. Just endless mounds of garbage.

"This world . . . it's a wasteland void of indigenous life. Anything that had lived here has long since died. And anything that's here now? It came from somewhere else. Including all of us." He sighed. "This planet is a refuge for the worldless. When people have no other place to go, they wind up here."

"Worldless . . . ," said Sahara. "You mean . . . homeless?"

Forlo nodded sadly. "A long time ago, I lost everything I had," he confessed. "And now I'm here."

Ogden took a look at the goggles in his hands. "If it were me, I'd augment like crazy," he said. "I'd want to see butterflies instead of spiders." He pushed one off his shoulder with a grimace.

"I wouldn't," said Sahara. "I'd force myself to see what was really there and get mad enough to do something about it."

Then First Citizen Forlo smiled. "Which is exactly why you're so important."

Neither of them were expecting that. "Us?" said Sahara.

"As friends of the new landlord, you can convince her to spend just a fraction of her fortune to make this world livable."

"Fortune?" said Sahara.

"Uh . . . what if she doesn't have a fortune?" said Ogden.

At that, Forlo let off a hearty laugh. "Of course she does! She bought this star system, didn't she? She must be wealthy beyond imagining!"

Ogden and Sahara exchanged a glance. Neither had the heart to explain. It was no wonder the planet had sold so cheaply. Ogden hadn't just bought Claire the star system, he had saddled her with all of this world's problems, too. This whole planet was a slum . . . and thanks to Ogden, Claire was the new slumlord.

PART 4

• • •

LET'S DO THE TIME WARP AGAIN

20

Murdrum, Birdrib, and Molévelom

ATTACKS IN INTERSTELLAR SPACE ARE NEVER RANDOM. FIRST OF all, the chance of even *finding* a ship in the vast void is far less than finding a needle in a haystack. It's more like finding an invisible needle in a billion haystacks, where each of the haystacks is furious that you're even looking and would rather die than part with that needle, which they may or may not be intentionally hiding from you. Plus, even for a space pirate, it's a poor business model to hope an unsuspecting craft might actually contain something of real value.

For those reasons, attacks on interstellar crafts are always very directed, very intentional, and serve a very specific purpose. In the case of Virgo Galactic Flight 3553, the purpose of the attack was to capture a single individual on board. An individual with skills worth their weight in gold (or whatever metal one's species considers precious).

• ● •

The tumbling of Noah and Jad's escape pod stopped abruptly. Then there were scraping and clanking sounds on the outside of the pod, making it clear that someone, or something, was trying to get the pod open. Noah and Jad, still awkwardly cozy inside the cocoon, tensed a bit at the sound. But the cocoon was hopeful.

"We've been found!" Kyle proclaimed. "We're being rescued!"

Jad's big bulbous Occuloid eye turned toward Noah. "What do you think?"

Noah, whose Occuloid skin was damaged enough to display both his shoulders now, shrugged. "Could be good, could be bad."

The Fauxlite, who had been tumbling around the pod for quite a while, oozing bioluminescence everywhere, had just regained consciousness.

"I'm never flying this starline again," he moaned. "And this time, I mean it."

Noah found the seam on the cocoon and pulled it apart just as the escape pod's hatch opened to dank humidity and a rancid smell. But even worse was the thing peering in the hatch. It was a horrific wide-mouthed blue creature. Even its teeth had teeth—in fact every one of its reptilian scales had its own mouth, and . . .

And wait a second, thought Noah, *I know this abomination....*

"Murdrum?"

"There you are!" said the Fractillian Abysmal Beast. "Do you have any idea how many of these tin cans I had to open just to find you? And don't think you can trick me with that Occuloid skin. I could smell you anywhere, Noah Prime!"

The battered Fauxlite took one look at the Fractillian Beast and crawled whimpering into the cocoon, apparently deciding that if he was to be eaten, he'd rather be eaten as a burrito.

Jad couldn't stop staring at the creature's gnashing scales. "Are we about to be eaten by all those little mouths?" Jad asked. "Or just the one big mouth?"

"Actually," said Noah, "I don't think we're going to be eaten at all."

As they stepped out of the pod, Noah could see they were in the shuttle bay of a large ship, its walls dripping with murky slime.

"Ever since I was rescued from Earth, I've been bragging to my friends about you," Murdrum said. "They want to experience your magic hands for themselves."

"Your hands are magic?" asked Jad.

"Long story," Noah explained. "How did you even find me?" he asked the beast.

"Your sister put out a distress call! Free back rubs if we rescue you, she said. Worth a detour of a few hundred light-years. So, who's your friend?" The beast sniffed but didn't seem to recognize Jad's smell.

"My name is Jadoon," Jad said. "You're a Fractillian Abysmal Beast, aren't you? I've heard of them, but I've never met one before."

"Not surprising," said the Fractillian. "Few survive their first meeting with my kind. But any friend of Noah Prime's is a friend of mine." He turned to Noah. "So where's your sister?"

Noah went back into the pod to retrieve the suitcase. Now the readout on Andi's handle was flashing symbols too fast for Noah to decipher. And it occurred to him why she had gone silent. All this time she was putting every last bit of her energy into blasting out that distress signal.

"She don't look too good," said Murdrum.

"She...uh...took a bad fall," Noah said. "We haven't been able to get her open."

"Hmm," said the Fractillian. "Let me try."

He studied the little singed suitcase from various angles, then set it on its edge, made a huge, heavy fist, and brought it down on the edge of the case like a sledgehammer.

Noah grimaced, imagining Andi shattering into a thousand pieces—but instead the suitcase popped open. All Andi's gears and panels began to spin and revert, and in seconds she had transformed back into human

278

form—although she looked almost as bad as the suitcase had. Tired and sooty and with the worst case of bed head Noah had ever seen.

"Finally!" said Andi to the beast. "Someone who knows what they're doing!"

Noah was overjoyed to see her and couldn't stop himself from throwing his arms around her, giving her a hug that she didn't have the energy to squirm out of. "I thought we'd never get you back!" Noah said.

"You almost didn't," she said. "If I'd hit the atmosphere at a slightly steeper angle, I would have burned up on entry."

"I'm glad you didn't!"

"So am I," said Andi. "Mostly."

The Fractillian peered into the escape pod to see the Fauxlite cowering within the cocoon. And the cocoon was crying.

"Friends of yours?" Murdrum asked.

"The cocoon's okay," said Noah. "But the Fauxlite's a jackass."

"Maybe you could eat him," Jad suggested.

"Nah," said the beast. "Fauxlites are poisonous." He shut the hatch. "We'll send them back into space. They can be somebody else's problem." Then he led the way into the deep dark recesses of the slime-covered ship.

• ● •

The Fractillian ship was a disorienting maze of unnecessary spirals that gave birth to even less necessary spirals. And no matter how deep you got, the more it felt you were in the exact same place you started.

Finally, one of the spiraling paths led them to what must have been the ship's bridge, because it was manned (or more accurately "monstered") by at least a dozen Abysmal Fractillian Beasts, all of whom looked similar, if not identical, to Murdrum. They were all busy, with their hands shoved into dark oozing holes in the ship's wall—the kind of dark holes that every kid's mother warned them not to stick their hand in.

As soon as the new arrivals entered, the crew stopped what they were doing and stared at Noah—although, to be honest, their faces looked the same from every angle, so they were, in a sense, already staring at him.

"This is the one I told you about," Murdrum told his crew, gesturing to Noah.

Several of them stepped forward. Murdrum introduced Noah, Jad, and Andi to first officer Molévelom and chief engineer Birdrib.

"So this is the one with the magic fingers?" asked Molévelom, a bit dubious. "But he looks so soft and flavorful."

"Yeah," mumbled Birdrib, drooling. "An oozy rat in a sanitary zoo."

Murdrum's many mouths frowned. "Dammit, I'm mad!

Anyone who tries to eat him will face my wrath! I tell you, he gives the best back massages in the known universe!"

Birdrib backed off, but Molévelom was still unconvinced. His many eyes narrowed into a plethora of glares. "Prove it," he said to Noah.

So Noah pulled up some nice wolverine claws and smiled.

"Who wants to go first?"

• ● •

After a dozen deep tissue massages, Noah was exhausted. His fingers hurt, and his talons had actually dulled. But the Fractillians were all in heaven—or whatever place Fractillians dreamed of going to when they died. *If* they died. Suddenly, Noah was everyone's best friend. So much so that he worried they might not let him go.

"Come with us into the Abyss," they said. "You'll be rich! You'll be popular! You'll be loved by gazillions!"

"Didn't I tell you?" Murdrum said, proudly. "The best in the universe."

"Great," grumbled Andi. "As if my brother's head isn't swollen enough."

"So, will you take us where we need to go?" Noah asked Murdrum.

Andi gave the coordinates of the star system.

"That's out of our way," Murdrum said, "but a deal's a

deal. It'll cost you a few more back rubs, but we'll take you there."

• ● •

The Fractillians gave them a cabin that was less slimy than other areas of the ship. It was actually kind of comfortable, with a large view port. Andi powered down to conserve energy, leaving Jad and Noah alone.

"Noah, I just want to thank you for...for getting me to leave my home," Jad said. "This is scary and all, but it's exciting, too. Is it weird to say I kind of feel safe with you?"

Then Jad put that third hand gently on Noah's head, not quite tousling his hair, but gently smoothing it. Noah already knew that this was how Jad's species greeted each other, but there was tenderness to Jad's touch that resonated. They were two different species, and yet they were two of a kind. In truth, Noah was more like Jad than anyone on Earth. If that didn't make them siblings, nothing did.

"Tell me about your friends," Jad said. "The ones we're trying to find. What are they like?"

"Well...Sahara's brave and kind and determined. She doesn't settle for anything but the best in herself. She makes me want to do better. And Ogden...he's smart and funny—although he doesn't always mean to be. He finds amazing solutions to problems—but half the time he's the one who created the problem." Thinking about them made Noah wistful. Sort of homesick—but not for Earth. Because for Noah, Earth didn't feel like home. But Ogden and Sahara did.

"I can't wait to meet them," said Jad with a smile.

"You'll like them," said Noah. "And I know they'll like you."

They fell asleep with the tops of their heads touching. That, too, was customary on Jad's world.

"It's been a long time since I had anyone to tap heads with," Jad said just before dozing off. "Thank you, Noah."

It was a custom Noah wished they had on Earth.

• ● •

The planetary palace—which Claire was told was her new home—was old. Way old. And the places that weren't too cold were way too warm, with no comfortable temperature in between. The polished stone floors were slippery, the staff was creepy, and bad smells wafted in from every direction. The view from Claire's balcony made it clear why. In the distance, massive garbage ships arrived at all hours of the night and day, leaving behind who knew what. Biowaste, toxic waste, interstellar junk. According to Slash, the palace stood in the middle of a no-dump zone, but wind knew no such boundaries, carrying the stench of intergalactic waste in from every direction. And as if that wasn't troubling enough, the Usurpers, most of whom were using unalive bodies of various shapes and species, stunk to high heaven. Slash promised to keep the worst of them away from Claire's sensitive human nose, but it didn't really help.

"My first official act will be to abolish zombies," Claire proclaimed. "If your people are going to be body-snatchers, then have the decency to snatch the living."

"The living fight back," Slash pointed out, "making them much harder to control. Only the strongest of us, like me, are capable."

"Well," replied Claire, "if you can do it, then so can the others. Tell them to stop being so lazy."

"Yes, Your Highness."

Claire appreciated the fact that Slash rarely gave her much of an argument. Things were so much easier here than back home. Slash was paying Claire visits, even when he didn't seem to have any business to attend to. And he smiled at her a lot as he regarded her, sometimes looking puppy-like in his attentions. She wondered how much of that was Slash and how much was Raymond. She found she didn't mind the attention. Although she never had any interest in Raymond as a person, he somehow seemed more interesting—attractive even—as a snatched body. She supposed some people were like pieces of furniture. Even the most hideous chair could be stylish in the proper light, with the right throw pillows.

"Once I'm in control, I will immediately ban the

dumping of garbage, too," she proclaimed. "It's gross. People will simply have to find another planet to put it on."

"An excellent plan, Your Highness," Slash agreed. "But more pressing is the decision on what we should call you."

"What do you mean?"

"As the sole landholder in this system, you need a title. You could be queen. Or empress. Or sovereign supreme."

Claire thought about it. "Queen" felt too pompous and self-important. "Empress" sounded like someone old and wrinkled. And "sovereign supreme" sounded like a fast-food item. She remembered hearing how Monaco had a crown prince. That sounded more her style.

"How about crown princess?"

Slash smiled. "Splendid! You shall be Her Majesty, Crown Princess Claire of Claire." Then he clapped Raymond's hands together. "Now all that remains is your coronation."

"A coronation!" exclaimed Claire. She might miss out on being prom queen one day, but this was certainly better. "I can't wait!"

Claire looked out the window—not at the distant dumping grounds, but at the palace courtyard below. "Will there be crowds and crowds at the coronation?" Claire asked, envisioning the grandeur of earthly ceremonies.

"Well..." Slash hedged a bit. "The monarchy's relationship with the planet's residents is...uh...strained at the moment. It will just be a few hundred of my kind, but I promise you, they will be as enthusiastic as thousands!"

"Hmm, well then, I'll have to make the masses on this planet love me," Claire said with her signature confidence. "Because if there's one thing I am, it's lovable."

"You most certainly are, Your Highness," Slash replied, his voice filled with the real Raymond's admiration just barely beneath the surface. And maybe a touch of mischievous anticipation. "You are exactly what this sad, sorry planet needs."

21

Full Bowling Ball

THE EARTHLING PTOLEMY WAS A GENIUS IN EVERY SENSE OF THE word. He wrote grand treatises on astronomy and celestial mathematics. He plotted the movement of planets. He cataloged the stars.

But his genius isn't what he's remembered for.

He's mostly remembered for getting one thing completely and spectacularly wrong.

He believed the Earth was at the very center of the universe and that everything, including the sun and stars, revolved around it. He was wise enough to acknowledge that the Earth was indeed a sphere, but when you see the universe from a geocentric model—that is, with Earth plopped in its center like a plum in a pie—every calculation you make after that is wrong.

Never was this so well illustrated as when Quantavius Kratz and Nell Knell set forth on planet Claire. Because as soon as they left the blue house, they were winding themselves deep down Ptolemy's path—and not just because Kratz saw himself as the center of the universe, but because he and Knell had simultaneously come to the conclusion that they were still on Earth, just trapped in the distant future.

When they came across their first mound of towering garbage, it only served to reinforce their belief.

"What more proof do you need?" asked Kratz.

And with a sad shake of her head, Agent Knell had to agree. "In the end, we turned the world into more of a garbage dump than it already was. Pity."

"Do you think humans went extinct?" pondered Kratz.

"Or we were killed by robots, that were then killed by better robots," theorized Knell. "Either way we're done for. Sad but not surprising."

After that, everything they saw and experienced just fed their incorrect assumption. If they had come across the town of B'light, they might have been set straight, but they bypassed it completely and were now heading toward a tall structure on the distant horizon.

"That may be some sort of monument to the fall of humanity," concluded Kratz. "Maybe we can find out what happened there."

"I thought we were here to capture Noah Prime," Knell reminded him.

Kratz waved a dismissive hand. "That miscreant seems like a small consideration when faced with the end of the world," he said. "And besides, if we find out how the world ended, perhaps we can figure out how to prevent it."

"And get rich in the process," added Knell.

Kratz smiled. "My thoughts exactly!"

He had to admit that his admiration for his highly intelligent and like-minded travel companion just kept growing. Clearly, the feeling was mutual because she took Kratz's hand, and together they made their way toward the monument to the fall of humanity, which was, in fact, the planetary palace.

• ● •

Sahara, after getting over the initial shock of the sad, sorry planet, began to find herself angrier and angrier. To see these poor people going about their business as if they were not relegated to the trash heap of the galaxy was infuriating. Being angry at them would be displaced anger, she knew—but she didn't know who to be mad at.

"We get by," Forlo told her, as they rode in his private hovercar toward the palace, which loomed on the distant horizon. "And sometimes we even forget."

"And it's better than our sister city, P'Light," chimed in their driver. "Our goggles are much better than theirs."

When they left the city limits, Forlo and the driver didn't take off their goggles, even though the law only bound them to wear them in the city. Perhaps to avoid having to acknowledge the state of the First Citizen's car.

"When you speak to your friend Claire, I'm sure you can convince her to help our situation," Forlo said. "Jobs, infrastructure. With a little help, our dignity can be real instead of virtual."

Ogden chose to stay out of the conversation. This was not his world, not his problems. He was here to undo his life's most massive screw-up and get Claire back to Earth. Of course, once he did, they'd have to deal with the fact that her parents were now in diapers, but that was a problem for another day. Right now, it was all about Claire.

He couldn't help but be distracted by the augmented-reality goggles, though, which he kept slipping on and off, comparing their projected visions to the stark reality of this world.

"If I had these goggles at home," Ogden said, "oh, the things I could pretend to do!"

"Life is more than pretending," Sahara reminded him.

"It doesn't have to be, if you pretend well enough," Ogden replied.

And to that, Sahara heaved a heavy sigh. "Ogden, you and I were on different planets long before we left Earth."

No argument from Ogden.

The going was slow. The farther they got from B'light, the less the pothole-ridden road seemed to make sense. It was as if the planners had rolled dice every few hundred yards to decide what direction the road would take.

In reality the road, which was centuries old, had not been designed for travel, but to spell out, in First Spiralese, and large enough to be viewed from space, the phrase: **"If you have any goodness in your heart, save us from this miserable place."** Unfortunately, money ran out early in the project, so they only got as far as **"If you have any goo."** And since goo was plentiful—especially in the trash industry—captains of garbage scows made sure to bring extra whenever they came to dump.

Their limo had trouble handling the hairpin turns, loop-the-loops, and occasional full stops and reverses of First Spiralese cursive—and while the hovercar looked fine with the goggles on, in reality, it was a rust heap with a faulty rear repulsor that left its back end dragging on the ground, shooting out sparks.

It should have been no surprise, then, that the limo completely broke down before it completed the first half of the already incomplete message, leaving them only halfway to the palace.

"I've called for a tow," the driver said cheerfully, never removing his goggles to assess the truth of the situation. "It should be here shortly."

"On this planet, shortly could be a week," the First Citizen told them. "Our best option is to walk the rest of the way. And, truth be told, if we approach in a vehicle, we'll be a target."

"A target for what?" asked Sahara.

"Let's just say, arriving at the palace is best done unseen."

Giving up on the cursed cursive road, they tried to make a beeline to the palace, which was easier now that they were within the no-dump zone that surrounded it. They were grateful for the relative lack of rubbish, but Ogden was still troubled.

"What if there are wild animals? Do we have anything to defend ourselves?"

"Oh, don't worry," Forlo told him. "There's no indigenous life left on this planet. Just what people brought with them. And no one brought anything too dangerous. Or at least nothing that's escaped."

Somehow neither Ogden nor Sahara was relieved.

• ● •

Meanwhile, the universe ejected the Fractillian ship back into normal space, and Planet Claire loomed large and ugly before it.

"That's where we're going?" Jad said. "Looks kind of bleak."

"Funny," said Murdrum. "That's the name of one of its cities. B'Leak."

Noah had to admit Jad was right. The planet looked like the result of a little kid mixing all their paints together. Just a brownish globe of celestial yuck. "Well, you get

292

what you pay for, I guess," Noah said. Fifty bucks for this planet? Made sense now.

"The palace is in the southern hemisphere," Murdrum told them. "We'll do a waste-dump and leave you with the trash, so hopefully you won't be detected."

Andi sighed. "It won't be the first time I was abandoned as trash."

"No one's abandoning you," Noah assured her. "We're right there in the trash with you—and as soon as we can, we'll get all your melted parts repaired."

Although Andi didn't actually thank him, he could see the gratitude in her eyes. Murdrum commanded his crew as they operated the controls with a slippery fluidity that matched their surroundings. The air hung heavy with a viscous mist, and the gurgling sounds of the ship's engine filled the eerie silence as they adjusted their approach for the steepest possible angle, hoping to get in and out quickly.

"Reports have been coming in that there's about to be an official transfer of power to the new planetary owner," Murdrum said.

"That would be Claire," Noah told him.

Murdrum nodded. "We'll get you as close to the palace as we can, but there's a no-dump zone around it. You'll have to get the rest of the way there on your own."

"We can handle that, right, Jad?" said Noah.

"Yeah, sure," replied Jad, but didn't seem too confident.

Noah put a friendly hand on Jad's head, as was the Tri-astral way. "After what we've already been through, this'll be a piece of cake."

"Right," said Jad. "What's cake?"

• ● •

Navigating between tottering piles of junk and twisted metal, the Fractillian ship came in for a landing, touching down with a wheezing groan. With a complete disregard for waste inspection protocols, the ship promptly opened its rear refuse aperture, disgorging slime-covered rubbish without waiting for approval from any inspector.

"You took too long," Murdrum scolded when the inspector arrived. "Our ship is a biological/titanium hybrid, and as such, it can only hold in its waste for so long!"

"I have half a mind to write you up!" shouted the inspector (which was both figuratively and literally true, since the inspector was of the same split-brained species as the two guards whom Ogden and Sahara had encountered).

The unapproved dump, however, was just a ploy to create chaos enough for Noah, Jad, and Andi to climb out from the slime-covered trash without being seen.

Noah and Jad emerged, coughing and spluttering among the miserable miasma—because while both had the ability to breathe underwater, neither could breathe in Frac-tillian slime. Andi—who only simulated breathing—had no such issues. But her disgust was real.

Jad, having three arms to work with, was free from the muck first and helped the others. Murdrum's argument with the trash inspector, accompanied by the clamor of other Fractillians chiming in, provided ample cover for the trio to discreetly vanish behind the towering mounds of garbage.

Noah noticed that no two piles looked alike, because every mound was from a different planet. One was full of broken, moaning robots—which made Andi shiver. Another looked like a mountain of half-digested jelly beans, and another seemed to be made entirely of green bones.

"I don't even want to know," said Noah.

"Andi, which way to the palace?" Jad asked.

"The palace is due north," said Andi. "Or due south, depending on the planet's preferred global orientation. But, regardless, it's that way," she said, pointing. "It's a day's walk from here by human standards—so I suggest you both engage a fast animal from your respective genetic soups."

Noah tapped into his inner cheetah, combining it with springbok; predator and prey merged into a single speedy skillset. Jad, although unsure at first, managed to pull up something called a NoseJoy Quickdart—which, in addition to speed, had the added benefit of making Jad smell like freshly baked cookies, a welcome shield against the stench of garbage.

"Everyone smells something different," Jad explained

with a grin. "Whatever your favorite smell is, that's what you get, times ten!" Which, Noah realized, was a great natural defense mechanism—because the aroma was so delicious and overpowering, it made him forget what he was doing.

"You biologics are so easily distracted," said Andi, clinging to Noah's back and steering him like a jockey on a racehorse. "Let's just stay on task!"

"So . . . what's our plan when we reach the palace?" Jad asked.

"First we find my friends, Sahara and Ogden," said Noah.

"And let's hope," said Andi, "that they haven't made an even bigger mess of things."

• ● •

Meanwhile, as Ogden, Sahara, and Forlo neared the palace, the challenge of entry became clear. The entire structure was surrounded by a high wall and a slimy moat. Since most arrivals and departures came by way of spacecraft, there was only one narrow bridge over the moat, which was patrolled by armed guards—because anyone who needed to enter the palace by way of the bridge didn't have any business being there.

"Don't bother," said Forlo, before they got close enough to be seen. "The guards are trained to vaporize first and ask questions later. Even if our hoverlimo hadn't broken down, we'd have to leave it and approach with greater stealth."

"But we're friends with the landlord," Ogden pointed out.

"True, but I doubt that your vaporized subatomic particles will be able to explain that. There's a tunnel system beneath the palace. We can get in that way."

Forlo led them through a tight gap in two rocks, which opened into a much larger, cavernous series of natural tunnels. The smell of garbage was replaced by the smell of mildew, which was an improvement.

Forlo took a double-ended flashlight from its stanchion on the rock wall and turned it on. Apparently, it was designed to show them not just where they were going, but where they had been, for beings that also had eyes in the back of their heads.

"This way," said Forlo. "Watch your step!" Which was hard with the rear beam of the flashlight shining in their faces. Sahara and Ogden followed Forlo cautiously. The flashlight illuminated jagged formations of stalagmites and stalactites, casting long, distorted shadows all around them. As they maneuvered through the intricate web of stone spikes, they couldn't help but feel they were traversing an otherworldly obstacle course. Every now and then, Ogden and Sahara stumbled over an uneven rock or narrowly avoided a low-hanging stalactite.

"They almost seem to be reaching for us," Ogden said, after sharply bumping his head on one.

"It's your imagination," said Forlo, curtly. "It's best if you believe that."

While the going was tough for the humans, Forlo seemed unfazed by the treacherous terrain, effortlessly navigating the narrow passages. His fluff-ended tail swished gracefully behind him, serving as a counterbalance to maintain his equilibrium. Ogden had to keep himself from grabbing onto it each time he stumbled. He assumed that would be a major social no-no.

The deeper they got, the moister the air became, and the cavern walls around them began to come alive with phosphorescent moss, casting a soft glow. The troublesome flashlight now redundant, Forlo turned it off in favor of the mosslight.

But just as they were beginning to find their rhythm and navigate the treacherous terrain with a bit more confidence, Forlo suddenly halted, causing Ogden and Sahara to abruptly stop in their tracks.

"Something's found us," he whispered.

"Is it an oh-how-cute-can-we-keep-it kind of thing?" asked Sahara. "Or an eat-your-face-off kind of thing?"

"We'll know soon enough," said Forlo.

And then it skulked out from the shadows.

A huge, shapeless, gelatinous creature.

"Stay back," said Forlo, although neither Sahara nor

Ogden were sure whether he was talking to the creature or them.

"What is it?" asked Ogden, taking a curious step closer. He slipped on the goggles, but the creature looked the same through them as it did in real life—as if the goggles had no algorithm for disguising it. It was decidedly blobby, however it did have internal organs of some kind that seemed to float randomly within its goo like bits of fruit in a holiday Jell-O mold.

"That . . . that can't be what I think it is!" said Forlo.

Then suddenly the thing lurched toward Ogden, who was closest, and engulfed him up to his neck in its blob-ness.

• ● •

Being devoured by a hungry blob was not on the agenda for Ogden's day.

"Get it off!" Ogden shouted. "Get it off!"

"This is amazing!" said Forlo, overjoyed and not helping Ogden at all. "No one's seen a Splunge for at least twenty years! They're supposed to be extinct! This could be the last one in existence!"

"Get if off me!" Ogden cried again. "It's eating me!"

"Don't worry—they're *detritivorous*. That is, they only eat dead layers of flesh."

"Oh!" said Sahara. "You mean like maggots?"

"That's not helping!" Ogden yelped, still convinced the

blob would dissolve him, just like the Blob did in the old movie and all its awful sequels and remakes.

For Sahara, though, watching the expression of horror and despair on Ogden's face was a source of unexpected joy. Of course, if he were actually in danger of being digested alive, she wouldn't feel that way, but seeing him in misery without him actually *being* in misery? Well, that was priceless.

It took a minute, but Ogden finally calmed down, took a breath, and went, "Ooh."

"Ooh what?" Sahara asked.

"Ooh, it doesn't feel terrible."

"It's taking off his dead skin," said Forlo. "He'll come out smooth as a baby!"

It made Sahara remember her mom taking her to a weird spa where tiny little fish nibbled off the dead skin and calluses from your feet. While Sahara had flatly refused to be living fish food, her mother had done a full hour of the treatment and loved the result. But dipping your feet in water was not the same as being enveloped by a hungry glob of gunk—even if it wasn't hungry for your living parts. Still, she stepped forward and shoved her hand into it because she couldn't deny her curiosity. And, yes, it actually did feel good.

The globulous creature purred like a cat, which was odd, because it had no mouth. It was little more than a giant amoeba.

"On Earth we have brain-eating amoebas," Sahara said thoughtfully.

"Why would anyone want brain-eating amoebas?" asked Forlo.

"Nobody *wants* them, but we're stuck with them." She pulled out her hand and looked at it. Soft and silky, smooth as a baby, as Forlo had said.

"I'd much rather have giant dead-skin-eating amoebas," said Ogden, relaxing into the gelatinous creature's embrace.

"I'm afraid that won't be possible," said Forlo. "Splunges can't exist off this world. The second a splunge is taken off-planet, it dies. It's one of the reasons they became extinct. Or nearly extinct, since there's this one left."

"If this is the last one, then it's doomed," said Sahara.

Forlo nodded sadly. "Probably so."

"So feeding it is the least we could do," said Sahara, kicking off her shoes and plunging her feet in.

As she did, Ogden held his nose and leaned back, submerging his entire head within the creature. And the creature began undulating in excitement. Ogden held his breath for as long as he could, and when he emerged . . . Sahara was looking at him funny.

"What?" he asked. "Is there some goo on my face?"

"Ogden . . . ," she began. "Your hair . . ."

"What about my hair?"

Ogden reached up to his scalp and felt skin instead

of hair. And then he remembered: Hair is just dead skin cells. And it wasn't just the hair on the top of his head— his eyebrows were gone as well. He had gone full bowling ball.

"Auughhh!" groaned Ogden. "This isn't what I signed up for!"

Sahara pulled her feet out of the creature, remembering that fingernails and toenails were just dead cells, too. But since they were thicker than hair, they hadn't been entirely digested. She took a close look at her fingers. Her nails were thinner but not entirely gone. Neither were Ogden's. A small consolation, now that he was a hairless wonder.

Ogden squirmed and pushed, and the creature, having had a full meal, got the hint and released him, leaving not even the slightest bit of slime on him.

"If you ask me," said Forlo, "I think you look much better without all that cranial fur."

"I liked my cranial fur!"

"Oh, don't be such a wuss," said Sahara. "It'll grow back. And look at it this way—you fed a starving creature." And, indeed, the creature was extremely appreciative, rippling and cooing and expressing amorphous, burbling affection toward Ogden.

"Who would have guessed that you had such a well-shaped skull?" Forlo said.

302

"I do?"

"Oh, very much so!"

"Do you think Claire will appreciate my well-shaped skull?" Ogden asked.

"I think she'll appreciate the fact that you're here at all. That you came to rescue her."

Ogden furrowed his ghost of a brow. "I don't know about that. I don't think she'd appreciate such a blatantly patriarchal idea as 'rescue.'"

"True," agreed Sahara, "but it's the thought that counts."

The Splunge, having been fed, and realizing Ogden had little left to offer, retreated happily into the shadows, and Forlo led the way through the cavern, which gradually led to a more engineered system of tunnels. Finally they stopped beneath a shaft, with a ladder leading upward to the palace grounds, and whatever they would find there.

• ● •

Manhole covers were much the same on Planet Claire as they were on Earth. Round, heavy, and awkward to open. One could not crawl out from under a manhole cover gracefully.

Luckily, this one was in a deserted side-niche off the palace's market square. But the square itself was bustling with activity. All sorts of species went about their business, and none of them looked at all well. In fact, it looked like Zombie Central.

"Usurpers," said Forlo, with undeniable revulsion.

"Like the ones who abducted Claire!" said Ogden.

Forlo shivered. "Nasty creatures. They burrow into the brain stems of other species—usually dead ones. They've been running this planet for some time now. It will be nice to have new management."

"What if they try to burrow into our brain stems?" asked Sahara.

"A risk we'll have to take," Forlo said. "But if they think we're just bodies already being worn, they won't bother us."

"So in other words, try to look zombie-like."

"I can do that," said Ogden, raising his hands and wriggling his fingers.

Sahara couldn't help rolling her eyes. "That's not zombie-like, Ogden. That's totally a 'Thriller' pose."

"Choreographed zombies are still zombies!"

"Just do what the other ones are doing!" Sahara said—which mostly consisted of heads lolling on necks, and appendages being loosely dragged.

The three of them zombied their way across the square toward the steps of the palace. And it would have been fine if Ogden's dragging foot hadn't tripped Sahara, sending her sprawling. Immediately, every Usurper in the square turned to them and began to close in around them, blocking off any hope of escape.

Because although the bodies Usurpers used were often dead, they never, ever tripped.

22

The Mobius Suite

AT THE SAME MOMENT OGDEN, SAHARA, AND FORLO WERE facing a zombie horde of Usurpers, Claire was being fitted for her coronation gown.

"The gown is going to be spectacular," the dressmaker exclaimed. "It's made of a gravity-resistant fabric that renders the wearer practically weightless. And if that isn't delightful enough, it will then be covered with one hundred fifty Rigelian ultra-doves that will cling to the fabric, and then be released to the skies the moment the crown is placed on your head! The effect of all those purple birds taking to the air will be breathtaking!"

Claire, enthralled by the description, replied, "I love the feel of the antigravity fabric on my skin. It's like I'm wearing a cloud. Once I'm crowned, will you make me an entire royal wardrobe?"

The dressmaker cleared her throat—or, more accurately,

cleared the dry, parchment-like throat of her host-body. "Yes, yes, of course," she said, "but let's cross that bridge when we come to it."

Suddenly, a commotion erupted in the courtyard, drawing Claire's attention. She glided to the window, her toes barely touching the floor, and gasped at the scene below. There were two humans and a long-necked alien who were being attacked by what could only be described as a horde of zombies.

"Get your claws off me!" shouted the girl.

"Help!" screamed the boy. "I have a very particular allergy to the undead!"

Claire recognized those voices. It was Sahara and Ogden. Once again, they had shown up uninvited to her party!

Leaving the unfinished dress with the dressmaker, she swiftly donned her regular Earth clothes and stormed down to the courtyard.

As she approached, she could see dozens of Usurpers in various states of rot pawing and grabbing at the three intruders, ready to tear them apart, or eat their brains, or do whatever it was that Usurpers did.

"Back off!" she yelled. "I command you!"

Reluctantly, the mob let go and cleared a path for her.

The third uninvited guest—a decidedly giraffish creature—smoothed its frayed lapel and spoke.

"You must be our new landlord! I am Forlo, the First Citizen of the city of B'light—"

Claire silenced him with a flick of her wrist. She had neither time nor patience for alien introductions. Instead, she turned her gaze to Ogden. "Why are you here? And what happened to your hair?"

Sahara stepped forward. "We're here to take you back home, Claire," she said, then glanced at Ogden's hairless self. "Before things get any worse than they already are."

Claire regarded Sahara with disbelief. "Home? Why on earth would I want to go home?"

"Uh, I think you mean, 'Why *off* earth would you want to go home?'" Ogden corrected.

"How did you even get here?" Claire asked.

"We came in a house that flew through space," Sahara told her.

"Was there a tornado involved?"

"Absolutely not!" snapped Sahara. "And don't go there again!"

Claire released a heavy, regal sigh. "Well, as long as you're here," she said, "you may all attend my coronation. But then you'll have to be on your way."

Then one more Usurper arrived, a smug grin on his face.

"Well, what do we have here?" Slash said.

And if anger could be transformed into heat, one hundred fifty Rigelian ultra-dove eggs could be fried on Ogden's head.

After all that Ogden had been through, he thought he'd be prepared for anything. But the sight of his archnemesis standing jauntily beside Claire Jenson, as if he had no better place to be, sent Ogden into a silent rage. He knew, of course, that Raymond had been usurped and sucked up into the alien ship that day, but he'd assumed that the aliens would quickly realize what a waste of life Raymond was and eject him into space. Or, even better, send him off to work in some remote mining colony, where he would spend the rest of his miserable existence enduring hell on earth. Or *off* earth, as Ogden had already pointed out. But no, because here Raymond was to ruin Ogden's otherwise highly interesting day.

Ogden narrowed his eyes to a burning glare. "Raymond Balding-Stalker. We meet again."

"No," said Claire. "This is Slash; he's just using Raymond's body."

"Living body or dead body?" Ogden asked.

"Living," Slash told him.

Ogden grunted. Not the answer he wanted to hear.

Then Sahara gasped, realizing . . . "You're the old man!"

Slash chuckled. "This boy is a much better host than that decrepit body. And the best part is that Raymond doesn't even mind."

"Of course he doesn't mind!" said Ogden. "Because he gets to be close to Claire!"

Then Slash gently touched Claire's shoulder, making Ogden seethe.

"What should we do with them, Your Highness?" Slash asked.

Claire tapped her chin, considering the options, and then declared, "To prove I am a benevolent ruler, we shall give them a suite within the palace. And then, after the coronation, we'll send them on their way."

"Excellent," said Slash. Then he turned to his partner in crime—the woman from the observatory, whose flesh had gone even greener than before. "This is UnEqua. She will make sure you are properly taken care of."

The woman straightened her crooked neck, looking down her nose at them with a moldier-than-thou expression. "It would be my pleasure," she said. But the sadistic twist of her thin-lipped grin left her hospitality very much in doubt.

• ● •

It took Kratz and Knell far longer than they expected to reach the structure in the distance. After hiking through rough trash-strewn terrain for hours, they finally crossed to a rocky, scrub-brush expanse where the only trash seemed to have been blown there by the wind. It was, perhaps, a perimeter around the hallowed ground of the monument—for they were still convinced the stone structure ahead was some sort of memorial to fallen humanity. It wasn't just ruins, it was clearly maintained—probably by the robots that replaced the robots that replaced humans.

They had found a knitting bag in the house and had filled it with snacks and bottles of water, as well as the alien weapons they had come with—the levitator, portal gun, and memory projector. But now the food and water were gone.

"We're FOBE agents trained in survival!" said Knell. "We should have thought to bring more water!"

"Well, since you're basically me, Nell, your training is rusty at best, as we haven't been an agent for over ten years, so don't beat yourself up."

"I'm not! I'm beating you up! For being you! For being *us*!"

When they finally got close enough to see a bridge leading to the structure's entrance, they picked up the pace, hoping beyond hope that there would be something to quench their thirst.

But then a laser blast passed so close over their heads, they could feel its heat.

"We're being shot at!" shouted Kratz. "Take cover!"

The second blast was even closer—hitting a leafless tree behind where they had just been, bursting it apart on a molecular level.

"Quick! Grab the levitator!" said Knell. "Send them sky high!"

311

Kratz reached into the knitting bag, but the weapons were hopelessly tangled in balls of yarn that they had neglected to remove from the bag.

"Hurry!"

"I'm trying!"

Another blast disintegrated a boulder behind them.

"It's no use!" said Kratz. "And even if I could get it untangled, we're no match for second-generation human-replacing robots! Run!"

And so they took off down a ravine that was out of their attackers' sightlines. Apparently, out of sight was out of mind, because their attackers didn't pursue.

"Well, what do we do now?" said Nell.

"Why are you asking me?"

They could go back to the house and rethink their strategy—but without water, they'd never make it back. They'd die out there in the unforgiving waste heaps, probably like the rest of humanity had.

It was only by chance that Knell, who had better eyesight than the original Kratz, spotted the footprints. One set seemed to be made by some hooved animal, but the others were clearly sneaker prints!

"Noah and his cohorts?" theorized Kratz.

"It has to be!" Knell concurred. "But only two sets of human prints. Weren't there more of them?"

Kratz pointed at the alien prints. "Perhaps the others were riding on the hooved creature."

"Or it ate them."

Kratz considered that. "Well, if so, then it will be too full to eat us."

They followed the prints to the entrance to a cave. It seemed dark at first, but as they moved deeper into the cave, and their eyes adjusted, they could see that the walls glowed with phosphorescent moss.

"Good thing we're experts at spelunking," Kratz said. "If we weren't skilled at exploring caves, we could become irretrievably lost."

The deeper they got, the more clearly they heard a rushing hissing sound. It was the sound of flowing water!

"Nell! Do you hear that?" He took off toward it.

"Wait!" shouted Knell. "We'll lose the tracks!" But he was already gone, and she had no choice but to follow.

It was, as they had hoped, an underground waterfall, spilling into a crystal-clear pool. Both of them scooped up the ice-cold water.

"Future water is much more quenching than water in our time!" Kratz said between gulps.

"I think that's just because we're so thirsty."

Then, when they'd had enough, they looked up, and nothing looked familiar. "Do you remember which way we came?" Kratz asked.

"Haven't a clue," said Knell. "We should have unspooled the yarn, so we could find our way back." But hindsight wasn't going to help them now.

"Well, we couldn't be too far off," said Kratz. "We'll find those tracks again."

Unfortunately, neither of them had anything resembling a sense of direction. Before long they were beyond lost. And all the while, they had the uncanny sensation that they were being followed by someone—or some*thing*—skulking behind them. . . .

• ● •

Above in the palace, Sahara was on her guard. These Usurpers reeked of deceit as much as they reeked of rot. As for Ogden, his mind was elsewhere. He was still miffed that Raymond got to be close to Claire. Perhaps, thought Ogden, he could convince Slash to snatch *his* body instead. It was a much better body, after all. At least Ogden thought so.

"The Mobius Suite is the best in the palace," UnEqua said, as she led them down a long corridor. "Nothing but the best for friends of Crown Princess Claire."

Then she pulled open a heavy door to reveal a lavishly appointed suite. A gleaming marble floor, gold-framed beds, a chandelier that hung with actual diamonds sparkling so brightly they seemed to warp space around them.

Forlo couldn't contain his delight. "Imagine! A room this stunning that's not even a hologram!"

"Uh . . . I don't see a bathroom," said Ogden.

"Down the hall and to the left," UnEqua said. "Of

314

course, it's not really designed for human anatomy, but, trust me, that won't be a problem."

As Sahara looked at the beautiful room, she finally dropped her defenses a bit, taking a deep breath. So Claire Jenson was going to be an actual princess. If she wanted to stay here, then fine—Sahara wouldn't begrudge her the chance to be galactic royalty. Of course, that would mean that they had come all this way for nothing . . . but still, it was the right thing to do. And on the positive side, after the coronation, with the entire planet at their disposal, Sahara was sure they'd be able to find out what happened to Noah. They could then find a ship to take them back home, where her parents were most certainly worried out of their minds.

"Well, what are you waiting for?" asked UnEqua, with growing impatience. "Step inside! Make yourselves comfortable."

And so they did. UnEqua, however, never crossed the threshold. She just stood by the open door.

"I hope you enjoy your stay," she said with a disturbing little giggle. Then she left, closing the door with a hefty slam.

After she was gone, Forlo sat down on one of the beds. "This mattress is certainly comfortable," he said.

Sahara turned to choose one of the remaining beds but accidentally bumped into a hat rack, which had hats for heads of multiple shapes and sizes, none of them human. It tipped over and fell to the floor with a hearty *clunk*.

"Oops," she said.

"I'll be right back," said Ogden. "I gotta go pee."

He moved toward the door, but then suddenly was facing Sahara again, looking a bit bewildered.

"This mattress is certainly comfortable," said Forlo.

Sahara turned and bumped into the hat rack. It fell to the floor with a *clunk*. "Oops."

"I'll be right back," said Ogden. "I gotta go pee." He turned to head out the door.

"This mattress is certainly comfortable," said Forlo.

Sahara bumped the hat rack. *Clunk*. "Oops."

Something was very wrong here. Fighting a tremendous sense of déjà vu, Sahara forced herself to look up at the diamond chandelier. It not only glowed but radiated waves of spatial distortion. No...not *spatial* distortion... *time* distortion.

"I gotta go pee," said Ogden.

But before he could turn, Sahara fought the inertia of her repeating actions just long enough to say, "Ogden, we're caught in a time loop!"

"This mattress is certainly comfortable."

Clunk. "Oops."

"I know, but I really need to pee! Does this mean I'm going to need to pee forever?"

They turned to Forlo, whose face was contorted in agony, tears falling from his alien eyes. He looked at

316

them helplessly and said, "This mattress is certainly comfortable."

"I gotta go pee."

"Ogden, I think we're in trouble." *Clunk.* "Oops."

• ● •

There are all sorts of temporal loops in the known universe. In fact, there's a perfectly legal and well-regulated industry creating them and selling them for all price ranges. Birthday parties that people want to relive or vacations worth repeating and repeating and repeating. It's the galactic equivalent of phone videos. And like most phone videos, they do nothing but take up time and space—except, in the case of temporal loops, they don't take up any space at all. Only time.

However, the type of loops Usurpers employed were unregulated and illegal. They were prisons—but more than that, they were sadistically crafted to allow those within the loop to be continually aware they were caught in one, able to make only the slightest, most unhelpful variations to the actions they were forced to repeat over and over, until time itself came to an end. For this reason, Usurper time loops were considered to be the absolute worst form of torture.

23

A Cold Passing of Wind

OVERSEEING THE PREPARATIONS, SLASH PACED THE COURTYARD that was in the midst of being transformed into a regal space, worthy of a coronation. A sense of majesty filled the air that was as oppressive as it was grandiose. Underlings scurried about, placing exquisite floral arrangements and polishing everything to a sheen. He looked up at the sound of dragging feet. He'd know UnEqua's limp anywhere.

"Are Claire's friends out of the way?" Slash asked.

"Yes," said UnEqua. "They won't be bothering us anytime soon. Anytime soon. Anytime soon."

It made Slash grin because he knew exactly what she meant. But it was only one of many problems to solve.

"We can't waste any time," said Slash. "I've received word that our next set of unwelcome guests is already on its way." He surveyed the room, ensuring every detail was perfect for the impending coronation. "We'll have to speed up the timetable," Slash said. "The coronation will have to take place tomorrow morning."

"Is all this ceremony necessary?" asked UnEqua. "We should just clap the crown on her pretty little head and get it over with."

"No—this has to follow planetary custom," Slash responded, gesturing toward the meticulously crafted, golden-trimmed throne and altar being installed in front of the courtyard's grand fountain.

"But the paperwork is all in order—we made sure of that."

"Yes, but everything must be perfect," Slash reminded her. "Because if this transition of power doesn't go by the book, it might be voided. We can't have that." Then Slash sighed. "The poor girl still has no idea what's in store for her."

UnEqua frowned with force enough to dislodge a tooth. "You have feelings for her?"

Slash's demeanor stiffened. "Not in the slightest," he said, his words carrying a hint of bitterness. "It's just the boy trying to exert his will—but he's weak. Pathetic. Sometimes I forget he's even there."

They stepped out of the way as a long red carpet was rolled out. That wasn't planetary custom here but was on Claire's home world—and this needed to feel real to her, too, or she might become suspicious.

UnEqua looked toward the rather garish throne. Claire would certainly get her fifteen minutes of fame. That is, if the throne's current occupant actually let her have it.

"Why is there a feline sitting on the throne?" UnEqua asked.

Slash gave her a mischievous grin. "That feline just happens to be Mittens the Cat."

UnEqua gasped. "*The* Mittens?"

"None other," said Slash. "He's offered to bring us in on his latest business venture, if we'll set up a meeting between him and the Fauxlites." Then Slash leaned in and whispered, "Apparently, Mittens found a Nascent Organic Aggregate Hybrid that was believed to be dead—and sent it to the Fauxlite preserve planet! Now it's just a matter of letting the Fauxlites know and being rewarded!"

"Ha!" laughed UnEqua. "Mittens always has the best and most profitable schemes!"

"It's even better than that," said Slash. "The N.O.A.H. is from Earth. Once we make the Fauxlites aware of him, they'll terraform the entire planet—which means no one from Earth will come around looking for Claire!"

"Elegant!" said UnEqua. "Two birds with one stone, as they say on that detestable planet."

"Indeed."

A team arrived with stunning floral arrangements that looked much more alive than they did. UnEqua sighed. "It would be worth suffering through Claire's ridiculous coronation if we could stay for what comes next. I would love to have watched."

"Not me," said Slash. "I want to get as far from this rock as possible the second that crown is on her head. Because it's going to get ugly...."

• ● •

Kratz and Knell, more lost than ever, trudged deeper into the labyrinth of the cavern, their hearts hammering with a mix of fear and frustration. They were convinced that walls contorted and morphed, confounding their senses and disorienting their every step. Passages appeared and vanished unpredictably.

In truth, the walls and passages didn't move at all—but it was much easier for them to believe they did than to accept how inept they were at spelunking. They were also convinced that the stalactites intentionally stretched and dipped toward them, repeatedly striking their heads with each malicious swoop.

That was actually true. Stalactites on this planet were unusually spiteful.

"We should have left ourselves a trail," Knell lamented. Now that it had occurred to them, they unrolled the ball of yarn as they proceeded, but it was too little too late, and soon, not only was all the yarn gone, but they couldn't even find the end anymore, leaving them without a lifeline to guide their way back to the waterfall.

Their paranoia deepened as the nagging feeling of being stalked intensified. Every rustle of distant movement, every hint of something slithering, sent their imaginations reeling.

Suddenly, a sound echoed behind them—a sickening squelching noise that raised the short hairs on the backs of their necks. Kratz and Knell spun around in unison, terrified of what they might see. It was worse than they could have imagined.

Emerging from the shadows was a gelatinous, amorphous creature, oozing toward them with malevolent intent.

"What is that thing?" Kratz said, trying to decide if he was more horrified, terrified, or disgusted.

"Some toxic waste mutation, no doubt," said Knell. "Some grotesque abomination that defies nature itself."

"It certainly is ugly!" said Kratz. "Whatever it is, something so hideous shouldn't be allowed to live."

"Agreed."

Kratz swiftly retrieved the levitator from the bag, no longer hindered by tangled yarn. The creature surged closer. Time seemed to slow as Kratz activated the levitation ray, capturing the gelatinous creature within its beam. In a swift motion, he flicked his hand upward with all his might, propelling the vile entity toward the cavern ceiling.

A sickening *splat* reverberated through the cavern as the creature was impaled upon a sharp stalactite and exploded into a thousand gelatinous pieces.

"There," said Kratz, triumphantly, "problem solved."

They continued their meandering journey through the caves...failing to notice that the many splatted remnants of the splunge still wriggled and squirmed, very much alive...and very, very hungry....

• ● •

Noah, Jad, and Andi waited for the sun to set, then approached the palace bridge under the cover of darkness, each with their own form of night vision. Andi had sophisticated radar, Noah could see heat like a goldfish, and Jad could smell movement like a SniffSnipe. In this way, they were able to detect the guards before they were detected themselves.

"Bad news," said Andi. "The guards are ArmaDeltoids. Titanium exoskeletons, with solid muscle beneath. We'll never be able to fight them."

"Maybe we can sneak past them," suggested Jad.

Andi shook her head. "They have natural multidimensional proximity detectors," she said. "Get any closer, and they'll know exactly where you are—not just here, but in every parallel dimension. Then they'll kill you in all of them." Andi sighed. "Of course, ArmaDeltoids do go into hibernation at subzero temperatures, but that's not going to help us on a planet this hot."

That made Jad smile. "Maybe I can help," he said.

• ● •

The sentries on duty outside the gate hated their job. Sure, disintegrating anyone who approached was fun and all, but working for Usurpers wasn't exactly something to be proud of. On top of that, the job itself was so uneventful, the awful green worms didn't even want to inhabit them. Which was a relief but also insulting. Weren't they worthy of having their magnificent bodies snatched?

The two ArmaDeltoid sentries were brooding on such things when a creature appeared. It arrived with none of the usual warning, and although they were fully capable of eradicating its existence in several thousand dimensions, they were caught off guard and fumbled with their weapons.

It smiled and waved one of its three arms. "Hi," it said. "Hope you like surprises!" Then it turned, bent over, and released a blast of frost from its rear end that enveloped the guards, dropping the temperature around them to zero degrees in a matter of seconds.

"Surprise!"

Instantly, the two ArmaDeltoids folded down into metallic balls like pill bugs, falling asleep in a deep hibernation that would last the length of an ArmaDeltoid winter, which was very, very long.

• ● •

"Wow," said Noah as he approached the two neutralized guards, "that was amazing, Jad! You're getting better at this!"

Jad shrugged. "I just channeled a frost-farting chill-hog," he said. "I once accidentally froze my entire class that way." Then Jad saddened a bit. "That was when my parents decided to pull me out of school and take me off-world."

Noah nodded in sympathy, remembering the time he'd done that emperor penguin mating dance in front of Sahara at the school dance. Educational humiliation was clearly not confined to the schools of Earth. "I'm glad you found a way to use it for good," Noah told him.

"Are we here for a pity party, or to find the others?" said Andi.

Leave it to Andi to mercilessly get them back on task. Having dispensed with the hibernating guards, the three slipped through the gate and onto the palace grounds.

24

Time Loops Are Funny That Way

RAYMOND LISTENED. RAYMOND WATCHED. HE TOOK IN EVERY-thing the Usurpers did. All their plans for the coronation. All the glorious moments he got to spend in Claire's shining presence. It took quite a lot of skill to be so passive, so invisible that Slash could forget Raymond was there. Raymond suspected it was his own lack of personal drive that would be his most valuable asset, because if Raymond needed to assert himself, Slash would never see it coming.

Raymond had no problem being an observer in his own life, especially now that his life had become so interesting—but the more he listened to Slash and UnEqua, the more he realized they weren't just talking about a simple coronation. Raymond couldn't see directly into Slash's mind, but when he tried, he knew something dark and terrible was in the works. The question was, how could he warn Claire? It would mean getting control of at least part of his body long enough to make a difference. So Raymond did what he was best at. He listened. He watched. And eventually, he developed a plan.

He waited until Slash was alone and lost in idle thoughts of his carefree larval days. Then Raymond launched an attack with the full force of his will...and, in order to shake Slash loose, began banging his head against the wall.

• ● •

Noah, Andi, and Jad quietly worked their way through the palace in search of clues as to where Sahara, Ogden, and Claire might be. Even this late at night, there was a lot of activity. Usurpers were running and limping and dragging themselves this way and that, making preparations of some sort.

"So, what's the plan?" asked Jad.

"We find out if our friends made it here—and we find Claire," said Noah. "Then we find a ship to get us out of here."

"And then what?" Jad pressed.

Noah took a moment to look at Jad. He knew what his friend was getting at, but this was not the time or place to discuss it.

"I thought you could come with us to Earth."

"I don't want to go to Earth. I want to go to Triastra.

Now that I'm learning how to control my animal traits, I can go back to my home world."

Noah took a deep breath. "We'll talk about it later."

"Why always later?" demanded Jad. "Why not now?"

Then Andi came between them. "Because right now, if we get caught, the two of you will have little green worms shoved into your brains, and you can kiss Earth and Triastra goodbye. Let's do what we're here to do—because it just so happens that I found something."

"What?" asked Noah.

"Be quiet! There's a lot of electromagnetic interference," she said.

They held still, letting Andi turn her head left, then right, then left again. "Yes! Yes, I'm definitely getting a reading on Sahara's and Ogden's life signs!"

"So they're here? And they're alive?"

"It would seem so. . . ."

Noah's sense of relief was so strong he felt he could slough off his skin like a snake and shed all the worry and tension he'd been carrying. He didn't even realize just how worried he had been until that moment. Jad saw his reaction and gave him a grin and a sentimental pat on the head with that third arm.

"I'm happy for you, Noah. I know your friends mean a lot to you."

"They're here, but . . . something's not right . . . ," said Andi.

328

"Not right, how?" asked Noah, afraid to hear the answer. "Were they usurped? Is that what you're trying to say?"

"No, nothing like that," said Andi. "It's like . . . it's like they have the hiccups, but over their whole body."

"That doesn't make any sense."

"I know it doesn't," replied Andi, just as frustrated as Noah.

"Maybe it's your sensors," suggested Jad. "Maybe they were damaged in the crash."

Although the suggestion infuriated Andi, she had to concede that maybe Jad was right.

"I'm also hearing chatter on all frequencies," said Andi, "about some sort of big ceremony. Maybe . . . a coronation?"

And just then, they came to a grand vestibule that featured a giant portrait of Claire Jensen, who was clearly the subject of all this pomp and pageantry.

"So, she's the one who got abducted?" Jad asked, looking at the portrait. "You know, aliens who abduct people usually don't make giant portraits of them."

"And they don't put them on thrones," said Noah, shaking his head in disbelief. "Has the universe lost its mind?"

"Yes, on a regular basis," explained Andi. "How else would you explain black holes and Social Media?"

At the sound of approaching footsteps, they ducked behind a pillar. A team of Usurpers with baskets full of bright decorations passed by. It was a close call, but it got them back on task.

"We can deal with Claire later," said Andi. "Sahara's and Ogden's life signs are directly above us. We just have to find the stairs."

· ● ·

Andi wound Noah and Jad through the palace hiding in shadows to avoid detection. Finally, she brought them upstairs and to a door in a long hall, then pointed at the door hesitantly. "They're in there, but like I said, their readings are strange—and there's another unidentified life-form in there, too."

"Is it a dangerous life-form?" asked Noah.

Andi shrugged. "I have no idea."

Well, dangerous or not, whatever it was, they'd have to face it. Noah reached for the door and turned the knob, pulling it open . . .

. . . to see Ogden standing there, as if he were on his way out.

"Ogden!"

"I gotta go pee," said Ogden.

Sahara, standing a few feet over, bumped into a hat rack and knocked it over.

"Oops."

Then, suddenly, reality glitched. Ogden's back was to them; the hat rack was standing again.

Noah blinked. "What the—"

"This bed is certainly comfortable," said a long-necked

creature sitting on a golden bed—yet despite its words, its eyes bore all the pain in the world.

Ogden turned toward Noah. "Help us!" he blurted, before saying, "I gotta go pee!"

"It's awful!" said Sahara. "Oops!"

Noah's instinct was to step inside to help them, because whatever was going on, they clearly were in distress. But luckily, every other animal instinct in him told him to stay back—and that made him hesitate long enough for Andi to grab him, keeping him from moving into the room.

"Noah, don't!" she said. "This is a Mobius room—they're trapped in a time loop. And if we step over that threshold, we'll be trapped in it, too."

"I hate this hat rack! Oops."

"This bed is certainly comfortable. Kill me now."

"I gotta go pee! For six weeks!"

That practically blew up Noah's brain. "Wait, six weeks?" said Noah. "But they only just got here."

"Time loops are funny that way," Andi explained.

Reality glitched. The loop repeated. Seven seconds start to end.

Noah turned to Andi. "Well, you seem to know about these things. What do we do?"

Andi pursed her lips. "Once a time loop is closed, it can't be undone. It would take more than all the energy in the universe to break it."

"So how do we get them out?"

331

Andi shook her head sadly. "That's beyond my programming," she said. "I'm sorry, Noah."

But then Jad stepped forward and tapped Noah on the shoulder. "Hey, I've got an idea. . . ."

• ● •

In the Mobius Suite, Sahara, Ogden, and Forlo could do nothing but suffer and suffer again the same bland seven seconds—and the greatest horror of it was that they remembered every single time.

When they saw Noah at the door, they managed to squeak out pleas for help in the midst of the repeating loop, only to be hurled back to the beginning. They saw Noah again, and he couldn't save them. Again.

But then something new was thrust into their repeating reality. Someone was now in the room with them: a creature with silver fur. They never saw it come over the threshold; it was just there.

"This bed is certainly comfortable," said Forlo.

"Yes, I know," said the creature.

"I gotta go pee," said Ogden.

The creature smiled with empathy. "So you said." Then the creature's third arm grabbed the hat rack before Sahara could knock it over, and to Sahara's amazement, the hat rack didn't fall!

"Hi, I'm Jadoon, but my friends call me Jad," the

creature said. "May I?" Then it wrapped all three of its arms around her.

Under normal circumstances Sahara would have said, *No, you may not!* and would have pushed the creature away. But these were not normal circumstances. Instead Sahara gripped onto its fur almost as firmly as its three arms gripped her. There was a sudden flash of light and darkness, a surge of extreme heat and extreme cold—

And suddenly, Sahara and Jad weren't in the room anymore. They were in the hallway, with Noah and Andi.

"It worked!" shouted Noah.

Jad let go of Sahara, and she practically collapsed to the floor. Noah caught her, holding her as tight as he dared without it seeming too awkward—but a little bit jealous that Jad had held her tighter. Still, he was holding her, which brought forth that darned blue-red mandrill blush in his cheeks—and, in true mandrill fashion, his butt cheeks, too. But he wasn't about to share that tidbit of information.

"Clever!" said Andi with an approving nod. "By teleporting, Jad never actually crossed the threshold, technically never entering the time loop. And by teleporting out before the loop repeated, there was no possibility of being trapped!"

"What about Ogden and Forlo?" Sahara asked.

"Coming right up," said Jad brightly.

Seven seconds later, Ogden was there beside them, and

seven seconds after that Forlo was with them as well, and the Mobius room was empty, save for a very unlucky fly that had been there for eons.

Forlo pulled out a handkerchief, blotted his brow, and heaved a massive sigh of relief. "Never have I so completely despised so comfortable a bed."

"Wait," said Noah. "Where's Ogden?"

But Ogden was gone, disappearing almost as quickly as he had appeared, into a bathroom down the hall that clearly was not designed for human anatomy. But any port in a storm.

25

A Very Dirty Iceberg

FROM THE THIN WINDOWS IN THE STONE PALACE, NOAH AND THE others could see Usurpers gathering for the coronation, wearing hosts of all shapes and sizes. Noah and Sahara tried to tell each other what had happened to them, but there was just too much to tell.

"I thought I'd never see you again!"

"I was afraid you were gone forever."

"I found the Fauxlites' zoo planet!"

"A blob ate Ogden's hair!"

And when words began to fail them, they just grinned stupidly at each other. Which was just fine.

In a moment, Ogden returned from the bathroom and raised a nonexistent eyebrow at their goofy grinning gazes. He tossed a glance at Jad, who just gave a three-shouldered shrug, as if to say, *Who can understand strange human behavior?*

"So, what do we do now?" Ogden asked. "Claire says

she wants to stay, so do we just leave her, or abduct her from her abduction?"

"There's something off about this whole coronation thing," Noah said.

"Ya think?" said Sahara, throwing him a half-hearted glare.

"Well, whatever we decide, we're going to have to find a way off this stinking planet," Ogden pointed out. "And I mean 'stinking' literally." Then he turned to Forlo. "No offense."

"None taken," said Forlo. "Believe me, those of us stuck here are the first to admit the planet stinks. That's one of many things your friend can help us with once she's in charge—and if it's your plan to prevent that from happening, I'm afraid I must object! Without her, who will take charge of the planet? Who will help us fix the mess the Usurpers made of it?"

Noah stepped forward, remembering what Sahara had called the creature. "Your name's Forlo, right?"

"First Citizen of B'light," he said, holding his head even higher than usual. "And I know I speak for my entire city when I say that Claire must stay!"

"Well, Forlo, First Citizen of B'Light, I suspect that this coronation is just the tip of a very dirty iceberg," said Noah.

"He's right," said Andi. "In my experience, Usurpers leave behind a trail of misery—so whatever they're planning for Claire won't be good for Claire, or for the planet."

But Forlo put his hoof down. "I remain unconvinced!"

Noah took a deep breath. If their little group couldn't agree on what to do, how were they going to get anything done at all?

• ● •

Raymond Balding-Stalker fought for his life—or at least his right to exist within his own body. But he knew that Slash was stronger. This was a battle he was going to lose. But if he could just manage to warn Claire, then that would be enough. He kept having to hurl himself against walls to keep Slash stunned and startled. It hurt, but that would be nothing compared to the pain he would feel if Slash did anything to hurt Claire.

All the slamming and banging against stone had left Raymond disoriented, not sure where he was headed, or where he even was. But then he saw figures ahead of him—and most of them were human. This, he knew, could be his only chance....

• ● •

Noah was the first to identify the figure barreling toward them down the hallway. His bloodhound sense of smell knew who it was long before they could see a face in the shadows.

"Is that ... Raymond?"

Raymond careened off the walls toward them like a pinball, moaning, groaning, hissing.

"Run!" yelled Ogden. "It's not Raymond, it's the Usurper in charge! He's taken control of Raymond's body!"

But Noah hesitated. "It doesn't seem to be in control of anything at all."

Raymond actually had a hand around his own throat, trying to choke himself. His other hand kept punching himself in the face.

"As much fun as this is to watch," said Ogden, "I still think we should run."

"No!" said Andi. "He's fighting the Usurper! I think he's trying to tell us something."

But clearly Raymond had no control over his vocal cords, because all that came out was gibberish that not even a brain tick could translate. He threw himself against the wall again, and that seemed to give him control over one of his wildly flailing arms. He raised his index finger, and it started twitching with clear intention.

"Look at his hand!" said Sahara. "I think he's trying to write something. Noah, can you figure out what he's writing?"

"Sorry, but I can't read invisible writing in the air."

"But I can!" said Andi, and zeroed in on Raymond's fingertip. "He's saying, 'Save her, save her, save her.' 'Stop them, stop them, stop them . . . before . . .'"

"Before what?" said Noah.

Then Raymond's fingers stopped moving, and his head turned in their direction. Noah could see the moment the

Usurper took over—he could see it in Raymond's eyes—all anger and ambition. But Raymond wasn't done fighting. He still had control of his legs, and in a bold move, propelled himself toward the grand palace staircase, then let his legs go limp, making him lose his balance, and sending him in a tumble all the way down.

Sahara gaped, and Ogden sighed.

"There are many times I've fantasized about seeing Raymond plunge down a staircase," said Ogden. "And yet that wasn't very satisfying at all."

· ● ·

At the bottom of the stairs, bruised but not broken, Raymond picked himself up and tottered off. He tried to resume his battle with Slash, but he had no strength left.

You fool! Slash bellowed. *Do you realize what you almost did! You could have ruined everything! I will make sure that you are pushed so far down, you'll never surface again!*

Then Raymond felt Slash's consciousness surround him and press harder and harder, until Raymond felt himself plunging into the very deepest part of his mind, where he couldn't see, couldn't hear, couldn't feel. Which meant that it would now be Slash instead of Raymond suffering from all the bruises he had just inflicted on himself. At least that was something.

· ● ·

Forlo, as obstinate as he had been, now held his extremely long tongue and put his tail between his legs. "Fine," he said. "Clearly the Usurpers are not to be trusted. I will assist you in any way that I can."

"Even if we can stop the Usurpers, we still need to find a way off this planet," Noah pointed out. "Can Miss Luella's house still fly?"

Sahara shook her head. "Maybe if Miss Luella repaired it."

Noah sighed. "She stayed behind on the World of Last Life. We'll need another way."

And so Ogden stepped forward. "I'll find a ship and save us all," said Ogden. "It's what I do."

Sahara threw a glance at Noah and said, resigned, "I'll go with him."

"I can find a ship by myself," Ogden protested.

"Yes, but you'll probably blow it up."

"Well, not on purpose!"

"You should both go," said Noah. "Two heads are better than one."

"Yeah," said Jad, "just ask our flight attendant."

• ● •

Slash was furious! To think that such a weak, insignificant individual as Raymond Balding-Stalker could dislodge him, even momentarily, from control of this body . . . how could he have let his guard down? And now those other

340

pesky humans and that long-necked local were loose in the palace.

They were running out of time; things had to proceed without any distractions.

"What happened to you?" UnEqua asked when she saw him so disheveled. "Did you decide to kill that body after all?"

"I've not killed him," Slash said, "but he did need to be subdued."

"And did I just see you dispatching a team of guards?" she asked.

"The prisoners have escaped," he told her. "Because *you* didn't secure them well enough."

"But no one can escape the Mobius Suite. . . ."

"They had help," Slash informed her. "There are three more of them. A human boy, a three-armed being, and an android. But they are pitiful, powerless creatures—even their android is damaged. They will pose no threat to the coronation."

"Are you sure of that?" she asked.

"Don't question me, UnEqua," he warned. "Now, let's get this coronation started."

• ● •

Although UnEqua didn't say it, she knew that if Slash had lost control of that human body, even for a moment, he had gotten weak, which meant he was compromised. He was always so full of himself, thinking himself the superior Usurper. But no more! It was time she took charge and, as humans say, kick him to the curb!

Of course, she couldn't do that in this decrepit body; she would need a more limber, more agile host. A dead one, though—she did not care to have internal battles with the living, such as the one Slash had just endured. But whom to usurp?

Ah, yes, of course! There was that girl from Earth, the one named after a desert. Yes, she would make an excellent host once she was recaptured. Then UnEqua would have the singular honor of ending the girl's life *and* taking over her dead body. Oh, what fun that would be!

• ● •

Andi just wasn't the same; the crash had fried much more of her circuitry than she was willing to admit. But her programming hadn't changed; her job, first and foremost, was to protect her brother from harm. Even when he did something so wildly irresponsible as chase an abducted classmate through the cosmos. She was supposed to be objective. She was supposed to see Noah as nothing more than a thing. A Nascent Organic Aggregate Hybrid, just a specimen in a test tube that just happened to be shaped like a human. But she had long ago come to feel he truly was her brother.

The Fauxlites who built her would laugh if they knew she believed she *felt* anything, but Andi knew her feelings were more than just simulations. And their parents knew, too—or at least they knew before they were turned into pearl earrings. There would come a time to find them and free them, but that day wasn't today. Today, she had to deal with Usurpers, which were even worse than Fauxlites.

"If we're going to find out what they're up to, we're going to have to access their computer," Andi told Noah, Jad, and Forlo after Sahara and Ogden had left in search of a ship. "And to access it, I'll need to find a quantum data node."

"Couldn't you just tap into their Wi-Fi?" Noah suggested.

Andi glared at him. "As if."

The ancient, musty palace breathed an eerie sense of lost history as they forged on. The walls whispered of long-forgotten secrets. Music now echoed from somewhere in the distance, filling the air with an ethereal melody that made the place seem haunted.

"That's coming from the courtyard," said Forlo. "I do believe the coronation has begun."

Finally, Andi found a data node in a dimly lit chamber. And in true Usurper form, it wasn't even one of theirs— it was a piece of stolen Fauxlite technology—which meant interfacing with it would be easy!

Andi placed her palm on the console and began to

extract data. But in an instant, she almost wished she hadn't.

"No, no, no, no, no!" she said, her voice trembling with fear. "No! It can't be!"

"What?" demanded Noah. "What is it?"

"Claire's in deep trouble. I know what the Usurpers are up to, and it's bad."

"How bad?"

"Imagine the worst-case scenario," said Andi. "Then double it. No—*triple* it!"

"Oh dear," said Forlo, with a hard swallow that sent his huge Adam's apple on a long ride. "I'm not sure I want to hear this."

"Andi, tell us!" insisted Noah.

Andi withdrew her hand from the data node. Then her eyes met Noah's, and she whispered words that were rarely, if ever, uttered aloud.

"The Tribunal of Ancients is coming."

• ● •

In the tapestry of existence, there were rules, sacred and absolute, that should never be violated.

Parallel universes should never be turned perpendicular.

Nuclear power should never fall into the claws of crustaceans.

And gravity should never be allowed to develop addictive habits.

These laws, and countless others inscribed in the annals of cosmic governance, were upheld and enforced by the stoic, stone-faced Tribunal of Ancients: three timeless entities who traveled the known universe, passing judgment on those who dared to trample upon sacred principles of existence.

Cloaked in righteousness and wielding the wisdom of epochs, they voyaged through the astral expanse, tracking down the worst violators, rendering verdicts, and making all things right. Or at least punishing those who made things wrong.

For quite some time the planet now known as Claire had been under the Tribunal's scrutinizing gaze. It had been in violation of too many laws for too long and had been slapped with citations enough to fill the libraries of eternity. Running a planetary dump without a license. Hunting indigenous life-forms to extinction. Horrendous nonhuman rights violations and enough parking tickets to put a boot on the entire planet.

Yet, to the astonishment of the Tribunal, every citation, complaint, and fine went unheeded and unpaid, as if the planet itself dared to challenge the very essence of universal law. Such brazen defiance ignited the fury of the Ancients, and so the three judges of the Tribunal set out to bring the responsible parties to justice.

The transgressors, once convicted, faced a fate more dreadful than the darkest of voids: execution by micro-singularity.

Within the depths of a personal black hole, the condemned were compressed into a point so impossibly small that they vanished from existence.

Until recently the rulers of the rogue planet had been a pair of Usurpers who sought to defy the cosmic order for their own selfish gain. Rumor had it that there was new ownership: a human girl. But that mattered little to the Tribunal. The universe demanded reparation from whoever was now in charge. In other words, the Tribunal didn't care who suffered, just as long as someone did.

And they were on their way.

PART 5

• • •

MOUNTAINS COME OUT OF THE SKY AND THEY STAND THERE

26

Coronation Crashers

Opulence! Spectacle! Magnificence! The palace court-yard was bedecked with flowers—shipped in from planets that had such things. Ropes of jewels lined the aisles and a sheer golden canopy had been unfurled to shield the glorious Throne of Tears from the harsh sun. It was all by the book—or at least as best as the Usurpers could interpret from the planet's historical records, made back in the days before the Usurpers took ownership and turned the place into a profitable garbage dump. A return to tradition! That's what was needed here, to make absolutely sure of Claire's installation as official ruler and sole responsible party for the planet's sorry state.

But within the courtyard, one would think all was well with the world. Or at least Claire did—and Slash and UnEqua were determined she would see none of the world's problems. Until they became *her* problems.

The coronation began with a choir singing hymns of hope, which weren't exactly comforting, as the choir was composed of various dead aliens, all controlled by Usurpers—but, oh, could those dead aliens sing!

As the ceremony began, Claire stood outside the court-yard in the grand archway at the back, waiting for her cue to proceed down the carpet toward the throne. Once there, UnEqua and Slash would pass planetary rule from the hands of the Usurpers into hers.

Claire could see that the courtyard was only half-full, and the attendants, like the choir, were all Usurpers in the unpleasant bodies of deceased hosts. She sighed heavily. So, just as Slash had said, none of the planet's people had both-ered to come. Well, once she was crowned, she would have plenty of time to win them over. The future of this planet was in her hands!

It was the first time Claire had thought about the future of this world, and her anxiety grew as the reality began to sink in. A whole planet. That was a lot of responsibil-ity. Her mother complained she didn't take good enough care of Cinnamon, her fussy little Pomeranian—how was she going to take care of a whole planet? She tugged at her delicate coronation gown to adjust it, but it was like pull-ing on a cloud. All she did was arouse the purple Rigelian ultra-doves that dotted her dress, and their flapping only compounded Claire's angst.

And imagine, this was all because of Ogden Coggin-

Criddle! Once she was crowned, she supposed she'd have to knight him or something for buying her this world.

The choir finished the last harmonious strains of their song, and silence fell. This was Claire's cue. With head held high, she moved forward to the generous applause of the crowd. Between the gravity-resistant dress and the flapping birds, her feet barely even touched the ground as she glided down the red carpet toward the throne. It was time to put all troubling thoughts behind her now, because this was her day, her time, her moment, and she was going to enjoy it.

• ● •

With the stealth of multiple species from two different planets, Jad and Noah arrived at the edge of the palace courtyard and watched Claire practically levitate down the red carpet toward Slash and UnEqua, who waited with the crown. Andi and Forlo, who were not nearly as stealthy, lingered behind, on the lookout for guards.

"How certain are you that the Tribunal is going to execute Claire?" Noah asked Andi.

"I'm absolutely sure. The coronation will seal the deal, and Claire will be held responsible for all the Usurpers' crimes."

"Then we've got to stop that coronation!"

"But it's us against all those Usurpers," said Jad, uncertain. "We're outnumbered."

"Just dig deep," Noah told Jad. "And let whatever comes, come. Your body knows how to defend itself; you just have to get out of the way, let it do what it does, and then figure out how to weaponize it. I promise you, Jad, these Usurpers won't stand a chance against what *we've* got!"

It was a rousing and inspiring little speech that Noah gave. He only wished he believed it himself... because deep down, he knew that they were in big, big trouble. He knew what had to be done: They had to get to Claire and get her out before the body-snatched Raymond could put the crown on her head. And despite what he had told Jad, Noah suspected it was not going to be easy. These Usurpers had taken over the bodies of dozens of different alien beings, each with their own strengths, weaknesses, and probably different attacks. It was like hurling yourself into a video game you'd never played. It might take half a dozen lives to figure out how to battle—but that wasn't helpful at all when you only had one life.

"Maybe you could grab her and teleport away," Noah suggested to Jad.

"Won't work," Jad said. "I can only teleport over short distances, and this courtyard is too big."

"I can scream," suggested Forlo.

"Uh, I'm not sure that's really going to help us," Noah told him, then turned to Andi. "Maybe you can shoot some laser beams out of your eyes and create a distraction."

"My power's low, and my weapons systems are offline. But I can grab a few Usurpers and throw them around."

"Good," said Noah. "Do that."

"I can act like a CloneFish, and project a bunch of fake images of myself," offered Jad.

"Cool!" said Noah. "Like Naruto!"

"Is that another friend of yours?"

"Kinda," said Noah.

"And I can scream," Forlo reminded them, eager to be of assistance.

"Fine," said Noah. "If all else fails, you can scream."

"Look," said Jad, pointing. "Is that her? The one covered in birds?"

"Yep," Noah said, and took a deep breath. "Here goes nothing."

Which he meant literally, because he employed octopus camouflage, glass frog transparency, and he even masked his scent like a puff adder, becoming as close to nothing as he possibly could. Then Noah launched himself into the courtyard with cheetah-speed, straight toward Claire.

He might have reached her, too, if there hadn't been a stray tentacle in the way.

• ● •

There's a First Spiralese word. It doesn't have a direct translation into English, as it's one of those idiomatic expressions that loses everything in translation. The word is "⟨glyph⟩" and one might be tempted to translate it as "epic fail," but that doesn't come close. The nearest thing to an accurate translation is "a personal disaster of mind-numbingly gargantuan proportions beyond which no further act can be imagined until time itself ceases to exist, and yet even then, the failure shall remain."

Noah's launch into the coronation was definitely a ⟨glyph⟩.

The tentacle, which a Usurper had inconsiderately extended out into the aisle, didn't just trip Noah. A suction cup caught on the tip of his shoe and ripped his shoe from his foot, sending him flying.

Suddenly, all his carefully planned animal traits were replaced with actual defenses that animals exhibited when they were about to painfully face-plant. Gone were the camo and the transparency and the absolute lack of scent. Instead, he sprayed like a skunk, inked like a squid, shot blood from his eyes like a horned lizard, and, rather than letting him hit the ground, his body decided now was the time to shoot a web from some nonexistent spinneret in the small of his back, like an accidental Spider-Man, where it stuck to a banner pole above the courtyard, leaving him trussed up like a piñata swinging uselessly back and forth.

The singular word he uttered was pretty much the same in every galactic language.

Claire heard a commotion but couldn't see what it was. All she saw were feathers and the flapping wings of the doves. Well, whatever it was, let the security zombies deal with it; it's what they were there for, right? If she was going to be royalty, she would have to learn to delegate and keep herself above such things, focusing her attention on the lofty matters of managing a planet.

She glided forward, until finally reaching Slash and UnEqua, who seemed edgy and eager. Slash held a bejeweled crown of light in Raymond's hands. UnEqua's flaking arms were folded, and she was tapping her foot.

"Move a little faster, dear," she said to Claire. "And ignore what's going on behind you, it's not important."

At last she arrived at the throne, where, according to planetary custom, various Usurpers hastily handed her a sword, a scepter, a golden scroll, a rock, and a loaf of bread that had its own opinions and didn't want to be held.

The commotion behind her seemed to be building, but UnEqua kept instructing Claire to pay it no attention.

"These are the ritual objects of transition," announced Slash, loud enough for the whole crowd to hear. "Do you, Claire of Earth, as owner of the Jensen star system, accept rulership of this planet, and all that it entails, including, but not limited to, duties, responsibilities, pre-existing liabilities, and consequent accountability?"

Blah, blah, blah—it sounded like some tedious terms-and-conditions clause that nobody anywhere in the history of any universe ever read.

"Yes, whatever. I accept."

Slash gave her a warm smile, although a corner of his lip was twitching. "Then by the power vested in me—"

"Just do the thing already!" said UnEqua, impatient as ever.

Claire knelt as best she could in an antigravity dress covered with birds and prepared to receive the crown.

• ● •

"That's a Darwin's bark spider web," said Andi. "Stronger than Kevlar. I don't think Noah's coming down anytime soon."

"Is this part of the plan?" asked Forlo, his eyes scanning the palace courtyard, where Noah, if not the center of attention, was drawing quite a lot of it from the crowd. The scene was both chaotic and mesmerizing, the radiant spray of the palace fountain contrasting with the dark, twisted forms of the Usurpers reaching for Noah as he swung back and forth above their heads.

"I don't think so," said Jad.

"Noah never plans to make a fool of himself," Andi chimed in, "and yet it's his greatest personal skill." Then Andi launched into the fray, fulfilling her promise to grab

Usurpers with her android strength and hurl them this way and that, drawing attention away from Noah, who struggled to free himself from the sticky entanglement.

Jad's mind raced, realizing that, with Noah in his current helpless state, the task of reaching Claire now rested squarely on Jad's three shoulders.

Leap, don't think. Rely on instinct, not reason.

It went against everything Jad was ever taught—because while instincts might save the day, they might also leave you swinging by a tether above a murderous mob of the undead.

Jad's thoughts focused on the CloneFish and its ability to baffle predators with multiple projections, but thinking about it didn't summon the skill. Jad recalled Noah's guidance to feel the need, rather than thinking of the creature. So what did Jad need right now? To be everywhere at once.

And suddenly, it happened! Projections of Jad were scaling the walls in three different places, while two more versions deftly dodged guards, and at least half a dozen more amused themselves by making faces at the bewildered coronation guests. The commotion in the courtyard reached a crescendo, and amid the chaos, the true Jad sprinted up the aisle toward Claire, who stood at the altar with Slash and UnEqua, in the midst of the coronation ceremony.

Jad skillfully evaded the pesky tentacle that had tripped Noah, getting closer to Claire, but was abruptly grabbed and taken to the ground by a beefy guard with even more arms than Jad—and although Jad spat acid and breathed fire, the guard wasn't letting go.

Andi was faring no better—because, although she had the strength of ten Usurpers, all it took was eleven to overpower her—and without her weaponry, all she could do was insult them, which, although satisfying, did nothing to loosen their grip on her.

Meanwhile, Noah valiantly fought off the grasping appendages. The strand of web that was coming out of his back was as strong as a cable and sticky as tar. He called up wolverine claws and sawed at the web until it finally began to fray—but as his eyes swept the scene, he spotted Raymond, holding the crown over Claire, about to place it on her head. There seemed to be no way to stop it now.

Then, out of nowhere, an earth-shattering sound bellowed forth: an agonizingly loud and terrible wail that felt like an entire team of trumpets blasting directly into everyone's ears. The intensity threatened to overwhelm Noah— he thought his brain would explode. The tremendous force of the sound wave shattered palace windows, sending fragments flying. It left seismic cracks in the stone walls. Usurpers fell like bowling pins, and the guard holding Jad was forced to release his grip, clutching his ears in distress. And, with a powerful gust, it sent the crown flying out of Slash's hands.

As suddenly as it had come, the sound faded, and an eerie silence enveloped the courtyard. In that moment, a lone voice broke through the stillness.

"There," said Forlo, triumphant. "I told you I could scream."

27

It's My Party, and I'll Die If I Want To

OGDEN AND SAHARA CREPT DOWN THE PALACE HALLWAYS, PEEK-ing into rooms, and out of windows.

"Now, if I had a spaceship, where would I hide it?" Sahara wondered aloud.

"You're assuming they're hiding it," Ogden replied. "They have no reason to. Maybe it's in plain sight."

"If it was in plain sight, don't you think we would have seen it by now?"

"Well, we already know that spaceships don't necessar-ily look like spaceships—and we really didn't get a good look at it when it appeared above Claire's party. Too many lights were shining in our faces."

"So we're looking for something that may or may not look like a spaceship."

"Correct," said Ogden.

"Which is basically everything."

"Correct," Ogden said again.

Sahara sighed and decided to give no further comment. Ogden's logic was never worth the time it took to argue. Besides, he might be right—which meant finding the ship might be even harder than they had anticipated. But then when she happened to glance out the next window, she saw something that most definitely did not look like a spaceship.

"What about that?" she said, pointing to a towering golden statue, at least ten stories high, in the middle of a nasty-looking garden.

"Uh...I think that's a statue."

"It's the right size for a ship is all I'm saying."

"Hmm. Good point," agreed Ogden. "Maybe we should get a closer look."

They found a set of stairs that led down to the ground level, and made their way to the garden, where a bumper crop of...*something* was coming in. Rows and rows of unidentifiable plants seemed ready to burst with ripeness.

But on the way to the statue, Ogden stopped dead in his tracks, and Sahara nearly bumped into him.

"What's wrong?" Sahara asked.

"Look!"

Sahara followed Ogden's pointing finger, to a very familiar cat meandering through the garden ahead of them.

"Is that Mittens? How did he get here?"

"He must have followed us all the way here, the poor thing!" said Ogden. "We need to rescue him."

"Okay, first of all," said Sahara, "I don't think anything about that cat screams 'poor thing.' And secondly, he bailed the moment we landed—so I think that cat can take care of himself."

But Ogden was already off, whispering, "Here, kitty, kitty," which was bound to be offensive to a telepathic alien cat. Sure enough, the instant Mittens saw Ogden, he froze, then bolted into the undergrowth of the garden, and Ogden pursued.

"Ogden, wait!" Sahara began.

But he was gone.

Fine, thought Sahara. She was more than happy to scope out the statue without him, although chasing after the cat was probably going to get Ogden caught by Usurpers, and she'd probably have to rescue him, for which he'd be completely ungrateful.

As she neared the massive statue, she caught sight of an undead usurped creature tinkering with it. The creature was a rotting twelve-legged centipede-thing with a semi-humanoid growing out of it, like some kind of nightmare centaur. It held a hose to the base of the statue, clearly fueling it. So she was right! This *was* a ship!

She would have quietly, carefully, tiptoed back the way she had come, but she inadvertently bumped into one of the bulging melon-like things that the garden was growing—and it burst in a cloud of neon-pink powder that covered her.

It drew the attention of the Centaur-pede, and it drew a blaster, taking aim.

"Appendages up!" it said. "Now!"

Sahara could have turned and run. But she didn't. Because even though her fight-or-flight response took over, suddenly the flight part ceased to exist. In fact, she wanted nothing more at that moment than to fight this monstrous creature with every fiber of her being. Only later would she learn that the powder she had been covered with was called aggro-spice, a Usurper crop, used to instill aggressiveness in their warriors. Sahara's fighting fury suddenly spiked to a level few humans had ever experienced.

The Centaur-pede got off one blast but missed. After that, he didn't stand a chance.

• ● •

Claire was not knocked down by the shrill sonic blast. It did ruffle the birds' feathers quite a bit, causing them to flap with panic and try to tear themselves free from her gown, but the force field that held them in place was too strong.

Her coronation was ruined. *Ruined!* Broken glass everywhere, sprawling, stunned, undead Usurpers littered the ground, and—was that the missing-presumed-dead Noah

Prime who just fell from a banner pole? Was he the cause of all this? The nerve of some people!

Well, this wasn't over yet! Because there on the ground between her and Noah was the glorious crown of light. If no one was going to put it on her head, she'd have to do it herself. Still skimming the ground on tippy-toes, she made her way to the crown, but Noah was approaching from the other direction.

"No, Claire, don't do it!" he shouted.

"You were *not* invited to this party!"

"You don't understand!"

"Oh, I understand plenty!" she snapped. "You're just jealous that Ogden didn't buy you a planet, too!"

She grabbed the crown just before Noah reached it and held it over her head, then, speaking as regally as she could, she proclaimed: "I hereby crown myself Princess Claire of Claire, now and forever, hallelujah, huzzah, amen, and whatever else!"

Then she slammed the crown down on her own head, where it stuck like a suction cup.

The moment it made contact, the force field holding the doves to her gossamer gown released them. The birds flew free, first winging around her, and then rising into the air before finally roosting in the eaves of the courtyard. It would have been breathtaking if anyone had seen it, but there was only the faintest smattering of applause because most every-one was still picking themselves up off the ground.

Claire glared at Noah. "That would have been much cooler if people were actually watching! But you spoiled it! You spoiled everything!"

"Claire, you don't realize what you've just done. Take it off before—"

"It's too late," said a voice from behind her. Slash stood up, dusting off Raymond's body. "The coronation is complete. Rule and responsibility have been officially transferred."

"Finally," added UnEqua. "Now let's get out of here."

And they turned to leave.

"Wait, where are you going?" Claire asked. "You can't leave yet. Look at this mess!" And now she realized it wasn't just Slash and UnEqua who were leaving—all the Usurpers were racing to escape the courtyard.

"It's your mess now," said Slash. "None of this is our problem anymore."

"Enjoy your world while you can, gullible human female," said UnEqua with a bitter laugh.

Then a massive object descended from the sky, eclipsing the sun.

28

Judgment Day

THE TRIBUNAL'S INTERSTELLAR VESSEL WAS AN AWE-INSPIRING creation, carved entirely out of rare granite from the deepest corners of the universe, and designed to resemble a mountain hurtling through space. This architectural marvel was not merely a vessel, but a symbol of justice, adorned with intricate engravings depicting countless civilizations throughout history. The mountainous vessel was much larger than the judges needed, but that was intentional. When it came to meting out justice, it was important to project an intimidating image of solid permanence. The sight of their craft made law-abiding citizens tremble and criminals run. But they never got far.

Within its grand halls, the trio of esteemed judges consulted their support staff of scholars and masters of interstellar diplomacy—their job being to assist the Tribunal in bringing order out of chaos wherever chaos might be found.

And right now, it was found in abundance on Planet Claire.

The ship dropped from intestinal space into normal space just beyond the planet's outer atmosphere. It didn't need to request permission to land; the Tribunal of Ancients had the absolute right to land anywhere and everywhere it so desired.

Wasting no time, the craft fired its thrusters and descended directly toward the palace.

• ● •

When it came to catching Mittens, Ogden's ignorance helped. He had no idea that the bulging pods around him were full of aggro-spice, so he had no problem bumping into them in his quest to apprehend Mittens. The cat, on the other hand, was being extra careful—he had already made a deal with Slash and UnEqua to catch a ride on their ship to the Fauxlites' home world. Going all wildcat right now was not going to be helpful—and might cause the Usurpers to leave him behind. The best thing to do would be to get out of the garden as carefully as he could, without bursting any of the aggro-spice pods. But before he could, Ogden pounced on him and grabbed him with those damnable hands with opposable thumbs. Curse human evolution!

"It's okay, Mittens, I've got you," said Ogden, falling to his knees. "You're safe now."

Oh, the irony. Mittens could tell that Ogden had no

idea what was bulging in the pods all around them. And so, to keep Ogden from moving too sharply, Mittens opened his mind and projected the truth of the spice pods into Ogden's. Unfortunately, Mittens was careless with his thoughts again and projected not just one truth but a whole bunch of unintended ones.

"What?" yelled Ogden, jumping to his feet. "You're the one who ejected Noah and Miss Luella? You're going to turn him over to the Fauxlites? Claire is being set up? You've been peeing in my lunch box? Mittens! How could you!"

Mittens decided this was not going anywhere good, so he clawed Ogden's arm just hard enough to make him let go and took off through the garden, determined to find Slash and UnEqua and get off this planet, happy to never see Ogden or his friends again.

• ● •

Noah knew that an eclipse could not be good, especially because the planet had no moon with which to eclipse its sun.

"What's going on?" yelled Claire. "Will somebody tell me what's going on?"

"A bunch of judges are coming to execute you."

"Excuse me?"

But with Usurpers rushing toward the archway, trying

to escape, Noah didn't have time to bring Claire up to speed.

"We can't let the Usurpers leave!" Noah turned to his sister. "Andi, can you do something?"

Andi shrugged. "Sorry, I got nothing."

So Noah called to Jad, who was closer to the courtyard archway. "Jad! Can you block the exit somehow?"

"I don't know—I'll try."

But as it turned out, Jad didn't have to. Because there in the archway stood Sahara, covered in pink stuff and looking more furious than Noah had ever seen her before.

"*I've had it with you rotten, stinking, good-for-nothing Usurpers!*" she bellowed.

"Oh dear," said Forlo. "It looks like she's been to the garden."

"*Just give me a reason,*" Sahara wailed, perhaps not realizing they'd already given her plenty of reasons.

Then one of the Usurpers, a reptilian alien, tried to sneak past her. Sahara wasn't having it. She grabbed the creature, let loose a bloodcurdling war cry, and in one smooth motion, ripped its head off. She actually ripped its head off!

"My God! She killed it!" gasped Claire.

"Well, technically it was already dead," Andi pointed out.

Then, out of the undead/redead creature's neck, a little

green Usurper squirmed, jumped into the ear of a passing rat, and scurried away.

Meanwhile, the sky above darkened as a mountain fell from the sky.

"I'd better go greet the Tribunal," said Forlo, "and try to spin things in our favor."

He slipped out behind Sahara, who tossed him a half-hearted glare, but let him go. Noah, however, was fool enough to engage her.

"Good going, Sahara," said Noah as he reached her.

"*Shut up*," she growled. "*I am so mad at you right now.*"

"Why? What did I do?"

"*I don't know, and I don't care! I'm just mad, so shut up!*"

Noah couldn't help but notice that the pink powder had a sharp scent, and just smelling it was tweaking his own sense of outrage. Wisely, he decided it was best not to ask questions. Instead, he slipped out of her line of sight. Then, behind her, he began slinging his newly discovered Darwin's bark spider web across the archway to keep Usurpers from leaving.

"*Who's next?*" bellowed Sahara, ready to tear anyone who approached her limb from rotting limb.

Then one voice rang out from across the courtyard.

"You dare stand in our way!" UnEqua snarled. Not even Slash was willing to take Sahara on in this state. He backed away, letting this be UnEqua's battle.

370

All the other Usurpers stepped aside, leaving a clear path between them, like this was an old-fashioned western face-off.

"You!" roared Sahara. *"I am so done with you!"*

"I've been waiting for this moment," said UnEqua, the shimmering waters of the fountain behind her seeming to glow like an aura of power. "Go ahead," she said, her rotting lips peeled into a horrible sneer. "Take on me."

• ● •

Sahara tore into UnEqua. Literally—ripping her limb from limb until UnEqua was on her last leg. Also literally.

Meanwhile, Slash and dozens of other Usurpers launched an attack on the others.

Claire was grabbed in a way that did not befit a princess. Andi, who had expended most of her remaining power, could offer no real resistance, and was easily subdued.

Jad, who was not a fighter by nature, tried to call up an animal trait but found only the fluffy pelt of a Triastral Furball Mink, which was really cute and melted hearts, but unfortunately *not* literally, so it wasn't very helpful at all.

Noah was harder to defeat, but in the end, he was also taken down—and not even rhino skull could save him from the stone that Slash hit him with. It wasn't enough to kill him, but it left Noah seriously stunned on the ground, head spinning.

But at least Noah had managed to web off the exit.

"Not to worry," said Slash. "We would have felt the ground shake if the Tribunal ship had landed. We still have time." Then Slash turned to one of his minions, a nasty thing that looked like it was right out of a *Predator* movie. "Fred, can you grab a flamethrower and burn down that web?"

Noah tried to rise, but his brain was scrambled in the worst way. He felt like a prizefighter who had taken one too many blows. "We have to help Sahara!" he told Jad as he fell back to his knees.

But Sahara needed absolutely no help from anyone. She was still a bottomless pit of aggro-rage. UnEqua had only one arm and one leg left, and Sahara was still pummeling her, sending unpleasant pieces of UnEqua's rotting self flying left and right.

If Sahara's intellect could rise above the rage, she would have realized that she really wasn't hurting UnEqua at all; she was just destroying the body of the dead host UnEqua wore. But she couldn't stop because it felt soooo good.

The shrewd Usurper, however, wasn't as helpless as she appeared. UnEqua took advantage of Sahara's fury, letting her tire herself out. Then, at precisely the right moment, UnEqua ducked Sahara's attack, and Sahara's momentum took her over the low railing and right into the fountain.

Once submerged in the shimmering waters, the aggro-spice was washed away. The instant the pink powder was gone, it was as if some spell had been broken—and with so much aggression suddenly washed away, Sahara felt limp and ready to fall asleep, as if all the adrenaline that had been coursing through her body suddenly turned to warm milk.

Coughing and sputtering, she tried to pull herself out of the fountain. But UnEqua wasn't about to let her.

"And now, pretty little human, you're mine!" said UnEqua, in cackling triumph. "I'll take your body now. But not alive. No, no, we can't have that! I prefer my hosts dead." And with that, she raised the ceremonial sword that had been given to Claire and drew it back, preparing to thrust it through Sahara's heart.

• ● •

Sahara would have died . . .

Noah would have been turned over to the Fauxlites . . .

Jad would have been usurped . . .

Claire would have been handed to the Tribunal . . .

Andi would have been recycled . . .

And Ogden would have become Mittens's servant . . .

Were it not for the sudden appearance of Arbuckle Middle School's least-loved science teacher, Mr. Kratz, and the love of his life—himself—but in the form of Agent Nell Knell.

29

Of Birds and Blobs

QUANTAVIUS T. KRATZ HAD NEVER ONCE, IN HIS ENTIRE LIFE, saved the day.

He believed that he had, of course. Many times. He was constantly telling people how everything would fall completely apart without him—that he was the mainspring that kept the world around him functioning.

But in reality?

No.

Just no.

And yet the universe has a way of giving everyone their shining moment, whether they deserve it or not. As it turned out, this was Kratz and Nell's moment.

If there was anyone to blame for what happened next, it was Mittens, because he was the one who locked Kratz and Knell in Miss Luella's basement in the first place, inadvertently bringing all of them to this exact moment in time....

•●•

In the midst of UnEqua's moment of triumph, a drainage grate sprang open in the middle of the courtyard, and Kratz crawled out with Knell close behind. It wasn't their arrival that made the difference, however—it was what they brought with them.

Blobs.

Hundreds and hundreds of blobs that had been chasing them through the caves below the palace for hours.

"Run, Nell!" shouted Kratz as the gelatinous creatures bubbled up through the drain. "Run, before they devour us!"

They were, of course, in no danger of being devoured, as Splunges only ate dead flesh. Not a problem for humans.

But a *big* problem for Usurpers.

The Splunges had been hoping for a small snack of dead skin cells and maybe a little bit of hair—but suddenly they found themselves in Splunge heaven!

At the sight of the creatures, the Usurpers panicked. Their home world had horror movies about things like this. They scattered, forgetting their prisoners, racing to escape, screaming in abject terror, as they hurried to the archway—but Predator Fred had not yet reached the web with the flamethrower.

"Splunges!" Predator Fred wailed. "How can it be? I thought we hunted them to extinction ages ago!"

The archway web held firm against Usurpers throwing themselves against it, sticking to it, and thus making an even denser barrier.

Meanwhile, the Splunges wasted no time. They moved faster than invertebrate blobs should be able to move and pounced on the panicking hoard.

UnEqua never saw it coming. One moment she was about to run Sahara through with a sword, and the next, a Splunge was on her arm, devouring what flesh remained, leaving only bones that clattered to the floor along with the sword.

With Jad's help, Noah got to his feet. What Noah saw, he thought was a hallucination brought on by being hit in the head. The scene looked like something ripped from his darkest nightmares—an army of zombies wailing in agony as they were devoured by living boogers. And was that Mr. Kratz in the middle of it? No, that part absolutely had to be a hallucination.

"What's happening?" Noah asked.

"Not sure," answered Jad, "but if it's bad for the Usurpers, it's good for us."

Meanwhile, Kratz and Knell came to the simultaneous realization that the palace was not a fun place to be, and they slipped back down the drain—because being lost in the caves was much better than whatever was going on up here.

And so, for once, Quantavius T. Kratz's astounding talent for creating monumental messes turned out to be precisely what the moment required.

• ● •

The Splunges were quicker than piranhas. In less than two minutes, they had stripped the flesh from every Usurper body, leaving nothing but brittle bones littering the courtyard. Well, bones, and a hundred little green worms squirming for cover.

UnEqua, in her unhosted form, wriggled out of the skull of her former host. This was a setback, nothing more. Sahara was still there, climbing out of the fountain—all UnEqua had to do was usurp her. She would have preferred Sahara dead, but that could be dealt with later. Right now, all she needed to do was get inside. So she coiled up and sprang toward Sahara's left nostril . . .

. . . just as a Rigelian ultra-dove swooped down from above, caught UnEqua in its beak, and swallowed her whole.

• ● •

Worms! The doves were thrilled by their luck. *Worms!* They had been stuck on that ridiculous dress for days with nothing to eat. *Worms!* Surely, this feast had been prepared just for them! *Worms!* This was a gift from the great Rigelian ultra-dove in the sky. *Worms!* They would give thanks, and lay eggs, and tell of this glorious day to their chicks and grandchicks. *Worms!*

• ● •

With their feathers aglow in a mesmerizing shade of deep purple, the Rigelian ultra-doves swooped down from their perches, their hunger rivaling that of the voracious Splunges. Their beaks seemed to shine like stars as they effortlessly plucked the Usurpers from their bony hiding places one by one—and with every morsel devoured, a soft and melodious *coo* filled the air, creating an otherworldly symphony of satisfaction. They wove between the bones, executing twists and turns with astonishing precision. And as the doves filled themselves, the once formidable foes were reduced to mere memories of malevolence. The Usurpers never stood a chance.

Noah and Jad watched the feeding frenzy with a strange mix of joy, wonder, and a little bit of horror.

"Have you ever seen anything so beautiful as the food chain?" said Noah.

Sahara made her way over the bone-strewn ground to them. "Did you see that? I thought there was only one of those gooey blob-things. Where did they even come from?"

"No idea," said Noah.

"The birds were mine," bragged Claire. "Sort of."

Then Noah turned at a strange gnashing sound and

saw Andi, looking more exhausted than he'd ever seen her, fall to her knees and double over. Gears popped out of her artificial skin, churning and grinding. Noah could tell she had lapsed into low-power mode and was converting back into suitcase form—but she was too damaged to make the transformation.

"Ugh, this is so embarrassing," she muttered.

"Let me help," said Noah, and gently guided the pieces of her singed and dented outer shell into place.

"I'm the one who's supposed to be helping and protecting *you*," she said weakly. "I'm sorry I've failed you, Noah."

"You haven't, Andi. You've always been right there."

"Shut up," Andi said. "Let me have the satisfaction of feeling sorry for myself."

Noah grinned. "Okay," he said gently. "If, just this once, you'll let me have the satisfaction of taking care of you."

Andi sighed. "Yeah, sure, whatever." Then she dipped her head, and Noah sat on her back until her outer shell closed and the latch clicked into place.

Just then, a sudden blast of heat drew their attention— and they realized that not all the Usurpers had been eaten. There was still one left.

Slash, who had been protected by Raymond's living body, had grabbed the flamethrower from the skeleton of Predator Fred, and had set the web on fire.

"Don't let him get away!" Noah yelled. But Slash was already gone.

And at that very moment, the ground shook with such bone-quaking force, it felt as if a mountain had fallen from the sky.

30

Take Us to Your Leader

THE GREAT SHIP OF THE TRIBUNAL, FINDING NO DESIGNATED landing area large enough, set their mountain down upon the palace's southwest corner, completely crushing it— because any planet without the consideration to construct a mountain-sized landing pad deserved a lesson in the importance of courtesy.

The three judges stood stone-faced as the landing ramp lowered. That is to say their faces were actually stone. In fact, the infamous carved heads on Easter Island were modeled after the Tribunal during their one and only trip to Earth—not to pass judgment, but for vacation. It was an idyllic spot—but the local life-forms began to worship them. Which was nice for the first five minutes, then was just annoying. It ruined their vacation.

The planet on which they had just arrived, newly

designated Claire, was not a vacation spot by any stretch of the imagination. This was business. This visit was about judgment, the rule of law, and punishment. But mostly punishment.

• ● •

Forlo watched the ship come down, and, as the ramp descended into the rubble of the palace's southwest corner, he strode forward to greet the three judges, to slow them down, and hopefully to create some spin in Claire's favor.

On his way, he had managed to make a quick stop in a cloakroom where he replaced his worn-out jacket with a long robe, heavily embroidered, very regal-looking. Just the kind of thing in which to greet Galactic VIPs.

The three justices were mostly head, with short, stout bodies and stubby stone legs. Forlo stood in their path as they descended the ramp, his arms spread wide in greeting.

"Honored Judges! I, Forlo of B'light, welcome you to our planet, and am pleased to give you an extensive tour before you settle in for the trial!"

"We have no wish to tour. We would like to begin this trial as soon as possible," said the chief justice. "Are you the ruler of this planet?"

"Guilty!" said the judge on one side.

"Not yet!" shushed the judge on his other side.

These were the Left Hand of Justice, and the Right Hand of Justice, standing like granite bookends.

"Me? Ruler? No, certainly not!" said Forlo.

"But you wear the robes of a king!" observed the chief justice.

Forlo looked down at the robe, seeing the royal crest on the chest for the first time. Perhaps his former rags would have been better. "If it pleases the court, I am merely the First Citizen of a single city."

Then the chief justice frowned. "It does not please the court." Then he spoke what were arguably the most common words uttered upon alien arrivals:

"Take us to your leader."

"But, Your Honors," said Forlo, "wouldn't you prefer to see the Usurpers who actually created the violations you've come to judge? Let me bring you to them instead!"

"Bah!" said the chief justice. "While we have no love of Usurpers, the law is clear. Upon ascension to rulership, the current landowner is responsible for any and all violations."

"*Guilty!*" yelled the Left Hand of Justice.

"Still not time," said the Right Hand of Justice.

"But surely you have more important things to do than trouble yourselves with the affairs of a small humble planet such as ours," Forlo pointed out.

"Yes," agreed the chief justice, "but time matters not, as we can be in many places at once."

"In fact, we even have a brother," added the Right Hand of Justice, "who dresses festively and delivers holiday gifts to entire planets on a single night!"

"Do not speak of him!" ordered the chief justice. "He is dead to us."

Suddenly, far-off wails of agony and terror erupted from the distant courtyard, and it drew the attention of the justices.

"What's going on there?" the chief justice demanded. "Out of our way! If the execution has begun without us, we will be greatly miffed."

• ● •

Slash raced up the grand staircase and through the palace's upper chambers to escape the humans. UnEqua had often dismissed his choice to have a live host, what with all the trouble wrangling its pesky consciousness. Well, Slash had the last laugh because UnEqua was now being digested in the belly of a bird. As were all their Usurper underlings.

Unfortunately, that left Slash vulnerable.

Slash felt the ground shake when the Tribunal landed. Time to make a hasty exit. It was just a matter of getting to the garden where his ship waited. That he would be the only Usurper to survive this planet didn't bother him. After all, usurping can be a dangerous game. And his new partnership with Mittens the Cat—one of the Galaxy's greatest criminal masterminds—was certainly a step up from UnEqua.

But before he could reach the ship, he was cornered in an upstairs hallway by the human N.O.A.H., whom

Mittens had told him about, along with that three-armed creature that had also been in the courtyard attack. It was a species Slash knew the name of but couldn't put Raymond's finger on it.

"You're not escaping," the N.O.A.H. said. "We're not going to let Claire pay for what you've done to this planet."

"It can't be stopped now that she's been crowned," Slash told him. "The Tribunal will judge her and execute her within the hour."

"You'd better hope that's not true," said the N.O.A.H., "because if that happens, I swear I'll pull you out of Raymond's brain and crush you between my fingers."

That made Slash laugh; bigger beings had tried!

Just then an image was projected into Slash's mind— the image of a laundry chute just a few feet away. If he was able to slip into it and down to the first floor, it was only a dozen yards to the garden where the ship waited! He was just a few feet from freedom!

But who had projected that thought into his mind?

At the sound of a sly meow, he realized, without even looking, that it was his new business partner standing behind him.

"Mittens!" said the human. "I should have known you were working with this creep."

And then it suddenly occurred to Slash exactly what kind of creature the boy's three-armed companion was. Oh, this was glorious and would play in Slash's favor!

"You're a Triastral!" Slash said. "I didn't think there were any of you left."

"What do you mean?" asked the Triastral.

The human N.O.A.H. seemed to panic. "Don't you talk to my friend! Don't you dare say anything!"

But Slash wasn't about to shut up now. This was an opportunity to fluster these two enough to slip past them and down that shaft.

"I've been to your planet; the Fauxlites have done wonders with it! Now Triastra is a dead frost world, void of life—but perfect for cold weather sports. What humans call skiing, sledding, and skating. And with no planetary life to get in the way, it's perfect."

"Wh-what do you mean, no life?" the Triastral said, taking the bait.

"Jad! Don't listen to him!" begged the human.

Slash feigned surprise. "You mean you didn't know? How terribly sad for you." Slash was a master of many things, but manipulating the emotions of sentimental species was something he excelled in.

"Cover your ears," the human N.O.A.H. said to the Triastral—who didn't have the wisdom to take the other's advice.

"Since everything and everyone on your planet was killed when it was terraformed," continued Slash, "I'll bet you're the last one! Although I hear that the Fauxlites have a planet where they keep specimens of everything. Is that where you escaped from? The World of Last Life?" Then Slash shook his head in mock sympathy. "What a pity. Yours was a beautiful species. But people do need their winter sports."

• ● •

Noah knew capturing Slash wasn't going to be easy, but he had never anticipated this. He could see all of Jad's fur rising, standing on end, but not in a cute furball kind way. It was more like the needle-fine quills of some alien porcupine.

"That's not true," growled Jad. *"You're lying! It's not true!"* Then Jad looked to Noah, pleading. "Tell me he's lying, Noah...."

Noah wished he could, but he didn't have it in him to deny the truth anymore. "We can talk about it later, Jad," he said. It felt like trying to talk someone off a ledge.

That's when Slash made his move, bolting toward a linen closet with a laundry chute that was just wide enough for Raymond's scrawny frame to fit through. Noah, with all his animal speed and agility, couldn't move quickly enough to stop him.

But Jad could.

Jad didn't just move—the anguished Triastral tele- ported to the spot, blocking the chute. And in Jad's eyes, Noah could see grief so white-hot it was like looking into the sun. And although it was the Fauxlites that Jad was truly angry at, it was Slash who was there to represent and bear the brunt of all the fury of every lost species of Triastra.

Noah could only hope that Raymond's consciousness was good and gone, because he knew there was no stopping what was coming next.

• ● •

Slash quickly found that Raymond's body was no match for a feral Triastral. Slash was slammed against the wall, the ceiling, the floor, over and over. A breath of blue flame set his clothes on fire, then acidic vomit doused it, only to burn in an even more terrible way. The Triastral gave off a screech loud enough to burst the eardrums of this human host, and Slash was speared by dozens of quills tipped with poison, not meant to kill but only to deliver intense, excruciating pain. Triastra might have once been a kind and gentle place, but its species certainly knew how to defend themselves.

Slash now knew that telling this creature the truth was a serious miscalculation. But there was always a way out, and Slash always found it. He would not let the last member of an extinct species destroy him. And then he saw his salvation watching from a dozen feet away, looking concerned but also very much amused.

The cat!

While the Triastral took out its anger on this human body, Slash let go of it and wormed his way up from Raymond's brain stem and out through his left ear. Then, seeing a clear line between him and Mittens, launched himself into the air.

For a moment, but only a moment, he was nothing but a small green worm flying through the musty hallway—but then he landed on the edge of the cat's right eye and quickly burrowed into a tear duct.

• ● •

Mittens. Went. Berserk.

He was not having this! He had partnered with the Usurpers to get off this planet, but partnering with one and being taken over by one were two very different things. Mittens fizzed up and jumped and yowled and sprang like a Halloween cat, doing everything within his power to shake the little green worm out—but to no avail, because he now felt Slash there, in his brain stem, trying to seize control of his body.

In any other circumstance, it would have been easy for Mittens to slip down the laundry chute and get to the spaceship, but he was too busy fighting for control of his own feline body. And he was losing.

• ● •

Slash was amazed he hadn't thought of this before! A Usurper in the body of a telepathic cat that was also a criminal genius—it was the perfect power play! If everything went right from this moment forth, he could be the most powerful Usurper who ever lived! Worlds would fall before him, making Slash a contender for domination of the known universe. So he burrowed deeper.

• ● •

Ogden arrived just in time to see the little green worm leap to the cat. He saw Mittens fizz up and bounce around the corridor—and he knew exactly what had happened.

"Ogden! Stop Mittens!" Noah yelled, which was easier said than done. But Ogden knew, no matter what, he couldn't let Mittens get away—not with a Usurper inside him—because this wasn't just bad for Mittens. It would be bad for everyone, everywhere.

Ogden considered Mittens, considered the hallway, considered his options. And all at once an idea came to him!

Because even hairless, Ogden was still full of harebrained schemes. . . .

• ● •

Noah could have gone after Mittens himself, but he couldn't just stand there and let Jad continue to rip into poor, defenseless Raymond.

390

"The Usurper's gone, Jad. It's in the cat now, let Raymond go."

Then weakly, frailly, Raymond said, "Whatever you are, please stop hurting me...." Noah's insistence, combined with Raymond's helpless plea, finally got through, and Jad was able to get all those alien animal instincts tamped down enough to let Raymond go.

Raymond collapsed onto Noah, grimacing and wracked with pain.

"It's going to be okay, Raymond," Noah said, although he wasn't sure if that was true.

Then Jad, still shaking from the ordeal, reached out toward Raymond.

"Jad, no," said Noah. "Don't hurt him anymore."

"It's not what you think." Then Jad placed a palm against Raymond's forehead. "The Touchbliss uses neural resonance to shut down pain receptors, so its prey feels no pain when it's eaten," Jad said. "But I guess I can use it any way I like." And then, in an instant, Raymond stopped grimacing, relaxed, and slumped like a child coming down from a tantrum.

"Is that thing in my brain gone?" he asked.

Noah nodded. "It's gone, Raymond."

Raymond turned to Jad. "Thanks for getting it out," he said. Then he passed out in Noah's arms.

• ● •

Ogden watched Mittens staggering, still fighting the losing battle with Slash. Time was of the essence here—because once Slash was in full control, his plan wouldn't work. Quickly Ogden went a short distance down the hall, then pulled open a door with a hearty, hefty *creeeeeeak* that made Mittens's ears perk up.

"Mittens," he said pleasantly, as if he were just calling the family cat. "Mittens, look over here! Look!"

• ● •

Deep within his own mind, Mittens struggled to regain the upper hand. Then he saw Ogden open the door. That was enough to give Mittens momentary control over his legs—because there is something deeper in a cat than consciousness or even curiosity. There is, in every cat, the overwhelming, all-consuming, irresistible desire to drop everything, to abandon any sense of decorum or restraint, and go through an open door.

• ● •

Slash, just beginning to latch onto the cat's brain stem, felt the surge of urgency as the cat ran toward the threshold. *No!* Slash screamed. *No, you mustn't!* But that was yet another miscalculation. Because anyone who knows anything about cats knows that you never tell a cat what *not* to do.

Mittens leaped through the door and into the room on

the other side, knocking over a hat rack that, admittedly, had been very poorly placed to begin with.

"Meowwowwwowww," Mittens wailed, avoiding the falling hat rack.

Look what you've done! yelled Slash in their joined mind, all his dreams of galactic domination crumbling to dust. *We'll never get out of here! We're doomed!*

Mittens turned and tried to race back out the open door, only to find himself turned back around, and knocking over the hat rack again.

"Meowwowwwowww."

Look what you've done! We'll never get out of here! We're doomed!

Mittens tried again, only to knock over the hat rack once more.

"Meowwowwwowww."

And now Slash had no choice but to resign himself to a very different eternity than he had planned, stuck in the mind of a very angry cat.

Look what you've done. We'll never get out of here. We're doomed.

"Meowwowwwowww."

• ● •

Meanwhile, on the other side of the doorway, Ogden looked sadly upon Mittens jumping out of the way of the falling

393

hat rack for the fourth time, and said, with far more com-
passion than you might imagine:

"Bad kitty..."

Then he slowly closed the door to the Mobius Suite,
never to be opened again.

31

All Kinds of Guilty

THE RESIDENTS OF B'LIGHT, P'LIGHT, AND S'LIGHT, THE THREE cities nearest to the palace, stood in awe as they witnessed the colossal mountain descending from the sky, a sight that could only herald the arrival of the Tribunal of Ancients. Whispers spread like wildfire through the bustling streets as the news spread.

In a momentous display of determination, thousands left their humble homes, venturing forth on a great pilgrimage across the trash fields, toward the palace—but on the way, encountered two mystical pilgrims heading in the opposite direction, prophets of past suffering and future prosperity. Word was, the two mysterious prophets were pursued by hundreds of overfed Splunges that had imprinted on the pair, believing them to be their parents. Tales immediately began to spread of K'Ratz and K'Nell, two holy harbingers of the future (even though they claimed to be from the distant past), who brought an extinct species back from the dead.

The mob of three cities crossed the hallowed ground of the no-dump zone that encircled the palace, and there they stopped outside the imposing palace walls, lining the edge of the moat. People from hundreds of different sentient species, at first brought together by a lack of hope, found themselves united by prospects of a future where they were more than mere squatters on a planetary vacant lot.

And so the people held a vigil, their hearts intertwined with the fate of their planet. They didn't know what form the Tribunal's justice would take, but one thing was certain—it would be a catalyst for change. The planet had endured eons of neglect. The time had now come for retribution, redemption, and, praise K'Ratz and K'Nell, rebirth!

• ● •

The three stoic granite judges stood before the new owner of the troubled planet: the chief justice in the center, flanked by the Left Hand of Justice to his right and the Right Hand of Justice to his left, which was confusing and intentionally so.

"Claire Jensen, earthling, you have been charged with 10,492 blatant violations of the Galactic Code of Planetary Rule," announced the chief justice, slamming down a massive tome the size of a dictionary on the empty throne in the center of the courtyard—because when addressing violations, a digital version simply did not carry the satisfying thump of a sizeable book.

The Right Hand of Justice stepped forward. "This planet is a dump, its many squatters are uncared for, most of its indigenous life has gone extinct, and pollution is creating a toxic primordial ooze from which some very nasty things may someday evolve. How do you plead?"

"My client pleads not guilty!" announced Ogden, who was Claire's self-appointed (and self-important) legal counsel.

All three justices chuckled, which, coming from stone heads, sounded a bit like a landslide. "I'm sorry," said the chief justice, "but 'not guilty' is not an acceptable plea."

"It's not?" said Ogden. "So what is?"

"*Guilty!*" shouted the Left Hand of Justice, who was beginning to sound like a Pokémon who couldn't say anything but its name.

"There's also 'mostly guilty,' 'somewhat guilty,' and 'shamelessly guilty,' to mention but a few," offered the Right Hand of Justice.

"But what if I'm not guilty of anything?" Claire blurted.

That made the judges landslide once more with bitter mirth. "Silly princess," said the chief justice. "Everyone is guilty of something."

Then Ogden turned to her. "If we're going to get you off," he whispered, "we're going to have to come up with something much more clever than innocence."

Meanwhile, on the sidelines—and feeling very much sidelined—Sahara clenched her fists in frustration.

"Letting Ogden do this is a terrible idea," she whispered to Noah. "He's going to get her killed!"

"Maybe not," said Noah. "Ogden's her best chance at a good defense because he thinks like an alien."

"It should be me, not Ogden...," mumbled Raymond, only semiconscious from his body-snatching ordeal yet still vying for Claire's affection.

Jad watched the trial, sad and sullen, from beside Noah, profoundly broken by the terrible news of Triastra. But even with such weight, Jad tried to help.

"The Magmadog from my world can melt stone with its breath," Jad said, "which means I have that power. If I do it right, I can melt all three judges."

"Uh...melting the Tribunal of Ancients would probably just make things worse," Noah pointed out, then put a gentle hand on Jad's rear shoulder. "But it was a good thought."

Forlo watched the proceedings with increasing dread. Although he really did not know the girl, and he had only first encountered humans for the first time a few days ago, he felt her termination would be a terribly sad thing. And what would become of his world without leadership? Was

398

his world destined to be a rubbish heap that no one wanted to claim?

As for Andi, she said nothing. Not even a string of broken symbols on her handle. Noah put his arm around the charred, dented suitcase. He didn't know if she could sense it, or even if she had any awareness at all in her low-power state, but he embraced her all the same.

Ogden, it seemed, was out of angles, because now he just stomped his foot and said, "This isn't fair!"

"Fairness and justice don't always go hand in hand," said the chief justice.

"Or claw in claw," said the Right Hand of Justice, in the name of inclusivity.

The Left Hand of Justice just pursed his thin lips, as he had nothing to add beyond a hastily reached verdict.

"But I never even knew this planet existed a week ago!" insisted Claire.

"Perhaps not, but you are under the jurisdiction of the world in which you were crowned and are obliged to abide by its laws," said the chief justice. "Whether or not you knew of this world's existence is of minor significance."

• ● •

Minor significance.

The phrase rang in Sahara's head. There was something there. Something important. Her heart started to pick up speed. Her intuition was piqued, and she had to figure out why.

Minor significance.

"Sahara, what is it?" asked Noah, sensing her gears turning—not in the way Andi's did, but in a very human way.

"Not sure yet. Let me think." Sahara found her thoughts drifting to Mr. Ksh—and how he said this was a real estate transaction, plain and simple. But real estate had rules.

Minor . . . significance . . .

Sahara gasped and stood. "That's it!" Then she propelled herself into the line of judicial fire.

"Stop these proceedings!" Sahara said. "I have new evidence the court hasn't heard."

Ogden gaped at her. "Excuse me, but *I* am the accused's legal counsel! Anything you have to say, you tell me, and I will present it!"

"Get over yourself!" said Sahara, and shoved him out of the way. "Claire is only fourteen," Sahara told the judges. "On Earth that is considered a minor, *and minors can't sign legal documents without a parent or legal guardian's co-signature*. And since Earth was the jurisdiction in which the contract was signed, that makes the star certificate she signed at her birthday party null and void!"

Claire gasped. "She's right!"

Ogden gawked. "Yeah, she is."

The judges were silent for a moment, then the chief justice said, "Excuse us." The three turned to one another, their mumbles sounding like seismic activity, and finally they turned back to face Sahara. "This is easily resolved," said the chief justice. "We shall bring her parents here, and compel them to sign a pre-dated contract, closing this particular loophole."

"Well," said Sahara, turning to throw Noah a secret little wink, "you could certainly do that under normal circumstances... but when the Usurpers abducted Claire, they used an age-regression weapon. Claire's parents are infants now."

"That's right!" said Ogden. "Which means—"

"That they won't be able to give their permission until they are no longer minors themselves!" blurted Noah, jumping to his feet.

"Which won't be for more than seventeen Earth years!" Sahara concluded, with a little triumphant bow.

"Well played," Ogden had to admit. "Well played. But I would have gotten there eventually."

The judges had another little seismic sidebar—and the kids knew, by the morose look on the Left Hand's face, that they had won.

"Seventeen Earth years might be convenient for you," the chief justice said, "but our docket is already full.

Therefore, it has been decided that we shall revisit this matter in precisely one galactic rotation from today. Anyone not present will be held in contempt of court."

"That's still not fair!" complained Claire, who had still yet to process the whole business of her parents being babies.

But it was Ogden who realized what they were saying.

"Correct me if I'm wrong," said Ogden, "but isn't a galactic rotation around two hundred thousand Earth years?"

"Yes . . . ," said the chief justice.

"But you must know the span of a human life is a whole lot shorter than that," said Sahara.

"We do . . . ," said the Right Hand of Justice.

"So . . . ," concluded Ogden, "you're using a loophole within the loophole to let her off the hook."

The Left Hand of Justice offered them a slim, resigned smirk. "Guilty," he said.

32

Siblings of the Stars

THE HORDES OF CLAIRIANS WATCHED AS THE MOUNTAIN TOOK TO the skies, leaving their world, and spiriting the Tribunal of Ancients off to judge other interstellar crimes. Murmurs rose within the crowd as they anxiously awaited news from within the walls of the palace. Or at least the walls that hadn't been crushed by the mountain.

One might think that there would be an air of celebration within the palace. But it was more like an air of relief.

The courtyard was a mess of fallen chairs and bird droppings. While Forlo went off to assess the Usurpers' ship, Ogden, Raymond, and Sahara struggled to get the crown off Claire's head, but it seemed to have somehow fused to her skull, becoming a part of her.

Finally, they gave up and decided it would take greater engineering than they currently had to remove it. Perhaps Andi would have been able to help, were she not currently a suitcase. The four sat, exhausted, among the courtyard debris. A Rigelian ultra-dove came to perch on Claire's shoulder, perhaps nostalgic for the dress or thinking she had more Usurpers to feed it. She didn't have the patience and shooed it away.

"What is it they say? 'Heavy is the head that wears the crown'?" said Sahara.

"It's not heavy, it's made of light," said Claire. "But it itches!"

Across the courtyard, by the fountain, they could hear Jad sobbing. Noah sat by Jad's side, trying to help his friend bear the grief of a world lost.

"There are worse things than having a crown stuck on your head, I suppose," said Claire. Then she heaved a sigh worthy of a planetary ruler and took a long look at Ogden, to the point that Ogden checked if there was something unsightly hanging out of his nose.

"I don't think I ever really thanked you for buying me the star, Ogden."

"Thank me?" Ogden was bowled over by the very idea. "I'd think you'd want to throw me out of an airlock!"

Claire shrugged. "Yeah, maybe," she said. "But when you bought it for me, you didn't know any of this would happen."

Then Raymond shoved his way between them. "I fought a Usurper for you, Claire," he said. "Are you going to thank *me*?"

"Thank you, too, Raymond." Then Claire shook her head as she looked at the two of them. "You're both very odd boys," she said. "But you know what? I'm starting to realize I kind of like odd boys."

"Join the club," said Sahara, tossing a glance toward Noah to prove her point. Then she went off to see how Noah was doing in his efforts to console Jad.

"So," said Ogden, rubbing his hands together like a greedy supervillain, "does this new realization mean that—"

"No," said Claire, and turned to Raymond, "and no to you, too."

Ogden began to bluster. "But you said—"

Claire put up her hand to stop him. "I know what I said. But 'liking' and *'liking'* are two very different things."

"Yes," argued Ogden, "but the *first* is a step closer to the *second*, isn't it?"

Claire had to consider that. "Could be," she finally said. "Give me two hundred thousand years to think about it."

"Fair enough," said Ogden. "Fair enough."

• ● •

Noah sat with Jad on the other side of the fountain, helping Jad come to terms with the greatest loss anyone could ever imagine. How do you get past such a thing? Even with the defenses of a million different creatures?

"Jad, I'm sorry I didn't tell you."

Jad took a long moment before answering, "At first, I was mad at you, but then I realized if it was me, and it was *your* world that was destroyed, I wouldn't want to tell you either."

"It'll be okay," Noah said. "Even though it can never be okay, somehow it will be. Because we adapt. I mean, that's what you and me are all about, right? Adapting."

"But I can't stop thinking of my ecto, endo, and exo. What you call your mom and dad." Jad turned away for a second, wiping away the tears. "Do you think my parents ever loved me?"

Noah knew that question intimately. He asked himself that every day. And on most days he came up with the same answer. "Mine did," Noah said. "In spite of what they were trying to do to my planet, they loved me. I'm sure yours did, too. And they would have come back if they could."

"Yeah, but how do you know?"

"I don't. And maybe I never will. But isn't it better to believe the best of them than the worst?"

Jad smiled. There was sadness in that smile, but sincerity and gratitude as well. "There must have been other Triastrals off-planet when my world was terraformed," Jad said. "Maybe I can find them." Then Jad hesitated. "Or maybe I should just go with you...."

But Noah remembered something Miss Luella had said and shook his head. "No, Jad. Friends don't let friends be sidekicks."

Jad nodded with understanding, then put a hand firmly on Noah's head, and Noah returned the gesture.

That's when Sahara arrived, looking a little sheepish. "Am I...interrupting something?" she asked.

"It's how Triastrals shake hands," Noah explained.

"Yeah," said Jad. "It's also how we reproduce."

Noah withdrew his hand with springbok speed. "AAAAGH!"

And Jad laughed. "Gotcha!"

Noah smiled. The fact that Jad could still laugh was a very good sign.

• ● •

Forlo returned to inform everyone that the Usurper ship had enough fuel in its RTR drive to get back to Earth. "The coordinates are still in the computer, Your Highness," Forlo told Claire. "So it will drop off your friends in the same spot where you yourself were first abducted."

"The scene of the crime," said Noah. "It'll be crawling with FOBE agents."

"After what we've been through," said Sahara, "Agent Rigby and her Nowhere Men don't scare me."

"Forlo, you said it will drop off my friends," said Claire, a bit concerned. "Don't you mean my friends and *me*?"

"I'm afraid your presence here is still required, Your Highness," Forlo insisted. "The legality of your reign might be in question, but the people don't know that. If they learn that this world now belongs to no one, and that it truly is an abandoned wasteland, it will crush them. For their sake you absolutely must hold to your role."

Everyone looked to Claire, awaiting her decision.

"But ... but what if I don't want to?" Claire's voice wavered, torn between this responsibility and her desire to simply go home.

It was Sahara who realized what needed to be done. Stepping forward, she spoke with conviction. "This planet doesn't need a crown princess—and it certainly doesn't need a landlord," she told everyone. "What it really needs ... is a First Citizen."

• ● •

Forlo stood in the middle of the parapet—the walkway directly above the palace gate—and gazed down at the crowd that had assembled across the moat. He had to find the right words to say to them and had no idea what they'd be.

He'd always been a smooth talker. As First Citizen of B'light, he viewed his duties as something of a salesman, always presenting the best side of the city to strangers, even if it was a fictional, augmented-reality side. But now he had to take over the reins of an entire planet, and there was no way to sugarcoat the challenge ahead.

He gave a little wave to the assembled, which they returned with cheers and hurrahs. Then he spoke. He needed no microphone because his voice rang loud and true.

"Greetings, fellow Clairians. Her Royal Majesty Crown Princess Claire has appointed me as our planet's First Citizen. And as my first duty, I am happy to inform you that the Usurpers have been erased from our world!"

A huge hurrah from the crowd lasted a full minute. Finally, when the clamor died down, he continued.

"Today, we stand upon the precipice of a new era...," Forlo's voice soared. The gathered multitudes raised their eyes, as if to follow the sound of his words, and for the first time in forever, their eyes were filled with something like hope.

"Today, my dear companions, we celebrate a triumph that shall resonate through the stars and inspire civilizations across the heavens."

Then someone in the crowd shouted, *"Yeah, but what are we going to do with all this garbage?"*

"Yes, well, we can discuss that later." Forlo cleared his throat and continued. "We are a testament to the power that resides within every sentient being, the power to stand against adversity and forge our own destiny."

Then someone shouted, *"Can we change the names of our cities to something less blatantly depressing?"*

"Certainly," said Forlo, "but we can talk about that another time!"

"Do we get a tour of the palace after your speech?"

"Can we make today an annual holiday?"

"Will there be commemorative coins?"

And rather than letting himself get bogged down in queries, he decided to end his speech with a bang.

"Today, we shout our victory cry to the universe!" Then he released one of his deafening screams that shook the ground, and effectively blew all impertinent questions out of everyone's mind.

• ● •

Forlo left the crowd galvanized and ready to face the future with a newfound sense of purpose and unity. Yet although he beamed with confidence when speaking to the Clairians, once he left the parapet, he looked subdued and worried, his mind burdened with the weight of responsibility.

He graciously accepted the congratulations of the princess and her friends, nodding his long neck appreciatively, but quickly tried to duck away, feeling the gravity of what lay ahead.

Ogden, however, caught up with him.

"That was a rousing speech!" Ogden told him.

"Thank you," Forlo replied. "But I fear words are all I have. Words and empty promises."

"Maybe it's not as bad as you think," said Ogden, with a little gleam in his eye to match the gleam of his head.

Forlo shook his head sadly. "We have no resources and still remain an impoverished world. I can rally hope, but how long will it last? We have no means by which to raise ourselves up."

"Yeah, about that," said Ogden. "I think I might have an idea. . . ."

• ● •

Like most everything else the Usurpers had, their ship had been stolen from a different species. Being worms, they had never evolved navigational skills, only borrowed them from bodies they snatched. That being the case, the ship was entirely automated. It made the trip home easy for Noah and his friends, since they didn't have to fly it. All they had to do was let the ship do its business unbothered by "disgusting sticky five-fingered hands" as the ship's AI put it. After having been used and abused by the Usurpers, it had a distaste of biological life-forms.

"Worms or walkers, you're all the same."

The kids decided it was best to leave the ship's AI alone.

"It's going to be a strange homecoming," said Ogden, as he peered out of a view port at the light show of stars as they soared through intestinal space toward Earth. "By now people will have figured out that this was an alien abduction. FOBE won't be able to keep a lid on it."

"It'll just be a new normal," Noah said. "One thing about us humans, we roll with it. Weird stuff never stays weird for long."

"My parents must be worried sick," said Sahara. She'd

been avoiding thinking about them as much as she could through all of this. She hated the torment her disappearance must have put them through. She wondered whether she should tell them the truth of what happened or make up an alien abduction story that was somewhat more acceptable. Scrawny gray extraterrestrials with big black eyes dissecting people on sterile operating tables. You know, the normal stuff. But no—perhaps honesty would be the best policy, whether they believed her or not. The important thing was that she'd be home soon. And that felt good.

"At least *you* won't have to spoon-feed your parents," Claire said morosely.

"Well, considering that they're babies," said Ogden, "spoon-feeding is better than the alternative."

Sahara whacked him. "Really, Ogden? Did you have to go there?"

"I boldly go where my mind takes me."

"Yeah," said Sahara. "Where no mind has gone before."

"I sincerely doubt that," said Ogden. "But point taken."

"I already miss them," said Claire.

"Your parents are still there," Sahara pointed out, "it'll just be . . . a different kind of relationship."

Claire bit her lip as she pondered the new, broader picture of her life. "I think every relationship will be different after all of this."

Sahara nodded, knowing exactly how she felt. "When

you've seen the secrets of the universe, it's kind of hard to come back to Arbuckle. But whenever you need someone to talk to—someone who *gets* it—I'll be here."

Claire said nothing, but the genuine look of thanks she gave Sahara was worth more than words.

"Hey, your parental situation could be worse," Ogden pointed out. "For the longest time, mine both thought they were Kratz. Better babies than *that*!"

"You know, weirdest thing," Noah said. "When we were at the palace—during the battle—I could have sworn I saw Kratz there."

"A clear sign of trauma," Ogden concluded. "Sometimes I think I see Kratz everywhere I go, but I'm sure he's still in a laboratory somewhere, being poked and prodded and experimented on."

"As well he should be," Sahara added, and they thought no further of it.

• ● •

Halfway through the journey, they convinced the ship's AI to let them rendezvous with another ship.

"One of the biologics on board is going to leave," Noah explained. "And the ship we're meeting has the technology to fix an AI of ours that's broken."

"You had me at 'leave,' " said the ship.

It was, of course, the Fractillians, lured back by

promises of deep-tissue back rubs. They said they'd be able to repair Andi, and they'd be willing to take Jad in search of other Triastrals.

"People thought the Splunges were dead and gone," Jad told Noah, "and now they're repopulating. If *they* can do it, *we* can do it, too. All it takes is three of us to keep my species going."

"And those Splunges," added Ogden, "might just be the best thing that ever happened to Forlo's planet."

Which piqued everyone's curiosity.

"Don't you see?" said Ogden. "Splunges are the best exfoliators in the galaxy. I mentioned it to Forlo, and he's working on a plan to turn the place into an expensive planetary spa! If they play their cards right, they'll be a top galactic vacation spot in no time!"

"I'd go there," said the ship, "if I had skin."

• ● •

The Fractillians sidled up beside them on schedule, the Usurper ship complaining about how it hated first dates.

Murdrum was the first to cross through the airlock connecting the two ships.

"So you survived," Murdrum said when he saw Noah. "I wasn't sure you would."

"Me neither." Noah introduced him to the others— although Raymond and Claire bailed to the farthest corners of the ship the instant they got a look at Murdrum's many mouths with many teeth.

Sahara was intimidated but respectful. Ogden was merely curious. "You look like something I've had a recurring nightmare about."

"Yeah," said Murdrum, "I get that all the time. I've got one of those faces."

Then Murdrum gave them news of Miss Luella. "Word is that the Fauxlites know Jad escaped the World of Last Life—but that lady you left on the planet refused to tell them how or where you went."

"I hope they don't hurt Miss Luella," Sahara said.

"They won't. They can't. She's claimed squatter's rights, so now they can't get rid of her. Not unless they want to face the Tribunal of Ancients—and nobody wants to do that."

"So . . . I'm a fugitive now?" asked Jad.

"Don't worry, Fractillians love fugitives and hate Fauxlites. As long as you're with us, you'll be safe."

Then Noah rolled up Andi. Or, more accurately, dragged her, since her wheels had melted off. It was so hard to see her this way. "You're sure you can repair her?"

"We'll do our best. I know how much she means to you."

"Yeah, well, she means even more than that."

Murdrum's various mouths smiled. "We'll bring her

back to you as good as new the next time we're in the neighborhood."

While Murdrum captivated Noah's friends with tales of life and death in the cosmic abyss he called home, Noah stepped aside with Jad, so they could have a final moment together.

"You once told me we were like family," Jad said. "I think that's true . . . littermates of the universe."

Noah smiled. "Siblings of the stars."

"We haven't known each other long," said Jad, "but I don't think anyone will ever understand us the way we understand each other."

"I think it's noble what you're doing, Jad," said Noah. "I hope you find other Triastrals out there."

Jad smiled and put that third hand tenderly on Noah's head—but rather than responding in kind, Noah used both his arms to give Jad a very heartfelt, very human hug.

"I'll miss you, Noah," Jad said, then whispered in Noah's ear, "Is it weird to say that I love you?"

"Not weird at all. I love you, too, Jad."

"Excuse me," said the Usurper ship, with increasing impatience. "But can you get this over with? I didn't ask for this coupling, I'm extremely resentful, and I think this Fractillian ship is getting ideas."

Ignoring the ship, Noah and Jad held each other for as long as they both needed to. Then Jad turned, and without looking back, crossed the airlock to the Fractillian ship.

"What was that all about?" Sahara asked. Noah couldn't help but sense a little jealousy in the question.

"Jad's a very complicated person," Noah said. "Like me."

They turned to look out of a view port. Intestinal space was as strange and stunning as ever. Soon it would push them out in orbit around Earth.

"When we get back, I guess you won't be staying in Arbuckle," Sahara said.

Noah sighed. They both knew it wouldn't be a safe place for him to be. "No. It'll be crawling with FOBE agents for months. Maybe years."

"Where will you go?"

"I'm thinking I might travel for a while and really get to know the different species inside me."

"Alone?"

The fact that Andi wouldn't be with him did change things. "Well, I do have this Usurper ship, which means I can go anywhere. Its AI might be annoying, but I'm sure we'll grow on each other." He thought the ship might comment, but it just gave him a cold shoulder. "I could see the wonders of the universe," Noah said.

But Sahara knew what he was really thinking. "Or look for your parents."

"Yeah," Noah said, in barely a whisper. "Maybe." But he filed that away in his mind for another day. "Anyway, Murdrum said I should take a tour of the Fractal Abyss.

He says it's like the Grand Canyon, only infinite and terrifying."

Sahara grinned. "Sounds fun. Bring me back a souvenir?"

Noah knew this was her way of saying goodbye but also a reminder that goodbye wasn't always forever.

"I will. I promise." Then Noah took Sahara's hand, gently squeezing it.

Sahara responded by squeezing his hand back. Which made him smile like a dolphin and chimpanzee combined.

33

On the Outskirts of D'Light...

IN A LITTLE BLUE HOUSE, IN THE MIDDLE OF NOWHERE, ON A junkyard planet that was cleaning up quite nicely, Quantavius T. Kratz and FOBE agent Jannell "Nell" Knell enjoyed a simple life. It was difficult at first, what with the plague of Splunges that had all but enveloped the little lopsided Victorian they called home. But locals had come to adopt the Splunges, and with the collective effort of the community, their home was soon freed from the blobby cling-ons, allowing Kratz and Knell to settle into a mostly carefree life.

The same locals, who saw them as prophets, brought them food on a regular basis, some of which was actually edible. Amid the bizarre circumstances of their existence, Kratz and Knell found a strange harmony, as if they were two halves of the same whole. Occasionally, they missed their former lives, but there was a peculiar yin and yang to falling in love with another person when, in fact, that other person was also you.

Aside from the occasional visits from the local populace seeking words of profound wisdom, they were mostly left alone, relishing the tranquility of their secluded sanctuary.

Until the day they had a most unexpected visitor.

Kratz and Knell went to the door together, figuring it must be another offering of food. Instead, they were faced with a strange humanoid creature that glowed, radiating an aura of ethereal light—although the light it gave off seemed somewhat false. A pretentious person (which Kratz most certainly was) might call it . . . faux light.

"Go away," Kratz told the glowing creature. "If you're looking for a spa, you'll find plenty of them in the city of D'Light."

"It's at the end of that long gully," added Knell. "You can't miss it."

"But you'll need a reservation," Kratz said. "I hear they're booked solid for months." He tried to slam the door, but the creature held it open, studying them with blazing eyes.

"I have no need of exfoliation," it said. "I'm here to speak to the two of you. You are both human, are you not?"

"Yes," said Kratz, adopting a dramatic pose. "We are humans from the distant past, trapped in a future time."

For a moment, the creature seemed confused, as if it

might comment on this but apparently decided it wasn't worth it.

"There is a boy," the creature said. "A human boy. We believed him to be dead, but there are rumors that he may still be alive and that he faked his own death." Then the creature put out its hand and projected upon its palm an image of a very familiar nuisance.

"His name," said the creature, "is Noah Prime. Can you give us any information on him?"

Kratz and Knell shared a knowing glance. Could it be that these dog days were finally over?

Turning to the luminous creature, they both said in voices that were eerily similar:

"What's it worth to you?"

ACKNOWLEDGMENTS

It should be no shock to anyone that this book couldn't have happened without the help and support of quite a few celestial beings! First and foremost, we'd like to thank our editors, Liz Kossnar and Lily Choi, who worked tirelessly with us to whip the book into shape, editor-in-chief Alvina Ling, publisher Megan Tingley, deputy publisher Jackie Engel, and editorial assistant Lauren Kisare.

But there are so many people in the Little, Brown star system who go above and beyond! In production, Marisa Finkelstein and Patricia Alvarado. In marketing and publicity, Stefanie Hoffman, Alice Gelber, Savannah Kennelly, Cheryl Lew, Christie Michel, and, of course, the unparalleled galactic entity Victoria Stapleton!

A shout-out as well to Little, Brown's remarkable sales team, including Shawn Foster, Danielle Cantarella, and Claire Gamble.

Thanks to artist Jim Madsen and designer Karina Granda for the series' iconic covers!

Thanks to our literary agent, Andrea Brown, for everything she does, as well as our entertainment agents, Steve

Fisher and Debbie Deuble-Hill, at APA; our contract attorneys Shep Rosenman and Jennifer Justman; and our managers, Trevor Engelson and Josh McGuire.

Neal would like to thank Claire Salmon, superstar, for managing tour visits, writing workshops, and all the various lifesaving assistant work that keeps the world turning, as well as Emily Varga and Amanda Adams, who organize all non-tour speaking engagements. Thanks to research assistant Symone Powell, social media managers Mara De Guzman and Bianca Peries, and Jarrod Shusterman and Sofía Lapuente for helping Neal's TikTok go viral.

Big-time thanks, one and all! These two high primates couldn't be happier!

GABY GERSTER

NEAL SHUSTERMAN is the *New York Times* bestselling and award-winning author of over thirty books, including *I Am the Walrus*; *Challenger Deep*, which won the National Book Award; *Scythe*, a Michael L. Printz Honor Book; *Dry*, which he cowrote with his son Jarrod Shusterman; and *Unwind*, which won more than thirty domestic and international awards. He invites you to visit him online at storyman.com.

LOU MELUSO

ERIC ELFMAN is a screenwriter and the author of several books for children and young adults, including the *New York Times* bestseller *I Am the Walrus*, *The Very Scary Almanac*, and *Almanac of the Gross, Disgusting & Totally Repulsive* (an ALA Recommended Book for Reluctant Readers), and coauthor of the popular Accelerati Trilogy. He invites you to visit him on X @Eric_Elfman or at his website, ElfmanWorld.com.